THE GLORY

Then the breath caught in his throat and he coughed and with the cough shouted: 'Gas! Hoss, it's gas!'

The gas, heavier than air, would roll down into the trench. He fumbled with the mask, knowing he must get it on or run; there could be no safety without it in the trench. And even as he rose to his knees, all hell was let loose upon them. There was the shattering roar which presaged the shell-burst and he saw, in slow motion, the ground ascend as the shell struck and felt the precursor of the impact patter, like rain, upon his steel helmet. He had the mask to his face when something struck it from his hand and the earth rose up before him like a black curtain.

His last thought was for Hoss, who had been standing when the gas came pouring over the ground, when the shell burst.

Then, nothing.

*Also in Arrow by
Judith Saxton*

THE PRIDE
THE SPLENDOUR
FULL CIRCLE

FAMILY FEELING

THE GLORY

Katie Flynn writing as

JUDITH SAXTON

arrow books

To Nancy Webber, whose enthusiasm
helped enormously, and whose editorial
alertness averted many a blunder!

Published by Arrow Books in 2001

2 4 6 8 10 9 7 5 3

First published in Great Britain in 1982 by Hamlyn Paperbacks

Arrow Books
Random House, 20 Vauxhall Bridge Road,
London SW1V 2SA

www.randomhouse.co.uk

Addresses for companies within The Random House Group Limited
can be found at: www.randomhouse.co.uk/offices.htm

The Random House Group Limited Reg. No. 954009

A CIP catalogue record for this book
is available from the British Library

ISBN 9780099549963

The Random House Group Limited supports The Forest Stewardship
Council® (FSC®), the leading international forest-certification organisation.
Our books carrying the FSC label are printed on FSC®-certified paper.
FSC is the only forest-certification scheme supported by the leading
environmental organisations, including Greenpeace. Our
paper procurement policy can be found at
www.randomhouse.co.uk/environment

MIX
Paper from
responsible sources
FSC® C016897

Printed and bound in Great Britain by Clays Ltd, St Ives PLC

Author's Acknowledgements

A great many people have helped me with research into the early twentieth century for this book, including Barbara Miller, who sorted through the early records of the Norwich High School for Girls and showed me some fascinating books and photographs, Adelaide and Alan Hunter, who found me magazines, postcards and cuttings dealing with the twenties in Norwich, and C. Wilkins-Jones of the Local Studies Library, who patiently photostated masses of material concerned with Norfolk during the Great War.

In the North-West, Adele and Reginald Mayorcas of Chester helped me with details of Jewish weddings, customs and even cookery; and in Wrexham, Maureen Jardine's knowledge of Judaism kept our mutual phones busy as I checked facts with her.

Librarians in Wrexham Library are always helpful particularly Lynne Butler and Marina Thomas, who make time to help me solve my many and various problems, no matter how busy they may be.

Lastly, I'm indebted to my father, Ivor Saxton, who told me many 'family' stories, and particularly school ones which helped me to understand the workings of a boys' boarding school; and to my grandfather, Alfred Saxton, whose sensible and delightful habit of photographing everything he could point a camera at, and saving newspaper cuttings, old menus, old bills and family documents, helped me to build up a picture of Norfolk and New Zealand at the beginning of the century.

THE NEYLER AND ROSE FAMILIES

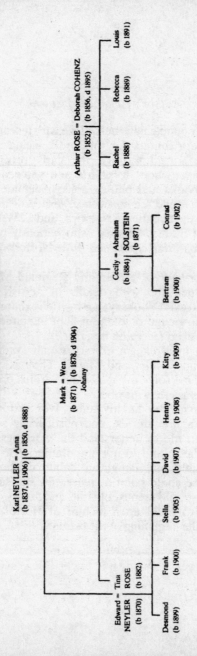

1: 1912

Tina was dreaming. She lay on her back in the big bed, one arm flung up above her head, her bedtime plait lying like a black rope across her shoulder and breast. A small sound, something between a squeak and a whimper, came from her half open mouth, and she moved her head restlessly on the pillow.

Ted, wide awake and far too hot even at six o'clock on this bright July day, touched his wife's shoulder. She kicked out, then whimpered again.

Ted rolled on to his stomach and leaned over her.

'Tina? Come on, love, you're having a nightmare. Wake up!'

Her eyelids flickered but did not open so he kissed her mouth gently, then with increasing firmness. It did the trick. Her lids trembled apart to show eyes still fogged with sleep. He smiled at her, their faces only inches apart, but she scowled, snuggling into the pillow again.

'Go away. 'Tisn't time to get up.'

'You were having a nightmare, sweet. Wake up, there's a good girl.'

She hunched up her shoulders and screwed her eyes tightly shut. 'No. I'm asleep.'

'How can you sleep in this heat? It's like an oven in here!'

It was no use; she was asleep again before he had finished speaking. Facing him now, she curled up and her breathing steadied into a regular rhythm once more.

Ted glanced towards the wide open windows. The trouble was, their room faced east and got all the early morning sun. In the nursery and the little slip of a room off

7

it, the three youngest children and Stella, who was seven, would be quite cool, for their rooms faced the pinewoods at the back of the house. And the boys, Frank and Desmond, would be sleeping still because their room faced west, towards the beech drive. Only he and Tina got the benefit of the early morning sun, blessing it in winter and cursing it in summer.

Even in bed he could see the cedar tree and imagine the flat slabs of shade which it would be casting on the lawn. He heard furtive sounds and knew that the servants were creaking their way down the attic stairs. He glanced at his gold watch on the bedside table. It was barely six, so why were the maids getting up? They had no fires to lay or light in weather such as this, and . . .

Recollection flooded in and he nearly groaned aloud. Of course, today was his father-in-law Arthur Rose's sixtieth birthday. Today he and Tina were to host a large birthday party, with Arthur as the gratified guest of honour. Later, there would be a family dinner party, also held at The Pride. In theory, the work would be shared between Tina and her three younger sisters, but in fact most of it would fall on the servants and inhabitants of The Pride. Sometimes he wished he had not built such a very large house! It seemed to attract guests as honey attracts bees. In winter the billiard room was always full, the playroom bulging at the seams with children. In summer he practically had to put his name down to play tennis on his court, and the garden swing seat, the croquet lawn and the terrace always seemed to contain sundry friends and relatives. So of course when the party had first been suggested, the decision to hold it at The Pride had been unanimous.

He wondered, a little wistfully, why it was that he, Arthur's only non-Jewish relative, should end up entertaining all those good Jews. Today, in my kitchen, kosher things will be happening, he thought. He teased Tina sometimes that she crossed herself and asked forgiveness in Yiddish before eating bacon, because her beliefs must be so mixed up. She had eloped with him when she was only sixteen and before then she had been a good Jewish housekeeper, running her father's house, knowing everything there was to know about the Jewish dietary laws. They had married in the face of fierce parental opposition from Arthur, and against all the odds the marriage had prospered and strengthened until it was the best thing in both their lives.

Religion was one subject which never worried them. Sometimes Tina went to Shul with her father and sisters. Sometimes she accompanied Ted and her own children to morning service at one of the churches in the city, or at Christchurch, which was so conveniently at hand. Ted told Tina that he wanted his children to have the choice between one religion and another, but in Texas, where they had spent half a dozen very happy years, they had attended a local church, and the children took churchgoing for granted.

Tina, brought up with Judaism but completely accepting her husband's beliefs, was happy so long as the children knew right from wrong and had a stable background, and Ted knew, without conceit, that nothing mattered to her which did not involve them both.

Thinking of his children's upbringing made him remember his own. He had been born and brought up on the South Island in New Zealand, his brother Mark almost his only companion on their farm in the mountains behind Dunedin. Owning his own farm had been his dream, yet when he and Mark had run a successful dairy business, been people of standing in the community, he had not been content. He had gone off to England and fallen in love with Tina. He was ashamed to think that in fourteen years of married life he had never once seen Mark. They had been inseparable until his marriage, united against a harsh and violent father. And after? When he was in England with his adoring wife? Mark, too, had married. He and his wife, Wendy, had been happy too, but not lucky, like he and Tina. Wendy had been killed and Mark had simply left the farm, his little son, and his wife's cousin who kept house for them. He had gone to Texas, in search of the big brother who had once been everything to him. And by a cruel twist

9

of fate, he had arrived in Humble, Texas, just as Ted and his family had left.

No one knew much of what Mark had gone through in the next few years. Unhappiness, misunderstandings . . . there must have been plenty of both, for Mark's rare letters were curt, raw with the pain of his loss.

Then a letter had arrived saying that Mark had come to his senses and was returning to Dunedin and his son. Later, they had heard that Mark had married again, to his first wife's cousin, whose name was Su. Ted supposed they were happy, but he knew that his own behaviour in the affair had not been good. During the four years that Mark had been in America he had written constantly to Su, suggesting that Johnny might be sent to England to be educated with his cousins; had even said that if Su agreed he would go to Dunedin and fetch the boy himself. But he had done nothing. Even when Mark was home and planning a wedding, when he could almost hear his brother's unspoken pleas for a brief reunion, he had let Tina argue him into putting off the trip. For Tina was jealous of his affection for Mark, and on this one point he had allowed her to persuade him against all his better judgement.

He knew that it was partly fear. Fear that he would be torn between life in South Island and life in Norwich, fear that he would want to stay with Mark. Whenever he acknowledged this, he saw himself too plainly and his conscience smote him bitterly.

To turn his thoughts from their painful, relentless track, Ted turned on his side and stared hard at Tina, trying to wake her. She *was* hot, he could see tiny sweat beadlets forming on her forehead. He stroked her silky skin and felt desire clutch at his stomach as he held the weight of her breast in his palm, rubbing his thumb over her nipple until it stood proud. Her lashes stirred and he saw the tip of her tongue moisten the fullness of her lower lip. He swallowed. In all the years he had shared her bed he had never known what it was not to want her. Even when she was huge with child, bad-tempered, weeping at nothing, she was the lodestar to which he turned, the magnet to his steel. He could not imagine life without her.

He put his arms round her and pulled her against him. His pyjamas had been abandoned long since and the touch of her excited him as it always had and always would.

'Go away! It's too hot!'

'I agree, sweetie. Take your nightie off.'

She giggled and then kissed his cheek, butterfly fashion, with her long, trembling eyelashes. He pulled the silly little silk straps down over her shoulders and her eyes opened into gleaming slits. As the nightie slid down to her hips he cupped his hand over her breast and felt her heartbeat quicken.

'Do stop it. Someone might come in!'

'They won't. It's very early. The servants are only just up.'

He pulled her nightie right off with only limited help from her and took her fully into his arms, then kissed her. She tensed, her mouth softening beneath his, and then she was clutching him, as eager, suddenly, as he.

The party, the heat, his own shortcomings, were forgotten as they made love.

In the nursery, luncheon was over and the little ones, David, Henny and Kitty, were washed, dressed and brushed to within an inch of their lives. Kitty was to give her grandfather a bouquet of roses and the little boys were presenting him with an immense box of cigars, and they had been rehearsed in their parts until they could have delivered the presents blindfold and in their sleep. Stella, who was seven and at the awkward age when she was neither nursery nor schoolroom, sat on the window-seat, watching the backyard.

'Mabel's gone into the kitchen. She's helping Ruthie with the tea.' Stella sighed and shot a meaning glance at Nanny Sutton, ironing hair ribbons at the nursery table. 'At least *she* isn't bored and shut up with the babies!'

Nanny Sutton finished ironing and stood the flat on its end.

'Nor need you be any more, miss! The boys are back

after their luncheon, so you can come along with me, see if they're ready for the tea party. But for goodness sake don't mess yourself up.'

Stella followed in Nanny's rustling wake, a smile already brightening her face. It was her life's ambition to be with her older brothers, but it was so rarely possible! They were at boarding school during term-time and though it was now the holidays they had their own ploys and their own friends, leaving little time for a child nearly half a dozen years younger than they. But today, because of the party, they might be with her until her bedtime!

At the door, she hurtled in ahead of Nanny, her voice high with excitement.

'Hello, Des, Frank! Nanny said I could . . .' She hesitated. 'You aren't in your suits! You'll catch it!'

Nanny's irate voice proved her point.

'Boys! What on earth are ye thinkin' of? Here's the little ones, bless them, sweet and clean as primroses and Miss Stella here a perfect picture, and you two sulky as bears just because of a stiff collar and a decent suit of clothes. Get *on*, will ye? Your mama wants you down in an hour, no more. Will ye get a move on, just?'

Nanny Sutton was twenty-five, extremely pretty, and Irish. When she was roused, her brogue deepened. Desmond looked across at Frank and winked.

'Sure and wouldn't we dress up as the Angel Gabriel himself for to please ye, Nanny?' he enquired innocently. 'For 'tis yourself we love dearly, me darlin' little bog-trottin' leprechaun!'

'Cheeky varmint!' Nanny Sutton took a half-hearted swipe at Desmond's golden curls. He was a great favourite with the servants and got away with a good deal more than Frank did. 'Now will ye get them suits on?'

'For you, Nan, anything!' Desmond bowed and smirked.

'Oh, get on with ye, Master Dessy! Just go to your room and get changed, the pair of ye!'

Desmond and Frank repaired to their room and began to don their best clothes. Frank, dabbing half-heartedly at his face and neck at the washstand, glanced out of the window

12

at the heat-haze shimmering above the lawn.

'What a spiffing day for Grandpa's party! Though I don't see why we have to dress up like this. It's only family.'

Desmond was pulling a face, tying his tie in the mirror.

'Yes, but it'll be the same for everyone. You don't think Aunt Cecy will let the cousins off because it's hot, do you? No, they'll dress up for the honour of the Solsteins, same as we are for the honour of the Neylers.'

'I suppose you're right. Even Nanny Sutton was glistening a bit, wasn't she? I suppose she'll bring the kids down?'

Desmond, finishing his tie, shrugged himself into his jacket and gave his brother a knowing look through the mirror.

'Noticed she was a bit pink, did you? Know why?'

'No. Why?'

Desmond was about to answer when the door opened and Stella pranced in. She was charmingly dressed in pink and white, her pinafore so starched that it would have stood up by itself, her hair ribbon perched, like a gigantic butterfly, on the back of her head.

'Nanny says I can stay with you if you're respectable,' she announced, with the air of one giving them a high treat. 'I'm so bored with the little ones! Even David's only a child, really.'

She bestowed her sweetest smile on them both, then turned and took the towel away from Frank, arranging it strategically on the towel rail so that the dirt was not immediately obvious. Frank's washing had not so much removed the grime as repositioned it.

'We're not. Respectable, I mean,' Frank said crossly, giving Stella a glare. She ignored it, turning, with a whisk of her long, dark gold mane of hair, towards Desmond.

'Oh, Dessy, I *can* stay, can't I? I'm so bored! You do look lovely in that suit,' she added, with serpentine cunning beyond her years.

Desmond, laughing, nevertheless turned back to the mirror for a moment, smoothing his curls flat with his palms.

'Oh, I suppose you can. But shut up. Frank and I don't

want you prattling.' He turned away from Stella, to give Frank a meaning wink. 'Is Nanny taking the kids down? Will she wear her uniform?'

'Not uniform. She's got a lovely, summery dress with frills. It's sort of yellow.' Stella, sharp as a needle, glanced quickly from Desmond's grinning face to Frank's puzzled one. 'Why? Do you have to stay with Nanny?'

'Of course not, we're handing,' Desmond said. He straightened his lapels and it struck Frank abruptly that Desmond and Stella had a lot in common. They both used their looks to get what they wanted, Stella tossing her pretty little head at Nanny and making eyes at servants, uncles, anyone she wanted to get round. Desmond might not do precisely that, but he teased Nanny by imitating her brogue, or complimenting her on a new dress, and he made up to the servants to clean his room or make his bed for him, to give him little extras, to make him hot buttered crumpets when schoolroom tea was dull. Frank, watching the two of them charming their way through life, sometimes wondered what was lacking in him that he never tried to do the same. It did not occur to him that it was not a lack but a strength, that he neither needed nor wanted to captivate others for his own ends because he made his own way, was content to do his own work.

'We'll go down then,' Desmond said, making for the door. He held out a hand to Stella and it occurred to Frank that he was the odd man out in this trio for another reason as well. Despite their protestations, there was nothing Stella and Desmond liked more than getting dressed up and parading themselves before an admiring throng of relatives.

When they reached the hall they could hear the hum of voices coming from the living room. They went in and Grandpa was there with their parents, and Auntie Becky and Auntie Rachel. They stood back politely, waiting to be noticed, and Frank remembered that whatever he had been going to say about Nanny, Desmond had not finished. He sighed. It probably hadn't been very interesting, anyway!

'Ruthie, Mama sent me to tell you they're ready for the urn

now. And she said to say could I help?'

Mrs Ruthven, scarlet and sweating, dashed a hand across her brow and turned away from the oven.

'All right, Master Frank, run and tell Mrs Neyler I'll be up directly. And then you can give young Mabs an 'and with them strawberries.' Mrs Ruthven, reared from kitchenmaid to cook in a blackbeetly basement kitchen, had not got used to working in a house where the kitchen and scullery, living room and dining room, were all on the same floor. 'Alice, can you come?'

Alice, Arthur's housekeeper specially lent for the occasion, smiled at Frank and took the other end of the trolley with the urn on the top and big jugs of milk beneath.

'I've got it, Ruthie. Has someone taken all the sandwiches up? What about the savouries?'

'They're ready. Nellie, get them savouries out on to the salvers and bring 'em up directly.'

Nellie, in her blue print dress with her best apron over it, reached for the oven cloth even as the two women, pushing the trolley between them, disappeared into the corridor. Frank glanced round. He was to help finish off the strawberries, but where were they? The kitchen seemed to be cleared for action. But Nellie, turning from the oven, remembered Cook's instructions.

'In the scullery, lad. Young Mabel's at 'em,' she said briefly, loading her salver and hurrying out of the kitchen in the wake of the urn.

Frank went into the scullery and there were the strawberries, a great, gleaming pile of them in Mama's cherished cut crystal bowl, with a smaller pile at the side which Mabel was speedily reducing still further as she hulled the fruit. She said nothing, but glanced up at him and grinned – the fascinating, three-cornered smile which Frank liked so much. He grinned back, then nudged her along the wooden bench on which she sat.

'Budge up, Mabs, or I can't give a hand. How many've you eaten? I bet you're busting!'

'I'm not! Too busy.' Mabel pushed a large berry into her mouth and chewed ecstatically, but her fingers never stopped their brisk work. 'Go on, take one!'

They worked side by side in silence for a while, then Mabel said a little wistfully: 'What's it like, the party? Bet them dresses are pretty, eh? My mum helped to make the cucumber sandwiches this morning. She said there were forty people coming!'

Ada Walters, Mabel's mum, helped out in the house and was always much in evidence at parties. Mabel's dad, on the other hand, seldom came indoors. He was the gardener and gifted at his work, but being a man of few words seldom hung around the kitchen to flirt with the maids or gossip with the cook.

'Dunno. We just went in and kissed Grandpa and the aunts, and then Mama collared me to run this errand and Dessy to hand cups. Is that the last of the strawberries?'

'That's right.' Mabel dusted her hands, purple-pink with juice, briskly together and pushed the bowl to safety in the very centre of the table. 'The trolley and all the dishes and that are there, see? My mum'll be through in a mo., and she'll take them in when Ruthie says. That way, everyone gets a squint at the party, see?'

'What about you? Why don't you bring the cream jug or something?'

Mabel, heading for the back door, turned and smiled condescendingly.

'The best part of the party's on the terrace, and I'm going to skulk. I'll see everything I want to see!'

She whisked out of the door before he could say another word and was gone. Frank sighed and made his way back into the kitchen, then along the corridor, through the green baize door, and across into the conservatory where the party was in full swing. He *did* like cheeky young Mabel!

'Here's the cake, Poppa! Ted's lighting the candles and then you must blow them out – all at once, mind! With one blow!'

Arthur allowed himself to be led to where the enormous, three-tier birthday cake, iced in blue and white and crowned with sixty scarlet candles, stood waiting. Ted lit

16

the last candle, then stood back, beckoning the guests nearer.

'Fine it is, Tina mine,' Arthur said. He felt tears come to his eyes, but he smiled through them at his family. 'Ach, it is good to be sixty and have my family around me. How I wish my dear Deb could have lived to see this day!' He blew his nose so vigorously that the nearest candles dipped and swayed alarmingly, and his son-in-law, about to put the matches down, held them ready for an emergency.

'Speech, speech!'

That was the Rabbi, his handsome, eagle-beaked face shiny with emotion and strawberries. Arthur had noted with awe the number consumed by his guest.

'A speech? You don't want to hear an old man talk! Don't I talk enough for you, hey?'

He looked proudly around him at his family. At Tina with her big, blond Ted; at Cecy, small and plump, standing close to her little, dark husband. Abraham was no beauty, but he was a good husband and father. Then there was Becky, watching the candles, and Rachel, his youngest girl, standing near her fiancé, Solomon Hurtz. His gaze rested longest and fondest on Louis, his only son. Louis was his pride and joy, so incredibly beautiful, with a height and assurance that made him the cynosure of all female eyes. At twenty, he stood at the threshold of life and Arthur knew he would grasp it with both hands. He had brought a young lady friend with him, and stood with one hand resting carelessly on her drooping shoulder. Arthur's heart swelled with pride. That Louis should have brought Sarah Kelpmann, rich, beautiful, and a good member of the Shul, to his old father's birthday party made his day. It showed that the boy had sowed his wild oats and was now settling down with a good Jewish girl of excellent family whose prospects it turned Arthur quite dizzy to contemplate. Landed Jewish gentry, that described the Kelpmanns! That his son, with his curly black hair, sparkling dark eyes and satyr's sensuous mouth, was the best looking man in the room Arthur never doubted. Nor that Sarah Kelpmann, given the opportunity, would leap at a chance to change her name to Rose!

'My dear, good children!' He held out his arms, then clasped them to his chest as if he were literally embracing his offspring. 'Such a party to make, and for the old man! Good food, that lovely cake, and after, just for family, a dinner party! What can I say but thank you all for making an old man very happy?'

There was laughter, then applause. The Rabbi, with a strawberry in one hand, cried: 'Old? Oh, Arthur!'

'Well, sixty feels old,' Arthur admitted. 'Fifty-nine, a boy, no less. Sixty, old.' He turned to grin engagingly at his assembled grandchildren. Tina's large brood; Cecy's two boys, Bertram and Conrad. 'If the old man's to blow out sixty candles, he needs a helper or two!' The little ones, dark-haired David, Henny with his plume of yellow fluff, Kitty with her dusky, clustering curls, ran to him, jostling and shouting with cries to be chosen. Stella hovered, not wanting to seem a baby. 'Three? Only three of my grandchildren to give me a hand? What about the men? Hey, boys?'

Little, dark Con, with his monkey's face and wiry body, caught Stella's hand and the two came forward. Desmond, smiling, self-consciously stroking his chin, was next, with Frank and Bertram close behind.

'That's better! Now we have a chance. But listen, chaps, we'll need strategy!' The eight young heads gathered close to his as his whisper made the little ones nod eagerly, the older ones choke on giggles.

'At the count of three! One . . . two . . . wait for it, wait for it . . . and *three!*'

The table rocked as the boys leaned on it, causing Tina to squeak with alarm and Cecy's little hands to fly apprehensively to her mouth, and the cake tilted perilously, but the candles went out to a man. Someone clapped, it was taken up by others, there were cheers, and then they were singing 'Happy Birthday' at the top of their voices and continuing, without a pause, into 'We all wish you *mazel tov*'.

Arthur, beaming, conducting with both hands, caught the Rabbi's eye and saw him cock a glance from the fair

Neyler grandchildren to their fair father, then look across at Bertram's dark, aquiline face and at Con's wrinkled monkey grin. The non-Jewish children were singing as loudly, and with as much enthusiasm, as any member of his Jewish family.

2

The tea party had been an enormous success, there could be no doubt of that, Tina told herself, and hoped fervently that the dinner party, and the subsequent bridge game, would also go off well. Bridge being Poppa's favourite way of spending an evening she had little choice but to propose it, and the family had agreed, with kindness if not enthusiasm.

At first, the gap between bidding the tea party guests farewell and sitting the family down to dinner had seemed an insurmountable problem. But then Ted had thought of the tennis court. So the women were advised to bring tennis skirts and the men flannels and straw hats, and though no one was particularly expert they enjoyed several sets, which were watched indulgently by Arthur and the older members of the party.

The only thing that had marred that part of the day for Tina had been her visit to the nursery. She had left the tennis party to check on the younger children and had found Millie, the nursery maid, supervising the eating of bread and milk by three nightgowned youngsters, all washed and brushed, whilst Stella, grimly determined to keep to her slightly later bedtime though her eyelids were drooping, ate bread and jam and an apple cut into quarters, and waited for her hour to strike.

'Well done, Millie. Everything went beautifully and the children looked lovely. I want to congratulate Nanny. Where is she?'

'She's changing out of her afternoon dress m'm,' Millie said. 'Back into her print, I daresay.'

Heaven alone knows what sent me along to Nanny's room, Tina told herself afterwards. Am I glad or sorry that I went? She could not answer the question since it raised an even harder one — having pried on Nanny, what was she going to do about it? In the end, as with all her problems, she took it to Ted, changing into his dinner jacket in his dressing room.

She opened the door, half fearing that Abe might have come up too, and be talking to Ted as he changed. But Ted was alone, already clad in black trousers and a white frilled shirt. She crossed the room, put her arms round his waist, and laid her hot cheek against his back. He turned round, still holding the ends of the black bow tie he had been in the act of tying, and kissed her.

'Poor darling, are you worn out? Never mind. In another three or four hours they'll be going home and it will all be over!'

'Oh, Ted, it's something much worse than tiredness!'

He always knew when she was genuinely distressed. His face became alert at once and he dropped the ends of his tie to put his arms round her.

'What's upset you?'

She had blurted out the whole story then: the trip to the nursery, Millie telling her that Nanny was changing out of her afternoon dress, her own visit to Nanny's small bedroom to thank her for bringing the children down looking so delightful.

Here Tina paused for a moment. Edward looked quizzical.

'Well? Tell me the worst! Had she gone off and left Millie in charge?'

Tina shook her head, her eyes on the floor.

'Oh no, she was there all right. *And* changing. In fact, she had h-hardly anything on at all!'

'And that upset you? Nanny's only human, you know. I expect she was feeling hot!'

'She was being human and feeling hot,' Tina said in a small voice. 'So was Louis. On Nanny's bed! In a c-compromising p-position.'

'My God!' Ted's face darkened. 'That little swine! I won't have him treating my servants like whores! I'll forbid him the house!'

'It's all right, Ted. I shall have to dismiss Nanny, so it won't happen again. But . . .'

'You will dismiss nobody! What good would that do? She's a damned fine nanny, you've said so a score of times. It's your unprincipled, immoral brother who's at fault, not the girl.'

His fury astonished her. She blinked nervously up at him as he shouted.

'But, Ted, I *must* dismiss her. I can't have a loose woman looking after my children!'

'She isn't a loose woman just because she succumbed to Louis's blandishments. Knowing him, he probably forced himself on her. I won't have the girl suffer for Louis's passions.'

'No, Ted, you don't understand! She was *enjoying* it! Truly! She was p-pressing Louis's head to her breast and he was mumbling on her skin and she was groaning, moving . . . it was horrible!'

He had been holding her close but now he put her away from him, looking down at her with gleaming eyes, slowly shaking his head.

'Tina, I'm ashamed of you! This very morning, when I . . .'

Her face flamed scarlet and she stood on tiptoe to put her hand over his mouth.

'Don't! There's nothing cheap or sordid about our love, Ted. We're married, it's different! What we do is . . . in the eyes of . . . well, with the approval of . . .'

He let her stutter herself into silence. They had been married in a register office, while she was still a minor, without her father's consent, and had kept well away from Norwich until Tina was pregnant and an annulment would merely have plunged her family into the sort of scandal they would most want to avoid. When she was quiet he took her shoulders and shook her gently.

'I'm not comparing our lovemaking with Louis's sordid

21

affairs, my darling. I'm merely saying that just because you saw Nanny at a very private moment you mustn't judge her by it. Physical ecstasy isn't something that can be turned on and off like a tap. She could have fought like a tiger to keep Louis at bay, but by the time you saw them . . . Damn it, she's probably as deeply in love with Louis as she can be by now! I'd like to wring his neck!'

Tina heaved a huge sigh and leaned her head against his chest.

'I see. But I'll never be able to look at her again without thinking about . . . that.'

'What about her? Hasn't it occurred to you that she'll feel just the same? She may even give her notice because of it!'

'She didn't see me,' Tina said bitterly. 'I daresay the Black Watch could have played the bagpipes marching round the bed and she wouldn't have let it disturb her.'

Ted's mouth twitched.

'You must forget what you saw, love. I'll have a word with Louis. I won't mention that you saw anything, don't worry.'

'Must you? Speak to Louis, I mean. If I'm not to dismiss Nanny, couldn't you just forget I told you? Then we can be comfortable again.'

Ted sighed. Sometimes his wife could be very difficult!

'Could you be comfortable if I didn't speak to Louis? Knowing that every time he came into the house he was just waiting for the chance to nip up to the nursery and get Nanny into bed?'

'No . . . yes . . . I don't know! Don't you *see*, Ted, that if I dismissed Nanny I wouldn't have to worry at all? Louis is my brother, I can't forbid him the house, but there are always other nannies wanting work.'

'That's the most stupid and immoral suggestion I've ever heard!' Ted was angry, and she hated him to be angry. She watched his face harden against her and could have killed Nanny, whose fault it was. 'Tina, don't you understand that with Louis, if it wasn't Nanny it would be the nursery maid? Or the cook? Can't you see that? Louis likes women!'

'You keep blaming Louis! It's never Nanny's fault! I wish I'd not said a word to you, then I could have . . .'

He caught hold of her and shook her till her teeth rattled.

'If you dare to dismiss Nanny Sutton, my girl, you'll answer to me for it! Is that clear? This house is run for your convenience and mine, not for Louis'. The truth is that you won't look facts in the face and see Louis for the rascal he is, but this time I'm going to make you. And now get into the bathroom and wash those tears away. Comb your hair and put on your best dress and come down to dinner with me. And for God's sake act as if nothing had happened. You may be sure Louis will!'

They sat round the table and Arthur beamed at them all and loved them, every one. He thought them happy and this pleased him, for he loved his family to be happy. Indeed, looking round the table at the façade each put on, they did seem to be a happy gathering. But beneath the surface the worries and miseries, the uncertainties and the disillusions, worked on each adult member of the party.

Tina was unhappy because she could not dismiss the children's nanny, and Ted was dreading having to tell Louis what he thought of his behaviour. Becky was eating her heart out because she was a year older than Rachel and still unmarried.

Rachel, sitting beside Solomon, was unhappy because she did not love him. He was suitable, Jewish, and he was fond of her. But he was so *dull*, so self-righteous! Last term she had been invited by Louis to the end of term ball at his college. She had gone and Louis, typically, had turned up with some dreadful, fast-looking female on his arm, introduced Rachel to a couple of his friends, and disappeared. But one of the friends, Frederick Sansom, had danced with her all evening, taken her into the summer-decked gardens for chicken salad and icecream, and rowed her down the river as dawn broke, to make discreet love in the shelter of some willow trees. It had been a night to remember, and Rachel could not forget it. Frederick had not been handsome or charming, but he had had a warmth and a liveliness of mind which Solomon patently lacked.

Four weeks had elapsed since that occasion, and Frederick Sansom had written to her five times. Day after day she nerved herself to write and tell him she was engaged to Solomon, or to write and beg him to rescue her from her loveless match. But as yet she had done neither. She had replied to the letters in the most colourless and guarded tones, and now she sat at the dinner table, crumbling her bread roll in thin, nervous fingers, and wishing she was brave, like Tina. Tina had thrown convention, parental affection and security in Poppa's face, and gone off with the man she loved. Would she, Rachel, have the courage to do likewise? She doubted it.

Louis was not experiencing any pangs of conscience because he had enjoyed the children's nanny; he considered such moments to be life's small compensations for the many dullnesses he suffered daily, such as this confounded dinner party. But he was unhappy because Sarah was furious with him. Most unfairly, for she knew nothing of the Nanny episode, she was angry because he had promised they would play bridge with the old man after dinner. So now she sat beside him, icicle cool, scarcely saying a word to him, though she laughed and flirted a little with her other neighbour, his confounded, cocky little nephew, Desmond.

'What's for pudding, Tina mine? That bird . . .' Arthur kissed the tips of his fingers extravagantly as the wreck of the roast goose was borne away. 'The recipe for that stuffing Alice would give her right hand to possess! You're still the queen of cooks, Tina mine!'

Cecy tried to strangle the jealousy which rose in her breast whenever Poppa praised Tina, and partially succeeded. She was not a jealous person by nature, but it was hard not to envy Tina Ted's astonishing good looks, and those tall, broad-shouldered sons of hers with their blue eyes and fair hair. She adored Abe, but he looked every one of his forty-five years and the beauty of his soul did not show in his dark-skinned, beaky face. Her own sons were clever and good looking enough, until they sat round

24

the table beside the Neyler boys. Desmond and Frank made her darling Bertram and even little Con look foreign, small; insignificant almost. But Tina was answering Poppa and Cecy banished her envy.

'Well, Poppa, there's orange and lemon sorbet, because the children love iced puddings, and then there's raspberry meringue or apricot mousse. We thought we'd have cold sweets after the goose, and I know how you love meringues.'

Arthur was delighted with everything, and, when the table was cleared and Ted had announced that they would have coffee and mints on the terrace, he was the first to get to his feet, offer his arm to Becky, and lumber off, leaning on her and on one of his sticks, anxious to get the coffee over so that the game of cards might begin.

It was at this point that Louis approached Tina.

'Can I have a word with you, big sister?'

He was laughing because he was over a foot taller than she, but to his surprise she went very red before nodding curtly and preceding him out of the room. In the hall she glanced up at him, her eyes having difficulty in meeting his. He thought she must have been arguing with Ted. They had quite violent rows at times for all they loved each other so desperately. He put his arm round her shoulders.

'Poor little sis. Are you tired? Look, I just wanted to tell you that I'm in Sarah's black books. I wondered if you could possibly get me off the hook?'

Her eyes rounded and her mouth dropped open.

'Me? Get you off the hook?'

'Who else? Sarah's mad as fire with me because I've agreed to play bridge. Apparently she hates the game, though she's quite good. I wondered if you could arrange something – perhaps play with two tables instead of three? Or I'd willingly fetch the Rabbi and his wife to make up numbers.'

'No, I could not! I wonder you dare suggest such a thing, Louis!' She shot her brother a fulminating look. 'I won't have you hurting Poppa so, and at his own birthday party!'

She turned her shoulder on him and made for the conservatory. Louis, following, touched her arm.

'Don't get your rag out! I'll calm Sarah down. I just thought I'd ask, that's all!'

He kept his hand on her arm and despite herself Tina softened towards him. Louis was abominably spoilt, that was the trouble, and she had done her share of spoiling him when he was small. No use turning on him now because he still wanted his own way!

'Look, Louis, would it help if I told Sarah that Poppa is always in bed by ten thirty? You might take her on somewhere else. I'm sure you'd find plenty to do at that time.'

'No. Leave it to me. She's a good girl, really.'

He crossed the conservatory and slumped elegantly into the vacant chair next to Sarah, then leaned across and began to whisper in her ear. Presently, Tina saw the girl smile.

She was a handsome girl, the heiress to old man Kelpmann's millions, with a magnificent figure — she must have stood quite five foot ten inches in her stockinged feet. For the first time, it occurred to Tina to wonder why Sarah had consented to come here tonight. Would such a girl seriously consider allying herself to Louis, a twenty-year-old student without a penny to his name?

Tina looked at her brother, at the broad shoulders, the curly black hair, the slight, but undeniably attractive, air of dissipation which hung about him. She thought wryly that had he lived a hundred years earlier he would have done very well in the Regency, when young bucks fought and womanised and drank deep. But in 1912 he would not get much tolerance from people who mattered if he continued to seduce servants and barmaids, and to offer gratuitous insults to young ladies. For she knew, though she supposed that Louis did not, what an insult to Sarah his seduction of Nanny had been.

There was one spark of light in the midst of so much darkness, however. Surely, having so recently slaked his appetite, he would behave with decorum when he took Sarah home, and would not try to seduce her in the front seat of his father's Delaunay?

If Tina has underestimated Louis, she had also under-estimated Sarah. When the brand-new, dark blue Delaunay drew up outside the Kelpmann mansion it carried one very furious but still virtuous young lady and one scratched and equally furious young man, nursing an incipient black eye.

'Damn it, Sarah, I was only trying to *kiss* you,' Louis said mendaciously, as the car stopped with a swish and scatter of the deep gravel. 'If that's what you're going to do every time you're kissed . . .'

'Louis, kissing I understand, kissing I enjoy. Mauling, however, is another thing entirely. You must learn to keep it for your kitchen maids and shop girls, because young ladies are not used to such treatment!'

'The young ladies I know don't punch,' Louis growled resentfully. He now knew how Sarah had learned the back-hand which had been much admired that evening on the tennis court! By punching ardent suitors in the eye, just as this particular ardent suitor had succeeded in getting his hand down the provocatively low-cut front of her evening gown!

'I don't think you know any young ladies,' Sarah said reflectively. 'Your reputation has gone before you, Louis, and rumour has it that you prefer the easier manners and morals of the lower classes.'

'Damn it, what a thing to say! And what about my sisters? Do you think they punch and scratch their gentle-men friends?'

'I daresay they would, if their gentlemen friends tried to do what you tried to do!'

Louis sighed patiently and put his hand, with a certain amount of caution, over hers as it lay on her lap.

'You're very young for eighteen, Sarah. I assure you that *all* men want to touch nice things, and that doesn't mean . . .'

She interrupted him without apology, her fine eyes sparkling in the faint light from the gas lamps which flanked the front door. Her lips were curved into a half-smile, and a dimple appeared in one flushed cheek.

'Louis, I'm by no means as inexperienced as you would like to think! I've been to a great many dances and parties when staying with my mother's relatives in London, and I've been kissed by any number of young men, and none of them behaved as you did. Look, it's absolutely useless your trying to justify your actions, because it's impossible, so the discussion's getting us nowhere! Do you want to take me out again?'

Fifteen minutes earlier, being punched in the eye in a country lane, nearly breaking his wrist when extracting his fingers from their warm and comfortable resting place, he had vowed he never wanted to set eyes on her again. But she was laughing up at him, her lively, sensual face caught in the golden light, the outline of that magnificent body, those splendid breasts, tantalising him with their nearness. He knew that he must see her again. Such stern resistance was made, he told himself, to be conquered.

'I do, Sarah,' he said humbly. 'I really do.'

'Then there must be no more nonsense.'

He sighed, then crossed his fingers behind his back.

'I promise you. Not until . . .'

'What?'

'I was only going to say not until you were willing! That's all! If you were willing there could be no harm . . .' He looked at her and grinned. 'Damn it, Sarah, you're laughing at me!'

'Oh, Louis, you're incorrigible.' But she was smiling, and he knew she had relented. 'Will you come indoors for a drink before driving home?'

Louis pulled a face and touched his swollen eye, the long scratch down one cheek.

'Like this? No, I think your father might put two and two together and make five. I'll come and see you in a few days, if I may, when the wounds have healed.

She chuckled softly, then said a little impatiently: 'Well? Aren't you going to come round and open my door?'

He put a tentative hand on her smooth, bare shoulder.

'But I've not kissed you goodnight yet. Surely you'll let me kiss you goodnight?'

She laughed again and leaned across towards him. He touched her lightly on the shoulders, drawing her near, and felt her firm breasts push against his dinner jacket. Only the throbbing of his eye kept his hands where they belonged. She kissed him and he kissed her too – the most gentle and decorous of salutations. Then, before he could forget himself, he jumped from the car and went round to open the door. He saw her up the steps and watched until the front door closed behind her, then started the engine, and drove back down the drive.

It did not occur to him at once, but when he had reached home and was garaging his car the thought struck him. He had enjoyed that brief, inglorious struggle with Sarah more than the entire seduction of the Neyler nanny! Could this mean that virtue would bring its own reward, in time?

It was a new idea and one to which he intended to devote some thought. Until that evening he had considered women as man's natural prey and nothing more. He had cared nothing for the mind behind the pretty face; all he had demanded was good nature allied to complete compliance with his desires. But Sarah, he reflected, was different. Time alone would prove whether different would also mean better!

3

Parties, Mark reflected as he drove back along the coast road towards the Peninsula farm, seemed to be in the air today. He had driven into Dunedin to collect the mail and had just finished reading a letter from Ted in which he had described his father-in-law's sixtieth birthday party and the family get-together which had followed.

Mark, who had been to see the principal of the largest school for boys in the city, was planning a party of his own, too. There were several reasons for it, the most overt one being that he and Su had been married three years, which was a very good reason for celebrating.

When he thought of the doubts and fears which had preceded his actually asking Su if she would marry him, he could only marvel at his own stupidity. But of course it had not been so simple then. There was the twenty-year age gap for a start, and the fact that he had fled from the farm and spent four wasted years in America fighting to get over the raw, scarlet pain of Wen's death. Throughout those four years, the longing for his home and for Su had seemed to him not natural and good, but evil, a betrayal of his perfect relationship with Wen. Yet though he always thought of the years in America as the wasted years, it had not been so. It had taken those years to make him see that another woman could not supplant Wen, because their life together had been perfect, and was over. Another love-affair could take nothing from Wen – indeed, it would give, because he would be able to remember the good times without stirring up the aching sense of loss which made him wince at the mention of her name.

Now, driving back to the Peninsula farm, he beguiled the time by remembering that other homecoming, more than three years ago.

He had been a little hurt when the ship had docked and there had been no one to meet him. It seemed strange that, after a four-year absence, there should be no one at the quayside. He had cabled, but had kept it short and succinct. Had he been too short, too succinct? So far as he could recall he had simply said he was coming on the *Boston Star* and asked them to meet him. Surely that was plain enough? The exact time of the ship's arrival would have been given in the local paper, so there should have been no reason for their absence.

He did not have much luggage, just a large and shabby

trunk, a suitcase, and a Gladstone bag containing a stuffed crocodile for Johnny, a pair of china figures for Toddy and Freda to put on their mantelpiece, and a feather boa for Su. He was doubtful, now, about the boa, which had got crushed on its long journey and looked somehow tatty and disreputable, as though it had once graced the shoulders of a dance-hall girl but had been cast aside as too shabby. Still, perhaps Freda could wash it, make it look perky again.

He went over to where the cabs and their patient horses stood and hired one of them, then helped the cabby to lug his baggage over and stow it in the capacious boot. The cabby was taciturn, not in the least interested in Mark or his homecoming, merely climbing ponderously back on to the box and clicking to his horse.

Going through the city, Mark pressed his nose against the window. It had changed, perhaps, but not enough to hurt. Still beautiful, with its gracious houses, tree-lined streets and quiet, green parks, it warmed his heart as did the backdrop of blue hills in the distance. Over there was Waihola, where he had spent his childhood, and as the cab turned on to the coast road he heard the mew of the gulls and the muted surge of the surf and thought of the enchanted beaches and the sting of the wind and the freedom that to him was part of New Zealand. He could not forget that he had found Wen's body on a beach, lying in the surf, but knew that it would no longer have the power to numb his enjoyment of the shoreline. It did no good to dwell on the sad times. Wen herself would never have permitted it, he knew that now. He would remember only the good times, the loving, the laughter.

When he saw the farm his heart jumped, but not because it was different; it seemed to have stayed exactly the same. He and his luggage were set down outside the white-walled garden. He opened the gate, remembering how he and Wen had made it Johnny-proof, for their son had been a terrible one for wandering. The proofing had been simply chicken wire to block the foot-high gap beneath the gate. It had gone, and Johnny, he guessed, would find it somewhat difficult now to wriggle beneath the gate! There was a good deal of difference between a two-year-old and six-year-old!

He looked at the house as he walked up the path towards it. The front door, when he left, had been painted green; it was green still. The roses had bloomed around it, deep red and palest yellow; they bloomed there still. They were taller, further up the stones, but they were still as colourful, and their scent, hauntingly sweet, brought tears to his eyes which blurred their brightness.

His hand went to the door knob, then drew back. After four years, he had no rights here. He should knock. He was a visitor, someone scarcely considered now, who had deserted them when they needed him most. They had made their own lives, and no matter how little he might like it he was alien here, wanting acceptance but not daring to demand it. He knocked.

There was no answer from within the house but he was content, for the moment, to stand in the sunshine and dream a little. On such a brilliant day he guessed that the farmworkers would be in the fields, and probably Su and his son had driven into Dunedin to meet him. He must have missed them. He knocked again, then cautiously tried the door knob, but the door resisted him. Locked, of course. Well, the back door was never locked; he would go round the back.

The back door was locked as well and that really startled him. They *never* locked the back door; friends, family, the hands, knew they could wander in and out at will. Then he chided himself. Things changed, and people too. Su was a very pretty young girl, living alone but for the boy. He knew she had not married, for, though he wrote rarely and though his letters were stiff and uninformative, Su had not treated him to such a correspondence. Her letters were frequent and lively, full of chatter about the child, the farm, her daily life. And Toddy told her of milk yields, wool yields, haycrops and horses.

He waited by the back door for another moment, then went over and peered through the window. At once, fear clutched at his heart. The fire was out in the stove! What was happening? A faint premonition of disaster touched him with its icy bat-wings. Not . . . Oh, God, don't let anything have happened to Su! Not that innocent, charming child! Dear God, take the farm, take me, take the whole of the Otago peninsula if You must, but let Su be unharmed!

He took to his heels and ran across the yard to Toddy's cottage. Freda would surely be in. She was always either in or at the farm. She must be in!

His impetuous knock was followed by an even more impetuous entry; he stood in the middle of the small kitchen, his heart beating like a drum, smelling the good, comfortable smell of baking, floor polish, fresh logs on a fire.

'Freda!'

She came hurrying through, a duster in one hand. She looked exactly the same, her bushy grey hair sticking out untidily round her head, her good-natured, weathered face placid as ever. She entered the room smiling, with words on her lips. The words died, the smile faltered. The duster went to her mouth. Round eyes stared at him above the yellow stuff.

'Mark? Oh, Mark!'

Then she was in his arms, kissing him, crying, breaking free to rub her eyes with the duster.

'Wait till Toddy sees you! You've been to the farm-house?'

He nodded. He felt calm now. He knew that they were all right, just by seeing Freda's expression.

'Ah, then you'll know they're away. Oh, poor Su, poor Johnny! They'll break their hearts to find they've missed your homecoming, honest, Mark. To think of them missing you! And Toddy was worried because they'd gone off quiet-like, only left a note, no address. But they won't be gone long if I know them, no fear!'

She patted his shoulder, her eyes tear-shiny.

'You could do with some feedin' up, I can see that! Sit down and I'll make coffee. There's some of them ring doughnuts you and Ted used to be so fond of in the jar in the pantry — cooked them barely an hour ago. Johnny likes 'em, too.' She glanced at the clock above the dresser. 'Toddy'll be up for his dinner presently. My word! To see his face!'

He enjoyed her voice like a good meal; the comfortable, New Zealand twang which he had sorely missed. He sat down at the table, sniffing the coffee pot as she added boiling water to the freshly ground grains.

'Away? Didn't Sue get my cablegram?'

She was in the pantry now, getting the cooky jar down from the shelf. She returned to put it down in front of him and bring the coffee pot over from the stove with two mugs and a bowl of brown sugar.

'There! I'll just fetch you some milk.' She bustled out and was quickly back. 'What cablegram?'

'Hell, didn't it arrive? I sent one from New York, asking them to send someone down to meet my ship.'

Freda poured the coffee and sat down, a frown creasing her brow. She helped herself to sugar, two heaped spoonfuls, then stirred it thoughtfully.

'A cablegram! So it was that . . .'

'They got it, then? And *left*? Ran away?'

His voice reflected his hurt.

'It can't have been yours which disturbed them.' Freda's sharp eyes had seen the change which came over his face at the suspected rejection. 'Look, Mark, it won't have been your cable. Toddy'll know. Johnny tells him everything, and . . .'

The door opened behind him and Freda's hand shot out, keeping Mark, who would have risen, in his seat, back to the door.

'Toddy, guess who's come visiting?'

There was the sort of silence that speaks. Then Mark turned and was on his feet in one movement and he and Toddy clutched each other, faces working with emotion.

'Mark!' Toddy's deep voice cracked with the depth of his feeling. 'After all these years! And the varmints away!'

'Where, Toddy?' Freda's voice was carefully disinterested. 'What sent them flying off, d'you suppose? I know you've been close with me and the others, but Mark's got a right to know. He's Johnny's father.'

Toddy went over to the dresser and took down a mug, then returned to the table. He poured himself coffee, added milk, and pulled up a chair as Mark sat down again.

'A cablegram; that's sure. But *where* they went . . .' He grinned across at Mark. 'Your brother Ted's caused the young 'uns a deal of worry, though Freda and I told them over and over Ted ain't the sort to throw his weight. Or poke his nose where it ain't wanted. Tell him straight and he'll back off, I told young Su. Not that they listened, I daresay.'

Freda tapped her husband's arm.

'Toddy, Mark sent a cable. He's thinkin' it might have been that sent 'em off. I told him no, but . . .'

Toddy's grizzled eyebrows rose and his mouth scoffed.

'You think young Su would have gone *anywhere* if she'd known you were comin' back? She'd have driven us all mad. that's for certain, gettin' the place ready, shampooin' all the sheep like as not. She'd . . . ' He stopped, to stare very hard at Mark. 'What did you say in that there cable, any road?'

Mark strained to remember. It had been such an innocuous cable!

'I think I said *Neyler returning on SS Boston Star stop Please meet.* Or something like that. No, I've got it! *Neyler arriving Dunedin on SS Boston Star stop Please meet.* That's clear enough, surely?'

Toddy was grinning, the relief written all over his broad, homely face.

'Oh, sure. Plain enough if you've been gettin' cables from Ted Neyler, askin' if he shouldn't send for young Johnny to come to England for schoolin' and upbringin' with his own kids. Clear enough when there hasn't been a mention of yourself comin' home!'

Mark felt light suddenly, as if he had woken from a nightmare.

'Then — it was just a misunderstanding? They thought I was Ted, coming to take Johnny?' He gave a crack of laughter and reached for a doughnut, cramming it into his mouth and speaking thickly through it. 'What a thing! How can we get in touch with them to bring them back? I can't wait to see them both.'

'That's goin' to be difficult.' Toddy's face was thoughtful. 'Johnny ain't secretive, but it was all done in such a rush, and not a murmur did he let out as to where they was goin'. Just goin' on a visit, that's all he said.'

'Oh, curse!' Mark absently reached for another doughnut. I've waited so long, he thought, that a few more weeks won't kill me. 'Well, what'll we do?'

Freda got up and went over to the stove.

'We'll let it be known that you're home, Mark. That's what'll bring 'em, feelin' foolish, you bet! It's a word-of-mouth country, this, and news travels fast. Give it time and one morning you'll wake up and they'll be squabbling up the garden path like kids, to see who'll be first in the door.'

'You're right. I'm really not in a hurry, though it will be marvellous to see . . . to see them. In the meantime, it's been a year or two since I worked the farm. Toddy'll keep me busy, giving me lessons.'

Toddy looked across at him, his faded blue eyes very bright.

'You're home for good, then? This ain't just a visit?'

Mark gripped the table top and bit his lip. Suddenly he wanted to put his head down on the table and weep like a baby, but it would only embarrass Toddy. Instead, he leaned across and grasped the other man's work-roughened hand.

'For good, Toddy. I'll not leave again.'

4

'A card! There's a card, Mark!'

Toddy burst into the farmhouse kitchen, his face shining,

evidence of his hasty journey from the stable to the back door. Mark, sitting at the table devouring stew and dumplings, dropped his spoon. Joe, one of the hands, stared. Even Freda, usually so calm, dropped her ladle back into the cauldron and exclaimed.

'I thought they'd never write,' Mark said, reaching out a hand. 'Can I see? Who's it addressed to?'

'Freda and myself.' Toddy sank down on to his chair and wiped his forehead with a large and rather grubby handkerchief. 'But you wouldn't expect them to send a card to anyone else, not when you consider they don't know you're here!'

Freda rescued her ladle and began to serve stew into another plate for Toddy. She carried it over to the table and plonked it down in front of him, then turned to Mark, her face eager.

'What's it say? Read it aloud, Mark!'

'It's quite short. It says *Having a good time, but missing you all very much. Home soon, I hope, love to everyone, Johnny and Su.*' Mark leaned back in his chair and cast a helpless glance at Toddy. 'I'm glad you've heard, of course, but what good is it? No address, and only a beach scene, which could be anywhere.'

Toddy spooned stew into his mouth, then spoke thickly through it.

'Use your eyes, lad. The postmark!'

Mark examined the postmark, then slapped his thigh jubilantly and waved the card under Freda's nose.

'Sydney! See, Freda? By God, they've gone all the way to Australia. No wonder none of the newspaper appeals reached them!'

'Sydney! Crikey, we ought to have thought of that,' Freda remarked. 'Johnny's grandparents are there. I remember Su telling me that she still wrote to them, regular as clockwork. Her uncle and aunt, of course. They've got a restaurant there, I believe. What'll you do, Mark? Write and tell 'em to come home?'

'I could do that, though it seems rather tame. What I'd rather do is . . .'

'Mark!' Freda was laughing, shaking her head. 'You wouldn't go all that way! She says they hope to be coming home soon. Suppose you missed them? Again!'

'You're right, of course.' Mark reached out and pulled his plate near him again, beginning to eat the cooling stew. 'I suppose I could send a cablegram, asking them to come back.'

'You do that. You'll find the Lengs' address somewhere in Su's desk. You'll look through it, surely, when you know that by doing so it'll bring them home quicker?'

Mark had steadfastly refused to interfere with Su's desk, not liking to examine the contents when the owner was far away. Su had done all the necessary paperwork on the farm in his absence and the desk, after so many years, was very much her property. But now, of course, he would feel differently. There was a reason to go through it; he would be searching for an address, not merely prying into what might be her private affairs. Mark finished his stew and took a slice of bread, using it to wipe up the last of the gravy.

'I'll do it! As soon as I've finished my meal I'll find that address. And when I cable, I'll be sure to make myself crystal clear!'

The waiting was hard. Being *almost* sure that she had fled because she thought his cablegram came from Ted, being *almost* sure that she had once loved him, made for disturbed nights, attacks of depression that were foreign to his old nature. Toddy and Freda were seen to exchange quick, worried looks when they thought themselves unobserved, but Mark knew that they were judging his behaviour solely on that of the old Mark. They scarcely know this me, he thought miserably once. They knew the old, easy-going Mark who had had Wen to bolster his confidence. They did not know the emotional cripple he had become without her, nor how easily the black moods had beaten him, once.

Fortunately, there was a great deal to do. He went over to his father's farm at Waihola, where he had been brought up, and was assailed by so many mixed emotions that he dared not go straight to the house. Karl had died during his time in America, Anna had been dead these past fifteen years or so, yet still they haunted the place: Anna with her fair, good-natured face, Karl with his striking looks and abrasive personality. And perhaps the young Ted, the young Mark, haunted the place too. His had not been a happy childhood in one sense, for his father's brutality had overshadowed it, but there had been compensations. His mother's overflowing love, the closeness which existed between Ted and himself. There was no substitute for that, because a woman's love was different. Better, perhaps, but still different.

I have not set eyes on Ted for fourteen years, but we are still close, he told himself, lurking in the big barn and staring towards the log cabin. It was a cabin still, with flowering creepers around the windows as there had been in his day. The new people had built on another room, but the main building was still logs, wattled with mud. Su had written to Ted, and Ted had authorised the employment of a farm manager, a youngish man with a wife and three small children. Despite their occupation, the place had changed remarkably little. Perhaps it might have been easier if he could have looked at the outside, traced the changes. The hurt was all in the mind, because you knew that if you walked up and opened the door the very air would be different, would repudiate the Neylers. It came home to him then that love and hate can run in harness, for he had hated Karl, yet loved him too. He wasn't so bad, the old man. He had mellowed with age, and his grimness had lessened. He had adored Wen, too, and his grandson.

As he walked away, down the hill towards the lake, it occurred to Mark that until he had returned to Otago Karl had, in a sense, not been dead to him at all; or no more dead than Toddy, Freda, Su. They had been away, that was all. It was only with his homecoming, and his visit to the Waihola homestead, that he was forced to acknowledge Karl was indeed dead. It would be a while, perhaps, before he was ready to meet the new manager and his wife.

Work on the Peninsula farm occupied him fully too, once

he and Toddy had got him into useful harness once more. Toddy had had ideas over the years which he had been unable to put into practice, lacking Mark to give him authority to do so. All he had done was to keep the place ticking over, the flocks in good heart, the crops bearing. He wanted to increase their beef herd. Beef was one of Scotland's most successful exports, he had heard, and he had also heard people say that the climate of the Peninsula was very similar to that of Scotland. Why not take advantage of the climate, then, and rear good beef stock?

Mark, grinning, said that it must rain a hell of a lot in Scotland and Toddy, also grinning, said he believed that to be true. As they spoke, the Peninsula was veiled in that light but persistent rain known to some as a Scotch mist.

Change must take place now that he was home, and Mark had a good deal of faith in Toddy's judgement. His own keen interest in farming reawoke as soon as he got back to his own place, and he and Toddy spent many comfortable evenings in the cottage, planning and dreaming.

He refused, however, to move back into the farmhouse. It did not seem like his home. He told Toddy and Freda that he felt like an intruder there, but this was not quite true. He felt like an intruder only in his old bedroom. Su had not used it, but had remained in the small room he had built on for her six years before, when she had first arrived at the farm to give Wen a helping hand when the baby was born. He remembered her so vividly, stick-thin and big-eyed, talking with the most appalling cockney accent and loving them, loving Johnny when he arrived, being just what they all wanted, only they had never known it until she was there. Su Yung, Wen's little Chinese cousin.

When he thought of her like that he knew a twinge of conscience over his present feelings for her, but he dismissed it briskly. She was no longer fifteen; she was a young woman and quite capable of either dismissing him or accepting him. Time alone would tell which she would do. And in the meantime, he did not wish to sleep in the big bedroom with the view of the harbour where all the most important things had happened to him and Wen. Their wedding night had been spent in that bed, Johnny had been born in it. One day, such memories would be sweet, but now because he was alone and uncertain still the sweetness was tinged with bitterness. It would take a lot of love to reconcile him to moving back into that room.

The day came when the ship carrying Su and Johnny was due to dock. He was restless and ill at ease all morning, shaving himself twice, cutting his chin quite severely so that he had to go out decorated with a sizable chunk of cotton wool, looking infuriatingly like a Santa Claus with a nasty attack of alopecia. He and Toddy left the farm, Toddy driving the trap. Sudden fear that they might not be on the ship after all, that he might not recognise them, that their attitude might be cold, impersonal, had assailed him, and he felt that with Toddy beside him he would be able to bear any or all of these things better. Of course, his thoughts, obediently saying 'they', really meant 'she'. Johnny was a child and as such his reactions worried Mark not at all. Su, on the other hand, was of an age to resent both his arbitrary leaving and his arbitrary reappearance. Even his cablegram might be resented! Who was he to demand their return, after all? He had listened to no one whilst he was in America, heeded nothing but his own wishes, his own fears. Was he to be paid out now?

They reached the harbour just as the ship was docking. There was a long line of tethered horses and carts, cabs and carriages, but Mark left that part to Toddy. Suddenly, he could not wait for the moment when he would see her, and he pushed his way to the quay, only to watch in agony as the gangplank was lowered. He saw her then, with her hand in the child's, standing as near the top of the gangway as she could get.

A whole new set of worries promptly reared their ugly heads. She was so young! His forty years lay on his shoulders like a ton weight. He could feel it dragging him down. How dared he aspire to her, who was so young and beautiful!

They joined him and he was seized with shyness, ruffling

41

the boy's hair perfunctorily, then staring at Su. She stood there, smiling, her dark eyes alight with amusement at his stupidity. But as their eyes met her gaze faltered, and she began to fuss the child, straightening his sailor collar, smoothing his thick hair.

He took her hand. It lay in his like a child's, the fine skin covering bones as fragile as a bird's. He felt clumsy, a great oaf, beside her. He saw that her long black hair had been tied into a knot on top of her small head, that she wore a dress with a skirt which was gathered on one side, reaching fullness at ankle level. There was a little cape round her shoulders, trimmed with fur.

'So you've come home at last!'

He had meant it to sound welcoming; with dismay, he heard his own gruff voice and knew it had sounded accusatory. Su knew it too. She stepped back, her colour rising, her hand sliding from his slackened grasp.

'I'm s-sorry. It was a misunderstanding, truly it was. If I'd known it was you, wild horses wouldn't have dragged me . . . Johnny away. He's longed to see his daddy, haven't you, Johnny?' Johnny continued to stare impassively towards Toddy and the pony cart. 'Did Toddy tell you how it happened? Your brother Ted kept writing, asking if he could have Johnny, to bring him up with his own children, and I was worried stiff — Johnny was my responsibility, yet what right had I to deny your brother? I shouldn't have gone, of course I shouldn't, but . . .'

'It doesn't matter.' Hang it, he had meant to sound understanding, not bored or impatient, yet he knew he must have sounded both. Desperately, he sought for something to say which could not be misunderstood, which might retrieve the magic he had dreamed about. He found it. 'Here comes Toddy!'

Toddy reached them and, without a word, bent down and picked Johnny up, holding him close to his weather-beaten face, beaming at the boy.

'Hi, Johnny, old sport! What did you think of the Aussies, eh? My, but you've grown! Did you see Ho John and Li? Were they well? Gee, you've sure done some livin', boy!'

Mark sensed the criticism in Toddy's action, and leaned over to take Johnny's hand as Toddy stood him down on the ground again.

'I'm sorry, Johnny. I'm afraid your dad isn't too used to children.' He squatted down so that he could look into the boy's face. He was a handsome lad, and big for six, and the smiles which Toddy's greeting had brought still lingered. But his eyes refused to meet Mark's. 'How are you, son?'

He thought Johnny's face flickered at the last word, and hoped he had at last said something right, albeit by accident. The word 'son' had been inadvertent.

'I'm all right.' Johnny still looked steadfastly down at his own stout boots and wrinkled stockings. He sounded sulky, but he might have been consumed with shyness. 'Where did you leave the trap, Toddy?'

Mark pointed it out and the small boy picked up his suitcase and staggered off, listing heavily to port. The three adults watched him go in silence for a moment before Toddy spoke.

'He's a grand lad. You're lucky, Mark. I wish he was mine. You'll be real proud of him once you get to know him.'

'I'm sure I shall, if he ever looks me in the eye,' Mark said a little resentfully. 'Damn it, the kid was two when I went, a charming, naughty baby. Now he's a proper boy, and if you ask me he's no keener to find himself saddled with a father than I . . .'

The words died on his lips, too truthful, too awful, to be contemplated. Toddy bent and picked up Su's suitcase and without another word the three of them made for the trap. Mark cast a haunted glance at the slim, upright figure walking beside him without so much as a word or a look in his direction. It had all gone wrong! It was plain that Su thought of him only as her cousin's husband and her own employer. She had had a crush on him once; Wen had teased him about it, said it was a fine thing when one's husband attracted fifteen-year-olds. Had she been right? Was it just a crush from which Su had recovered as one recovers from a head cold? Her letters had been so warm and friendly, so full of artless confidences, that he had allowed himself to believe otherwise. Of his own feelings there could be no doubt. He loved her and wanted to marry her. The thought of living at the farm and watching her marry someone else sent a shaft of pain through him.

In the trap, Johnny sat beside Toddy on the driver's seat and chattered ceaselessly. Behind them, Mark and Su exchanged only the most banal remarks and then fell silent. Miserably, Mark sought for subjects of conversation which would bring him back on his old friendly footing with Su, and could think of nothing. If he talked of America, she would think about the years he had left her to carry on alone, selfishly wrapped up in his own loss and sorrow. If he talked of their lives before he left for the States, she would think of him as Wen's husband, a father figure.

The result was, of course, that he sat beside her, stiff-faced, and endured the journey. She was wearing some sort of perfume, very faint, flowerlike; he remembered enough to know that it was different. Four years ago she had smelled of baby powder, soap, and peppermints, of which she had been inordinately fond. He cleared his throat.

'That perfume — what's it called?'

She turned to him, eagerly almost, probably as glad as he to end the too-long silence.

'I'm not sure. One of the boys bought it for my birthday last year.'

His discomfiture increased. Not once, in all the time he had been away, had he sent her so much as a birthday card. Nor had he remembered his son's anniversaries. Guilt swamped him. He turned his face to the sea and said nothing more. He hated himself.

For a month he remained in Freda's cottage, only visiting the farm at lunchtime, when as many of the hands as possible ate there. He avoided speaking to Su, because he was afraid that when he told her he could not spend the rest of his life in Freda's tiny spare bedroom she would announce that she was leaving. That, he thought, would be

44

unbearable. As things stood, at least he saw her daily, watched her laugh with the hands, move about the kitchen serving the meal, bend over Johnny's books. And during that month, he took Freda's advice and tried to get to know Johnny.

'Mark, he's your son – Wen's son, if you like to look at it that way. Have you *no* feeling for him? No recollection of how you and Wen adored him?'

He could be truthful with Freda, whereas with anyone else he would have prevaricated.

'No, I haven't. My mind's muddled where the boy's concerned. He's changed, you see, so that I can't associate this big chap with the naughty, loving kid I left. He seems to belong to Su, and he doesn't like me one bit! I suppose I resent the time Su gives him, too. Teaching him lessons, taking him walks, riding out to see the Dodmans with him. He absorbs all her time and energy, you know. If I do happen to go over to the house, hoping for a word with Su, he appears. Just a pair of narrowed black eyes and a resentful mouth. No matter how politely I ask him to do something, what's more, he ignores me and turns to Su for her approval before he'll do it. I'll try, but I think I'm batting on a losing wicket.'

Freda chuckled.

'You wouldn't be the first to resent his own child, and I know Johnny doesn't help, but you must persevere! Take him for a walk one afternoon, just you and the boy. Don't let Su insist on accompanying you. Take him down to the beach, teach him how to fish, or row – something Su can't help with. You'll find he'll chatter away easily enough once you're by yourselves.'

'That's not a bad idea. I've had the feeling once or twice that it might be easier to get to know him without Su there. He feels a bit torn between us, perhaps.'

'Perhaps. And then why not take Su out somewhere one evening? You've got to get things sorted out between you. You'll have to move back into the farmhouse eventually, even if you have to get a maid of all work to move in as a sign of respectability. And why don't you ask her to marry

45

you? All this talk of the age difference is bunkum, and you know it. She's a pretty girl and she's had plenty of offers, but she's turned them all down without a qualm. Toddy and I, we always had the feeling that she was waiting for someone, and why shouldn't it be you?'

'I'd love to ask her, but suppose it spoils even what we've got now?' Mark said miserably. 'Suppose she just goes?'

'And leaves Johnny? I don't think you need fear that! Now take my advice, there's a good fellow.'

He did. Despite some grumbling on Johnny's part, he took the boy into Dunedin and between them they selected and purchased a small sailing dinghy with a pair of oars. Johnny was not a successful actor, and it soon became obvious that he adored the boat and enjoyed his afternoon sailing lessons with Mark more than almost anything else he did. Mark, who had not sailed a boat himself for more years than he liked to admit, was pleased by his own skill as a teacher and soon extremely proud of Johnny. The boy was only six, after all, yet he handled the boat with confidence and competence; and, though his attitude to his father could be somewhat ambiguous, when they were sailing together they were the best of friends.

'And now,' Freda announced firmly, after she had seen Mark and Johnny returning from the beach, each talking as hard as the other, 'you must tackle Su. There's a play on in Dunedin tomorrow night. Ask her to go with you, and to have a meal afterwards. And even if you don't ask her to marry you, you might at least get on a friendly footing. I'm sure Su is as miserable as you are — she wants to be friends, if nothing more.'

'Suppose she won't come out with me?'

'Of course she will! Why shouldn't she? I tell you I'm sure she's as keen to get something sorted out as you are!'

It took the sort of courage that Mark was rather short on at the moment, but he forced himself to go through with it. He strolled over to the farmhouse that afternoon and walked into the kitchen, determined to ask her at least to go to the theatre with him.

She refused.

'I'm terribly sorry, Mark, but I can't leave Johnny alone all that time, especially in the evening. If it was an afternoon performance we could take him as well, but I don't think they do matinees.'

Johnny, sitting at the table devouring Bovril sandwiches, smirked, and Mark, sorely disappointed, lost his temper.

'If I'd wanted to take Johnny to the theatre I'd have invited him, not you! Very well, we'll forget it.'

He turned and slammed out of the house, and went straight across to the cottage, where Freda was peeling potatoes at the sink. He was so upset that he stuttered out his explanation.

'She w-won't come! She can't leave Johnny! That damned b-brat!'

Freda straightened, and dried her hands on a tea-towel.

'Less of that language, Mark, if you please. Here, finish them potatoes!'

With that she swept out of the house and returned ten minutes later, flushed with victory.

'You can call for her at six o'clock tomorrow evening. I'll take care of master Johnny!'

Mark, having finished the last potato, cast the knife down on the draining board and turned to hug Freda.

'You're marvellous! Of course I know she doesn't want to come and you bullied her into it, but I can't stand this uncertainty any longer.'

'Doesn't want to come? Nonsense! She's as mixed up as you, that's the trouble. She's convinced herself that you still think of her as Johnny's nanny and nothing more. I told her that even if you do think that (and it's up to you, Mark, to convince her that she's wrong about it!) you would still expect her to have some time to herself. You left Johnny for them other lads, I told her, pretty severely. If you won't leave him for Mark, then what's he to think? That took her aback, I can tell you. "Oh, I'll go then. Tell him I'd love it," she says, quick as a flash.' Freda tutted, regarding him with mock severity. 'You two! I'll be glad when this charade is over, I tell you straight!'

He called for Su the following evening, sharp on six

o'clock. Su was ready, and looking splendid in a dark blue silk skirt and jacket, the skirt fashionably gathered at one side, the jacket tight fitting, with a low V neck which ended in a large butterfly bow just below the breasts. A white blouse with a heavy lace jabot, and a blue silk hat with a plume of ostrich feathers which curled around her face, completed the ensemble.

'You look so pretty,' Mark said spontaneously, and was rewarded by her flush and the gratified little smile which curved her lips. 'I wish the trap was a bit smarter!'

Beneath the brim of the hat dark eyes sparkled at him with delicious coquetry.

'You look pretty good yourself. Once we're on the road, though, I'm going to take my hat off! The feather tickles. But I'll put it on as soon as we reach the outskirts of Dunedin.'

'Good enough. Then you won't mind if I do the same with my tie?'

For the first time since her return, they were at ease together, and when he drew the reins in a sheltered part of the road where it ran between trees, and suggested that they might talk since they would arrive at the theatre very early otherwise, she agreed peacefully. He looked into her calm face and knew that, in some mysterious, womanly way, she had made up her mind about him, about their relationship. He realised too that she might have decided to reject him, yet it no longer frightened him. If she had made such a decision then it would be up to him to change her mind, for her resolve could not be stronger than his!

He drew the trap right on to the verge, then loosed the pony's head so that she might crop the grass, keeping the reins over her back so that she did not get entangled in them. Then he turned to face Su, and smiled. He had prepared a beautiful speech about responsibility and the boy, the farm, the fact that Su had not yet met a man she liked well enough to marry, all working up to a peroration which was to be his own proposal. He spoke not one word of it. Instead, he took her face between his hands, seeing the lean palms and the long, tanned fingers curved round her heart-shaped countenance.

'I love you.'

He half whispered it, and knew that he was right, that the best way is always the straight way, in the end. Love was what it amounted to; all the other things, responsibility, convention, even his proposal of marriage, were only important because he loved her.

'I love you too.'

An hour before he would not have believed she could say such a thing. Now, he simply lowered his head and kissed her lips.

What followed was inevitable. Lovers' talk, sometimes happy, sometimes wistful, boring to everyone save the lovers themselves. They laughed at each other's diffidence, at the many ways they had planned to gain the other's love, then discussed their life to come.

It was nearly midnight before it occurred to either of them that they had missed the play, left it too late to get a meal, and were, in fact, ravenously hungry.

'Never mind!' Su snuggled close to him, tucked in against his dark suit jacket, blissfully happy. 'I'll make you something nice if you come back to the farmhouse with me.'

'I'll accept that kind invitation, ma'am, though it seems pretty shabby of me. I was supposed to be entertaining you, not vice versa.'

'There'll be other times. Oh, Mark!'

He squeezed her small waist.

'Oh, Su!'

Presently, they drove into the farmyard. The cottage was in darkness but a light burned in the farmhouse window. Mark got down, then held up his arms to Su.

'Down you come. You can go in and cook me a meal whilst I rub the pony down and put the trap away. How about a beer, too? I'm pretty thirsty.'

'All right, though I could rub the pony down; I'm a farmer too, you know.'

He smiled at her, then pointed to her suit.

'Not in those clothes! Where's your hat?'

The hat had been carefully placed on the seat between

them some six hours earlier. Now, one look at it was enough. It would never be the same again.

'Goodness, that hat cost me a week's wages,' Su exclaimed. 'How furious Freda will be! She thought it a great extravagance and scolded me soundly for buying it. And the suit, of course.'

'What did you buy it for?' Mark asked, leading the pony into the stable and pretending not to notice that Su was following him. 'It's almost as beautiful as you are!'

'For this evening.' She smiled naughtily at him. 'I thought if I looked very grown up and stylish you might treat me less as a little girl and more as a woman!'

He was incredulous.

'Never! When could you have bought it?'

'I cadged a lift from Joe the minute Freda said she'd sit with Johnny. Joe went into town for more cattle cake. I didn't tell Freda how much it cost. She guessed it was expensive, and she barely had time to denounce me for a spendthrift before you arrived to pick me up. And now she'll have to admit that it was money well spent, since it was Su in the suit you asked to marry you, and not the ordinary Su.'

He was rubbing down the little mare, but he turned at that, raising his eyebrows at her in the light of the lamp he had lit in the stall.

'Who's jumping to conclusions? I don't remember actually asking you to marry me at all! I just took it for granted that you would!'

She put a hand, cool and small, on the back of his neck.

'True. Ask me now.'

He finished the pony, stood back, then took her in his arms. He rested his chin on the smooth crown of her hair.

'Will you marry me, Su, and make me the happiest man on earth, etcetera, etcetera? I don't care now that you're just a baby, and that I'm far too . . .'

'So you're back at last.' Toddy's would-be accusatory tone could not mask a certain satisfaction in his voice, nor the scowl on his face hide the gleam in his eyes. 'I'll finish off here, Mark. You go on in. Did you have a good evening? Where did you go for a meal?'

'We didn't actually eat,' Mark said guiltily. 'But Su's going to cook me something now. I'm afraid I'll be a bit late in, but I'll come quietly and won't slam anything.' He still had his arms round Su, and now he turned her so that they both faced Toddy. 'Are you going to congratulate us?'

'What for? For taking leave of your senses? Keeping the poor lass out till this hour and not feeding her!'

'We're going to get married.'

Toddy walked around the pony, checking that Mark had finished with her, then doused the lantern and walked out of the stable.

'I knew that! It took you enough time, the pair of you, to come to your senses and realise what everyone else has known this past month! A fool could tell you were plumb crazy for each other. Tell Freda to bring some grub with her when she comes to the cottage. She's made you a late supper.'

They were left, standing in the stable doorway, staring open-mouthed at each other as Toddy stumped towards his cottage.

———

5

———

It was a fine Saturday morning, and the children were in the tree-house. Strictly speaking, it was several tree-houses in two trees, the first a yew and the second a great tall chestnut in whose lofty branches only the older children were allowed to perch. The yew had stout platforms on three of its boughs, and the boughs themselves were so close that climbing it was like climbing the stairs.

The top platform in the chestnut tree needed considerable agility and nerve to reach, and was reserved for Desmond, Frank and Bertram – not that they ever succeeded in keeping Mabel and Conrad from climbing up there whenever the fancy took them. Indeed Mabs, in her black stockings and black button boots, with her skirts tucked shamelessly into her bloomers, could climb like a monkey and was totally fearless. Neither Desmond nor Frank could forget the day they had been playing tennis when the ball, walloped by Desmond and sped on its way by a fair gale, had disappeared through the trees and into next door's orchard. Mabel, watching, had galloped to the chestnut tree and ascended it with almost shocking ease, not even bothering to discipline her skirts, so that the wind, billowing them out like a balloon, did its utmost to pluck her from her perch. The boys had watched, terrified, as the great trunk swayed and the branches whipped to and fro, but Mabel slid down to the ground and trotted over to them, remarking placidly that the ball was clearly visible from the upper platform, and telling them precisely where to find it.

The boy who will admit himself worsted at tree-climbing by a small girl has yet to be born, however, so Desmond and Frank thanked Mabel casually and went to fetch their tennis ball. They were careful, after that, never to enter into competition with such a superb tree-scaler!

But on this particular Saturday there was no wind and, though the colours of the leaves proved that summer was limping to its close and autumn would not be long arriving, it was still a glorious day. The four youngest children were playing at tea parties in the yew tree; from his loftier perch Frank could see the little pink china cups and saucers and the little woven baskets containing food, either real or make-believe, set out in the centre of the platform.

'When'll the Sollies be here, Frank?'

Desmond, his eyes half closed, was gazing out through the leaves in the direction of a distant boarding school's grounds. He had recently discovered that from this particular spot he could watch the boarders as they strolled in their garden, or played tennis, and it was a favourite pastime now to climb up here with a pair of binoculars and watch. Frank disapproved of this new craze and sincerely hoped that his own fourteenth birthday would not bring a sudden preoccupation with anything as soppy as girls!

'It's Saturday, you loon. They won't be here until after luncheon.'

'Of course. Damnation! Well, where's Mabel, then?'

Frank had a grubby piece of string round his hands and was trying to work out a new form of cat's cradle. He shot a quick, sly look at Desmond through his lashes. He only hoped his brother did not count Mabs as a girl. She was his, Frank's, friend and companion. He had no desire for Desmond, who thought her a silly kid, to suddenly decide she was worth his attention!

'Probably caught in the kitchen, peeling spuds or stringing beans or something. You know how Ruthie grabs her. It isn't fair, really. It isn't as if she's paid to help.'

'I daresay she's quite glad of the chance to nick buns and that. Anyway, she helps Mrs Walters, doesn't she?'

'I know. But it isn't as if Mrs Walters gets off early or something because Mabs helps her. She just gets through twice as much work!'

'Mm hmm.' Desmond flung himself back suddenly on the platform, abandoning his vigilance. 'I forgot, on a Saturday the girls go home, or most of 'em. It's a dratted weekly boarding school!'

'You weren't watching those daft hens?' Frank sighed disapprovingly. 'I wonder why they go back to school a week before we do?'

'Because we're term boarders, not weekly. We'd probably *starve* if our terms were as long as theirs. One of those girls is quite pretty, though. Lovely legs.'

'Don't be so bloody stupid,' Frank said sharply, resorting to term boarder's language. 'I'm going to fetch Mabel. She doesn't keep on!'

Desmond rolled on to his stomach.

'Don't bother. I'll go.'

Before Frank could gather his wits – or free his hands from the over-intricate cat's cradle – his brother was disappearing down through the leaves. Frank, left behind, sat down and felt resentful and uneasy. Why Mabel? She was three whole years younger than Desmond, and not a bit grown up for her age. A vague, formless worry began to nag at his mind. Mabel was *his* friend! Desmond had better leave her alone!

In the absence of a companion, Frank decided he might as well climb down. He supposed he could go along to the kitchen as well as Desmond, and then they could both escort Mabel to the tree.

He had barely reached ground level, however, before Mabel and Desmond came into the clearing, Desmond carrying an enamel jug and Mabel a string bag full of iced buns.

'It's our elevenses; Ruthie said we might as well have it out here as it's such a nice day. The littles must go to the conservatory, though.'

Elevenses were always served in the conservatory on sunny days. Drinks of milk, iced buns and apples or bananas were handed out indiscriminately to anyone who happened to be playing, so that Mabel got her share and even daft 'Arry, the gardener's boy, if Ruthie happened to be in a good mood. Luncheon, on a Saturday, meant that Desmond and Frank ate with their parents, a doubtful privilege, though the food was always much better than nursery fare. Best manners as well as best clothes must be donned, however, and usually conversation was confined to the older members of the company.

The littles, hearing that elevenses were being served, promptly deserted their 'house' and made off towards the conservatory, only Stella glancing back, rather wistfully, before diving into the wood.

'Ruthie forgot mugs for the milk, but Mabel says if we go back she'll change her mind about letting us stay here. We'll drink from the jug. You first, Mabel.'

Mabel tilted the jug and solemnly drank. Her dark eyes were lowered, looking into the jug, and her remarkably thick black lashes lay on her cheeks. Her pinafore was stained with one or two tiny pinkish marks and the hem of her blue gingham dress dusty and too short, so that her petticoat dipped into view. Her hair was done in a long, thick braid this morning, and seeing her in profile as he moved towards her to take the jug Frank was reminded of Red Indian maidens in books, with their remote, stern little faces and their high cheekbones.

'Hurry up, Frank!' Desmond jerked his brother's elbow and took the jug from him, hastily gulping down the remaining milk. 'Now let's go back up the tree for a bit. We can eat the buns and watch the world go by.'

'Watch the boarders, you mean,' grumbled Frank. 'Let's not climb right to the top for the buns. We'll only have to climb down again to take the jug back.'

Rather to his surprise, Desmond agreed without demur and the three of them stretched out on the lowest platform, a mere eight feet or so from the ground. They lay on their stomachs, eating the buns and arguing softly what they should do next. Frank wanted to give his rabbits a run on the side lawn before luncheon, Desmond wanted to play hide and seek, which made both Frank and Mabel stare, and Mabel herself wanted to dam the stream.

They were just growing heated when the sound of someone pushing through the undergrowth brought instant silence. They lay very still, hearts beating. No grown-up, except for Walters the gardener and daft 'Arry, knew about the platforms in the chestnut tree. They knew that somewhere in the wood the children had a tree-house in a yew – a lovely safe place for them to play. They had no idea that platforms had been built in the great chestnut tree and the children had no intention of letting anyone find out. They craned their necks to see through the screen of leaves into the clearing. It was far too soon for the little ones to be returning after their elevenses, and Walters or daft 'Arry would come along the path, not push through the woodland. They were astonished when Nanny Sutton emerged from the trees, then turned to someone behind her.

'It's all right, Louis, there's no one here. The kids have all gone in for elevenses, and if we stay here and someone calls I can say I was looking for them.'

The children exchanged startled glances as Louis followed Nanny into the clearing, put his arms about her, and began to kiss her with a fervour which shocked Mabel and Frank into an involuntary glance at each other. But presently Louis led Nanny over to the lowest platform in the yew and they sat down upon it. It was sturdy and well built, and scarcely creaked as Louis dragged Nanny Sutton across his knees and into a reclining position in his arms.

'How long'll the kids be gone? I don't fancy any interruption for the next few minutes.'

'Twenty minutes or so. Longer, if Millie gets in a flap with the iced buns. Which she will, because she's very partial to them herself and tries to keep a couple back.'

Louis laughed deep in his throat and began to kiss Nanny again whilst the three watchers exchanged glances. They loved Louis, but what on earth was he doing here, kissing Nanny? Everyone knew he was going out with Sarah Kelpmann and all the grown-ups were as pleased as if he had done something rather clever. When Louis kissed the side of Sarah's neck or turned her hand over to kiss the palm, their mother gave a little smile and Grandpa beamed so widely that one felt he would presently begin to applaud. The children had accepted that Louis was doing the right thing in kissing Sarah. But kissing Nanny Sutton?

As they watched, however, Frank realised that this was going further than mere kisses. To his horror, his charming, respectable uncle began to unbutton the front of Nanny's dress and, having opened it out, plunged his hand inside, convulsively squeezing some part of Nanny and causing her to give a moan of pain. Frank hissed in his breath, then saw that Nanny was not attempting to stop Uncle Louis; on the contrary, she was giving him every help and encouragement in a number of things, all of them unlikely and wicked, which Uncle Louis promptly began to do.

Frank looked at Mabel. She was watching without expression, her face once again reminding him of a Red Indian, so impassive was she. He glanced at Desmond and quickly away. Then he reached out and shook Mabs's arm and nudged his brother. This was the perfect moment to escape unseen, whilst the couple on the platform were so engrossed in what they were doing.

Frank sneaked, on his knees, to the back of the platform and then dropped to the ground. His feet thudded against the leaf mould, but he knew he would be safe enough. Mabel, following, landed more lightly still, and Frank stood for a moment, looking up at the platform edge, waiting for Desmond.

Mabel jerked at his sleeve, rolled her eyes upwards and then shook her head. He got the message that Desmond would not be following and took Mabel's hand, leading her the quickest way out of the wood.

They crossed the kitchen garden and walked quickly through another belt of trees and down to the stream. Some day, Mother threatened, she and Walters would turn the stream from its present bed so that it could run through the garden proper and not just through the wood where no one could see it. The children sincerely hoped that it would be as expensive and arduous an undertaking as Pa protested. They loved the stream, with the tall beech trees growing beside it and its deep, fern-fringed banks. Frank broke their companionable silence.

'That was Uncle Louis and Nanny!'

Mabel slanted an enigmatic look at him.

'Yes, I know.'

Without having to consult one another, they sat down on the bank to remove their shoes and stockings. Then, with the shoes laced together and dangling round their necks with the stockings stuffed into them, they began to paddle downstream to where the water would dive under the cart-track which bounded the property just there, and emerge in the meadow on the other side.

'But Mabs, he's going out with Sarah! Why was he kissing Nanny? And squeezing her?'

Mabel shrugged and kicked up a foot, sending a shower of sparkling drops ahead of her.

'My mum says your Uncle Louis's a devil for the women. Perhaps that's what it means — that they kiss more than one.'

'Well, if that's so . . .' He hesitated, then turned to another subject, or at least another facet of the same subject. 'Why wouldn't Des come away when we did? He's changed, you know, Mabs. It was just the sort of thing he would do now, stay and stare; I suppose he thinks Nanny's a girl!'

'I know what you mean, Frank. I been thinking of getting that girl who's in my school to come up here, before you go back to school, specially for Des. Do you 'member me telling you about Suzie Canning?'

'No . . . oh, yes! You don't mean . . . '

'I do, then.' Mabel nodded solemnly. 'She and Des would get along fine.'

Frank was silent, digesting this information. Mabel had told him about Suzie when he first came back from school – how Suzie was turning into a 'real nasty creature' because she sold 'looks' for a farthing, 'touches' for a halfpenny, and 'feels' for a penny. He had been mystified until Mabel had explained, and then both disgusted and fascinated. Familiar with the anatomy of small sisters, he felt, first, that money so spent was money wasted, and secondly, when Mabel had told him about the enthusiastic response evoked amongst the boys, that in some way Suzie was preying upon ignorance and that, when the payers had seen – or touched – or felt – what she had to offer, their fury at the deception would be very great.

Mabel had speedily disabused him.

'She sits in her grandma's outside privy, holidays Monday Wednesday and Friday, from nine until ten in the morning,' Mabel assured him. 'School times, it's four until five in the afternoons. And there's always a queue; some of the lads go back twice in the same day! I tell you, she's making a mint!'

Now, remembering this, he felt he must question Mabel further.

'You think *Des* would give her farthings? Honest?'

Mabel grinned. She had a delightful grin, a three-cornered smile which dispelled all the impassivity from her small face and made her look twinklingly alive.

'Farthings? He'd give her pennies! I daren't walk past him in the house if there's no one around.' She adopted a recognisable imitation of Desmond's voice. 'Mabs, why don't we go for a stroll in the wood one evening?' She returned to her own tones. 'And he's forever pinching my bottom and rubbing up against me.'

'Well, I knew he'd got a thing about girls, but you! You're only a kid! Younger than me, even. Now if it was . . .'

Mabel interrupted him.

'It will be. He'll start mucking about with girls like Suzie, and then it'll be kitchen maids, and then bigger girls — he won't ever be with us again. Not proper.'

'You're right. I didn't know how bad he was, but I do see that you're right.' He shot a suspicious glance at Mabel. 'Why are you laughing?'

'You make growing up sound like measles! And then I thought what your Uncle Louis'd say if he knew we'd seen. And Nanny Sutton, who tells us off and scolds, lying there with her chest all open and groaning and carrying on!'

Frank laughed too.

'I suppose it *is* funny, in a way. But . . . well, I'll be fourteen in nine months! Will I get like Des?'

Mabel's sharp gaze softened as she took in Frank from head to foot.

'You won't be horrible with it, like Des is. You'll be grand, Frank, when you grow up.' She patted his hand. 'Are the Sollies coming after luncheon? What'll we do?'

'Yes, they'll be here. We'll build the submarine, I expect.'

Some time ago the children's imaginations had been fired by undersea warfare, and they had begun, using as the main part the body of an ancient carriage found in the loft, to build themselves a play-submarine. Up in the dim and dusty loft they had played some memorable games in their sub, but it had recently been borne in upon them that they would soon need another. Warfare was best if there was an enemy, for one thing, and the rapid growth of Stella and David and the fact that they constantly besieged their elders for a place in the *Waterspout,* as the submarine had been christened, made it clear that if war was to be waged in peace a second craft must be built.

They had received with cries of joy a number of tea-chests from Uncle Louis and had borrowed tools and advice from Mr Walters. But the second submarine still needed a good deal of work to make it playable.

'I'll bring some food, if I can,' Mabel said magnanimously. It did not seem strange to her that she, very much the poor relation of the crew, should be the only one capable of nicking food. Nursery meals were not easy to purloin, and Ruthie did not encourage the children of the house to wander around her kitchen. Mabel, on the other hand, constantly working there, had many and various opportunities of slipping food into her pockets, to say nothing of the fact that Ruthie would often show her appreciation of Mabel's hard work by slipping her a bag of buttered scones or a basket of fruit 'for the crew'.

'That'd be spiffing. Here's Des at last!'

Desmond strolled through the trees, sat down on the bank and shed his shoes and socks. His cheeks were flushed and his eyes very bright.

'Paddling? I don't blame you. It's hot enough!'

He said nothing of the scene he had left and neither did Frank or Mabel. They talked of the submarines, and the Sollies. Safe, childhood topics.

'More pie, Louis?'

Tina presided over the luncheon table, slipping the wide silver pie-slice beneath the next wedge of plum pie and handing it across the table to Louis, then catching Ted's eye so that the small silver cream jug was also nudged in her brother's direction. She did not offer more pie to the boys, for she was sure that such rich food could not be good for young digestions. Ruthie should have provided a nice rice pudding, or caramel custards perhaps, but she had probably forgotten that the boys lunched with the grown-ups today.

Louis poured cream over his pie and dug his spoon into

the golden pastry.

'Ruthie makes a superb plum pie, as good as Alice's,' he remarked. 'Don't make me feel greedy, boys. Have some more!'

Frank and Desmond, who had been watching him with unusual intensity, blushed and disclaimed any interest in the plum pie. Tina put in a few words about the inadvisability of the young being encouraged to eat hot pastry and cold cream in the middle of the day.

'Oh, rubbish,' Louis said blandly, keeping his eyes on his plate so that he would not see the small figure stiffen with annoyance over her baby brother's words. 'Look at the stuff you used to guzzle when we were children! Pickled onions, and salami, and . . .'

'Really, Louis, if you're in a mood to reminisce . . .'

'Touché, little sister!' Louis's more recent past was not a subject upon which he wished to hear his sister's opinion. 'I'm sorry, boys, I cannot influence your mama into giving you any more pie!'

'Influence! Well, well, the less said the better, perhaps.' Tina smiled a trifle maliciously at Louis. 'And what have you been doing today? Dancing attendance upon Sarah?'

Louis found himself the object once more of two pairs of blue eyes, trained on his countenance like machine guns. Whatever was the matter with his nephews today? But his limpid gaze fixed itself on Tina's face, supremely innocent.

'That's why I didn't get here until one o'clock. I had to meet Sarah. I've arranged to take her for a run this afternoon in Poppa's motor. We'll go over to the Horning Ferry for tea. After that we'll hire a boat, I daresay, and I'll row her up the river. Very romantic, don't you think?'

Frank and Desmond exchanged glances. Louis had been at The Pride at eleven o'clock, not dancing attendance upon Sarah but kissing and cuddling Nanny!

'You met Sarah this morning? Oh, Louis, you should have invited her here to luncheon,' Tina said at once. 'She would have been very welcome − she's such a charming girl. I do believe she's having a good influence on you as well. You haven't been nearly so . . . well, so wild, dear, since you took up with Sarah.'

'I couldn't. She had a luncheon engagement,' Louis explained. 'But I'll take her home to dine with Poppa, I expect.'

He sounded a trifle resigned.

'I don't know where you get your energy from,' Ted remarked. 'Taking Sarah rowing, on a warm afternoon like this!' He smiled at his brother-in-law. 'I'll take the last piece of that pie, please, my love. That's about all I'm capable of on such a day!'

It was fortunate that, at the moment he had remarked on Louis's energy, he had not been watching his eldest son's face. It was a study.

'I wouldn't be so energetic if I'd not had a quiet morning,' Louis began, 'but . . .'

Desmond, catching Frank's eye, suddenly gave a most awful snort which he tried, without success, to turn into a cough. He choked and spluttered, turning scarlet, and Frank, banging his brother on the back, began to snigger beneath his breath. Louis looked at them, then quickly away. Tina, leaning across the table, smacked Desmond's hand sharply.

'Des, what on earth's the matter? You'd better both leave the table and apologise to Uncle Louis for this behaviour when you're calmer.' She turned to Louis. 'Thank goodness you *didn't* bring Sarah back to luncheon, if the boys are going to behave like hyenas!'

With Frank and Desmond gone, Louis was able to finish his plum pie in peace. Remembering his own youth, he could only sympathise with their abrupt fall from grace. How often had the giggles caught him at the most inappropriate moments! They were nice kids, though, Tina's boys!

'Did you hear Uncle Louis? What a whopper, a quiet morning! And he said he didn't get here until one o'clock!'

The two boys stood in their bedroom, still pink-faced from their recent attack of untimely mirth. Desmond began to remove his collar and best tie, shaking his head reprovingly at Frank.

'Our uncle is without doubt a terrible liar. But I don't blame him for not telling Mama what he had been doing. You should have waited, Frank, I can tell you!'

He proceeded to give Frank every detail of the passionate scene which had been enacted below his perch. Frank, striving to follow a story which sounded anatomically impossible as well as dreadfully sinful, comforted himself with the thought that Des must be exaggerating. Must he not? Yet he was uneasy. The recollection of his uncle's hand plunging into Nanny's bodice, the convulsive closing of that hand, the groan which had been wrenched from Nanny's lips, made him realise that he did not really understand grown-ups at all.

He was spared having to comment on Desmond's tale, however, by the thump of feet in the corridor outside, closely followed by the bursting open of the door. Con stood there, hair on end, monkey-face wreathed in grins.

'Are we late? Sorry. It was the porridge. Here comes Bertram.'

Bertram, smooth and unruffled as ever, stalked past Conrad and greeted his cousins.

'Hello, chaps. Sorry we're late. It was the porridge.'

Frank, wrenching off his suit in favour of play clothes, turned to stare.

'Still? Con, you're a rum 'un.'

Con grinned deprecatingly.

'If you could have seen it this luncheon, you would have thought me mad. It had whiskers growing on it, and no end of mould. But it's been awful at home. Mama cries at every meal and Papa storms and then goes all icy. And today our Nellie started bawling when she put the dish on the table. So I ate it.'

'You never! With the whiskers and the mould? *Why*, Con, when you've held out for ten days? You weren't starving, were you?'

Con shook his head, his grin never faltering.

'Of course I wasn't starving, you oaf! Bertie got me food, and Cook kept slipping me bits and pieces. Mama insisted that I had milk and biscuits to make up for no breakfast or luncheon, and I had a proper meal at night. No, I changed tactics when I realised that Papa didn't actually want me to eat it, he just wanted me to give in. And the women wailing . . . well, it got a bit much.'

'So you did give in, in the end! Oh, well, you did pretty well for a kid, Con.'

That was Desmond, patronising as ever. But he had reckoned without Bertram.

'You don't understand, Des! He ate it *all,* every scrap! Mama wept and tried to snatch it away from him, Papa kept saying, "That'll do, Conrad. Now I've proved my point you may leave the rest," and Nellie wailed, "It'll kill 'im, Mr Solstein, it'll kill the boy!" It was a triumph, I tell you. And when Con had eaten the last little smear, he pushed the empty plate away from him and said . . .' Bertram, the grave, the sensible, was suddenly convulsed with mirth. He could not go on with the story, so Conrad took it up.

'I said it was the only decent porridge I'd ever tasted, and if they wanted me to eat porridge in the mornings they must always serve it with whiskers and mould. And Nellie started to giggle, and Mama clapped her hand across her mouth and she was laughing and crying at the same time, and then Bertie and I went off. Only Papa didn't even smile.'

Frank could imagine his Uncle Abe's ugly, self-righteous face, set in disapproval, furious because he had suddenly realised he had lost the battle he thought won.

'I just hope they don't take you seriously, Con, and offer you porridge with whiskers every morning!'

Bertram wiped his streaming eyes on a clean pocket handkerchief and pulled himself together.

'Don't worry. They won't do that. Con was s-sick all over that turkey carpet in Papa's study! Oh, you should have seen . . .' and he was off again, his face turning scarlet.

Presently, when they were sober once more, they set off for the stables and the submarines, Frank eyeing his cousin Con with considerable respect. To have the nerve to stand out against his father, and then to have the nerve to eat cold ten-day-old porridge! Frank had always been a bit scared of Uncle Abe and thought him a stern and unsympathetic father to his two sons. So different from their own dear Pa, who adored and spoilt them all indiscriminately.

'Wait until Uncle Louis hears,' Frank said, as they climbed into the loft. 'He and Mama have talked over the porridge story, wondering how it would end. They won't dare say so to you, but I bet they're pleased, Con.'

Desmond, starting to take a tea-chest to pieces with Walters's big claw-hammer, looked up at the mention of their uncle.

'Have you told them about Uncle Lou and . . .'

'No! Des, you mustn't! Really, we shouldn't have been there. It was spying, and eavesdropping, and all sorts.'

'It doesn't matter, then,' small Con said placidly. He picked up a piece of tea-chest, fitted it into place, and began to push tacks through it. 'I like Uncle Louis. He lightens my life.'

Frank grinned at this, but he saw Bertram and Desmond exchange a glance, and then the two of them disappeared down into the stables, with a furtive air which made him turn apologetically to Conrad.

'Des is taking Bertie down to tell. But you won't say anything to the others?'

'Of course not.'

At the end of Frank's conscientious recital, however, Con squatted back on his heels and frowned at Frank.

'Well, I know Uncle Louis kisses people. I thought you and Des knew as well. We were at Grandpa's once and Uncle Lou caught Nellie in the downstairs cloakroom and pinched her bottom. She let out such a squeak that I ran in, thinking it was Stella messing about — we were playing hide and seek. And there was our Nellie, pushed right into the coats and things, with Uncle Lou sort of leaning on her, and Nellie's skirt up round her waist, most peculiar! So I said: "What are you doing to Nellie, Uncle Lou?" and he said a mouse had run up Nellie's skirt and he was trying to catch it.' Con snorted. 'It sounded silly, but Nellie's face was so red, and Uncle Lou wouldn't turn round and talk; he just sort of spoke over his shoulder. So I went away. But in the carriage going home I asked Nellie what Uncle Lou had really been doing — it was just Nell and me, because it was the time Bertie and I had measles, only I got better first — and she said Uncle Louis was a right varmint and he'd pinched her bottom, and that was why she'd squealed out. And not to tell, if I pleased, because she would get into trouble if my mama thought her flighty.'

Con ran out of breath and beamed triumphantly at Frank.

'Well I never!' Frank's astonishment was genuine, for he had always thought the Solsteins' Nellie the height of respectability. But now that he considered the matter, he realised that she was no older than Nanny Sutton and every bit as pretty. 'And there's something else I meant to ask you about, Con.'

He told Conrad, without going into too much detail, that Desmond had started some bottom-pinching on his own account, with Mabel as his victim.

'She doesn't like it at all,' he finished impressively. 'I ought to say something to Des, only he *is* the older, and he may just say something smart.'

'You tell him to leave our Mabs alone,' Con said fiercely. 'If he wants a stupid girl, let him find a stupid one, not our Mabs.'

But in the event it proved far less embarrassing to tackle Desmond than Frank had anticipated. He stumbled and muttered his way through a couple of short sentences before Desmond, far from denying it all or pretending to be offended, simply said: 'Oh, you needn't worry about that stupid kid. She's only a child! Now that I've seen what I saw this morning I shan't bother Mabel again. No fear!'

'Then who will you bother?' asked Frank, expecting to hear the name of the High School boarder with the lovely legs, or a sister of one of Desmond's friends. Instead, Desmond gave him the benefit of his most superior look.

'Nanny, of course!'

Frank stared at him, round-eyed, for a moment, then

laughed scornfully.

'Oh, yes, I can just see Nanny going for a walk with you in the woods, or letting you pinch her bottom in the laundry-room! She'd give you a clip that'd send you into Suffolk!'

But Desmond neither rushed at him nor grew hot and flushed as he so often did when he was laughed at or disagreed with.

'Don't forget what I saw, baby Frank! And what I could describe in every detail to Mama. Nanny likes working for us, I've heard her saying so. And no wonder, with Uncle Louis . . .'

'Des! You wouldn't! Tell, I mean.'

'I shan't have to,' Desmond said cryptically. 'I'll play you at chess, if you like.'

And when he lost, he only smiled, patted Frank's head in a manner which seemed more consoling than congratulatory, and left the room, humming a sprightly tune.

Frank put the chess pieces away thoughtfully. Desmond had taken a big step away from him today, but they were returning to school in a week; then he would just be old Des again. Neyler Major. Until Christmas.

6: 1912

'Of course I'd love a party! But you said a combined party, for us and for Johnny. What did you *mean*?' Su, enveloped in an outsize apron, was baking bread. Mark laughed, and crossed the kitchen to kiss the tip of her nose.

'That smells good. I hope it's one of those milk loaves! I went into Dunedin earlier in the week, and whilst I was there I had an interview with the headmaster of the boys' school. I've arranged for Johnny to start there as soon as the school holidays are over.'

'Mark!'

'He's running wild here, love. You do your best, but he's ten now and needs more work than we can give him, and he's dropping behind boys of his own age. Where is he now, by the way?'

Su turned back to her baking board, but her shoulders drooped.

'Rabbiting. With Sam, in the high pasture. Why?'

'Well, there's a good reason for sending him to school! There's no one his own age to play with, so he hangs about with Sam, who's thick as porridge and as cunning as a weasel. *And* nearly three years older than Johnny.'

'Boarding school.' Su tried to assimilate the idea. Not to see Johnny every day, not to read to him at bedtime every night. Not to set his schoolwork, not to cook his meals or darn his socks. Not to see him coming into the house after spending an afternoon rabbiting with his friend Sam, dirty, tired, happy as Larry! 'Oh, Mark, I'll miss him terribly! I don't think I can bear it!'

Mark had been watching her face, his eyes full of concern for her, and now he took her in his arms, swaying her gently from side to side.

'It's for his good, darling! I know what you were thinking, you were thinking about the good times. But think deeper, my love!'

She obeyed, wrinkling her forehead. Other things. Johnny's truancy, the times he ran off and just did not bother to return until he was ready, careless of the anxiety he caused. His obstinacy which meant that sometimes he hurt himself, either physically or mentally, refusing to listen to advice. His increasing dissatisfaction with her teaching, his grumbles that the work was either dull or 'babyish'. His eagerness to play with other boys, and the diffidence he was beginning to show in the company of his peers.

'I do see what you mean, I suppose. But have you told Johnny? What does he think?'

'When I first sounded him out he was furious, and said he'd run away,' Mark admitted cheerfully. 'But when I told him that behaving like that simply proved how badly he needed the discipline of a decent school he took me a bit more seriously. He tried bursting into tears and when that didn't work he tried to punch me on the nose. Unsuccessfully, I might add. He's getting quite interested in the idea. I think he'll stick to it and end up enjoying it, once he's made some friends.'

'Well, I suppose you're right, and he needs school. But I've been so careful these past years never to make him feel an outsider, or unwanted. I'd hate him to feel that.'

'I know. In a way, it's a bad time to send him away, when he's becoming difficult and a bit headstrong, but we didn't do it a couple of years ago because you couldn't bear it, and I won't see the boy ruined by either of us. Darling, you fret over him like a mother hen, you know you do!'

'What does Freda think?'

He sighed and kissed her, then pinched one of the hot scones standing on the table and bit into it.

'I haven't asked her. How could I, when you didn't know? But I did tell Toddy, and he's all for it. Especially when I explained that he'd only be a weekly boarder, and come home every Friday night until Monday morning.'

He watched Su's transparent face light with relief, and congratulated himself upon his acumen. He had deliberately let her believe that Johnny would be a termly boarder, knowing how much less terrible, by comparison, weekly boarding would seem.

'Home every weekend! Gracious, that's nothing! He'll enjoy it, and he'll have every weekend to play on the farm and boss us about. Oh, Mark, you're the most wonderful, clever, darling man!'

'Tell me something new! Let me go, you insatiable woman, and put the kettle on. Scones need tea with them, and I could do with some butter, too!'

Johnny accepted the idea of school in the end because he knew Su wanted him to go and thought it was for the best, and Su was the most important person in his life. His father was a good companion, but he had always known that, though Mark loved him, there was an ambiguity in his attitude to his son. Had Johnny realised that Mark was jealous of him he would have been astonished and more than a little gratified. And had Mark known that Johnny was equally jealous he would have been just plain astonished. But Freda knew. Knew, too, that boarding school would probably improve the relationship out of all recognition. It had not occurred to any of the Neylers that it was strange that Mark and Johnny got on best well away from Su, but Freda had noticed. Johnny's horizons were so narrow that he concentrated too much on Su.

Freda, a childless woman, had given all her maternal love to Johnny. She hated the thought of him going, for she realised, in a way that Su and Mark did not, that the Johnny who returned from boarding school would not be the Johnny who had left.

But she loved him truly, so gave her blessing to the scheme.

Johnny sat in the trap with his suitcase on the floor behind him and Toddy's thigh rubbing his own. His parents were in the back, strained and awkward in the face of the impending parting, but Johnny watched the barrel-sided bay mare jogging along the road and felt the cold wind plucking at his hair, and was reconciled to the thought of boarding school because he would play games, team games, for the first time in his life. Also, he knew his education had been neglected, and he was a competitive boy who liked to be at or near the top. But what had finally decided him was the knowledge that if he continued to fight he might win the battle, but lose the war. He would stay at the farm and find himself disciplined more and more firmly, whilst Su's affection and companionship, which he valued more than anything else, would stray from him because he was 'difficult'. Better, by far, to accept a degree of parting, knowing that when he returned at weekends he would have almost all her attention and affection to make up for their time apart!

So when he finally kissed his parents quite warmly, shook Toddy's hand, and humped his suitcase into the school hall, he was sure he was doing the right thing. It was also in the back of his mind that the intimacies between Mark and Su, which he hated and most bitterly resented, could take place whilst he was out of the way and would not even have to be thought about.

He had reckoned without Freddy Fawcett.

Freddy was his roomer; the younger boys shared two to a room and Freddy, a thick-set, fair-haired boy with twinkling blue eyes and a cherubic countenance which hid a mind like a sink, fell to Johnny's lot. A little lost at first in the echoing corridors and crowded classrooms, Johnny turned to his roomer as to an old friend, and on that first evening, as they got ready for bed, told Freddy about his father and Su.

'Your pater married a *Chink*? I call that disgusting!' Freddy drawled the words in a man of the world fashion, for he was a good deal more sophisticated than Johnny. 'Got her in the family way, I suppose? Doin' the decent thing, eh?'

'I don't know what you mean,' Johnny muttered, knowing only too well. 'Su's beautiful. She had heaps of boy-friends before my father came back to Otago and married her. I like her awfully.'

Freddy's twinkling eyes scanned Johnny's countenance and saw there was more here than he had realised. Freddy's father was a notorious womaniser, his mother a meek, much maligned woman who adored her son, so Freddy had rather naturally assumed that Johnny would be contemptuous of the woman in his father's life. Instead, it appeared to be the other way round. Despite his prodigality with his father's money Freddy was not popular with his classmates, and he had hoped to make a friend of the new boy; it would not do to antagonise him by making remarks of a derogatory nature about Chinese women, evidently.

'Nice, is she? Your pater's done well, then, because I've

heard Chink women are good lays — my father says so, and he should know. Now that you're out of the way, I daresay your father's got her in his room and . . .'

His conversation became obscene and Johnny, not understanding that this was Freddy's way of championing the woman in his roomer's life, weighed the pros and cons, decided that an ally was only worth so much, and hit Freddy on the point of the jaw.

Against all the laws of commonsense this instant and open sign of disapproval started a friendship which would last all the time they were together and do Johnny and Freddy a great deal of good. Freddy, nursing a bruised jaw, put the word about that 'young Neyler' was both aggressive and capable. Johnny, not a boy to bear a grudge, was impressed by his roomer's immediate apology and explanation that his words had been meant in a complimentary fashion.

In the days which followed, Johnny grew to understand why Freddy spoke as he did. In Freddy's eyes, it was natural and right that a man should both want and take the woman of his choice. When Johnny let it be known that he felt slighted by Su's preference for her husband, Freddy told him bluntly that he had his facts muddled; an adult male wanted at least one adult female of his own and women were the same. A boy of Johnny's age could in no way take the place of a mate.

It was a startlingly frank way of explaining sex and marriage but it was easily absorbed by Johnny, a farmer's son. Freddy, a farmer's son too, could not understand why this basic fact of nature had escaped Johnny, but as the boys grew to know one another he realised that Johnny's circumstances were very different from his own. Johnny had only seen the man-woman relationship working between Mark and Su and no one else, for Freda and Toddy, the only other married couple he knew at all well, were not in the habit of exchanging so much as a kiss in public. He could — and did — accept mating as natural in farm stock, for the procreation of the species, but he had thought Mark's preoccupation with Su disgusting. All in all, Johnny's education was lacking in certain areas.

Johnny, for his part, was puzzled by Freddy's attitude to his parents. Joe Fawcett treated his only son with sublime indifference, but Freddy adored him. Beryl Fawcett worshipped her constantly erring husband and her swaggering son, yet Freddy thought little of her. Johnny had always assumed that feeling begot feeling; this was certainly true in his own case, for he loved Su who loved him and suspected Mark, who suspected him. Now it seemed that you could love someone who did not love you at all. Or Freddy could. It was very strange.

After a week, Freddy found himself less puzzled by the fact that Johnny's pater and Johnny could both love a Chink. Freddy had absorbed, without ever thinking about it, his father's precept that women were made for man's pleasure, and that when their period of supremacy was done they could and should be cast aside. A Chink, he felt, should never actually be married! Yet he respected Johnny, and Johnny respected Su. He found himself eager to meet Johnny's people, and wanted Johnny to meet his.

Though neither knew it, the boys were educating each other, both broadening their minds in a way which would have been impossible under different circumstances.

Johnny found his first close friendship very satisfying, and actually accepted an invitation to visit the Fawcetts' sheep station on the first weekend of the term. He also invited Freddy to accompany him home on the following weekend.

He wrote and told his parents of this change in plan, and as he sealed the letter he felt independence push out the last echo of complaint with his lot. He was growing away from them, living a life of his own, and it was good!

7

Mabel was cleaning up the tree-house, because in a few days the boys would be back and it would be in use once more. It never occurred to Desmond and Frank, of course, that during its long winter loneliness the tree-house got messy; bird-droppings, piles of dead and rotting leaves, the scatterings of prickly nut husks, piled up on the platforms, transforming the tree-house into a sort of repository for anything that could be blown on the wind. But Mabel knew, and enjoyed this annual clean-up because it meant that the boys, and therefore the summer, were almost here.

Today she was armed with a bucket of hot soapy water and a cloth; yesterday she had done the main job of clearing the rubbish, using the hand-brush which hung all summer, unobserved and unremarked on, in the thick, tussocky growth of shoots around the roots of the elm next to the chestnut. It was not easy, for all her nimbleness, to scale the tree with the full bucket, but she had managed it and was rubbing away now, enjoying the smell of the wet wood as, board by board, she cleaned. Very soon she, the boys and the Sollies would be occupying their eyrie once more.

She had a lot to tell them, too, this year. She emptied her bucket airily through the green of the leaves, then hoped, too late of course, that there was no one prowling about below. But no one was. On the second platform she stopped, rubbed her hot face with her bare arm, and gazed across to where Stella was strolling round the lawn, her arm around the waist of her friend Heather. Stella was a pupil at the Norwich High School now, and Mabel often saw her setting out in her green tunic and cream blouse, with her black felt hat on the back of her head. Mabel, a pupil at the Bullock Street Board School, was in with a chance of going to the High School too if she got a scholarship and viewed the possibility with faint alarm, but it increased her interest in Stella. She had taken the examination several weeks previously and awaited the results with mixed feelings. She was in the same class as Suzie Canning and they were best friends, drawn together by the fact that they were easily the two most intelligent girls in the scholarship class, but even if Suzie got a scholarship Mabel knew full well that her friend would never be allowed to use it. So if she did get through she would be alone at whatever school she qualified for; no one else in Bullock Street stood a chance of passing.

Her parents were torn by two perfectly natural desires — that she might get a scholarship and continue with her education, and that she might take Mrs Neyler's offer of a job as kitchen maid at The Pride.

'That'd be nice, Mabs, to have you workin' with me,' Mrs Walters had said wistfully. Mabel pointed out that she worked with her mother quite a lot already, and was told that it was not the same. Mabel thought it was — boring work, and long hours; she had no desire to be a kitchen maid to anyone. But time would pass before she had to break it to her mother that nothing would induce her to work in the kitchen. It had given additional impetus to her studying, however, to know what fate might have in store!

Sitting in the chestnut tree and wondering about her chances of getting a scholarship made Mabel think about Suzie. The two girls might have been thrown together at first because of their brains, but now they were genuinely fond of one another. Suzie had strange morals, perhaps, but she was a good friend. She was a year older than Mabel and had the kind of beauty that rarely blossomed in Bullock Street Board School. Smooth, light-coloured hair fell gleaming to her waist, rippling like a fall of heavy satin. Her eyes were almond shaped and green, fringed with incredibly long, dark lashes. Her brows were two wings of black above those unusual eyes, and even at thirteen her figure was bidding fair to be exceptional. But it was not for these attributes that Mabel valued Suzie. It was her quick wit, her humour, and her courage in adversity which drew Mabel to the other girl. Suzie's mother was a Frenchwoman who had run away from her hulking bully of a husband when her baby was little more than a year old. By the time Suzie was four she was an orphan, her father having succumbed to a thirst for meths and a conviction that he was a skilled diver, proving himself incontrovertibly wrong one hot summer day when he had made his unsteady way to the topmost diving board at the local swimming pool and died as a result of his amazing leap.

'Couldn't he swim, then?' Mabel had asked Suzie, fascinated by this weird tale.

'Dunno. Didn't really matter, 'cos the pool had been emptied. Splat!'

Splat must have been an understatement, Mabel concluded, and viewed Suzie with even more respect, for her friend lived with her sour and disapproving grandparents, a reminder of a son they had feared and despised and a daughter-in-law they had scarcely known. Yet Suzie, who should have been meek and downtrodden, was lively and easy-going, never blaming her parents for their desertion or her grandparents for their mean, grudging attitude towards her.

'They can't help being old, and they didn't ask to be landed with me,' she said, when questioned about her grandparents. 'No good grumbling; but they wouldn't let me take the scholarship, they want me to earn.'

'What'll you do?'

'Depends.' Suzie pulled a face. 'I in't going to work in a factory, that's for sure! But a shop'd be different. Selling pretty clothes, or food, or shoes — I wouldn't mind that. I say, any chance of me visiting your place, come Saturday?'

Suzie adored visiting the Walters, loving their tiny, crowded cottage which looked so quaint from the outside though it was really dark, damp and inconvenient. But it was a home with love in it, and Suzie appreciated that and was frank enough to say so.

Mabel, dreaming up in the chestnut tree, suddenly

remembered that tomorrow was Saturday and Suzie would be having her dinner with them, and began to climb down as fast as she and the bucket could make it. A problem was going to arise fairly soon, and she would have to think how best to tackle it. Suzie, who had been such a good friend this past year, would not expect their friendship – and visits – to cease just because the Neyler boys were home, nor did Mabel intend this to happen. But she must make it plain to Suzie that there must be no 'carryings on' with the boys. It would lead to trouble, she was sure of that.

So when Mabel went to meet Suzie the following day she broached the subject as soon as they climbed off the tram and began the walk up the long, beech-lined drive. To her intense relief, Suzie admitted that she was thinking about giving up her money-making scheme completely.

'No one who's more than a month past their fourteenth birthday in't coming near nor by,' she said darkly. 'No fear, not any more! That's dangerous!'

Mabel, with no idea of what her friend was implying save that obviously someone had got difficult – perhaps demanding his money back? – nodded sagely and told Suzie that Des, Frank and Bertie were all above the legal limit and that Con, though younger, was exceptionally strong for his age. Suzie cocked a quizzical eye at Mabel, but forbore to say anything other than that she would not dream of suggesting any of the boys might like to visit her. Suzie respected her friend's innocence but did not envy her for it. Armoured against the world by her knowledge of its various sins and wickednesses, she thought herself far more of a match for what life might hurl at her than her little friend.

'Ted, do pay attention! I'm trying to talk to you! I asked you what you thought about the Walters' idea of sending Mabel to the High School?'

Ted and Tina were sitting in the drawing room whilst outside rain fell steadily. Ted was trying to read the paper. He grunted at Tina's impassioned words, then glanced up at her over the spectacles he had lately taken to wearing.

'What? Who's Mabel?'

'Oh, Ted! Mabel Walters!' Tina's voice came out in a wail of exasperation. She knew full well how Ted hated being dragged into discussions of affairs over which he had no control, but this was important and she was determined to get his opinion before she said anything further to Mrs Walters.

'Oh, that Mabel. Go on then, fire away. What's she done now?'

'Mabel's got a scholarship, and she passed well − so well that they've been given their choice of schools. She's a very clever little girl. Well, Ada was telling Ruthie that she thought she and William might send the girl to the High School and when I came into the kitchen she asked me what I thought. I said I'd talk to you, because it might be better for the child to go to one of the more practical schools. You know, with more emphasis on useful subjects and less on academic.'

It seemed she had caught Ted's attention at last. He put his paper down and frowned across at her.

'She should go to the High School, of course. The Public Day School Trusts provide about the best education available, I think, which is why Stella's there, and why Kitty will go when she's old enough. I don't believe in boarding school for girls but I do believe in giving them the best you can manage.' He picked up his paper again, hopefully. 'Is that all?'

'Ted! How can you prefer reading the paper to talking to me! You're very unkind, and as it happens that isn't all. Mabel brought the most extraordinary child to the house last week − if it *was* a child! Skirts almost to her ankles, hair looped up on top of her head! Just the sort of girl I don't want Des mixing with, and he and Frank were both with them. Of course I don't want to interfere with Mabel's friends, but . . .'

'Then don't.'

'What?' Tina blinked. 'Oh, but I wasn't interfering. It's just . . . Ted, you're horrid to me!'

Ted put down his paper and stood up. He walked over to

Tina's chair, then pulled her to her feet. His expression was rueful.

'Poor darling! Let's go for a ride in the motor, just the two of us. It's raining too hard for a stroll in the grounds, but we could go round to Bishopsgate, or up to the Sollies on Ipswich Road, or out into the country to the Mainwarings.' He paused, then smiled at her. 'As a matter of fact, I'd rather like to visit Abe; we're working hard over bringing the Motor Show to the city, but it occurred to me the other day that Abe does most of the dull work and I do most of the exciting things. Poor Abe sits in the car showroom and does the ledgers and sells, whilst I go off to meet the big manufacturers and try out the cars. So I thought he and I might go up to town for a few days next week and do some business, see some new models. I could sound him out on the idea tonight, if you like.'

'I don't know about Abe, but *I'd* love to come,' Tina said with alacrity. 'Nanny takes excellent care of the little ones and the boys amuse themselves very well. Why, if Cecy came too . . .'

'Heaven preserve us! All I said was . . .' Ted flung an arm round her shoulders and led her towards the door. 'All right, all right, I'm not being horrid to you again! It'll just teach me to make rash statements, that's all.'

The car was kept in the erstwhile stables, in what had once been a loose box at the end for sick animals. Ted, holding up a huge umbrella, ran out, fastened the doors back, then bent to the task of starting the engine, turning the handle with increasing vigour until at last the engine roared sweetly into life. Tina, standing in the shelter of the side door, muffled in a long raincoat and with her own umbrella rampant, darted out and flung herself breathlessly into the passenger seat. Ted slammed the door on her, then went round and climbed behind the wheel.

'Here we go,' he shouted, for the engine's roar in the confined space of the garage sounded painfully loud to unaccustomed ears. 'We'll go and visit the Sollies and suggest a trip to town.'

Tina furled her umbrella and snuggled up beside him,

patting his arm and almost purring with contentment. A trip to London! This evening was turning out better than she had hoped!

'Ted,' she said presently, when they were heading down the drive towards the road. 'What I *meant* to talk about . . .'

Without taking his eyes off the road he leaned over and patted her knee.

'I thought as much. You've not forgotten! Look, young lady, if you want to come with me to London, you'd best forget about little Mabel's friends, and her education. Leave both problems to her parents.'

Tina glanced sideways at him and did not fail to note the sternness of his profile.

'Edward Neyler, sometimes you're Teutonic, you are really!'

'Teutonic!' He pretended to lurch in his seat, pressing a hand to his heart. 'What a rare insult! My darling, all I do is save you from yourself. I just make sure that you remain as sweet as I know you are.'

'You try to rule me! You want to make me think like you do! You won't let me . . .'

The car slowed, then came to a halt beside the kerb. The rain continued to bounce off the windscreen, and even above the noise of the engine they could hear it striking the roof and sides of the vehicle.

'Tina.' Ted turned from the wheel and caught her hands in his. His palms were warm but his eyes were cold. 'Darling, just because we employ Mabel's parents, it doesn't give you the right to pick the child's friends. Nor, to be blunt, does it give you the right to "advise" Mrs Walters to send her daughter to some school other than the one your daughter attends. If you want to come to London with me, you must remember that everyone is a human being with rights and desires, not just you and your family!'

Tina coloured hotly and her gaze faltered.

'I didn't mean . . . but Ted, that girl was dreadful, not a bit like sweet little Mabel! And I truly thought that perhaps a more practical school would be best. The thought that

Mabel would be at Stella's school didn't worry me.' She glanced quickly up at him, then down again. 'Well, not much.'

He pulled her towards him and kissed her lightly on the mouth.

'That's my own girl; it's settled then. If Abe and Cecy want to join us they shall, but I'll book us a suite at Wilde's Hotel first thing tomorrow morning.'

The car drew out into the middle of the roadway once more and proceeded on its way. Tina snuggled up against Ted again and sighed happily. She wanted her own way, of course she did; she still thought that Ted was soft with the servants. But it was lovely to see herself being effortlessly managed into good behaviour so that she appeared in the best possible light in Ted's eyes. He outmanoeuvred her, persuaded her, even bribed her – but she loved every minute of it!

'We're having a tennis party at the weekend, Mabs. Pa said we should ask our friends, so how about asking Suzie?'

Mabel and the boys were in the stable loft. The craze for submarines had suffered a temporary setback with the fine weather, but it was wet today and though the *Waterspout* needed little doing to it the younger craft, *Tornado*, still lacked certain essential items of equipment such as guns and a conning tower.

Mabel reached for one of the few remaining apples and bit into its wrinkled sweetness, watching the boys as they hammered empty tins into gun barrels.

'Suzie plays a good game of tennis,' she acknowledged. 'But your mum wouldn't want us at one of her smart parties.'

'It's a party for us, not Mama, and you're always at our summer parties, so why not Suzie?' Des demanded. 'And you're a cracking good tennis player.'

'Mm hm.' Mabel finished the apple and hurled the core at Desmond, who ducked and grinned. 'But a tennis party's more . . . oh, more grown up than the usual sort of party. It sounds it, anyway.'

'Well, I'm fifteen,' Desmond said. 'We're having Una and Richie, and the Sollies of course, and that girl who stays with the Tatsons. You *must* come, Mabs, otherwise what shall we do?'

'Without,' Mabel said, smirking. 'What about numbers, though? Your mama's crazy about even numbers. Many's the time I've heard her beating your dad about the head because he's asked someone home and unevened her dinner table.'

'That's why we want you and Suzie,' Desmond said patiently. 'We've got to have ten, and Mama says we can count Stella as one, because she's beginning to play tennis, though very badly. But Mama says we must include her more. Of course, we shan't get many sets with so many and only the one court, but we can play croquet, and Pa's putting up the net for quoits − deck-tennis, I mean − and . . .'

Frank, patiently hammering away at the tins, turned and winked at Mabel.

'Say yes, Mabs, or he'll pester you to death. He says he thinks Suzie's got . . .'

Desmond shouted and launched himself across the loft, landing squarely in the middle of Frank's back. Frank tipped forward and the *Tornado* lurched beneath their combined weight.

'Get off, you swine!'

'Then shut your bloody gob!'

There followed a brisk exchange of blows and insults until Mabel, well used to such behaviour, picked up the hayfork and began jabbing both contestants indiscriminately.

'Stop it, you two, or someone'll hear and we'll be for it,' she said breathlessly. 'I'll ask Suzie if you're so set on it, Des.' Her fork landed on Desmond's behind and he reached back, thumping wildly in the general direction of Mabel. She, not one whit worried by this, merely increased the pressure on the fork until Desmond, swearing, removed himself from on top of Frank and cast himself down on the pile of hay Mabel had vacated.

'All right, all right, there's no need to be so damned vindictive, Mabs. I wasn't going to hurt precious boysie! I just didn't want him repeating . . .'

Frank, spitting dust and hay out of his mouth, rolled over and grinned at his brother.

'Forget it, Des. If I'd known every word you uttered had to be treated as a state secret . . .'

'Frank! Oh, for goodness sake, you two!' Mabel threw the hayfork down as Desmond began to growl, and headed for the ladder which led down into the stable below. 'I'm going. You can fight without me. Look, I'm meeting Suzie tomorrow. I'll ask her if she'd like to come to the party. But I can't promise anything.'

Desmond hastily abandoned his seat in the hay and followed her to the top of the ladder.

'Is she coming to see you tomorrow? If so we'll ask her ourselves; then we'll know straight away if she can come or not.'

Mabs was halfway down the ladder, but her head was still just in the loft. She stopped and flashed a glance pregnant with mischief at Frank.

'No, we're meeting in the city. We're going to have coffee and cakes at the Salonica.'

'Why on earth?' Desmond's fair brows rose.

Mabel shrugged and grinned across at Frank. Plainly the whole thing amused her very much.

'Dunno. Just for a lark. The thing is, Suzie got a scholarship too but her grandparents won't let her use it and she'll be starting work in a few weeks. She won't have trouble finding a job, she's so smart, and she dresses ever so nicely. But once she's working there won't be any time for larking. See?'

'We'll come too,' Desmond said eagerly. 'We'll treat you. Won't we, Frank?'

'I don't mind, though girls' larks are pretty slow,' Frank said. 'I suppose we could, though. We could tell the parents we were going to the museum and catch the tram into the city. Now that we're older we don't have to ask permish anywhere near so much.'

'No,' Mabel said firmly. 'It's a lark for the two of us, see? Me and Suzie. I don't want to get wrong with her by letting you come along. Whatever plan she's got, it'll be just us.'

No more was said and Mabel continued on her way down the ladder, leaving the brothers to continue their work. Desmond hammered away for a while, but presently he suggested that whatever Mabel had said they might go along to the Salonica next day to see the fun.

'We could. I've been there with Mama. Their cakes are prime,' Frank agreed. 'But it's a swanky place for kids – is that why Suzie chose it, do you suppose?'

'Probably. She's a little cracker, that girl. If you're game then, we'll go. There's no law against two fellows having coffee and cakes there on a Saturday morning.'

Frank continued to hammer, nodding his agreement. He had no particular desire to annoy Mabel and even less to cross the deeply carpeted confines of the Salonica. But a lark was a lark, and he rather agreed with Desmond, for once, that a ringside seat was not to be missed!

'A table for two, please, miss,' Desmond said to the waitress who came forward as they entered the low-ceilinged, sunny room. 'By the window, if that's possible.'

The waitress was in a black dress with a white frilled apron, and a white cap was perched on her glossy curls. She smiled at Desmond, then turned to smile at Frank.

'This way, sirs. A table for two.'

But halfway across the room Frank suddenly remembered their plan. In a voice which came out much higher than he intended he said: 'Four! A t-table for four, if you please!'

'A table for four. Two young gentlemen and two invisibles,' the waitress said cheekily, and led them to the most favoured table, where they could sit and survey through the windows the market place spread out beneath them – for the Salonica Refreshment Rooms were on the first floor – or watch the other customers as they sipped their coffee and ate their cakes.

Frank, taking a seat beside his brother, was glad he had

put on his best clothes. It was early and there were only half a dozen other customers in the place, all ladies and all immaculately clad in light summery gowns. Desmond was smiling up at the waitress as she stood, little pad and pencil poised, waiting to take their order.

She thought them a handsome couple, both so tall and fair, broad-shouldered in their dark blazers, their beautiful, deep young voices occasionally cracking into falsetto as they argued over what they should order.

'If you was to order coffee, then I could bring the trolley over and you could choose your own cakes from there,' she remarked at last, since the discussion over the respective merits of chocolate éclairs and cream doughnuts seemed to be getting dangerously heated. 'You can have whatever you like, see? There's lovely cream meringues an' all.'

Relieved of the responsibility of mutual choice, the boys did as she suggested and presently the coffee pot and cups and the silver cream jug arrived in front of them. Desmond insisted on telling the waitress that they were expecting a couple of young ladies, and would be obliged if she would bring fresh coffee and the trolley of cakes over as soon as their companions arrived.

Agreeing with a smile the waitress, who was in fact only Desmond's age though she felt centuries older, went back to the kitchens for another order. She wondered with a good deal of curiosity what sort of 'young ladies' would presently join the boys. They were a right couple! Lads of that age, she knew, often took up with proper little tarts — but they did not usually then take them to the most respectable coffee house in the city!

Twenty minutes later, when both boys had succumbed to temptation and eaten a cake each, Mabel and Suzie came in. They were scarcely recognisable as the children Frank and Desmond knew. Mabel wore boots with heels, a long dress and a hat. The very thought of Mabel in a hat would have convulsed Frank at any other time, but somehow today, in conjunction with the grown-up dress and the way she walked, it no longer looked funny. It made him wish he had never come; this was not a lark, it was an attempt to grow up, and he hated it! The two girls crossed the room in the waitress's wake, arm in arm, and Frank saw Suzie looking wonderful in a peach-coloured, gauzy dress, with her hat tipped forward so that it shadowed her small face. He could appreciate that Suzie looked very grown up without a qualm. It was just Mabel who must stay the same.

The waitress, catching Desmond's eye, steered the two girls over to their window table. Mabel, so self-conscious that she had not looked at anything except the distant windows, suddenly focused on the boys and became scarlet with embarrassment, then succumbed to a terrible urge to grin. She clapped a small hand hard over her mouth, but giggles bubbled out from between her fingers despite Suzie pinching her arm and frowning down at her with the utmost severity. Frank, also infected, began to snigger, but the two older ones were solemn, Desmond pulling out a chair for Suzie who, after one cold, infuriated stare, sank into it.

'Might we have the trolley . . . ? Here we are, ladies!' Desmond said affably. 'Which cakes do you prefer?'

Suzie turned gracefully towards Desmond, then cast her enormous, expressive eyes in the direction of the trolley.

'What a surprise to see you here, Mr Neyler! I say, look at those meringues!'

Both girls stared with unabashed greed at the creamy confections spread out before them.

Once coffee had been poured and cakes chosen, however, there came one of the small, awkward silences that can be so difficult to break. But Suzie, having accepted their presence, did not intend to let her 'lark' lose all its savour.

'Well? Didn't you two take us for young ladies out for a good time? We've been round the smart shops, and bought some hat trimmings and some ribbon, and made the shop-girls wrap it neatly for us. We even went into Garlands, and I was very gracious to the young lady on the haberdashery counter. Wasn't I, Mabs?'

Both girls dissolved into irritating giggles. At least, they irritated Frank and Desmond, who simply could not see the joke.

'Well? What's so funny about Garlands?'

Suzie pulled a face and took a large bite out of her meringue which promptly exploded softly, showering her with pieces. She said a short, sharp word and both boys blinked, then she turned to beam at them.

'What's funny? Why, by this time next month I'll be a young lady on the haberdashery counter in Garlands myself. I got a job there, that's why the lark! Though I bet they never recognise me in my shop blacks after seeing me in this!' She indicated her finery with an eloquent wave.

Desmond began teasing Suzie, telling her she would be the prettiest girl ever to serve on haberdashery and easily the prettiest girl at their tennis party, and Frank turned with relief to a second cake, offering the plate to Mabel as he did so. It struck him that there was something sad, almost wistful, in her expression as she looked at the older girl.

Frank frowned. Surely Mabs did not envy Suzie? And then, suddenly, he knew that it was not that. Mabel thought it a shame that her friend was being forced to cast aside her scholarship in favour of a job in Garlands. She must realise, as Frank did, that being forced to grow up before one was fourteen was not a lark at all, but a wretched business.

'Mabs! Have another cake! Go on. Des and I are rolling at the moment, because Uncle Louis tipped us yesterday.' Frank spoke impulsively, wanting to make Mabs smile, to take that haunted look out of her eyes.

He succeeded. Mabs eyed the plate with her head on one side, like a sparrow, then pounced on a cream meringue.

'All right then, money-bags! Take the éclair, Suzie. They're really good!'

The four of them laughed together, the boys beginning to boast and show off, the girls to nudge each other. A party of smart ladies at the next table smiled indulgently. Frank knew that Garlands was forgotten. But he was terribly glad that Mabs would be safe from the world for a while yet.

8

'Today Poppa's gone to Cecy's house, which is right and proper. She'll give him a *cholent* at lunchtime and so on. But tomorrow he must come to us. It's Alice's weekend off, and I'd feel guilty not to do my share.'

'Tomorrow? But Tina, love, you know Sunday's the only chance I have to get out into the countryside! Old Blake's got a boat for sale which sounds just what I've been looking for, and I told him we'd pop over tomorrow and take a look at it. I thought you might get Ruthie to make a picnic and I'd bring some wine — make a day of it.'

Tina and Ted were in the kitchen talking, whilst Ruthie scraped new potatoes at the sink and enjoyed the almost plaintive note in the master's voice. Ruthie was a feminist and it always amused her to watch tiny Mrs Neyler dealing with her tall, commanding husband. She could charm him with a glance, make him laugh with a few words, or reduce him to silent disappointment with a frown. Yet he was one of the foremost businessmen in the county, always thinking up something new and profitable. He sold cars, ran a kinema for the moving pictures, built office blocks and beautiful houses. She knew, of course, as all the servants knew, that Mr Neyler was the boss over the things that mattered. But Mrs Neyler knew how to get round him, nevertheless!

'Not tomorrow,' Tina said firmly now. She glanced meaningly at Mrs Ruthven's broad back. 'Ruthie, why are you scraping the potatoes? I thought Mabel helped out on a Saturday?'

'So she do. She've gone to pick a foo raspberries,' Ruthie said. 'I'll goo and give her a holler.'

She rolled out of the back door and presently could be heard 'hollering' in the kitchen garden.

'Now that you've got rid of Ruthie I suppose you think we can quarrel,' Ted said approvingly. Tina was mixing something in a big yellow bowl and he put his arms round her waist and rested his chin on her shoulder, peering down at the mixture. 'Why can't we go today, then? And what're you cooking?'

'Ted, you're impossible,' Tina said, dabbing his chin with a floury hand. 'Have you forgotten the children's tennis party? I'm up to my eyes as it is. And tomorrow is Poppa's day. I'm cooking in a kosherish fashion right now, so don't think you can persuade me to change my mind!'

'Well, how about taking Poppa with us?' Ted suggested, clinging to the faint hope of retaining his outing. 'Imagine it, my love! The whole family packed into the Rover, a picnic on the bank of the broad; champagne, if you like. Then coming home late in the moonlight, singing the old, sentimental songs, breathing the good fresh air . . .'

'Topping up with oil every ten miles, breaking down, you swearing fit to give Poppa a heart attack, the children cross and argumentative – oh, I can imagine it all too well,' Tina said. 'Goodness, Ted, it would be awful! Family motor trips are fine for us and the children, but it would be fatal to expect Poppa to enjoy our sort of outing. Besides, he hates fresh air. He thinks night air injurious. He . . .'

'As it happens the car's going like a bird at the moment. No, honestly, don't snort in that disbelieving way. And you could pack Poppa a special kosher picnic. You need a break. Be a sport, my love!'

'It's out of the question,' Tina said, but she softened the remark by turning in his arms and kissing his chin, keeping her hands well clear of his dark jacket. 'Poor darling, you *do* enjoy your outings, but . . . I know! Why not go today instead? Ruthie can get a picnic in no time at all, because there's heaps of food for the tea this afternoon. You could take the little ones. Actually, it would be . . .'

'What do you mean, "*You* could take the little ones"? What about you? Why can't you come?'

Tina shrugged helplessly, pointing to her mixing bowl and then waving vaguely round the kitchen.

'How can I? Not only do I have to prepare the meal for tomorrow myself, but there's the children's tennis party this afternoon. What sort of mother would I be to abandon my children at party time? Besides, Cecy's coming over, and the girls.'

'And with my four favourite Roses present, you expect me to take a picnic out?' But Tina saw the look he shot at the golden summer day through the kitchen window. 'Don't you need me here?'

Tina shook her head.

'Not really. As I was saying, it's Nanny's afternoon off, so I've been wondering how on earth to keep the little ones amused. If you took them with you it would be wonderful — a real help. And then I'll arrange an early dinner so that you and I can go out for a drive this evening. What do you think of that idea?'

'Not so dusty. And it would mean I'd see Blake's boat.'

Mrs Ruthven surged back into the kitchen at that point with Mabs, bearing a colander full of raspberries, in her wake. Tina, who had heard all about the exploit in the Salonica from a friend who had been having coffee there at the time, looked narrowly at Mabel, then dismissed her. Small, skinny, with straight black hair and black eyes, she seemed very ordinary to Tina. It seemed that the Walters had decided to send their daughter to the High School, but clever though she might be she would never compete with Stella for beauty. Tina caught the thought back guiltily. How absurd, when Stella was nine, quite four years younger than Mabel!

'What delicious raspberries, Mabs! Can I take some of them for the picnic?' Edward grinned down at the girl and she smiled back, and immediately her face was transformed into pixie-like prettiness. Tina, catching sight of the smile, reflected that the child had character and, with her boys in mind, would have to be watched.

'Well, Ted? Will you go today?'

Ted nodded, taking a handful of raspberries out of the colander and popping them into his mouth.

'All right, then, if it'll help. What's for dinner tonight, and what time's early?'

'We'll dine at seven.' Tina turned to the cook. 'What's for dinner tonight, Ruthie?'

'Iced cucumber and yoghurt soup, my special lobster mayonnaise with a crunchy salad, and pears in brandy with whipped cream,' Mrs Ruthven said. 'You said not to serve a savoury, ma'am, because of having a big tea for the tennis players.'

'There, Ted, a dinner worth hurrying home for! And you'll pack the master a lovely luncheon to eat by the broad, won't you, Ruthie? Enough for the three little ones too, of course.'

Mrs Ruthven agreed at once.

'Beer for you, sir, and milk for the children. Cold chicken's nice, I always think. But we've plenty of food, I'll put you up something a bit special. How about some of them strawberries?'

Edward groaned, patting his waistline.

'I've got a weakness for strawberries. And chicken. Don't worry that I'll be late home, not if it means missing your lobster mayonnaise. Seven, you said?'

'Not a moment later,' Tina said gaily, pushing him gently towards the kitchen door. 'Go and tell Nanny to get the little ones ready.' She prodded his back where a roll of flesh showed against his jacket. 'You're getting fat, my darling!'

'Rubbish!' Edward said, but even in his own ears his tone lacked conviction. 'I'll go and fetch the children, then.'

He disappeared round the kitchen door and Tina, closing it gently behind him, bustled back to her cooking bowl, smiling at Ruthie and Mabel.

'There, all settled! Thank goodness the little ones won't be underfoot when the guests are here. Are you looking forward to the party, Mabel? I hope so, since you're working so hard to make it a success! Have you a nice tennis dress?'

'I've the skirt and blouse the High School wear for games,' Mabel answered politely. 'They're very nice.'

'Of course. I expect you're getting the uniform together now. I'm coming to watch the tennis, of course, and from what my sons say you really should win!'

Since a trip in the car with their adored father was the height of bliss, and the thought of seeing a boat one degree better, it took David, Henny and Kitty only a few moments to get ready. Nanny co-operated eagerly. She had plans of her own for the afternoon which would be all the better for having most of the morning free as well. If her employers had known that she was being picked up by Louis and taken to Wymondham Gala and Fête, they might not have been so ready to allow her to leave early. But they did not know, and Ted was grateful for her cheerful co-operation as they got the boys into their sailor suits, thick stockings and sturdy boots, and Kitty into a pink and white smock dress and white stockings – though her shiny black boots were every bit as stout as the boys'.

As soon as the children were dressed they rushed out to the Rover, cramming themselves into the back seat with squeaks and giggles and dragging the lap robe over them, although this was speedily discarded since the day was warm.

As soon as the picnic basket was aboard they set off, talking and shouting cheerfully as they drove along. Ted, driving serenely with the wind ruffling his hair, felt totally happy. It was often thus. An easy-going and good-natured man, he needed only a fine day, a smooth-running car and the company of his children to have his good fortune brought home to him so forcibly that only in song could it be released.

He began to bellow; tunelessly, alas, but the children knew what he meant to sing and joined in. 'I'll be your sweetheart,' they carolled, and Kitty's little pipe, Henny's husky tones and David's choirboy soprano mingled with Ted's flat and tuneless bass to make a beautiful sound on a sunny day.

They reached the broadland village without incident and drove down the main street, then turned into the Blake boatyard. Mr Blake was nowhere to be seen; the sheds, the yard, and even the boats bobbing at anchor, were deserted. Everyone promptly abandoned the car, David holding Henny and Kitty firmly by their hands.

'Blake will be having his luncheon,' Ted said, consulting a large gold hunter. 'We should have stopped and eaten our picnic on the way down. We can't very well sit and eat it here, in someone else's yard.'

The children were hungry and three faces fell at the thought of having to wait, without so much as a bite, whilst the Blakes finished their meal.

'I know!' Ted said suddenly. 'I'll drive a bit further down the street and through the village, and turn down a lane I know. There's a bit of a staithe down there and we can eat our luncheon overlooking the broad. How will that suit you?'

The children, with squeaks of enthusiasm, promptly piled back into the car. Ted walked into the house, acquainted the Blakes with both his arrival and his intention of lunching before seeing their boat, and then returned to the driver's seat. He duly drove down the village street and turned into a dusty, tree-lined lane. They emerged, as he had predicted, on to an open space where the boarded bank proclaimed a safe mooring place for craft. Despite the brilliance of the day the staithe was deserted and the broad likewise. Spread before them like silk, not a ripple disturbed the surface of the water, and it seemed as though the whole world snoozed in the breathless noon heat.

As soon as the Neylers arrived, however, silence was at an end. Ted, a born organiser, had everyone working at a task within minutes. Kitty unpacked the basket and arranged the contents on the tablecloth which Ted had spread in the shade of some alders. Henny and David searched for dry sedge and twigs to build a fire and Ted himself filled the tin kettle, lit the twigs, and made himself a cup of tea. He had no particular desire for a cup of tea, since there was beer in the picnic basket, but knew how dear to the heart of a child is a fire, burning merrily in the open air.

As soon as the picnic was spread out everyone fell to upon cold chicken, salad and fresh bread rolls, then turned their attention to a large skep full of cherries which the thoughtful Ruthie had included instead of strawberries, which were inclined to travel badly.

Ted, reclining on his back with his straw hat tipped over his eyes, heard the shrill voices move away from him towards the edge of the water. He said drowsily: 'I'll just have a little rest to let my luncheon settle and then we'll go back to Mr Blake's place. Be good, won't you?'

He heard David say obediently, 'Yes, Daddy,' before he drifted off into delicious slumber.

Left to their own devices, the children were good, at first. They tidied up the picnic things and threw the crumbs into the water, then lay on their stomachs and watched the shoals of tiny fish which appeared as if by magic to browse upon their sudden largesse. When this amusement palled, David showed the younger two how to make boats out of leaves and twigs, and then how to drive the craft across the broad with the aid of leafy sallow branches, which were dipped into the water and sloshed vigorously around to cause waves which carried their tiny craft, bobbing and lurching, further from the shore.

Unfortunately, a slight disagreement over who had upset whose boat led to Henny, a stocky and determined child, swiping his elder brother with a soaking wet branch, whereupon David retaliated. Within seconds a fight was in progress, both boys dipping their branches in the water and lashing each other mercilessly. Kitty, despite her four years and her pink and white appearance, joined in lustily, and it was only after a particularly brilliant swipe by David had actually bowled her into the dust that she retreated, stumbling into Ted's recumbent form and inadvertently waking him.

Sitting up suddenly, still fogged with sleep, Ted received a wet and dusty branch right across the face. He gasped and swore, and Kitty swung round, catching him across the face for a second time, uttered a cry of 'Daddy, Kit's all wet!' and, running across to claim his protection, trod on his hand.

Ted's shout of pain and rage frightened his daughter and she promptly burst into tears, putting small, dirt-streaked hands to her face and knuckling her eyes vigorously as she wailed. David and Henny, grimly battling on, were first aware of their father's participation in their game when their weapons were grabbed, snapped across Ted's knee, and tossed into the water. One glance at their father's face, usually so mild but now red with temper, put both boys to flight. Kitty, tugging at Ted's jacket, was crying steadily, the tears channelling white lines down her face, and the boys, fleeing in opposite directions, were out of sight in seconds. Ted hesitated for a moment, then, with a sigh, relinquished thoughts of revenge on his sons and turned instead to his woebegone little daughter.

'Come on now, Kit, you aren't hurt,' he said. He knelt before her, holding out his handkerchief. 'Spit on this and I'll clean you up a bit.'

Kitty paused in her howling to say testily: 'You c-could dip it in the w-water, Daddy,' and then howled louder than ever as the significance of her remark made her remember the battle. Also, she felt a lot safer from Daddy's wrath whilst howling and hiccuping.

Ted silently stood up, went to the edge of the staithe, soaked his handkerchief and returned. Mopping Kitty's hot and dirty little face he said: 'That's enough, Kitty, or I'll give you something to cry about.'

Two blue eyes, framed with dusky lashes, opened and gazed at him searchingly, then Kitty stopped in mid-sob and said in a trembling voice: 'You won't hit the boys, will you, Daddy?'

Feeling the grittiness of the mud drying on his face and knowing his shirt was smeared, its stiff collar drooping, and his three children resembled nothing so much as three ragamuffins, Ted found it quite an effort to say truthfully: 'No, I won't hit them. If you can find them, Kitty, you'd best tell your brothers to come back here whilst I pack the car. Don't be long.'

The boys returned once Kitty had assured them that it was safe to do so, and Ted did his best to clean them up. Their hair was so muddy that he had to get them to kneel on the edge of the staithe whilst he poured water from a picnic mug over their heads, and then rubbed them dry on the lap-robe. Then he found he had no comb on him. But at least they looked clean. He tried not to notice their rumpled hair and crumpled, damp clothing. Boys will be boys, he thought, climbing back into the driving seat. They've got the mischief out of their systems now, and they'll settle down for the rest of the afternoon.

He knew his children a little less well than he imagined. David and Henny were both inventive and high-spirited and the battle had merely whetted their thirst for action. But their father, driving into Blake's boatyard, was unaware of that.

Old Fred Blake, telling Mr Neyler that the boat for sale was in fact his son's, and was moored on the opposite side of the broad, suggested that the children 'might prefer to goo to Platt's landin', together, and git some fishin' ', but Edward felt he wanted the boys under his eye.

'Besides, they'll enjoy the trip across,' he said, giving them a minatory glance which was lost on them completely, since they had every intention of enjoying such a voyage.

And enjoy it they did. They leaned from the boat and dabbled their hands in the water, spying for fish in the clear depths. They saw a swallowtail butterfly, huge and colourful, fluttering over the reed beds, and a flock of moorhen chicks paddling along like a flotilla of tiny ships.

Once ashore, they congregated by the boathouse until young Mr Blake, a mere stripling of fifty-five or so, joined them. He owned a trim bungalow with two boathouses built over the broad and a glorious garden, landscaped by himself, with groves of small trees, and miniature lakes, streams, islands and bridges. Kitty was enchanted by this child-sized world. It seemed built especially for her, and as soon as the Blakes and Ted had disappeared into the larger of the two boathouses she and the boys wandered off on a tour of inspection.

At first, it really was a tour of inspection. They crossed tiny bridges, explored wooden slopes, examined an artificial ruin and some wooden pagodas. Heavy booted but on tiptoe, at first they treated the garden reverently. Then David was struck by the possibilities of one particular island. With its thatched pagoda, its surrounding streams and its beds of irises, it would have been easy to defend had it not had two bridges, one to the east and one to the west.

It was the work of a moment to explain to Henny and Kitty that he would defend the island and they would attack it, and then he positioned himself in the centre of his property and announced that the attack must begin. The response was immediate and the fun fast and furious. David ran, skidding and shouting, from one bridge to the other to repel the enemy, pushing Henny into the stream, never noticing when his brother's desperately anchored boots scored the bank into twin furrows, nor when Kitty, following her leader, trampled almost flat a very fine clump of Japanese iris, the blue and lavender *kaempferi,* which had taken the Blakes months of anxious cosseting to rear.

David did not notice, but someone else did. Young Mrs Blake, a gimlet-eyed woman in her fifties with a passion for gardens and a deep dislike of children, had seen from afar and, on wings of fury, traversed the garden at astonishing speed, unnoticed at first by any of the three combatants.

'Come you outer that!' Mrs Blake shrieked, arriving on the scene like an avenging angel. She saw the furrows on the bank and moaned. 'See hare, you young varmints, what . . .' She spotted the bent and bleeding irises and her sudden scream of rage brought David off the island by the far bridge and sent all three children scuttling for their father and the boathouse.

Mrs Blake, still buoyed up by fury, followed them, announcing shrilly as they all arrived more or less simultaneously in the boathouse that 'Gardings in't no place for damned kids!'

Ted began to apologise but she shouted him down, her

mouth working, her cheeks bannered scarlet.

'There's a dam' big hoole in the stream-bank, and them iris what took Father and me such a power o' work to raise, they've tromped 'em flat. Thass too bad!'

Ted, seeing that action spoke louder than words, slapped both boys briskly across their tingling ears until they sought refuge behind their sister, gave Mrs Blake a handful of cash to 'make good the damage', and promised that the boys should suffer more fully for their sins when he got them home. The two male Blakes, eyeing their termagant female with a degree of embarrassment, mumbled that the iris would doubtless survive, and that it didn't do to expect old hids on young shoulders. Then, before Mrs Blake could voice further complaints, old Mr Blake steered the Neylers out of the boathouse and back to the dinghy.

'Don't you worry yourself, sir,' he said to Ted, clearing his throat and patting Ted's shoulder in an avuncular fashion. 'She hev got a bee in her bonnet regardin' that garden, and thass the truth. Silly old mawther! Now we'll go back to the yard an' talk business.'

Poor Ted, still simmering, cast his offspring a speaking glance and ignored them completely until Henny leaned too far out over the side of the boat and dropped his sailor hat overboard. Instead of helping his brother to regain his headgear, David smacked his head for carelessness and Henny, stung, seized David's hat and flung it from him. A fortunate breeze, springing up, carried the small object a good way off, twirling it merrily, and Henny crowed over David, who was about to begin a proper fracas when a glimpse of his father's face sent him sinking into his seat once more.

'Boys will be boys,' Mr Blake said tolerantly, rowing in pursuit of the floating sailor hats. 'I've 'ad four of me own, sir, so I should know!'

'Boys will have sore bums!' Ted roared, forgetting himself. 'Letting me down, behaving like hooligans . . . can't take them anywhere . . .' His words became lost in incoherent threats, his fury even greater because David and Henny were, by now, in the extreme stern of the boat and he was in the bows and therefore unable to inflict the swift punishment which would have given him so much satisfaction.

By the time the bank was reached and the boat moored safely, it would have seemed churlish to have whacked the boys, now the picture of innocence as they jumped ashore, helped their sister out of the boat, and then stood meekly waiting for their father, dripping sailor hats in hand.

'Get into the car and stay there,' Ted said, scowling at his offspring. 'I want to talk business with Mr Blake and I can't do so whilst I'm wondering what you three are up to. Stay in the car! Do you hear me? If you want to see one solitary strawberry when we get home this evening, don't move out of that car.'

With that he turned on his heel and marched into the house. Mr Blake, tipping them a wink, followed. The door closed behind them. Silence descended on the boatyard.

The Rover was parked at the top of a slight slope overlooking the broad, and directly in front of her, joined to the edge of the staithe to increase the mooring area, was a stout wooden platform which extended into the water for a distance of several yards, a sort of cat-walk, so that it and the staithe formed a letter L. The yard being deserted by visitors and workmen alike on Saturday afternoons, the boys and Kitty had no one to complain to, no one to watch, and no one to watch them. However, they were all a trifle subdued by their vigorous afternoon and climbed into the back of the Rover, where Kitty, cuddling down on top of the lap robe, almost immediately fell asleep.

'What did we do, Davie?' Henny enquired presently, his voice expressing injured astonishment. 'All we did was tread on her old lilies by accident, and – and anyone's hat could of fallen in the water! It isn't fair! I don't wanna sit in the car all afternoon!'

'We got a bit muddy after luncheon,' David pointed out, trying to be fair to their absent persecutor. 'But you're right, it isn't fair. I bet old Blake's giving Daddy beer right this minute! I'm thirsty too. Is there any milk left?'

At once the picnic basket was lugged out and rifled, and

though the milk was no more, there were two bottles of beer which, as David said, 'would have to do'. Presently, with a bottle of beer in one hand and a chicken leg in the other, David said brightly: 'Let's play we're driver and navigator, exploring Africa in our car!'

No sooner said than done. No orders had been given forbidding them the front seat so they climbed over, with their provender, and David settled behind the wheel to take first go as driver. Like most small boys, David had a very fair idea of how to drive a car from watching his father closely on outings, and though he knew they could not get down to start the engine he fiddled with various levers, twisted the wheel and finally, not without difficulty, released the handbrake.

By this time, David had swigged half the bottle of beer, and was delighted when the car began to trundle slowly down the slope. This was proving to be an excellent game and they had not disobeyed a single one of their father's commands!

'Spiffing, Davie,' Henny shouted, his voice a little slurred, his bottle emptier even than his brother's, for he had not got the car to drive, but merely had a road-map spread out on his lap. 'This must be Africa. I c-can see giraffes! Wake up, Kitty, Davie's taking us for a drive!'

But Kitty slumbered on and David, suddenly realising his responsibilities as a driver, began to tug fruitlessly at the handbrake, looking anxiously ahead to where the broad loomed. However, they were heading straight for the wooden cat-walk, which was not on a slope but ran flat and straight right out into the deeper water of the broad. He calculated that the car would stop of its own accord before it reached the end of the cat-walk.

The big car trundled down the last slope of the staithe and on to the wooden planks, which reverberated beneath the unaccustomed weight. All might have been well had David only continued to concentrate on his steering. Instead, he leaned over and began to heave again at the handbrake, allowing the car to head where it would for a split second.

It was their undoing. The right-hand wheels spun for an instant in space, then the car turned turtle.

The boys saw a confused kaleidoscopic view of sky, water and spinning landscape, and then they struck the water, the sudden shock of it making them gasp, even as the weight of the car above them pushed them under. Kitty, perhaps not even waking, did not cry out. David knew a second of guilt — what would his father say to this? Henny's frightened yelp was lost as the water surged into his mouth.

There was a tremendous splash as the car hit the surface, but soon enough the ripples which surged against the staithe settled back into calm. Quietness descended once more and the moorhens, which had fled when the leviathan suddenly crashed in amongst them, came back to paddle indifferently across the muddied water.

Ted, returning with Mr Blake, their business satisfactorily concluded, looked unbelievingly round the empty yard where the Rover had stood when he left it barely forty minutes earlier.

'What the . . .' Ted took off his straw hat and scratched his head. 'Oh, no!' He turned to Mr Blake. 'The young devils! I reckon they managed to get her going and they've gone joy-riding into the village! I'd best chase after them.'

But Mr Blake had him by the arm.

'Mr Neyler, sir! There's tyre marks on the cat-walk. Look!'

Ted ran across the yard, his heard suddenly thumping with fright, half expecting to see the car in the water on the far side of the cat-walk, with three repentant figures perched on the hood, for the water was not deep near the bank.

He saw only water. Calm, still.

He saw the tyre marks, but they ended halfway along the cat-walk — they *must* have gone into the village! He was turning away, almost faint with relief, when he noticed how muddy the water was further from the bank. Beside him, old Mr Blake began to run along the cat-walk. Ted stood still, and the world suddenly stilled too, so that an uncanny pause seemed to grip the moment. He saw, faintly through the muddied water, the dark shape of the car a foot or two below the surface.

Wheels uppermost.

9

Stella stood in the kitchen with her nose pressed against the window pane and watched the first cold flakes of snow drift down from a leaden sky. All the buildings which surrounded the kitchen yard had slate roofs, and Stella traced the slow spiralling of the flakes from the bare branches of the beech trees right down on to the roofs. It looked chilly and forbidding out there. Behind her, she knew, all was warmth and light. Ruthie was making a cake, Ethel and Edie were sitting on either side of the fire, praying that the bell would not ring, and Millie was making Stella's tea.

She did not have to turn round to verify the scene, for she had been home from school for thirty minutes and routine had taken over. Tea in the kitchen was her favourite time of day, now.

For Stella's life had changed so drastically since the death of the little ones that she felt she was no longer *that* Stella Neyler; that Stella, a pretty, heedless creature, had died as surely as the little ones on that day in July.

After the first shock of their loss, Tina and Ted had sent the children away. They had gone to Cromer, staying with Alice's cousin Maude, and had remained there for six weeks, until the school holidays were all but over. Twice a week they telephoned their parents, once a fortnight their parents spent Sunday with them. In between they went for long walks, played games on the sand, ate strange but delicious meals and tried not to think about the little ones.

Stella still remembered the awkwardness of those Sunday visits. Mama and Daddy, clad in black but with bright, artificial smiles, had taken them for car-rides and picnics. But the smiles were apt to slip if they thought themselves unobserved, and they held each other's hands tightly when they went walking. Too tightly. Eyes were shiny for no reason, one was suddenly kissed or hugged with undue fervour. The children breathed sighs of relief when the visits were over, and returned to their Cromer world, glad to be allowed a fortnight before the next descent.

On their return home, they found other changes. Nanny Sutton had left, and the nursery wing was locked up.

For the boys, going back to their boarding school, this was not so hard. For Stella it was a cruel deprivation. She knew no other life save the nursery one; her little bedroom, leading off Nanny's, had been her refuge in times of trouble and her favourite place in times of happiness. It was small, to be sure, with large boxes for toys all along one wall and a chipped little dressing-table with a mirror the right height for a nine-year-old and whitewashed walls on which her successful drawings were pinned. But it was cosy and familiar, unlike the guest suite, to which she had been promoted.

'It's just right for you, separated from the other bed-rooms and with your own private bathroom, just like a grown-up guest,' Mama had said, pointing out the guest room's advantages. But Stella hated the new room with its pale carpet, fitted wardrobes and velvet curtains. There was nowhere for her toys, she was not allowed to pin anything to the walls, and though she had brought Gungy, an earless, eyeless toy monkey, and Alison, a doll with eyes that swivelled and real hair, they seemed no more at ease in this new magnificence than she did. In her old room she had formed the habit of curling up on the window-seat, feet on the cushions and fingers in ears, whilst she committed poetry, tables and spellings to memory.

Here, she had a real little desk and a table lamp, but the basket chair creaked frighteningly, and the table lamp sometimes cast funny shadows on the smart wallpaper. She had a gas fire, but was bidden to use it sparingly, and to treat the bathroom with respect.

Treating the bathroom with respect was not difficult. In the old days bathtime had been a communal affair, with Nanny supervising, the small room hot and steamy, the other children wanting their turn, leaving boats bobbing on the surface of the water, while Kitty sang, slapped the flat of her hand on the water, squealed, ducked . . .

The new bathroom had pink tiles, one mirrored wall, matching towels. Here Stella bathed herself, washed her own hair. She hated and feared bathtime and was, suddenly, afraid of drowning. Once she had driven Nanny mad by ducking her head beneath the surface and holding her breath for as long as possible, emerging, scarlet-faced and panting, to Nanny's scoldings and Kitty's admiring squeals. Now, she ran a tepid inch or two of water, soaped herself with thumping heart, took a flying leap back on to the bathmat and dashed back into her chilly bedroom. There she would crouch before her lonely gas fire, dripping and shivering, until boredom and a sick feeling from hanging her head down drove her to bed, still damp-haired, uneasily to sleep.

Above everything else, she was lonely. The maids were kind, especially Millie; and Ruthie, too, welcomed Stella to the kitchen, understanding how bereft the child was. But Mama did not approve of her spending so much time with the servants. When she came into the kitchen and found Stella there, a slight but definite frost seemed to form; Stella, recognising it without understanding the reason for it, soon learned to slip out of the back door as Tina entered the room. But now that Christmas was behind them and the hard cold of January had arrived, it would be too chilly to hang about in the yard or the coach-house. She would have to retreat to her room after tea, and she dreaded the thought of the long, lonely evenings.

The war, of course, had made changes in everyone's lives.

Uncle Louis had left Grandpa's house and was living in London somewhere and learning to fly an aeroplane at Hendon airfield. He wanted and intended to go to the war when he had got his 'ticket', whatever that might be, but Stella knew that Mama and Grandpa thought it was just a phase, that Uncle Louis would realise that his place was with Grandpa and the business and not in France. Anyone could fight in France, Mama had once said, but only Louis could cope with Grandpa and the factory. He and Sarah were to marry in the spring, their wedding having been postponed last summer after the death of the little ones. Stella never doubted for one moment that Uncle Louis would go away, once he had married Sarah. She understood that this must be so, even though Mama could not see it that way. Uncle Louis had explained it to her, kindly and rationally, but she worried about him because he was her favourite uncle. Indeed, her only real uncle, for though Daddy had a brother she had never met him.

Behind her, Stella heard Ruthie lift the now filled cake tin and carry it across to the oven. She listened and heard the bell go; Ethel − or was it Edie − got to her feet with a martyred sigh and the kitchen door opened, swished shut. Millie poured milk into Stella's blue mug. Outside, darkness was falling as well as the snow. In the reflection on the window glass Stella could see the quiet, domestic scene. Her tea was set out, her milk poured. She even saw Millie's mouth open, preparatory to calling her name. She turned back with pleasant anticipation to face into the warm and cosy kitchen. Faces were flushed from the warmth, and everyone smiled or looked good humoured. They had mourned the little ones quite as fervently as her parents, but they did not have time to let the loss continue to weigh on them. She basked in their smiles.

'Oh, Millie, that looks delicious!'

Stella's praise was genuine for Millie liked to 'keep her hand in', as she always said, and her teas were beautifully presented. Today there was a thick hedge of mustard and cress in a horseshoe-shaped container, egg sandwiches in white bread and potted meat in brown, two tiny fairy cakes with pink icing and silver balls on top, and a slice of fruit cake. A plate of thin bread and butter, a jar which looked like a pineapple filled with raspberry jam, and the blue china mug full of milk.

'It don't take long to make things look nice,' Millie observed. She smiled at her solitary charge. 'I see your calendar marked out again! Never you mind, my chick, the time'll soon pass. You're too much by your own, together.'

Stella, used to the anomaly which caused Norfolk people to address one person as a crowd, nodded, her mouth full of egg sandwich.

'I know. Daddy says he might let me go to boarding school soon, though. Then I wouldn't get so lonely because I'd only be here in holiday times, like the boys.'

Millie, tidying away the remnants of tea-making, turned and stared, dismay evident in her large, light blue eyes.

'Oh, miss! You'd 'ate that, surely?'

'I wouldn't, I'd like it. You don't know what it's like, Millie, being alone when you're used to . . .' She paused, aware that there were some things which should not be said, however true they might be. 'I miss living in the nursery,' she finished lamely.

'You in't the only one,' Millie said briefly. 'If you go, miss, I will an' all.'

Stella's hand stopped, sandwich-laden, halfway to her mouth. Her dismay was as complete as ever the nursery maid's had been. Millie was the last link with her old nursery life, and to part with her, unthinkable. Her protuberant blue eyes, her flyaway hair that would never stay under her cap, her knobbly legs and the big-knuckled, chilly hands — they were as familiar as and a good deal dearer to Stella than her own mother's.

'You wouldn't! Oh, Millie, you wouldn't go!'

Ruthie murmured something warningly, but Millie was not to be turned from her purpose.

'I would, miss! I'm right fond of littl'uns; I wouldn't know what to do with meself if there weren't no childern here. Who d'you think does your mending, and keeps your room tidy? To say nothing of polishing up in the nursery and keeping it all nice.'

'Millie, thass enough!' That was Ruthie, coming straight out with it now. Millie flushed and hung her head, then she tossed back a hay-coloured lock and faced Stella.

'Well, I do, Miss Stella.' Millie glanced defiantly at Ruthie, then back at Stella, sitting white-faced at the table. 'And let me tell you, it have struck me, times, there's more life up in that there nursery than in the rest of the house, lately!'

She turned and fled then, into the darkness of the scullery, and Stella scraped her chair back, ignoring it when it fell over with a clatter, and flew after her. In the small room, smelling of cabbage and earth and scouring powder, she flung her arms round Millie's stringy waist.

'Do you really go up there, Millie? Can I come? It *was* a good place, wasn't it? I miss it so terribly – and Nanny, and them.'

Millie's scrawny arms were round her, she was pressed close to Millie's bony chest. And for the first time since the tragedy, she knew a sense of comfort and protection as great as that engendered by Nanny's comfortable, well-padded embrace.

'Yes, my woman, you shall come up there with me! There's nothing frightening in a place where kids ha' been playing. Do you come with me tomorrer, when I goes up there!'

'Come you outa that, the two of you,' Ruthie called. 'The bell have rung for Miss Stella to go to the study. You'd best cut along there, love.'

Carefully, Stella detached herself from Millie's arms.

'Daddy probably wants to talk about boarding school. I'll tell him I've changed my mind, Millie, and don't want to go after all.'

But Millie really did love children; far too much to let Stella make what she now realised would be a great sacrifice.

'Look, my woman, I was talkin' daft just now. You go, if the master'll send you. I'll stick on here, and that's a promise!'

*   *   *

'Miss Kelpmann to see you, ma'am.'

Tina, knitting khaki mittens for the men in the trenches and warming her toes in front of a lovely fire, put her work down and rose as Ethel stood aside to let Sarah into the room.

'Sarah, my dear, this *is* an unexpected pleasure! I thought that, with Louis being home, we should see very little of you. Louis's with you, I presume?'

Sarah stood in the doorway for a moment, tall and striking in an earth-brown coat with a fox-fur collar turned up to frame her pale, patrician countenance. But it was the look in her large eyes which brought Tina hurrying across the room towards her.

'Sarah! My God, what's wrong? Is it Louis?'

Sarah shook her head and came into the room. She undid her coat and sank into the chair which Tina indicated, then put one hand to her brow. Worried as she was, Tina still noticed that the little fur hat she wore exactly matched the reddish-chestnut of the fur collar and that, in turn, her Russian boots were the same dark brown as her coat. Even in obvious distress, Sarah was elegance personified.

'Oh, Tina! He's postponed the wedding again!'

Tina sank into her own chair and picked up her knitting, but made no attempt to start work on it.

'He's a thoughtless scamp! Why, for goodness sake?'

Sarah pulled the little fur hat from her shining dark hair and leaned forward earnestly.

'Oh, if only I knew! He says he'll be getting this certificate or whatever shortly, and then he'll go to some wretched place outside Liverpool, and then he's going to ask to go to France! Yes, really, with the RFC, of course. And Tina, there's no earthly need. He could just as easily apply for a flying job in England! They *need* pilots, and though I dare say you'll think I'm prejudiced, I do think Louis is good at his job. As for postponing the wedding, whyever should it be necessary, whether he's in England or France?' She fished a tiny square of cambric out of the pocket of her coat and dabbed at her eyes with it. 'I'd rather have some happiness than none!'

'I can't understand it,' Tina muttered. She reflected that she would dearly have liked to smack Louis. How could he behave so to someone as eligible as Sarah? She bit the thought back, trying to substitute the word charming instead. 'Do you have any suspicion that . . . well, that there might be someone else?'

Sarah shook her head hopelessly and stuffed the handkerchief back into her pocket.

'He says there's no one else, but I suppose he would. He says it wouldn't be fair to me to marry me and then go off and perhaps get himself killed, but that really is for me to decide! He's put me in an unbearable position, Tina! I dare not go round to the Bishopsgate house, in case Mr Rose has a heart attack when I say that Louis is going to France. And that means I can't enlist your father's support for the marriage. As for my parents, if Papa knew that Louis wanted to postpone the wedding again goodness knows what he'd say. I don't mind telling you, Tina, that several times Papa's been very difficult about my marrying Louis! It has taken Mama and me all our time to bring him round. There were rumours . . .' She paused delicately. 'But I daresay you heard them, too. I promised Papa that Louis's philanderings were a thing of the past, but if I admitted that the wedding was to be put off again . . . well, I don't think I could persuade Papa that Louis was not keeping a dozen mistresses!'

Tina stood up.

'Where is he now? I brought him up, so perhaps I can talk some sense into him. The trouble is, dearest, that he believes you'll wait. I shall disillusion him on that score.'

Sarah got up too, her eyes beginning to sparkle once more.

'Would you? Oh, Tina, that would be such a help! He met me as we'd arranged, to talk over wedding plans, and just told me about the postponement and walked out, back to the Bishopsgate house! I didn't know which way to turn, truly!'

'I'll speak to him,' Tina promised. She crossed the hall to

the cloakroom and got down her blue wool coat with the silk lapels. 'Is your car outside? May I borrow it to save ringing for James and letting the whole house into the secret?'

'Of course! Dickson's outside still, I daresay. Unless he's gone into the kitchen to chat to the maids.'

Dickson was a handsome young man with dark hair and a rosy complexion; Tina had little doubt that he was at this very moment sitting on the kitchen table, swinging gaitered legs and flirting with Ethel, who was a pert and handsome girl much sought after by young men despite her occupation, for 'skivvies' were not generally thought to be much fun to 'walk out' with, due to their job being a living-in one, with very little spare time.

'I'll ring and ask the girl to send him round.'

Tina, as it happened, was in luck. She arrived at the Bishopsgate house to find her father was dining out with a friend, Becky had gone round to visit Cecy, and Louis was alone. In fact, he answered the door when she rang and seemed pleased to see her, waving a chicken leg hospitably at her and taking her straight into the kitchen where he sat her down in Alice's favourite chair by the range and seated himself opposite, his wicked face alight with curiosity.

'Excuse me continuing my meal, sis, but it's Alice's night out and she didn't trust that young flibbertigibbet Annie alone in the house with me, so she sent her off to visit her mother in Bull Close. And since Poppa's gone a-visiting and Becky's with the Sollies, here I am, alone and starving, forced to subsist on cold chicken and a few other trifles. Want a cup of coffee? It's good — Alice made it before departing. Becky makes lousy coffee and Rachel's staying with someone this week.'

'Yes, I'll have a coffee, but I'll make it myself, thank you.' Tina felt sorry for Dickson, stuck out in the car in the cold, but she could scarcely send a maid out to fetch him in when there wasn't a soul in the house save herself and her brother. 'Louis, what's this about putting the wedding off again?'

Louis took a large bite out of his chicken leg and spoke thickly.

'What sort of life would it be for Sarah, married to me when I was off with the RFC? Can you see her in a little flat in town whilst I finish my course? She would go mad! And then, when I leave to fight . . .'

'Louis, that's just making excuses! You know very well that her father's giving her — both of you, I mean — a very beautiful house on Ipswich Road as a wedding present. As for a little flat, why on earth should she? You can spend weekends with her here in Norwich.'

Louis looked sulky. He stretched out his well-polished shoes and scowled at his reflection in the gleaming toecaps.

'I don't want her old man's charity, I want a wife who can be with me. If we're married, we should be together. At least until I go to France.'

'Go to France! Louis, your place is here. Even more if you've a wife. You'll break Poppa's heart, and Sarah's.'

Louis's brows rose and his expression became knowing.

'Indeed? Like you did? But he survived, Tina mine!'

'Don't rake up old forgotten stories,' Tina said sharply. 'Tell me the truth, Louis. Is there someone else?'

'Only Sarah. Truly, old girl.'

It relieved Tina's mind more than she had believed possible. She had suspected for a long time that Louis was having an affair with someone, and when she had asked the question she had been watching his face. There had been mischief there, and a certain triumph, but no trace of deceit, none of the little tricks she had come to expect when Louis was lying to her. For the first time it crossed her mind that her brother might actually be sleeping with his fiancée, but she banished the thought as soon as it was born. Such a thing was impossible, Sarah being such a closely guarded, well brought up young woman. And yet the predatory air which Louis wore when he was not having an affair with some woman had been noticeable, of late, by its absence. Shocked by her base suspicions, Tina burst into rapid speech.

'Only Sarah? Well, that's wonderful, Louis! And when

111

you lose her, what then? Because you will lose her, if you try to put the wedding off again.'

It set him back on his heels, she could see that. The dark brows drew into a frown and there was an arrested expression on his face.

'Lose her? But she's crazy about me!' He grinned suddenly, his brow clearing. 'There are hundreds of pretty girls, Tina, but only one Louis Rose.'

'You've forgotten one thing, Louis.' Tina was keeping her temper with difficulty. The conceit of the man! 'Sarah isn't just a pretty girl. She's an heiress. And she's got style.'

Louis did not answer for a moment but transferred his gaze to the flames, flickering in the fire. It was almost, Tina thought, as if her brother were weighing the pros and cons! And when he spoke, it was wearily, as if he were tired of the discussion.

'All right then, if it means so much to everyone! I'll marry her at the end of April. Tell her, would you?'

Tina got briskly to her feet and buttoned up her coat.

'If you wish. Shall I tell her you're here, and alone in the house?'

He got to his feet, holding the kitchen door for her, and shook his head.

'No. I'm leaving in a few minutes.'

She crossed the hall, then turned in the doorway, her expression puzzled, the finely curved brows arched.

'Leaving? But you're here for another three days!'

He almost pushed her out of the door, into the chilly, snowy darkness.

'I was. But even though I may be forced to marry Sarah, none of the rules say I've got to spend the remainder of my leave here!'

Before she could say one of the words burning on her lips, the door slammed and she was alone, unable to vent her spleen on anyone with Dickson watching her, jumping down to start the car engine, and with something so final in that slammed door that she knew instinctively that had she returned to beat upon it there would have been no answer.

More than a little shaken by the vehemence in Louis's

112

last remark, Tina climbed into the car, settled herself into the deep leather upholstery, and planned what she would say to Sarah. She wondered at her own lack of satisfaction, for even if Louis had been ungracious in his defeat, defeat it undoubtedly had been. She had won, hands down, and Sarah would be married in the spring.

Sitting back as the car slid through the thin fall of snow, she tried to plan her wedding outfit and decide on presents. But all she could think of was the fact that Louis, who had courted Sarah with such ardour, no longer seemed to want to marry her, but seemed determined to join the rest of the army in France.

The roads were a little treacherous so Dickson drove with great care, which was as well, since by the time they reached The Pride again Tina had tidied away her tears and fixed a bright smile to her face. Sarah was a bride-to-be once more, and Louis's resolve to go to France might easily be weakened by a wife.

But in her heart she acknowledged that he would go.

Louis had a small, brightly painted two-seater Ford Tourer whose engine, lovingly tended, could do a good speed on a deserted road. He left a note for his father propped up on the kitchen table explaining that he had been called away, donned his thickest overcoat and a long striped scarf, and threw his few possessions into a Gladstone bag. Then he and Flossie, his car, set off on the road back to London.

Despite the fact that he was to be married, he knew a wild and exultant happiness as he drove. The snow had stopped and the sky was clear, the moon and stars bright in the deep blue-black above. The wind was cold but Flossie's engine purred, there was a bag of peppermints handy so that he could suck one as he drove and a flask of brandy in his pocket to keep out the cold. One way and another, he enjoyed the journey.

He threaded his way through London to Golders Green, parked the car in a mews garage and made his way softly across the courtyard to a cottage with a blue painted back door, robbed of colour by the moonlight but as familiar to

Louis as his own hands on the steering wheel. He unlocked the door, slipped through it into the small, red-tiled corridor, then locked the door behind him. He stood for a moment, head cocked, listening. Nothing. He had woken no one. Then, very quietly indeed, he mounted the stairs with their squeaky treads. At the head of the stairs was a tiny landing with two doors leading off; he opened one of them and let himself into the darkened bedroom.

'Darling?'

His whisper was barely audible, but it woke the sleeper in the old-fashioned double bed. She stirred and sat up, and in the dimness he saw her smile, saw her arms come out to him. He knelt on the bed and reached for her, kissing the sleep-blurred mouth and eyes, pressing her softness harshly against his still driving-coated chest.

'I've come home early. Are you all right, my love? How's the boy?'

She snuggled against him for a moment, then kissed the side of his face and settled back against the pillows as he began to undress.

'He's got a name, Lou! Call him James, not the boy! It's lovely to have you back so soon, but − why?'

He stripped naked and stood for a moment smiling down into the cradle at the foot of the bed without answering her. The child within, dark-haired, its small face scowling in sleep, stirred as though conscious of the scrutiny and Louis turned quickly back to the bed.

'He's grand.' He murmured the words as he slid between the sheets and turned to take her in his arms. 'My son! Sarah Sutton, you've done me proud!'

And Sarah Sutton, once the Neylers' nanny and now the mother of Louis's son, relaxed in her lover's arms and let her mouth soften beneath his lips. It was only when he began to tug impatiently at the neck of her nightgown that she spoke again.

'Lou, why've you come back so soon? Is it all arranged − the wedding, I mean?'

'Button your lip, Say. I've been away nearly a week and all you want to do is talk.' Persuasive fingers slid down the neck of her nightie and began to caress her swollen breasts. 'Can we make love? Is it all right now?'

She sighed and began to unbutton the gown, then, with his help, wriggled out of it. The curtains at the window were drawn back and in the moonlight the new fullness of her body pleased him immensely. Anticipation made his touch suddenly tender, almost hesitant. He stroked her waist, and then down the smooth curves of her buttocks, pulling her gently closer.

'Well? Is it all right?'

'Baby's nearly eight weeks old, so I suppose so. The doctor did say after six. But do you think we should?'

He raised his eyebrows at her, continuing to caress her back, their bodies just touching. He felt the shudder run through her and felt the push of hardening nipples against his chest.

'Do *you* think we should, Say? I don't want to do anything you wouldn't like!'

She giggled, a delicious bubble of amusement deep in her throat, knowing her own weakness as well as he did. She adored him, she adored making love, and tonight, after their long abstinence, she could not even pretend coyness or unwillingness.

'I think . . . perhaps . . . we should.'

In the past, Louis had been a sensual and demanding lover, greedy, sometimes rough, always taking rather than giving. But tonight he made love to her leisurely, wooing her in a way he had never bothered to do before, taking delight in the full ripeness of her body, teasing her with kisses and caresses until she was completely relaxed and eager for him, the baby in the cradle, who must not be woken, totally forgotten. Then he took her engorged nipple in his mouth, playing with it, drawing off some milk, until she was clutching him, pushing her hips forward, mutely appealing for consummation.

'Oh, Lou, you're driving me crazy! Oh, Lou, I want you so!'

It was a delicious loving, made more so because they felt like prisoners released from their recent abstinence. When they were quiet at last, Sarah with her head on his chest, Louis on his back, one arm behind his head, staring up at the ceiling, they had never felt more in accord. It was easier to ask the question which had to be asked, and to answer it truthfully.

'Louis, are you going to marry her?'

He stroked the rich, tumbled brown hair away from her brow, and sighed.

'Yes, dammit! If I'd put it off again she'd have smelt a rat. As it was, I nearly gave the game away to my sister Tina. Your one-time employer, sweet Say. She asked me whether there was anyone else.'

'And you told her . . .?'

'Only Sarah, I told her. Which couldn't be truer.' He grinned, his caressing hand still smoothing her hair. 'When I think of the times I've said "Sarah" and meant you! I never thought having two women with the same name could be so convenient!'

'I'm glad. That you're going through with it, I mean. When you go to France, you'll have a wife to write to.'

'And you. If you think that I'll marry and forget you and the boy you're wrong! This' – he slid his hand down to caress the curve of her stomach – 'this is for ever.'

'Or until I meet another man and marry him.'

'Why should you do any such thing? I've *got* to marry Sarah so that I can afford to keep my mistress in luxury. And my son.'

She laughed, and turned her head to kiss the hand near her face.

'Oh, Lou, you'll have other sons! Do you think Miss Kelpmann will be barren?'

He turned her on to her side, then put his arms round her waist, holding her close and covering them both with the bedding.

'Forget it now, Say. Sleep. God knows, the morning will come soon enough, and the boy will start his demands on you.'

She sighed and cuddled down and very soon she slept. But Louis lay awake and thought. Many things had touched

116

him about young Sarah Sutton – young she was not, he reminded himself, since she was four years older than he, yet she seemed young. He had been at the house when Ted had returned after the children's fatal accident. He and Sarah Sutton had been out in the country, making love under a haystack, and he had brought her as far as the bottom of the drive and then driven the rest of the way up himself, to visit his sister.

He had barely assimilated the news before Sarah was back, and the full shock of her loss broken to her. Tina had been white-faced, shocked, silent. Sarah had screamed and then keened, and he had not comforted her, nor gone to her, nor tried to ease her pain. Later, he had been deeply disgusted by his behaviour. To stand by as she blamed herself – who was blameless – and agreed to leave at once, refusing money, swollen-faced with grief. It had been, he thought, the worst thing he had ever done.

Afterwards, anxious to make what amends he could, he had followed her in his car and picked her up, asked her where she would go, what she would do. By then he was bitterly angry with Tina for virtually turning the girl from the door and it helped to ease his own sense of shame. But Sarah was conscious of none of it. She sat beside him in the car, all her tears cried out of her, shaken now and then by a deep, dry sob, and waited for him to tell her what to do next. It was not until a fortnight later, when he had moved her and her belongings into the mews cottage in Golders Green, that she had told him she was pregnant. Even then, he had admired her. She had told him, neither accusingly nor reproachfully, of her condition, and waited for him to turn her out, or suggest an abortion, or send her back to her mother in Ireland.

He had not, at that stage, intended to live with the girl. He shared a flat in Hendon with a fellow flier, and had merely meant to visit Sarah. But something about her, the gallant way she had kept her condition a secret, or the way she immediately began to plan what work she might do to keep herself, changed his mind. He moved in with her, took over the finances of the small house, and, with considerable

117

amusement, insisted that the neighbours should call him Louis Sutton. When his son was born, he knew that he could never leave her to struggle with the boy alone. He adored the child, was proud to tell the neighbours that they had a son, and wanted to give the boy the earth, to acknowledge him openly.

And yet, side by side with his love for Say was his love for Sarah Kelpmann. Sarah had character, determination, a lively and original intelligence. Poor Say had a placid disposition, a generous spirit, and a straightforward attitude to life. One day, he suspected, he would love Sarah deeply and possibly only tolerate Say.

In the moonlit bedroom he turned cautiously away from her to lie on his back. Immediately, she turned round too, snuggling up against him, underlining her own dependence and the depth of her love. Yet she had done everything in her power to get him to marry Sarah Kelpmann! Did she know that he was not by nature faithful? That if she had not borne him a son he would have moved back from her a little, gradually allowed her to drift away from his life and back into her own? Perhaps. She had said something of the sort, just before he left for Norwich earlier in the week. He screwed up his eyes and brought the scene clearly back into his mind. Say feeding the baby in the low armchair by the fire in their tiny sitting room. Himself sitting on the table, kicking at the dining chair nearest to him. Say smiling up at him, speaking.

'You're not a one-woman man, Lou, you've got time and energy for two. I'd rather you married Miss Kelpmann now and went on loving me than blamed me later.'

'And you the mother of my boy? As if I would.'

She had smiled almost indulgently, as if she knew him better than he knew himself.

'Oh, Lou! Marry her, to please me!'

He had muttered something and left the room but he knew now that she had been right. If he lost Sarah Kelpmann, in the very depths of his mind he would blame Say. Because, dammit, he loved them both, in his way!

He turned on his side at last to settle down to sleep, and

118

knew that he would go through with it now whatever might happen. By the end of April Sarah Kelpmann would be Sarah Rose, and he would have two homes: a large house on Ipswich Road and a mews cottage in Golders Green. But the thought did not worry him. Things had a way of working themselves out, if you trusted to providence to guide you!

10

It was a beautiful wedding. The synagogue was decorated with branches of early lilac, white, mauve, and purple, and the poles of the Chupah were wreathed in vineleaves, cunningly twisted, with the pink and lavender motif of the lilac echoed in the hothouse blooms peeping from between the foliage.

Ted was sitting with the boys but Tina was with the wedding party, an 'interferer' in place of her dead mother, for she had helped to bring Louis up. Watching his wife's small, determined face as she, in turn, watched the bridal couple, Ted thought wryly that the Jews knew what they were talking about when they referred to the parents or parental representatives at a wedding by that name. Tina, bless her, could no more stop herself interfering in the lives of those around her than she could have stopped loving him. It was, he knew, both her strength and her weakness. And because it was part of her he could be indulgent about it, stepping in when he saw that her strong-willed 'guidance' was going to cause unhappiness, applauding her when it caused joy.

This was Ted's first Jewish wedding, and he noticed that apart from the bride − who looked absolutely radiant in white wild silk, with a coronet of lilies of the valley shining in her dark hair — Stella, who was a bridesmaid in blush-rose muslin, and Tina and Mrs Kelpmann, there was not a woman in sight. They were all up in the women's gallery, behind him. Mrs Kelpmann was crying steadily, the tears making glistening tracks down her bunchy, olive-skinned face. Would Sarah look like that one day? It seemed impossible — certainly Sarah would never have chosen to wear plum-coloured velvet and sables!

Mr Kelpmann was not crying; he was standing, very straight and upright, with one hand lightly touching his wife's, and as the bridal couple moved slightly — the ring was about to be placed on Sarah's finger — Ted saw Mr Kelpmann's expression change as his eyes fell on Louis. Ted looked away quickly, and when he looked back Mr Kelpmann — 'You must call me Ernest' — had controlled his features once more. I hope Louis realises that this time there's got to be no messing about, Ted thought, or my irrepressible brother-in-law might live to regret it. Ernest Kelpmann was a powerful man and he adored his only child.

There had been a lot of Hebrew spoken, but suddenly English words caught Ted's ear.

'Blessed thou art, consecrated to me by this ring, according to the law of Moses and Israel.'

The ring slid on to Sarah's forefinger and she raised her eyes to Louis's face. Her smile was sunlight on dark mountains, day dawning. Yet it was a private smile, meant for Louis alone. Louis was still holding her hand; Ted saw his fingers tighten, saw his brother-in-law's glance soften yet burn, and then they turned back to the Rabbi and the Chazan to drink the toast, their private moment over for now as Louis grinned his reckless grin and put his foot on the wineglass, symbolically significant in some way no doubt but to Ted it looked remarkably like the end of freedom. No more wine, women and song, for the cup is broken and the free man fettered. He grinned to himself, but then the choir broke into a chant of heavenly beauty and the couple moved down from up by the Ark to walk through the congregation.

As Tina passed him she crooked a finger and he slipped out of his seat, crooking a finger in his turn to his two sons. Desmond and Frank, as tall as he now, fair hair water-flattened, dark suits drawing attention to their broad shoulders, followed him out.

Outside, the sun shone brightly and up the road a laburnum tree, leaning over a little cobbled courtyard, was already spilling its bright gold. A small crowd had assembled and Ted grinned at the servants who clustered near, anxious to see the bride and to offer their good wishes to the happy couple.

He saw Mabel, looking extremely nice and rather grown up in a gown which looked vaguely familiar. And next to her, looking straight at the boys, that friend of hers, what was her name? Sally? Susan? The one Tina disapproved of so strongly. Ted, watching her, blinked as she caught Desmond's eye and one of her own long-lashed orbs closed in a wicked, twinkling wink. He glanced round, but Tina was busy, talking to Ruthie and the maids, calling Sarah over to show her bouquet. It would never do if Tina knew that already Desmond was bidding fair to rival his Uncle Louis over his interest in women!

The cars were waiting to take the wedding party and all the guests back to the Kelpmann house, where the reception was to be held in a vast marquee erected on the lawn. Desmond, standing beside Tina, murmured something and slipped away. Ted knew where he had gone but pretended not to notice. The boy was only human, the girl both young and extremely pretty. It would do more harm than good in any case to try and stop Desmond talking to her. Frank had followed his brother and the four of them stood in a small group until Tina, ending her conversation, called the boys to join her in one of the cars. Ted watched them drive away. The wedding is over, he thought sentimentally, and today a new life will begin for them both. If it was even half as happy as his own married life had been, they would be fortunate indeed.

*   *   *

'Suzie!'

Suzie, watching the bride, had been aware of Desmond with the tingling excitement that always overcame her when she was attracted to a man and knew it was mutual. He was, of course, much too young for her; Suzie, at nearly fifteen, usually sought companions of at least seventeen. But he looked much older; you could have taken him, she considered, for nineteen or twenty quite easily. Besides, there was something about him, though she did not quite know what. Louis had it too – though he, of course, was out of her class, and would not spare a second glance for someone of her age. Suzie, who made a point of knowing most things, knew that he and Sarah Sutton had been lovers right up to the time the Neylers' nanny left the family. She suspected, though the suspicion was completely unfounded, that Louis still had another woman tucked away somewhere.

'Oh, hello, Des.'

Her voice was calm and friendly, her smile the same. It was as if she had a little voice inside her, advising her how to behave with men, and with Desmond the little voice advised that he should be allowed to do all the work, all the pursuing; that he would not value her if she showed the slightest sign that she would welcome his attentions.

'Suzie, you look grand! Meet me this evening? At the tree-house?'

He spoke so low that only she could have heard, she told herself. Frank was telling Mabel about the ceremony, his voice still at the stage when it sometimes ascended the scale for a word or two, coming out as a squeak instead of the deep, masculine voice which was almost identical with Desmond's.

'I was surprised, Mabs; it's very colourful. Odd, in places. Do you know, before Uncle Louis went under the sort of canopy thing, he lifted Sarah's veil and they smiled at each other. Uncle Abe says it's tradition that the groom lifts the veil so that he can tell he's getting the right woman – not being palmed off with some spotty sister that they couldn't marry off. Weird, isn't it?'

122

'He'll lift more than her veil tonight,' Desmond said salaciously, and noticed Mabel's blush with interest. Three months ago, she would not have known what he was talking about. On the other hand, Suzie merely smiled and made as if to turn away. But as she did so he heard her murmur, scarcely above a whisper:

'Nine o'clock?'

'It's a date.'

Then their mother called them and the boys turned away. The colour in Mabel's cheeks was fading and Suzie caught her friend's arm.

'Shall we go out for tea, now we're so fine? To the Corner House, if you like – my treat. I'm rich this week. Want to know why?'

'Yes. Why?'

'I've left Garlands.'

They were walking away now, leaving Ada and William, and all the other servants from The Pride who had come down to see their dear Mr Louis wed, to make their way back home. Mabel shot a glance at Suzie.

'No! But I thought it wasn't so bad, and the money was all right. Where are you going next?'

'Nursing. That way, maybe I'll get to France one of these days.' She shot a dancing look at Mabel out of the corners of her long, green eyes. 'I don't mean to be poor for ever, Mabs. I'm going to marry a rich feller and live in luxury, I am.'

'I don't blame you. I suppose you didn't fancy munitions or working on the land or anything like that because . . .'

' . . . because there's no men in jobs like that. That's the idea. Perhaps I'll nurse a rich, fat old major, and marry him. Or a dashing young captain, who's an earl really, and then I'll be an . . . there's no such thing as an earless, I suppose?'

Mabel giggled and elbowed Suzie briskly in the ribs.

'Fool! If you're aiming for an earl, why did you say you'd meet our Des in the tree-house tonight?'

Suzie groaned. Mabel must have excellent hearing to have caught that low-voiced conversation!

'Meeting Des? Oh, that's just a bit of fun. I don't mean anything by it. Why? D'you still think he's too young for me?'

'I don't know that I ever thought he was too young for you. I thought you might have trouble if you messed around with Des. And I still think it.' Mabel could be frank to the point of crudeness when she liked, and she faced her friend frankly now. 'You don't want to take your drawers off for Des, I'm telling you, Suzie, or you'll get more than you bargained for. You'll end up rocking a cradle and that won't get you an earl!'

'I don't see why. I've given lads a good time before, and I'm not nursing a big belly yet.' Suzie looked curiously at her friend. 'I didn't know you knew about . . . well, that!'

'I'm not any too sure,' Mabel admitted. 'I'm repeating what Ruthie said to Nanny Sutton, ages ago. Only it was Louis she meant, of course.' She pursed her lips, then began to speak in a very good imitation of Ruthie's motherly tones. ' "Thass oonly fair to warn you, gel, that them as takes their drawers off for Mr Louis gits more'n they bargain for. You'll be rockin' a cradle in nine months." That's what Ruthie said,' Mabel finished, returning to her own voice.

'And you deduced from that . . . ?'

Mabel frowned and scratched her head.

'Lumme, that something *happens,* of course! No one's ever said what, so I don't know.' She raised a brow. 'Do you know?'

'We-ell, I know you can have a lot of fun without rocking no cradle,' Suzie said a little defiantly. 'You've got to be careful, that's all.'

'Oh. Well then, be careful.' They were on the Walk now, heading for the Corner House. 'Aren't you going to tell me what people do? When they make babies?'

'I am not!' Suzie sounded disproportionately indignant, Mabel thought. 'You'll find out for yourself soon enough.'

Once in the Corner House at the window table they favoured, eating cream cakes and drinking tea and eyeing the dresses of the ladies around them, it crossed Mabel's mind that, for all her talk, her friend might well be as ignorant as herself. Comforted, she continued her tea.

Louis and Sarah honeymooned in London. At first, Poppa had been taken with the idea of the two of them going to Yarmouth where, so many years before, he and his beloved Deb had been so happy. But then, in January, the town had been heavily attacked by Zeppelins and since then the east coast had been sporadically bombed, so he had suggested London. The theatres were still doing business as usual, the restaurants too.

Louis, of course, was all in favour of a London honeymoon. There would be opportunities, he thought optimistically, of getting over to Golders Green when Sarah was otherwise engaged.

So they travelled up to their hotel by car and made their way to the suite of rooms which Poppa had reserved for them. He considered it his right to pay for the hotel, he explained, and had also given Louis a generous cheque to pay for other pleasures during their stay.

And now, even as Desmond tiptoed across the croquet lawn towards his rendezvous with Suzie, Louis, who had been banished to the bar for a drink whilst his bride prepared for bed, tapped on their bedroom door.

'Sarah? Can I come in now?'

She opened the door and he slipped into the room. The curtains were firmly drawn across the wide windows which overlooked the park and the subdued, pinkish glow from the bedside lamps was the only illumination.

Sarah's hair was loose. That was the first thought which occurred to him, for he had never seen it loose before, flowing in deep, rippling waves down to her waist. She was wearing a white satin nightgown, quite grand enough to be a ball-dress, and she had bathed and powdered herself — he could smell something flowery which almost combated another scent: Sarah was nervous, despite her apparent calm.

He took her in his arms. She had always seemed almost as tall as he but now, barefooted, she seemed much smaller and more vulnerable. He decided to be gentle with her. Releasing her from his embrace he pushed her gently towards the bed.

'Lie down whilst I undress.'

She sat on the edge of the bed, brushing her hair, scarcely glancing across to where he was hastily stripping. He glanced at his maroon silk pyjamas, then decided that it would be a waste of energy to put on garments which would so soon come off. He sat beside her on the bed, put his arms round her, then rolled her, quite gently, on to her back and began to kiss her.

At first, she responded well and eagerly, almost as he would have expected an experienced woman to respond. But with the first attempt at real intimacy, she tensed and drew back a little. Not before time, Louis thought prudishly. A decent virgin of just twenty should not part with her nightdress willingly. He was subconsciously judging her by Sarah Sutton's standards, for Say had never allowed the light to remain on whilst they made love; he had never seen her naked in anything but moonlight, and then only, so to speak, by accident.

Suddenly, as if she could read his thoughts, Sarah began to resist him. Strenuously. Louis had expected coyness, perhaps a few tears, and was prepared to deal with such maidenly faltering in his best and most seductive style. He was not prepared to be kicked, scratched, punched, and finally to find himself kneed in the groin.

'Look, Sarah, I'm not going to hurt you. I'm . . .'

An expletive he had never expected to hear on a woman's lips was hissed at him.

'You are hurting! For God's sake, what do you think you're doing? Ouch! Stop it! *Ouch*!'

All Louis's good resolutions deserted him. It had always been like this, right from the start! On their very first date she had blacked his eye and scratched his face, and for what? For daring to try to touch her breasts, when if she had not worn such a provocative dress he would never have dreamed of doing such a thing! Well, this time it would be different. And to think that he had allowed her to retain her

126

nightdress, when the bloody thing was confoundedly in the way!

He hurled her on to her back and ripped the nightdress off her, hearing the material rend with a good deal of satisfaction. She screamed at him and hit out and he captured her wrists, then began to force her legs apart with his knee. With some difficulty, for she was wriggling like an eel, he got both wrists clamped in one hand and shut her mouth with his own, then he tangled the other hand in her loosened hair and pulled it savagely until, beneath his mouth, he felt her lips part. He dared not loose her, though she was responding to him now, moving her body into a more comfortable position, her breathing steadying. In the muted light he watched her thick, white eyelids droop and then widen with pain and shock as he took her. She jerked convulsively, and tears welled up in her eyes, but she neither screamed nor tried to tear herself loose. He admired her then, wanting to explain to her, to move less savagely, to give as well as receive pleasure, but unable to do so, transported by a lust to which she was a stranger. And presently, when he was sated, he knew that he was forgiven. She cuddled up to him, sighing, and took his hand and put it on her breast, and laughed at the great black bruise disfiguring one cheek and the scratches on his chest.

They slept for six hours, heavily, and he was woken by her, kissing him. She was lying on her stomach leaning up on her elbows, and her mouth was on his own, firmly, and then her tongue probed at his lips and her breathing quickened.

Desire was roused to white heat by the sheer unexpectedness of the caress. He reached for her and she came willingly into his arms, though having deliberately begun to seduce him she proceeded to make him work hard for her capitulation.

An hour later, she remarked, in a slow sleepy voice, that her nightdress was ruined, and that it had cost twenty guineas.

'You shouldn't have fought,' Louis reminded her. 'If you hadn't, it wouldn't have been necessary to tear it.'

'You raped me,' Sarah said in a wondering voice. 'Now I think back, you raped me! Shame on you, Louis Rose!'

'Did I? I suppose I did. And you enjoyed it. Shame on you, Sarah Rose!'

'Mm hmm. Oh, Louis, I love you so!'

'You must do. You've scratched half the skin off my shoulders and it still stings!'

He propped himself up on an elbow and looked down at her. She pouted at him, her skin shiny, her hair tangled, her poise quite gone. He let his eyes linger on her mouth, beestung into soft plumpness by kisses which had known little of tenderness. He had marked her beautiful body, he knew that. Bruises on her wrists and breasts, on her soft inner thighs. With tenderness now, he kissed her lips.

'I'm sorry, darling. I didn't mean to be rough, but . . .'

He stopped talking.

'Who blacked your eye for you then, Des?'

Frank's far from innocent remark earned him a baleful look from his elder brother.

'What black eye? You did it, Frank, when you shot your elbow out last night over the billiard table. And don't you forget it!'

Frank, undeceived, grinned.

'Was it Mary? She's getting a big girl, isn't she? Lovely tits, as the upper school would have it.'

'Think what you like.' Desmond's tone was airy. The two boys were in their room, getting ready for a shopping trip into the city with their mother. They were only home, officially, for the wedding, but it would be a couple of days before they were returned to school, possibly four or five if they played their cards right. 'I say, Frank, have you got my blue tie with the white polka dots on it?'

Frank was sitting on the window-seat, with a copy of *Chums* before him, open at a Frank Shaw adventure story. He had been reading, with only half his attention on his brother, but now he looked up, his face darkening.

'You've not been mucking about with Mabs? Des, if you . . .'

'Not with Mabs, old bean. What riles me about Mabs is that you've no desire to muck about with her yourself, yet you're dead against anyone else having a go at her. You want to grow up, young Frank.'

'That's just where you're wrong,' Frank said placidly, returning to his story. 'You being a year ahead of me is a great help, because if you're an example of what growing up's like, then I don't want to do it.'

'If I have any more of your lip you won't live to do it,' Des said. 'And answer your elders and betters, will you? Where's my blue tie?'

'Don't know. Look for it. Lazy bugger.'

'Hey, just you look as well! Lazy bugger yourself! You're the younger, and if I say move, you move.'

Usually the boys avoided direct conflict since they were of a height, of a build, and of a boringly identical strength, so that a fight between them tended to last for hours rather than minutes. But on this occasion, though neither knew it, there was just sufficient needle in both remarks to make them throw caution to the winds. Frank was uncomfortably aware that there was more than a grain of truth in Desmond's accusation — he would have killed anyone who hurt Mabel, but he had no desire to start what he termed 'nonsense' with her himself. And Desmond, smarting under the recollection that Suzie was nothing but a little tease, who would let a fellow go so far and no further, was jumpy and quick to take offence at what he imagined to be a slur on his manhood. They met, head-on, like stags in the rutting season, and it was thus that Stella found them when she came in to tell them that their mother was waiting. Locked in what appeared to be mortal combat, they swayed and staggered around the room, butting, punching, wrestling, whilst Stella squeaked and circled them, her small, shrill voice almost unheard above the rich medley of threats and swear-words pouring from her brothers.

'Boys! What are you doing? Stop it at once! Remember you are supposed to be gentlemen!'

Their mother's outraged voice had the effect of bringing them both out of their fury. One last push, a muttered 'You swine!' and then they were shaking their heads sheepishly and muttering, being forgiven, departing to the bathroom to wipe away bloodstains – Desmond's nose had bled copiously over them both, a tribute to a lucky head butt from his brother – and to tidy themselves.

'I didn't mean to nettle you over your eye,' Frank said, as he cleaned up. 'It's ages since we fought.'

'True. I rose to the bait like a fish to a fly, I suppose,' Desmond admitted. 'I'll tell you who it was, anyway. Suzie.'

'No!' Surprise and a degree of envy fought for supremacy on Frank's face. Surprise won. 'What was she like? As hot as Mabs painted her?'

'Yes and no. But when I come home in the summer I'll make jolly sure it's yes and yes! C'mon, let's get back, or Mama will ring a peal around our ears.'

Frank, following his brother down the stairs to where their mother would, by now, be impatiently awaiting them, wondered whether it would be politic to tell Des that, by the summer, Suzie would be a nurse and probably far away. He decided, perhaps a little regretfully, that it would not. He must keep his own counsel – for the time, at any rate.

'Well, Say my dearest, I've got my ticket, I've done most of my training, and any day now I'll be off to France. We really ought to get the boy saying "Dada" before then, though.'

It was a lovely bright day towards the end of May, and Louis, Sarah, and the baby were out walking in the park – or rather Louis and Sarah were walking whilst baby James rode in style in his perambulator.

'Oh, Louis, we'll miss you, Baby and me! Do you get a leave before you go?'

Say was wearing a white muslin dress with little blue flowers scattered over it, and a blue ribbon tied up her hair. She looked young and innocent, and although he knew that strictly speaking she was neither of these things he still felt his heart move at the sight of her. She was a good girl, was his Say! Nevertheless, both duty and desire prompted his

130

next utterance.

'I get leave, but I'll go back to Norwich and my wife. Of course.'

'Of course,' she echoed, ashamed of a natural wish to have his company, and Louis put his arm round her shoulders and squeezed her lightly. She was growing plump; not that he objected. It was nice to have a plump woman and a slender one, he considered, for then one made fewer mistakes in bed. Awful, to roll over, grab a tress of thick hair, clear the back of a pearly neck for his passionate kisses – and discover himself murmuring the wrong name! Fortunately, this had not yet happened. He was training himself to call them both either by their given name of Sarah or by a love-word – darling, sweetheart, my love – during moments of passion.

He acknowledged ruefully that each Sarah had cause to be grateful for the existence of the other. Living with Say was a little like living with a contented and affectionate cow; living with Sarah more like cohabiting with a tigress who could love you one minute and rake you down the next. Lovemaking with Sarah was strenuous, she made him work for her and fight for what he wanted, but when he got it, God, it was sweet! He never quite knew where he was with her. She was unpredictable, beautiful, capable of sweetness, fierceness, sulkiness, generosity.

He found her exciting but exhausting. He knew that, had it been she in the Golders Green mews, he would probably not have won his flying certificate. But Sarah Sutton was different altogether. With her he could relax and be himself. On his weekend leaves he walked slowly around the summer city, or sat in a pub drinking and talking, or slept in the square garden, stretched out on a deckchair, Say content to lie on a rug at his feet and make daisy chains or sing lullabies to their son.

But now he had come to say goodbye to her for a while. He would see her when he had leave since he intended to go back to Norwich via London on each occasion, and to spend either the greater or lesser part of each leave with his mistress and the boy, depending on whose companionship he felt most in need of.

No one knew about his double life. The chaps at Hendon had known there was a woman, the chaps at Filton, where he had completed his training, assumed that he had married her. Walking with Say's hand tucked into the crook of his elbow, with the precious burden before them in the high perambulator, he mused idly on the undoubted fact that he felt a lot more married to Say than he did to Sarah. Sarah was excitement and escape, Say and his life with her the very stuff of marriage − bills, lines of washing, plain cooking.

'I'll leave after luncheon,' Louis said now, squeezing Sarah's shoulders again. 'Poor old darling; but you'll manage very nicely. You always do.'

Her smile was a little sad, a little abstracted. She told herself continually that one day he would go and that, when he went, she must make a good life for herself and her son without him. She knew Sarah well enough to guess what an exciting and challenging wife she would make. And yet each parting hurt a little more, made the possibility that there might be no return a little less easy to bear.

'Yes, we'll manage, Baby and me. We'll write, as well, as soon as you send us an address.'

She kept a brave face until she waved the little car off that afternoon, then she went indoors and wept over the washing.

'London's been bombed! Father always said a Zeppelin would get there one day!' Sarah scanned the newspaper eagerly, heedless of the sudden, icy stillness of her husband on the opposite side of the breakfast table. 'Oh, Louis, Golders Green's been badly hit. You had a flat there, didn't you? I do hope all your friends are all right.' She glanced up. 'A motor omnibus was hit and a score of people killed. And a great many injured. Do you . . .'

Louis plucked the paper out of her hand, scanned it quickly, then stood up, throwing his napkin down on the table where it knocked over the marmalade pot. His coffee cup was untouched; his toast, buttered but not yet spread with the marmalade, lay on his plate. Sarah stared up at him, her mouth dropping open.

'Louis? What . . .?'

'I'll have to go.' He walked round the table and patted her shoulder. 'I've scores of friends living in that area. Some of the fellows are in France already, but they left wives and children. I'll not be above a day, but I must go at once.'

'Of course you must.' She was immediately practical, immediately understanding. 'And I'll come with you. There might be something I could do.'

He was in the doorway, but turned at that.

'No, darling. It may be . . . a bit gruesome.'

She was on her feet, following him.

'War's gruesome, Louis. I'm coming. I'll just get my dark coat.'

But when she went round to the garage ten minutes later, the little car had gone.

Louis drove into the mews close and parked his car outside the cottage. Passing down the main street, he had been appalled by the damage. Houses with the frontages sheared clean away so that one saw the cracked washstand, the warm rug by the bed; the tiny, intimate details of the life that had once filled the house bared to the world at last. Louis turned away his head. He felt, obscurely, that the little back-to-back houses were like plain, fat little women who had found themselves stripped by the blast and were trying, in vain, to hide themselves. He would have liked to catch hold of the walls and close them around such pathetic, embarrassed nakedness, and failing that he would not stare at them.

But in the mews all seemed quiet and placid enough. There were geraniums in the windows of No. 4, salmon and scarlet, and the books which had lain on the sill of No. 7 lay there still. He walked briskly to his own front door, and rang the tinkling little bell. No answer. It was then that he remembered the motor omnibus and the people killed. He fished for his key and opened the door. It was quiet and cool, the low-ceilinged living room deserted. He went through to the kitchen. There was a fire burning, and the smell of cooking. He glanced out of the window, and saw Sarah. She was pinning washing on the line, nappies over one arm, the other reaching up. Her hair was untidy, wind-tugged, and in the loose grey gingham dress her bulges looked less appealing, but his heart, nevertheless, lurched with pleasure because she was all right. He opened the back door and whistled. She turned towards him, and he saw the pink fly to her cheeks, her eyes brighten.

'Louis! Oh, darling, is anything wrong?'

She ran into his arms and he patted her shoulder, trying to stifle an impatient desire to be sarcastic and biting at her very ingenuousness. Anything wrong indeed, with half the main street torn asunder by bombs!

'I thought there might be. I thought you might have been caught in the raid.'

She smiled up at him, then gently detached herself from his arms to pick up the washing, which she had cast down on seeing him.

'No, I'm all right. And Baby too. The noise was dreadful, but no one we know was hurt. Except Mr Tollworthy, the butcher. He's in hospital.' She returned to the line and began pinning the rest of the nappies out, speaking loudly above the rollicking wind. 'I would have let you know, but I didn't think.'

'No. Anyway, a letter wouldn't have reached me before tomorrow. We've got to arrange something, because I'll go mad with worry now, knowing that no one would contact me.' He gazed at her back view. When she stretched up like that her skirt lifted unbecomingly, revealing thick, wrinkled stockings and over-chubby calves.

She finished with the washing and turned to him, taking his hand and leading him back into the house.

'Worrying's silly, Louis. We'll be all right.'

'It won't do! London's going to be the most dangerous place in England for the rest of the war.' Inspiration struck him and he caught her shoulders. 'Of course! You must come home, to Norwich!'

Her eyes widened, then narrowed with laughter.

'Norwich? To Ipswich Road, I suppose? Oh, Louis, if only I could! But I'll be all right here.'

'I'll get you a little flat. This place is rented, and I daresay a flat in Norwich would cost no more. We'll choose one in a part of the city where the family don't go much. Why on earth didn't I think of it before? You'll be Mrs Lewis − you can remember that − and I'll be Robert Lewis, your soldier husband. Then I can divide my leaves up between you. God, it's the best idea I've ever had!'

She gazed up at him, adoration shining from her eyes.

'Could we? I'd love it, of course, because I've friends in the city. But we'd be found out, Lou, that's the rub. Someone would recognise you, or me, or both of us. We wouldn't be able to stroll in the streets or anything without being afraid.'

But his quick mind had already grasped both the advantages and the disadvantages and he had an answer ready.

'Yes we would! I'd keep special clothes at the flat, ready for Robert Lewis, and if anyone saw me by chance they'd think how like Louis Rose was, not that I *was* Louis. It'll work out whilst the war's on, at any rate, and when it's over we'll think again. It might be better for you to live in London then, because in peacetime I come up to town quite a bit for Poppa. But for now you'll live in Norwich, somewhere where you won't keep running into the family. And everything'll be prime, you see.'

'Louis, it wouldn't work. We'll find some means of keeping in touch so that you know I'm all right. But going back to Norwich − it would be far too risky. I'll stay, and it'll all be for the best.'

The flat was more of a bed-sitting room really, on Pottergate. It was next door to a pub, the landlady was fat and good-natured and made a great fuss of James, and Louis left mother and son there with no qualms.

'Your furniture will go into store until I get you somewhere better,' he told Say as he prepared to leave her. 'I'll send you an allowance, of course, and I'll see you every time I'm home. And I'll write. Now take care of yourself, and if you need anything either write to me or speak to Mrs Tuddenham.'

He had three more days of his leave left and she knew that he would not see her again. He had brought her straight back, after giving notice to the landlord of the mews cottage, and found her a room in a boarding house for one night. Then he had found the flat and moved her into it, barely remaining with her for an hour before rushing off back to his wife.

Now, in the stuffy, over-furnished living room with the gas-ring in the corner, he was saying goodbye to her. He kissed her, his mouth clinging for a moment, then he put her from him and instructed her again on how she was to behave.

'And take care of James,' he ended as he turned from her to go back to his other life.

She stood at the top of the stairs and waved, not liking to go rushing into the road because he had hidden his car further along so that no one would see him with the vehicle and later put two and two together. She knew that with the change of venue their relationship would change, but she did not know how. Time alone would tell that.

11: 1916

Dawn was breaking as Louis's aeroplane gained height, and the first rays of sunshine glinted on the edges of the retreating night-clouds in the lightening sky. It was 4.15 and this was the dawn patrol, a routine flight which could be boring or exciting, depending on whether the German aircraft were also dawn patrolling, trying to spy on or bomb the trenches below them.

Louis yawned jaw-crackingly and turned to glance at Nick, flying on his right and a little behind him in the formation. Nick raised a hand, and then, with a grin, mimed someone drinking, then clasped his head. They had had a hard night of it at the local *estaminet* the night before, and Louis's mouth felt like the bottom of a birdcage. He swallowed, and licked his dry lips. A cup of hot coffee would be nectar now, but he wouldn't get anything to drink until they landed in about an hour's time. Roll on breakfast, he thought longingly.

They were over the Allied trenches now. It was always grim down there, in winter a sea of mud and bodies, in summer a sea of dust and bodies. Now, in the March chill, it was gleaming clay, puddles reflecting the steely, cloudy sky. The shell holes were pools of thick, treacherous mud; horses could and did fall into them and were entirely swallowed up. Men, too. Louis shuddered and looked ahead to where Flight Commander Tillett led them. He saw the captain waggle his wings, then the nose of his aeroplane lifted as he began to climb again, straight up into the cloud cover. This probably meant that, having seen the sky clear above the trenches, he was checking that there were no enemy aircraft coming from the east, whence they always came. If everywhere was clear he might signal them to break formation and go off separately, keeping their eyes peeled for enemy formations of course, and then they would make their own way back to Petitpasteur, and breakfast.

The cloud, cold and clammy, closed round Louis and immediately he was alone. He could not see the wing tips of his own aeroplane, let alone anyone else's, but he held his course with the supreme confidence of one who flies in formation with men as experienced and skilful as he, and presently burst out into brilliant sunshine, the sky deep blue, the clouds a snow-scape just beneath his wheels. And company; the rest of the flight, all in exactly the same positions as they had held upon entering the cloud.

But there was nothing else of interest, save for some fast

vanishing specks in the east; German bombers, probably, making their way home after shedding their deadly loads over the trenches. They were a good way off, but it was possible that the captain would decide to chase them, or send a pilot or two in pursuit. Louis watched the leading aircraft eagerly, but instead the captain made signs that they were to split up, some going one way, some another. He tapped his wristwatch, then held up one finger, then gestured back towards the aerodrome. Louis, breaking away to the north, waggled his wings in acknowledgement; he would be landing in an hour, old Tilly might rely upon that! With a thirst like his he was not likely to be tempted into strafing balloons or chasing off to terrorise the German trenches. No, today he would be a good boy and patrol along his territory until it was time for breakfast.

It was as he broke away from the others, doing a rather showy roll, that a thought occurred to him. There was a farmhouse out in this direction where only the previous day he had gone with Nick. They had bought an excellent meal there — scones, new-baked and thick with cream, the real clotted sort. Afterwards, they had been pressed to accept delicious sandwiches made out of smoked ham. Louis swallowed. And though the coffee was only ersatz it had been good!

If he continued to fly in this direction, he could be over that farmhouse in five minutes. And landing in the big pasture at the back in five minutes and thirty seconds. And drinking hot coffee and eating ham and eggs in . . . say ten minutes? The prospect was irresistible. He continued to fly towards the farmhouse, noting absently that the area had been heavily shelled since he last passed over it. Last night there had been shelling, and he had heard the whine and crump of bombs, too.

He knew his plan was going to come to nought two minutes later, but for a moment he could not bring himself to believe it. The place must have taken a direct hit. The grey stone walls still stood but where the roof had been there was only a smoking ruin, and plainly nothing could have escaped from the fire that had raged in the farmhouse.

He circled, remembering the old couple, the woman's beaming, toothless smile and the old man's friendliness, the way they had pressed the ham sandwiches on the two young men who were in their country, fighting their war. The talk, almost philosophical, of their son and daughter, both dead in the war, and of a nephew, fighting in Egypt. It was impossible that the old people had lived, and yet . . . the ruins were still smoking, and the place was a good way from the village. It was all too probable that no one had yet been near the farm, and if not . . .

He knew he would land. Impossible to fly back to Petitpasteur not knowing whether those good people were alive or dead! He knew, of course, that they were probably, almost certainly, buried in the ruins and as probably dead. But if they were down there, suffering . . .

He landed neatly, climbed down from the cockpit, and walked over to the farmhouse.

He found them almost at once. They were both very dead, without dignity or individuality. They must have been sitting or standing close together when the bomb hit them, and now they were just fragmented. Louis walked away from the jumble which had once been the farmer and his old wife towards the stabling, which was, paradoxically, standing as untouched as though there had been no bomb, no blast, no sudden deaths. He had best take a look, make sure that there were no beasts waiting to be milked or fed or something.

Afterwards, he wondered what had taken him along to the darkest end of the apparently empty stable, to peer right inside the last stall. Could it have been providence? But for whatever reason, he went along to the end stall and saw its occupant.

'Hello! You gave me a fright! You aren't hurt, are you?'

The small, skinny child curled up beneath the manger neither moved nor spoke. Only the eyes glinted, to show that it lived. Louis moved closer. He tried in French.

'*Bonjour, mon enfant. Que faites vous?*'

Not a movement nor a sound. Louis moved nearer. He put out a hand. Still nothing. Making a quick decision, he lifted the child up beneath her armpits, for she was definitely a girl, with a skimpy, thin little cotton dress and shoulder-length hair. She hung in his hands like a rag doll; her head even lolled a little to one side. But beneath his right hand he could feel the thunder of her heartbeat. She was deathly afraid.

Louis loved children and had always been at ease with them. Now he simply sat down on the floor, cross-legged, and cuddled the little girl as unselfconsciously as though she were his own little niece. He sang to her, he played games with her, going 'round and round the garden' on the palm of one small, grubby hand, burying his head in her neck and blowing raspberries against her soft skin, teasing her in a mixture of English and French over her silence, her dirty face, her lack of movement.

He was hours overdue, and never even thought of it. His thirst no longer mattered. Nothing mattered but bringing this filthy, tattered girl-child back from whatever far country she had been driven to by the bombardment.

It was when he began to play 'This little piggy went to market' that he knew he was winning. She withdrew her foot from his fingers with a little jump. And then she laughed — a small enough sound, certainly, and although he knew it was a laugh he also realised how nearly it might have been a cry. But it was a beginning.

Thirty minutes later, he took her to the pump in the yard and solemnly washed a small part of her face, 'so that I can see if you can smile at me'. She could, and, presently, did. When he climbed back into his cockpit and wedged her on to his knee she showed not a trace of fear, though when they landed and his mechanic came running towards the aircraft she shrank back, her eyes widening and darkening like a cat's.

He picked her up, for she was featherlight, and walked with her to the squadron office. Captain Tillett was there, worried in case he had managed to crash his aeroplane and kill himself. The story, briefly told, was explanation enough of the child's presence.

'What's her name? And what was she doing there? I've

140

been there myself, but there was never any mention of a child.'

Louis shrugged.

'I don't know, and I doubt whether she can tell you. Her shoes are almost worn through; I'd say she's walked for weeks. And the dirt on her isn't just ordinary muck, it's engrained filth. If you ask me, she just turned up at the farmhouse last night, and hid in the stables to avoid the strafing. What with the noise and the shock of the farmhouse coming down, I daresay she's not yet able to think straight.'

'I see. Well, you'd better take her to the base hospital. The girls down there are wonderful. They'll see her right.'

So Louis put the child into the squadron's ancient lorry and drove her to the hospital, and tried to leave her with the prettiest nurse he had seen for some while. But the child would not be left. She clung to him, and when the nurse took her and Louis turned away she spoke for the first time.

'Non! Non! Avec vous, monsieur!'

He returned to her side at once, explaining that the nurse was good and kind, and was merely taking care of her because she was a little girl and needed food and a nice hot bath.

'If you tell me your name, I'll come and see you tomorrow,' he assured her, in his best French. 'And then, if you would like it, I could take you to my home and you could meet my family.'

'Josette,' she murmured, clinging to his hand. 'I am Josette. You swear you will come back, monsieur?'

He put a hand to his heart, squatting down so that their heads were level.

'I swear it. You'll be good with this lady?'

She glanced indifferently up at the nurse, then back at him. She nodded vigorously.

'Yes. If you will truly come back.'

It took them a month to make all the arrangements and to get Josette respectable once more.

'There was nothing physically wrong with her,' Louis

told Nick. 'But she had worms, and fleas, and lice, she still doesn't know her surname and she had no idea where her relatives might be. She and Maman were walking when the aeroplanes came over and Maman fell. Then, later, Maman died. And she went on walking, because she didn't know what else to do.'

'And she's been cleared to go to England?'

'That's right. She's a Belgian, and England's full of 'em at the moment, so there's a slight hope that someone might recognise her, I suppose. But more to the point, my sister's got a little girl, Stella, about Josette's age, and she's said she'll give Josette a home and bring her up like her own. She will, too. She's a sharp little lady, my sister Tina, but she needs this kid as much as Josette needs her.'

'Why's that?' Nick suddenly did a double-take. 'Hey, you say she's a *Belgian*? and she *walked*? Good God, man, it could be a couple of hundred miles!'

'That's right. Kids are odd little creatures, but they can cover the ground when they decide to keep moving. Tina lost her own younger children in an accident in the summer of 'fourteen. That's why she'll welcome Josette.'

'I hope you've explained to her that England's an island, or she'll probably set right out to walk back to you,' Nick remarked. He had not been able to help noticing how very attached to Louis the small girl had become. 'Does she understand that she's to live with your sister and her daughter?'

'She does. She's sharp as a needle, you know,' Louis said with almost paternal pride. 'Only until the war's over, mind you. Then she's going to live with me!'

'Hmm! What will your wife say to that?'

'Oh, by then Josette will have settled with the Neylers and probably wild horses wouldn't drag her away,' Louis said with airy optimism. 'It'll all work out for the best. Things always do!'

Desmond thundered down the stairs, skidded across the parquet flooring in the hall, and then, just outside the dining room door, adopted a careless pose and sauntered into the room. Because it was Saturday morning no staff members presided over breakfast, only two prefects, and the boys were talking freely, opening their letters and eating vast quantities of toast and jam. The butter, which was rationed, had gone long since and the jam itself, being rhubarb and ginger, was detested by every pupil of Pursell's School from old boys to the very youngest midget in the juniors, but food was food. On weekday mornings two rounds of toast only were allowed, so at weekends one ate one's fill.

Desmond grabbed a chair and flung himself into it. He was immediately hailed by Frank, sitting opposite him in deep conversation with his friend Puggy.

'Des, there's a letter from Mama and Daddy. I bags first read.'

'Be my guest. Where's my egg?' A boiled egg apiece was a Saturday morning ritual and Desmond did not intend to miss out just because he was late. 'Come on, did someone bone my egg?'

'No, young man, no one's ate it,' the cook said placidly, entering the room. 'It'll be like a bullet now, and cold, too, but I daresay you won't mind that. If you 'adn't been late, acourse, you could have 'ad it 'ot. I heard you thunderin' down the stairs, so I brought it through.'

'Ta, Cooky, you're a princess,' Desmond said, decapitating his egg. It was hard. 'Any bread and butter for your favourite customer, Cooky?'

'It's all gone long since. You'll 'ave to make do with plain bread,' Cook said tartly, but she snatched a slice of bread from the plate and presently returned it, smeared with either butter or margarine; it was such a scraping that Desmond could not tell which. Nevertheless, he thought, devouring it and giving Cook a grateful beam, it was better than nothing. And it was Saturday. If Frank was in the right sort of mood they could take themselves off to the Copper Kettle and get themselves coffee and cakes.

'It's from Mama, with a bit on the end from Daddy,' Frank remarked, reading the letter. 'Mama's going on about the Belgian child. She's dark-haired, and has dark

143

eyes. Mama says she's teaching Stella French faster than Stella's teaching her English.' He broke off to chuckle and help himself to a pale and tepid cup of tea. 'Auntie Ray's nursing somewhere in France, and Aunt Cecy made a cake with grated carrots instead of dried fruit – ugh, horrible!'

'Shut up! Let me read it!' Desmond grabbed the pages and skimmed them with only faint interest. Josette – soppy name – interested him not at all. Girls were fine, but ten-year-old girls did not count as such in his book. On the other hand, it seemed as though Stella and the new brat got on pretty well. That would mean he and Frank would have peace during the summer vac, to say nothing of Easter, which was almost upon them. So good would come out of evil, in fact. He grinned at the thought. One could scarcely describe the taking in of a ten-year-old brat as an evil action, but it really would be jammy if it got Stella off their backs!

Daddy's few lines were typical of his father. He had gone up to London to see if the army was interested in putting him in khaki but it appeared it was not, or not yet, at any rate. He had a contract to make special boots for officers and was putting men and women on to the work at more than he had ever paid anyone before. He was giving free cinema shows to the wounded soldiers twice a week. He was their loving father.

Desmond finished the letter and shoved it back into its envelope and then into his jacket pocket.

'We go down to Austin's for our fruit today, Puggy. You coming, or shall little brother and I go off on our tod? If so, we can bus.'

Puggy, thus appealed to, shook his head and stood up.

'Not today, Neyler. I'm playing in a match after grub, so I'll go and punt a ball about. I know you two. You'll be up to something, and I want to be in tip-top condition. We're playing King's, and they're good.'

'Tip-top condition?' Frank got up too and punched his friend lightly in the shoulder. 'With all that soggy school toast inside you? And about ten gallons of Cook's worst tea, laced with snail's milk? You'll be lucky if you can trot, let alone gallop!'

Puggy grinned and punched Frank back. He was a thick-set boy with greenish eyes, ten million freckles and ginger hair. He was also a very fine rugger player.

'Do me less harm than cream cakes and black coffee,' he observed. 'Why aren't you playing, Neyler?'

'Because I went to Ely last time, and young Horton-Smythe needs a game,' Frank said. 'I might watch, though, so do your best, laddie!'

Desmond snorted. He had got his cricket colours at the end of the previous summer and was longing to sport his white blazer with the purple raven on the pocket, but he had little time for rugby, which he considered a crude and dirty game, easily leading to black eyes, broken noses, and the consequent loss of the good looks of which he was so fond. Frank and Puggy had acquired their first fifteen colours this year despite their youth, and at match times wore purple blazers with silver ravens on the pocket and velvet caps with tiny peaks and silver tassels on the crown. If his brother watched the match in all the glory of his blazer and cap, then Desmond would not do so for the world.

'I'll do better than you would,' Puggy jeered. 'Going to give us the benefit of your support, Des?'

'No, it's a game for ruffians,' Desmond said. He had remained seated, finishing off the last of the toast, but now stood up. 'Well, if you're not coming, Pug, we might as well go. Ready, Frank? Shall we catch the bus?'

During the autumn and winter terms the pupils of Pursell's had to walk or bicycle everywhere to keep them fit for rugger and football, but in the summer term they were allowed to travel by bus since the headmaster did not believe that cricket was as exacting a sport as 'footer'. However, an exception had been made for the Neyler boys, when they visited the greengrocer for their Saturday order.

The whole business had come about after their father had visited the school and had been impressed by everything except the quality of the food.

'It's like food on board ship in the sixteenth century,' he grumbled to their mother. 'I'm not having my sons going down with scurvy, or losing all their teeth by the time they're twenty. Boys need decent fruit and vegetables as well as meat stewed to rags and great suet puddings.'

Accordingly, he arranged with a greengrocer in the town that each Saturday during termtime his sons might go into the shop and spend up to five shillings between them on fruit, the bill to be settled by him at the end of each term. The town itself being out of bounds to the boys except on special occasions, he had made his arrangements with Mr Austin, a greengrocer who was right on the outskirts of Cambridge.

And then one day Desmond was forced to go for the fruit by himself, since Frank was in sick-bay. Seeing a chance to gain additional privilege, Desmond had pointed out to his house tutor that with the weight of oranges and grapefruit in his bicycle bag making him unsteady he had been forced to unload half the fruit and to make two trips. His house tutor, a sensible and easy-going man, agreed that in future the boys might catch a bus 'when necessary' to fetch their weekly order. It immediately became necessary on almost every occasion for a while, since one must not allow privileges to lapse. And now they frequently caught the bus, not just as far as Mr Austin's, but right into the centre of Cambridge, for there were a hundred good reasons why it might take them most of the morning to fetch their fruit and, unless they were seen, very little fear of being apprehended.

Today, however, was sunny and relatively mild.

'No, let's walk,' Frank said now, as they clattered across the hall to the front door. 'We can always get a bus back.'

They were dressed in sports jackets and flannels, their caps in the regulation position on the extreme back of their heads, but when they were well clear of the school both boys stuffed their caps into their pockets, removed their school ties, and tried to look as though they came from anywhere but Pursell's. It would not do to be seen in Cambridge sporting the school colours. The dons and other college officials were quite capable of informing on them to their teaching colleagues at the school.

'Here, I brought our civvy ties. Is yours the red or the blue?'

'Doesn't matter.' Frank slung the red tie round his neck and tied it, then scrutinised the road ahead. 'There's old Ma Hogman! D'you think she'll notice our ties?'

Desmond whipped his cap out of his pocket and was about to jam it on his head when, by some trick of fate, a bus drew noisily up at a stop some half a dozen yards ahead of them.

'Quick, run for it!'

Before Mrs Hogman was anywhere near they were on the bus, making their way to the top deck, triumphantly bound for the town centre.

As they climbed down from the bus Frank remembered something.

'Des, I meant to ask you. Did you see the notice board this morning? Anyone mention Tufton?'

Tufton had been head boy last year, and had beaten Desmond for taking a shop girl to the cinema when he should have been attending a demonstration of small boat sailing organised by the prefects. There had been no love lost between them after that, for Desmond considered himself too old for beatings. He frowned now.

'Tufton? No one said anything. Why, what's happened to him? Nothing pleasant, I hope.'

'Killed. At Verdun. There were four of ours.'

'Oh.' Desmond looked blank for a moment, then pushed his hands into his pockets and began to saunter non-chalantly up the street, gazing into the shop windows as he went. 'Well, he was a swine so I can't feel any great loss, though I wouldn't say that to anyone else, of course. Four of ours, you say? D'you know the other names?'

'I wrote them down so I can tell Uncle Lou when I write. He won't have known them. They would have been midgets when he was here if they were here at all. And over there I shouldn't think subalterns have much to do with the elite of the Flying Corps. Tuffy had only been out three weeks.'

'Three weeks!' His voice subdued, Desmond added:

'Who were the other three?'

Frank fished a crumpled piece of paper out of his pocket.

'Paget, Carruthers, Coe; that's William Coe's elder brother. He was called out at suppertime a couple of days ago and didn't come back. We guessed then what it must be. I can't remember Carruthers at all but Paget played in the old boys' match last year. Big fellow with a yellow moustache. Remember?'

Uneasily conscious that in just over a year he himself would be taken for military service unless he had managed to get into a classified job by then, Desmond tried to change the subject.

'That reminds me, I've not heard from Suzie lately. I wonder if she's in France? She wrote to me a couple of times when she first went into nursing, but I've not heard for ages.'

'Don't show your ignorance, Des. Girls can't nurse in France until they're eighteen. Anyway, she writes to Mabs, so I think she must be all right.'

'And Mabs writes to you. I see. Well, next time you write to Mabs you might ask her to remind Suzie I exist. Come on, here's the Kettle. Going to risk it?'

It was not, in fact, as much of a risk as it might have appeared. The Copper Kettle was an attractive little tea-room with a wide window looped with net, giving an excellent view down the street in both directions. At the back the tables were partitioned off, and there was also a very convenient rear exit so that if one were careful one could slip out if a house tutor's wife, or a couple of prefects, looked like entering. And now that the younger masters had been caught up in the war effort, so that even the older ones were involved with sporting and other extra-curricular activities, it was less likely than ever that they would be caught.

Accordingly the boys went in and sat down at their favourite table, a sheltered nook near the back, and beckoned the elderly waitress. All the staff, except the older women who could not stand the pace of war-work, had been employed elsewhere by now.

'Coffee and cream cakes, please,' Desmond said, giving the waitress the benefit of his most charming smile.' 'Have you any meringues?'

Presently, with a plate of mock-cream cakes between them and a jug of coffee steaming in the middle of the table, Desmond leaned towards his brother.

'See those girls over there? What d'you think?'

Frank followed his brother's meaningful glance. Two girls, both personable, wearing fashionable light wool suits and with their hair short and curled, were sitting at a window table. They were glancing now and then towards the two boys in their alcove in what could only be termed an interested fashion.

'Des, will you never learn? It'd be bad enough just being caught in town, but to be caught talking to girls . . .'

'We shan't be caught! We could take 'em to the cinema this afternoon, since you aren't playing in the match. Or we could meet them down by the Cam after dark this evening. Be a sport, Frank. Let's go and see if we can click with 'em!'

Frank hesitated. They were very pretty girls; the smaller of the two had a roguish look in her dark eyes and he admired the way her suit clung to her small, high bosom. He nodded, only half reluctant.

'Righto. I don't suppose they're interested in us, but it wouldn't hurt to have a word with them.'

They finished their coffee and cakes, paid the bill, and got up. Crossing the room and heading for the door, Frank saw Desmond preparing himself for the usual opening gambit just as the two girls got up as well and came towards them. This threw Desmond slightly, Frank realised, but his brother gathered his wits and held out his hand to the taller of the two girls.

'Good morning! Miss Ferris, isn't it? I was just saying to my friend that . . .'

'Why aren't you at the Front?'

That was the taller of the two, the one Desmond had addressed. She was blushing deeply, colour spreading patchily across her face, but she held her ground, repeating the words loudly.

'Pardon?' Desmond was completely bewildered.

'At the Front! Why aren't you fighting in France? The army needs you, but my friend and I don't! We've got no time for a couple of windy shirkers.'

Briskly, she pressed something into Desmond's nerveless fingers. Her small friend, eyes downcast, came forward and fumbled something soft into Frank's hand. Then the two girls marched out, heads held high.

Frank opened his fingers and stared down at a pigeon's feather. For a moment it meant nothing to him. Whatever had that girl been prosing on about? And then he realised he had been given a white feather. He felt warmth rise in his cheeks. Desmond stood there, crimson-faced. Someone sitting at one of the tables muttered that they should be ashamed of themselves. Frank turned round, clenching his fists. Bland female faces beneath feathered hats, linen cloches, avoided his gaze. Every face seemed suddenly condemnatory. He wanted to explain, or to hit someone, but instead he shoved Desmond in the back, then walked past him, opened the door, and pulled his brother outside. Cool, crisp air! After the malignant stuffiness of the Copper Kettle it was like wine out here! The girls had disappeared.

The boys walked blindly, away from the Copper Kettle, around corners, until they reached Regent Street, with Parker's Piece on their left. Frank jerked his head at the green grass, and the two of them walked out to where some philanthropic soul had propped an ancient wooden seat against a gnarled tree-trunk. They sat, wordless for a moment. Frank opened his hand again to let the feather flutter free, but the wretched, crushed thing clung to his sweaty palm and he had to wipe it off against the slats of the bench. It was not even white, he noticed, with wry humour. Stupid little sluts. They had not even had the commonsense to pick up white feathers to round the insult off nicely. They had just grabbed for the first thing they saw — and for the first two boys they saw as well. One each. Neat.

It occurred to Frank then, sitting quietly on the bench whilst the fresh March morning erased the stupid, spiteful

150

words from his mind, that if he looked eighteen to a couple of girls he probably looked eighteen to a lot of people. And it followed that in that case he would be accepted into the army without any fuss. In a way, then, the girls had been justified in telling him that the army needed him, because it was true. Conscription had come in at the beginning of the month and any young male who was not in an essential job ought to be fighting in France! His blood raced for a moment, then doubt cooled it. He was a good shot, he enjoyed the OTC manoeuvres carried out two or three times a week on this very piece of ground, he was head of his platoon whilst Desmond was a mere squaddy still. It had not occurred to him to try and join the army because he knew himself to be too young and believed the war would be over before he was old enough to take part in the conflict. Yet that morning, when he had read the list of the old boys who had died at Verdun, he had had a cold feeling, an intimation of mortality, perhaps. What could happen to a big, tough ex-head boy like Tufton could also happen to him. Yet thousands of soldiers did not die; look at the generals. They seemed to be all right. And more than four of last year's sixth form had gone to France. Uncle Louis had been in France for ages, and to be a flier, like him, would be prime!

When he thought that Desmond was calm enough, Frank suggested that they make their way back to Mr Austin's shop and thence to school. But all the way back along Regent Street and Hills Road Desmond brooded and muttered about the stupidity of the two girls and the cruel unfairness of what they had said and done.

Frank, on the other hand, bore them no ill-will; he was too excited by the thought that they had put into his head. Why should he not take up the challenge and join the army?

12

'My arms are stiff! When we come in on Monday, Esther, let's have a change round. I'll rinse the sheets, and you can jolly well mangle them.'

Mabel and her friend Esther Smallwood were changing from overalls and caps back into their outdoor clothes after a session in the laundry of the Norfolk & Norwich hospital.

'I wouldn't mind that. Just look at my hands!' Esther exhibited small, pink hands, the fingers wrinkled and ancient-looking from constant submersion in water. 'It isn't so bad in the summer, but this evening the water was icy!'

'I know. But if you don't get a move on the Figg mutters about "young ladies what in't never done a hand's tarn, together", and that's maddening. Are you ready?'

The two girls called goodnight to the regular laundry workers and made their way out of the hospital to the main road. They usually walked home together since their homes were not far apart, though Esther's father was a timber merchant living in a mansion and owning two motorcars, and Mabel's father was a gardener living in a cottage and owning two bicycles. But the war, and Mabel's scholarship, had made them as nearly equal as it was possible for two girls to be.

'You're doing post next week, aren't you?' Esther said presently as they trudged along the sandy pavement. 'I'm doing clerical work for my father.'

'Yes, I'm postlady. And I'm on at the hospital from four till six as usual, and I'm due to help with the allotment as well. We'll be busy, holiday or no holiday. Still, I daresay we'll have time for a bit of fun!'

'I daresay. And it's all to help the war effort. My brother says the home front is just as important as the fighting.'

Esther's brother was a subaltern in France. Mabel had been watching her friend's face once when Esther had been skimming down a recent casualty list. It had made her glad she was an only child.

'I suppose that's true. Everyone works hard now, don't they? Mrs Louis Rose drives an ambulance and helps in the wards, and my mother's full time at Bolton & Paul's. Even Mrs Neyler works hard. She does nearly all her own housework!'

They reached the end of Esther's drive but paused for a moment, Esther swinging on the wrought-iron gate as she spoke.

'Will you call for me on Monday if I don't see you before?'

'You'll see me before then, delivering your post,' Mabel reminded her. 'And I might take your fare on the buses if I'm doing that on Monday, or . . .'

'I know. If I died tomorrow I'd half expect to meet a High School girl on the gate with a temporary worker band on her arm, explaining that she was standing in for St Peter! But do call for me!'

'Righto. Cheerio for now!'

Walking the few hundred yards along the Newmarket Road which separated the Smallwood home from The Pride's driveway, Mabel thought about the changes the war had made in everyone's lives. Women who had never so much as dusted their own bedrooms now scrubbed floors in hospitals, drove motor buses, manufactured parts of aeroplanes, or worked on the land. Her own horizons had widened remarkably, but she loved the opportunities to see how other people lived, and hoped sincerely that after the war was over people would not return to their old dull and narrow paths.

Reaching the dark driveway, Mabel struck up it without a qualm, well used to returning in the late evening after her work was over. She wanted to visit the house tonight, though, so did not strike across the top of the drive and into the pathway through the trees which led to her parents' cottage. She knew that Mrs Neyler would be in the kitchen, preparing the evening meal, so she made straight for the back door, tapped, and slipped in.

Her guess had been right. Mrs Neyler was taking a meat pie out of the oven. On the bottom shelf Mabel glimpsed jacket potatoes and a rice pudding. The war was a great leveller when it came to food, too. Mr Neyler refused to take advantage of his position, and there was little difference in the way the Neylers and the Walters ate now.

'Hello, Mrs Neyler. Is my mum here?'

Tina, who had heard the door open, straightened and smiled.

'No, dear. She came in for a few minutes, but she left half an hour ago. You're on holiday now, aren't you?'

'Yes, we broke up for Easter today. Only of course our war-work goes on. I'm doing the post on Monday, and I was wondering . . .' Mabel hesitated, then glanced down at her boots and up again, to meet Mrs Neyler's dark blue eyes. They were very like Frank's eyes, she thought. 'Well, Frank will be home by then, won't he?'

'Yes, that's right. And Desmond, of course.'

'I was wondering whether Frank might come with me to do the deliveries. I do rather hate the post job.'

Tina smiled, half teasing.

'Not worse than mangling sheets, surely? Your mother was telling me about it. It sounds horrid.'

'Not as horrid as the post. Last winter I took an official letter to an old lady in Suffolk Street. I had to read it for her, since her sight was failing. It — it wasn't a nice letter, and though I stayed for a bit, and made a cup of tea, I've never forgotten how awful it was.'

'That's too bad. I suppose it was a sad sort of letter? Frank will enjoy coming round with you on Monday, I'm sure.' Tina turned to the oven and began to take the potatoes out. Curiosity and delicacy were fighting a battle, and curiosity won. 'What did the letter say, dear?'

'Her boy had been killed.'

'Dreadfully sad. Frank will be home tomorrow morning,

154

so if you pop in at luncheon time you may make arrangements with him.'

Making her way home, Mabel remembered the letter. I was too young to know I should have lied, she thought with anguish. Reading the letter aloud to the old lady had been almost as wicked a deed as writing it had been.

It had been brutally brief. Your son has been court-martialled and shot for desertion, it had said.

'Well, love, they've found a use for me at last, even though it's only as an organiser! They won't send me to the Front, but I'll free some other fellow to fight for his country, and that's what matters.'

Tina stared across the kitchen at Ted, the angry words held back, with the tears. He had longed to be part of the war and now he was. Weeping or reproaches would not change the army's mind about accepting his services. It would merely make him less happy.

'Ted, darling, I'm very glad for you! It's what you wanted, and knowing you're in a safe job makes it easier for me to bear you being away from me.'

His delight was transparent and he kissed her, beaming.

'You're a woman in a million! You'll manage without me, I know. You did it once before, my clever girl!'

'Of course I will. Look, this meat pie's cooked to perfection. Could you fetch Ruthie and the girls? They trooped out to the garage with William to watch him doing an oil change, of all things!'

'I know. I asked them to bring me down some apples from the loft, so that I could have a few words with you before they came in. I'll give them a shout.'

He went to the back door and shouted, while Tina began putting meat pie out on the plates. They all ate in the kitchen now, the girls, Ruthie, herself and Ted. It was rather cosy, sitting round the scrubbed wooden table in the warmth of the fire, though a far cry from pre-war dinners!

In response to Ted's call the children came hurriedly into

the kitchen, closely followed by Ruthie. Tina, watching the children settle, mutter grace, and begin to eat, realised what secret lives Stella and Josette led. Like two little mice, or two sisters, they whispered and giggled together over private jokes, shared a bath at bedtime, pooled their pocket money. With Ted gone, it would fall to her to live more closely with her daughters. It might be fun to get to know them better!

'Actually, I don't mind delivering round here.' Mabel stood on tiptoe and pushed a bundle of letters through a letter-box, then descended the steps to join Frank on the gravel sweep once more. 'It's impersonal, you see. No one wants to chat to you, or asks you to read the letters for them. The other girls hate doing round here because there's so much walking up and down drives, but I rather enjoy it. They have lovely gardens, some of them.'

'I like it today,' Frank agreed, smiling at the bright sunshine. 'But yesterday – by gum, didn't we get wet? I was half drowned by the time we got home. Even my rubber boots were squelching.'

'I don't mind a bit of wet,' Mabel said with airy inaccuracy. 'It would be much quicker if we just pushed through the hedge into next door's garden, but I daresay they'd complain and we'd only catch it.'

'We couldn't, it's holly,' Frank said briefly. 'Go on. You were telling me about the concert you gave at school for wounded soldiers.'

'So I was. Where had I got to? Oh, I know, the little ones. They did a black and white minstrel show. Stella and Josette took girls' parts so they didn't have to black up, and they looked so pretty! They had frilly muslin dresses, and little ballet shoes, and they did a topping dance! The men cheered and clapped! And then there was a toy symphony. That was awful!'

'I believe you!' Frank laughed. 'I suppose they had combs and triangles and all those fearful noise-makers?'

'Well, yes, but that wasn't the reason. There was this man at the back, you see. He was pretty bad. I think he only came because he was related to one of the mistresses. She did a lot to help and wanted this chap to come. He had awful scars on his head and neck, Frank; purply, raw-looking places. Then, when a girl began to whack a big tin tray to start the symphony off — oh, it was awful!'

'Why? Do go on, Mabs! What happened?'

'He went a bit mad, I think. He howled like a dog, and he was crying real tears and banging his head against the wall, and not even the biggest girls knew what to do. The other soldiers got up and stood round him so we couldn't see, and someone called for a car and they took him away. Then the soldiers came back and sat down and said carry on, only they were . . . twitchy. I don't know how else to describe it. We knew they were longing for the whole thing to be over, only we didn't know how to end it. And then Miss Leman — she's a wonderful woman — stepped forward and said would the men like to put the chairs back against the walls and come through to the kitchens for a buffet tea. We'd meant to serve it to them in the hall, but this way they all milled around and helped to get the cakes out of the tins and made their own tea, and cracked jokes about how handy they were. And before we knew it everyone was comfortable again. We'd got them boxes of home-made sweets and a string bag of fruit each, because everyone else gives cigarettes, and they really liked them, you could tell. Then they went home.'

'I wonder what happened to the man who went a bit mad?' Frank said. 'Poor devil!'

'Yes, I know. I wonder, too. Now tell me about your school. What do you do towards the war effort?'

'Not as much as you, I don't think. Des and me are in the OTC and we've learned how to shoot and drill and read maps. Bayoneting, attacking, using cover, throwing grenades — that sort of thing. I'm pretty good. I command my platoon already. Daddy's leaving in a day or two, you know, and I reckon I'll be next.'

'No, Desmond will. He's a year older than you.'

'Doesn't matter. I want to go and Des hates the thought. You know what he's like about getting his hands dirty, and in the trenches you get more than dirty hands! People get in by lying about their age and that's what I'll do. I look a lot older than I am, you know.'

'Oh, really? Where's your beard, then?'

He grinned down at her from his considerable height, not annoyed by the slur on his apparent age as Desmond would have been, but amused by it. He is older, Mabel thought, and was dismayed.

'I can't help being blond. Fair-haired fellers always seem to have pretty feeble beards. Daddy can still go two days without shaving and no one would notice. It isn't that which counts, you know. It's height, shoulders – general strength, I suppose. You could take me for eighteen.'

They reached the roadway again and Mabel stopped, pulling Frank to a halt too. His very coolness and self-confidence was convincing.

'But you wouldn't, Frank! You wouldn't join up and go out there. Your mum and dad would mind terribly, and I daresay Des would as well. And what about school – your future?'

'Daddy can't say much considering he's off himself in a few days, and Mama cares for Des more than she does for me. As for school, I've had enough of it. And if everyone says "I must think of my future" and doesn't go and fight, there won't *be* a future. Or not a future worth living, at any rate.'

They walked the rest of the distance between the drive-ways in silence but as they turned up into the next property Mabel tried another tack.

'Why, Frank? What brought this on? You're happy at school, for all you may pretend you hate it, and you aren't the aggressive type. You don't want to kill people, do you?'

'Not ordinary people, no. But the Huns aren't ordinary people, Mabs. They do things that make your blood run cold! The stories I've heard . . . there's a chap who writes in *Chums* who's pretty straight, and from his reports it just doesn't bear thinking about that the Huns might win and come over here.'

'Are all those stories *true*?' Mabel shuddered. 'But even

so, you're under age! I know you'll go when you're eighteen, but before then why *should* you? Desmond won't.'

'He won't, not till he has to. But Mark Neyler's gone.'

'Who's he? What does he matter?'

'He's Daddy's brother.'

Mabel scowled.

'Just because your uncle's a fool you don't have to follow his example and be a fool as well.'

Frank did not take exception to this remark but reached over and rumpled Mabel's hair.

'Oh, Mabs, Mabs! There are other reasons. My grandfather, Karl Neyler, was a German, you know.'

'Was he? I didn't know, and it doesn't matter. No one could accuse your family of being German sympathisers! They're all as English as anything.'

'Then two girls in Cambridge gave Des and me white feathers. It made me think. You see, I *look* eighteen and I'm as strong as any eighteen-year-old, so in a way if I don't fight it could be because I'm afraid. If I was a weedy type it would be different, but I'm not. I'm more capable of defending myself than a good many lads who'll be sent out now that there's conscription, and anyway I'm itching to go! I want to prove that I'm capable of kicking the Hun in the guts. And I'm going.'

'Frank, don't.' The day seemed grey now, though the sun still shone. She could sense his determination, but she had to try to stop him. 'Please, Frank! I've got a friend at school whose brother's a subaltern, and she told me once that young officers only last two or three weeks in the trenches. Her brother's been there six months and he's experienced, but the new ones . . . oh, do listen! Think of the casualty lists! Hundreds and thousands are dead already. Don't go, Frank!'

'I know all that, old girl, but I'm not going to be an officer. No fear! I'll enlist as a squaddy and get all the fun and none of the responsibilities. I'm a crack shot, and I reckon it's cushy out there if you keep your head down! Look, I wouldn't go if winter was coming on because I've read the letters in *Chums* about mud and blood, but it'll be *summer,* damn it! I'm not keen on cricket and it's end of year exams, and I reckon the war'll be over by September, so I can get back to school for the rugby season. I'd never forgive myself if I missed out on this!'

'All right then, I'll tell!'

He laughed at her, running his hand through his thick fair hair which the summer sun would bleach to an even lighter shade.

'You wouldn't, my flower! I'll write to you and tell you what's going on. News from the Front! You'll be quite a heroine at school with a fellow of your own in the trenches.'

'A fellow of . . . Frank, don't be silly!'

'I'm not being silly, you are. You must know very well that I like you more than I like anyone else.'

They were halfway up the drive of yet another house, with the trees overhead shutting out the sunshine and the curve of the carriageway in both directions ensuring privacy. He moved close to her so that their bodies touched and put his arms round her as naturally as if he was always hugging girls. They stood thus for a moment, hearts pounding, then he bent his head and Mabel felt his lips, cool and firm, touch hers.

Her body knew what to do better than she. Her arms went round his neck, her mouth softened beneath his, and when he moved his tongue with gentle intimacy against her full lower lip she shuddered with pleasure and made no attempt to stop him. But neither did Frank attempt to go further; instead he released her.

'There! Now does that prove you're going to have your own fellow in the trenches?'

Mabel sighed and they moved up the drive towards the house once more, but this time with Frank's arm around her shoulders.

'If I'm your girl then surely you see that I don't want you to go? I don't care if other girls think you're a coward or if you've got a German grandfather, I just want you here, whole and safe!'

'That's very nice of you. But I'm not here, I'll be stuck away in Cambridge as soon as term starts, and then I'll be at university. And all the time you'll be growing up, getting prettier, probably marrying some damned chap whose only claim to you is that he's on the spot.' He swung her round to face him, holding both her shoulders now. 'Mabel, I want to *deserve* you! How can I deserve you if I won't fight to keep things as they should be for you!'

'That's not the reason, though. You want to go despite wanting me,' Mabel said shrewdly. 'Don't you see? I want you without any old nonsense about deserving! I want you because I . . . like you best.'

'What's wrong with saying "love"?'

'It's soppy, that's what,' Mabel said austerely. 'I don't *know* about love, but I know about like. I like you best.'

He laughed and squeezed her, then set off towards the house once more.

'I wish I had a ring to give you . . . something special. To show you that you're mine. A token, something to remind you . . .'

'Half a sixpence? Like in *Kipps*?'

They laughed and continued with their delivery of the mail, but that evening, just before Mabel went to bed, a note was pushed under the cottage door. William brought it through to the kitchen where his daughter was dutifully making cocoa as a bedtime drink for them all.

'Note. For you, Mabs.'

Mabel took the envelope and knew she was blushing as she spread out the single sheet of paper it contained.

'*I'll pick you up at seven,*' the note said briefly. And then, in smaller letters, '*Look in the envelope.*'

She put her fingers into the envelope and fished out the small object which she knew, instinctively, would be there. A sixpence, mangled in half. She crumpled the note into a ball and threw it into the fire in the kitchen range.

'It's from Frank. He's calling for me at seven to deliver the post.'

She took her drink up to bed and put the half-sixpence under her pillow, and next morning slipped it into her pocket before leaving to meet Frank.

'I had the devil's own job to get that coin in two,' Frank

161

greeted her, displaying his own half-sixpence. 'I hope you appreciate that I cut myself quite badly with the chisel? Don't laugh, you Jezebel, give me a good-morning kiss.'

'I don't think we ought to kiss any more until we're courting properly. Not until we're engaged. Or is it married?'

'Good Lord, if Des could hear you now he'd know I'd taken leave of my senses,' Frank exclaimed. 'You're a silly little kid with a moral code fifty years out of date and no brain, and now that it's too late and I've plighted my troth I find you think kissing's the seventh deadly sin. What have I done?'

'Don't be a fool. I didn't say that! It isn't sinful so much as more-ish,' Mabel explained. 'I don't think we ought to start a habit like that — not if you're going so far away.'

'You cunning little serpent!' Frank said. 'Are you trying to bribe me to give up the idea of joining the army, with your lily-white body as first prize, so to speak?'

Mabel, who had indeed allowed a vague plan on those lines to form in her mind, blushed fierily and hit him as hard as she could.

'I hate you and you're very insulting! As if . . . I just said . . .'

He grabbed hold of her and tried to kiss her, but she fought stoutly, furious at his embarrassingly accurate guess, and finally broke away and tore into the trees. There he caught her, as she must have known he would, and they kissed, wildly and innocently, before going down to the sorting office, arms entwined, to deliver that day's mail.

Both knew that the subject of the army would lie fallow for a while, though it would be uppermost in their minds.

13

It had been a gargantuan row with Mark that made Johnny run away. It was one of those very violent rows which blow up from time to time between people who are secretly jealous of each other. Since neither knew they were jealous, however, each put the row down to a weakness in the other's character, Johnny deciding that Mark was narrow-minded, Mark that Johnny was a libertine.

For once, the row had not involved Su in any way, though a woman was definitely responsible. Johnny was tall and strong, looking a good deal older than his years. His thick black hair and eyes were the only signs that his mother had been Chinese; his height and build came straight from his German grandfather and his personality was his own. What Mark thought of as a libertine streak was, in fact, no more than a certain precocity, brought about partly because he looked older than he was and partly because he was mixing with boys of sixteen and seventeen.

Freddy Fawcett's father had at last left his long-suffering wife and moved away to Canterbury, taking with him his latest mistress and his son. This would have left Johnny high and dry, had he not already begun to form a tentative friendship with Phil Rawson, who was two years older than he. And Phil, in his turn, introduced Johnny to Shirley.

Shirley worked in the coffee shop nearest the school. She was a buxom, rather simple-minded girl of about sixteen, whose generosity might have been termed promiscuity by some. The boys who benefited, of course, merely said that Shirley was 'good fun'. Johnny, going for a walk with

Shirley down by the sea one evening, thought her very good fun indeed, for he was a perfectly normal healthy young animal. Offered cream cakes, he ate them every one. Offered Shirley's temptingly rounded body, he enjoyed it with very much the same appetite.

Since more than half Phil's class were members of the Shirley-club, Johnny was very pleased with himself when it became obvious that she liked him best. His enthusiastic and puppy-like approach may have had more to do with it than his performance, but this, fortunately, did not cross Johnny's mind. He thoroughly enjoyed the spring term, despite missing Freddy badly at first.

But then came the long Christmas holidays, and Johnny began to make excuses to visit Dunedin, until it occurred to him that Shirley's chief attraction had to do with being a girl. And if one girl was willing to accommodate him, surely other girls might be equally willing – and girls, furthermore, who lived nearer home!

He soon found a suitable candidate in Chloe, the young woman who helped with the farm work now that several of the men had gone off to fight in the war. She was older than Shirley, quite nineteen, but even more attractive, being the possessor of the finest bosom Johnny had ever seen and a physique much improved by all her hard work on the farm. She had a boyfriend fighting in foreign parts; she often spoke longingly of 'Billy', and as soon as Johnny began eyeing her up he could not help noticing that she was doing the same to him. She missed Billy, she told him, and her eyes continued the story. One evening spent together in the hayloft was sufficient to prove their mutual interest; henceforth she literally as well as figuratively took Johnny to her bosom.

Su, blissfully unaware of Johnny's chief preoccupation, thought that life had never been so smooth. He and Mark did not quarrel so much, the boy worked hard on the farm during the day and at his books in the evenings. He slept like a log, admittedly, but always rose betimes. If, after the second week of the holidays had passed, she noticed that he was sometimes worn out after the evening milking, she put it down to his youth and let him slumber on the couch with his mouth and book both open and both unregarded.

Johnny and Chloe restricted their sessions in the hayloft to Tuesday and Thursday evenings, after milking. This was because Su and Mark visited friends on those particular evenings; on Tuesdays the Dodmans, on Thursdays the Campbells. And twice a week was enough to satisfy Johnny, if not Chloe.

Then, one warm Saturday afternoon, Mark announced that he was going to take Su over to Dunedin to visit a sale of work in the Presbyterian church hall, and then go and have a word with the manager who ran the Waihola homestead for Ted.

'Come with us, Johnny,' Su urged, but Johnny, very conscious that he had a holiday task of gargantuan proportions untouched, declined the trip.

'I'd better get my maths done,' he told her. 'I've got to do it, and the place will be quiet, being a Saturday afternoon.'

So when his father and Su left, Johnny settled down at the kitchen table with his work spread out round him, contentedly figuring. The contentment was genuine, for maths was his favourite subject. It never crossed his mind that Chloe, like a love-hungry mare, might come seeking her stud.

Yet that was exactly what happened. Within five minutes of Mark and Su departing, Chloe slipped into the kitchen.

'Johnny, your ma and pa went! Toddy's give me the afternoon off. What d'you say?'

'Well, why don't you go down to the beach?' It was a hot, sunny day, the sort of day when Johnny would have enjoyed a swim had it not been for the maths. 'I might come down later, if I finish this before teatime.' He frowned down at the sum in front of him.

'Oh, Johnny!' Chloe pouted. She was clad in a cotton blouse and a short, practical skirt. She bent forward, examining his book upside down, and Johnny noticed she was not wearing anything beneath the blouse. Two buttons were undone and he could see bare skin through the gap. 'Ain't there some other time you could do them sums? It seems such a waste!'

Johnny sighed and bent over his work again. He really must get on. He wanted to be finished by the time Mark and Su returned. A swim would be nice, of course, but he could swim in the evening when the maths was off his conscience.

'It's got to be done, Chloe. If you go down to the beach I might join you there after tea. Su and my father will be back for tea and they might come down as . . . oh!'

Chloe, losing patience with subtlety, had undone all the buttons on her blouse. Two large, melon-shaped breasts faced Johnny across the scattered papers. Chloe leaned forward and her breasts swung amongst the papers, nosing into them like a couple of impatient, pink-tipped balloons. Johnny swallowed.

'Aw, come on, Johnny! We ain't never done it on a real bed!'

Enlightenment dawned. So it was not a swim she was after! Slowly, Johnny closed his maths book.

'That's true. But . . . I don't know . . .'

Chloe moved round behind him and leaned on his back. Johnny felt the soft fullness of her pushing against his spine through the thin cotton shirt and her fingers beginning to slide across his shoulders, and swallowed again. He stared unseeingly at the answer paper in front of him. He could not, at that moment, have added two and two with much hope of getting a correct result.

'Aw, come on, Johnny!'

He turned and clutched her, burying his face in her ample plumpness. In less time than it takes to tell they had got themselves through the kitchen and across the hall, and were disporting themselves on the Neylers' big, soft bed. Chloe undressed him; Johnny, quick to learn, undressed her. They had never made love naked before, never seen each other's bodies in full daylight, and their lovemaking, for obvious reasons, had been mutually silent.

But not now! Chloe crowed and groaned, uttered small shrieks and mutterings. She also bucked and reared beneath him, bit him, and scratched him.

Johnny, not to be outdone, was equally uninhibited.

Their lovemaking became mobile, first here, now there. They rolled off the bed on to the floor, progressed to the washstand, returned to the bed. And all the while Chloe cackled like a hen laying an egg.

It was the noise of Chloe enjoying herself, in fact, that brought Mark, returning to the house for some papers, round to his bedroom window.

At first, he could scarcely believe his eyes. He saw a naked man coupling with a naked woman, first on the floor, facing away from the window, then moving on to the bed where, with cold shock, he recognised his son and Chloe. He knocked on the window, his temper such that afterwards he realised he had actually cracked the glass; neither Johnny nor Chloe heard a thing.

Fury, which was possibly partly envy, brought Mark round and bursting into the bedroom before he had thought what he was going to say to the evildoers. Fortunately, perhaps, words were not needed. The pair of them had left the bed again and were on the floor, on Su's beloved white fur rug. Mark's roar made Chloe jump quite perceptibly, and brought Johnny's head round, his eyes widening with dismay.

'Dad! Oh! Oh crumbs!'

For the rest of their lives, the people involved would remember the next ten minutes with the most acute embarrassment. Chloe, naked as the day she was born, trying to scramble into her skirt and blouse, clumsily fumbling with buttons and fastenings, copiously weeping. Johnny, trying to get a word in edgeways as Mark roared and Su came in, round-eyed, begging for an explanation. Then Chloe gave up the unequal struggle with her buttons and rushed from the room, her big breasts bouncing as she ran, her sobs becoming wails of terror and despair.

Johnny was in his trousers; that was about the extent of his attempt at regaining his respectability and, since the fly-buttons were unfastened, Su was not taken in.

However, Su's presence at least calmed Mark down a little. He had been attempting to roar at Johnny and lay him out cold at the same time, but now that his wife had arrived Mark sobered a little.

'Come into the kitchen,' he said gruffly, and they followed him meekly through, Johnny not daring to look at Su nor she at him. Once there, the row really got into its stride. Mark, cuddling Su, told Johnny that he was an animal and would in future be treated like one. Su, sobbing, moaned, 'Suppose she has a baby? Oh, Johnny, what will we do if she has a baby?'

Su's tears hurt Johnny far more than Mark's ill-aimed blows or abuse.

'She won't, don't worry, Su,' he said earnestly. 'Girls don't have babies with me.'

This ingenuous remark led to the story of the girl in the coffee shop and the preoccupation with 'Shirleying' which had gripped the upper school last term. This, not unnaturally, led to another eruption from Mark, together with the grim warning that the headmaster should be told, the guilty boys expelled for corrupting his son's youthful innocence, and the practice of after-school fornication stopped once and for all.

Having made that decree in his most impressive voice, Mark grabbed Johnny — very unfairly, since his son was sitting meekly down on a kitchen chair at the time — and leathered him with his belt. It was the first time in his life that Johnny had ever been beaten, certainly the first time that he felt his beloved Su was actually in agreement with his punishment, and it left him trembling, sick and furious. What would the school say when they found out who had put an end to Shirleying? And how would he face Chloe, knowing that he would never again dare to do the exciting and altogether delightful things she had taught him that very afternoon? Glowering at his parents, he slunk out of the kitchen and locked himself in his own room, where he twisted and turned, gloomily counting the pink, raised welts on his back and buttocks. Life in future would scarcely be worth living, here or at school. He would go! He would run away to somewhere he could be sure of appreciation and a place in the adult world.

It never occurred to him to try to join the army. Instead,

he thought of that other running away, when he and Su had fled together. He had loved his grandfather and grandmother, still wrote to them, and had long promised them a return visit when he grew up. Well, he would go to them, and nothing would make him return to New Zealand, where they treated him as a child when he was as adult in most ways as his father!

By the time Mark and Su were in bed, Su having fastidiously changed the bed-linen, they were already realising that they must not make a mountain out of a molehill.

'I'll tell him that such behaviour is irresponsible, and must stop,' Mark promised. 'But I shan't say anything at school. It was probably nine days' wonder there, and Johnny'll warn the boys that they've been twigged.'

Even as he spoke, Johnny was tramping the coast road. By the time his parents woke next morning, Johnny was stowed away on a ship bound for Australia.

For the first two days, the Neylers searched the district. Then they informed the authorities that a boy of fourteen who could be mistaken for seventeen or eighteen had run away from home, and the authorities suspected the army.

Johnny, landing at Sydney, had little difficulty in persuading his grandparents to keep him. He was young and strong, a good worker, and quite willing to be employed in any capacity, provided that he was not despatched home. They wrote to Su, but two days before she got the letter Johnny took off once more on a cattle-lorry bound for the outback. He had seen his grandfather addressing a letter to Dunedin, and he had no intention of being so speedily collared.

He might have felt differently had he known that Mark, worried by reports of the state of affairs in Europe and fired with patriotism by the sight of all the uniforms in Dunedin, had lied about his age and joined up.

'You can cope, love, because you coped before,' he said tenderly to Su as he prepared to embark for the battlefields of France. 'Toddy's here, and Freda of course, and this time I'll write every day and let you know what's happening. I'd hate myself if I didn't fight for my country and my wife!'

'I'll cope. They say the war won't last much longer anyway,' Su said, her voice carefully bright though her eyes were wet. 'Take care of yourself, darling.'

Bereft of Mark and Johnny, she prepared to be very lonely.

Frank had laid his plans carefully and thought them foolproof as, indeed, they proved to be. On the last day of the holidays he got on the train with his brother and a pile of luggage, to get off again at the first stop, leaving Des with a note, forged, purporting to be from Ted Neyler to the headmaster of Pursell's School.

The note explained that Desmond and Frank had fallen victim to mumps during the holidays and that Desmond, stricken first, had recovered first also. Frank, the note continued, was still very poorly and would not be returning to school until half-term.

Desmond also had a number of letters, written in advance by his ingenious brother, to be posted weekly along with his own parental bulletins.

'I'm going to join up in London,' Frank said, drilling Desmond in the part he was to perform. 'It's easier not to be noticed in a big city. You'll have to stand buff for a few weeks, old fellow, and then it'll be too late. Once I'm trained and at the Front, the army won't give me up just because the parents make a fuss. Don't forget to post the letters each week, though. I don't want Mama and Daddy finding out too soon.'

'I'm not putting them in the same envelope as mine,' Desmond muttered. 'Then, if there are questions asked, I'll say you must have left them with some bit of fluff in Cambridge to post for you. And I'll say I knew you were off on some lark, but I didn't know what. I don't see why they should expect me to stop you just because I'm the oldest. It isn't fair! Why should I get stick because you run away?'

'You do that − post the letters and deny all knowledge,' Frank advised. 'Look, why not say that we both wanted to

170

go, and tossed for it, and I won? Say you gave your word, then they won't blame you.'

'Yes, that might work.' Desmond hated the thought that his parents might secretly believe him to be windy, even if it was true! 'If I say I gave my word not to split, Daddy wouldn't expect me to go back on it. Though Mama's a different kettle of fish! Anyway, Daddy's in the army himself, so he can't blame you all that much.'

'Suppose I meet him in France?' Frank's grin faltered, then returned. 'But I won't. I reckon he's in London for the duration. Anyway, it'll be over by Christmas, everyone says, so all I'm doing is having my share a bit earlier, or I'll miss out! I bet hundreds of fellows are doing the same.'

'Maybe. If it wasn't the summer term, and I wasn't in the eleven . . .'

'Don't you go changing your mind, Des!' Frank said. 'You've got to be in school to keep my cover!' The train began to get up steam and he raised his voice above the racket. 'Cheerio. I'll write. Care of Tilly Catcher.'

The train steamed out and Frank's adventure began. He got to London and sold his luggage, or most of it, having spent the journey cutting out all the name tapes and burning them with a box of matches he had bought. Clothing sold would disappear utterly; clothing found would start an immediate hue and cry.

He reached Liverpool Street Station and made his way to the nearest recruiting office. Though he did not know it, the staff there was recruiting for a big offensive planned for the early summer. Questions were not likely to be asked of a tall, upstanding youth who gave his age as eighteen and looked every month of it. By the time he went to bed that night he was in the army, and next day, in company with a number of other youngsters, would be sent to a training camp on the Downs for a few weeks before being despatched to France.

That first night, wrapped in blankets and lying on a rickety camp bed, Frank felt the first faint stirrings of doubt. This was to be an adventure – but it was so like school! Boys everywhere, and adults stamping and shouting and ordering one about. But soon he would not be classed as a boy any longer, and would be able to prove his manhood by shooting at something other than a wooden target!

Without the slightest conception of how he would really feel when he first saw bullets tearing into living flesh, Frank turned on his side and slept soundly till morning.

Flanders. A city of canvas tents pitched on marshy ground, criss-crossed by duck-boards. Mark was a lieutenant by March, training other men for the big battle which was said to be imminent. They were stationed a few miles outside Steenbecque and for the most part the men were New Zealand infantrymen who had already fought their way through the fronts in Egypt and Gallipoli. They were experienced fighters, certainly, but new to the war as it was being fought in Europe. Mark had been trained for this type of warfare, and now he was passing his knowledge on.

Sometimes, as he lectured, he thought how odd it was that he should be expected to teach something he only knew from his own teachers. But he did his job well and was liked by the men. Off duty, he and a few fellow officers would go into the town, which was packed with refugees, and have coffee and the plainish cakes which was all that was available, and buy postcards to send home. It intrigued him to see the women doing work the men had once done, and doing it well. And their traditional tasks, lace-making, sewing, and cooking, still went on as before.

He wrote to Su about the good things, never about the bad; never mentioning the fever which sprang up amongst the men billeted in this low and marshy area, nor the violence he taught. And her letters speaking of the farm and her life there were a great joy, as were Toddy's brief notes, Freda's scribbles. It gave him immense pleasure to know that they were cutting corn or clamping potatoes; he could see the scene so clearly in his mind's eye when he read the words. The seasons were upside down here; even the stars overhead no longer danced in their familiar places. He had given a lecture only last week on the stars – one day, if

172

you were lost in no man's land with the stars your only guide, knowing them might make the difference between a safe landfall and a bayonet in the belly.

Then, one miserable, rainy day when he and Jamie Jamieson were squatting on boxes in their tent, gloomily contemplating the unceasing downpour, a hand threw a bundle of mail into Mark's lap. He sorted the letters out, and the first one he opened was from Su. Jamie, reading his own post, jumped as Mark suddenly leapt to his feet, knocking the box backwards into the mud.

'Christ! Su's pregnant!'

Jamie righted the box and grinned up at the older man.

'Good on you, mate! When's it due?'

'At the beginning of July, but it's her first child, so she says it will probably be late.' He glanced down at his friend and read the startled look aright. 'She's my second wife. Johnny — my son — he's not Su's child, though she treats him as if he was.'

'And she's pleased, is she? The wife?'

'Pleased? She's in seventh heaven! We've been married a while and not a sign until now.'

'That's great. You'd better write back at once, tell her we're on the move again. Our letters travel even further than we do, and that's saying something.'

'I will. But we'll be in France before she gets it.'

Mark refolded the letter and returned it to its envelope. It would be read and reread many times in the weeks to come, and always with increasing pleasure. He knew how unhappy it had made Su when she thought herself unable to bear him a child. It had not made him unhappy — Johnny was sufficient proof that having children was not all honey — but now that he knew she was pregnant he found his joy and pride so great that he wanted to tell everyone he met. He longed to see his child safe in Su's arms, longed to be back on the Peninsula once more. Yet it gave him, he told himself, an even better reason for fighting this war. To make the world a better place for Su and his child. For his son or daughter. He had not much minded which at first, but as the brigade marched across into France his desire for

173

a daughter crystallised into a positive longing. A little girl, just like Su! That would be the best thing that could happen.

Weighed down with all the impediment of a continental war on their backs – the rifle and ammunition, the bedroll and greatcoat, the gas mask, steel helmet, water bottle and entrenching tool, to say nothing of the emergency rations – the men could not hurry. Mark had a horse on the march now, and as he rode beside the column of men he often thought of Ted. Ted wrote too, long, newsy letters, and nothing could hide his longing to be in France with Mark, where the action was! Mark, lean and tanned and fit after his years on the farm, his hair untouched by grey, had given his age as thirty-eight and been believed. Poor Ted had not been so lucky, and he chafed against the restrictions of the Ministry and longed for a horse between his knees and the comradeship of soldiers.

When, after days of marching, being billeted in barns to recover their strength and then marching on again, they neared Armentieres, Mark saw an aeroplane with the British colours clear on its wings and remembered that Ted's young brother-in-law, Louis Rose, was in the Royal Flying Corps and stationed somewhere near here. How strange it would be, after all these years, if he and Ted and this Louis should meet up, in the middle of the biggest war the world had ever known, in a country which was foreign to them all! His heart contracted at the thought of seeing Ted. The years could not change his feeling for his brother; Ted was dearer to him than any other person on earth except for Su.

As the column clattered into the church square he glanced up at the clock, long stopped at half past eleven – giving the square its name of Half Past Eleven Square – and vowed that when this lot was over he would find Ted. Go to England and find him, if necessary. They were too near to miss seeing each other again as they had missed each other in America, a decade ago!

He had seen no action yet, or he might have qualified the thought.

174

14

It was raining again, a fine, drizzling rain that did not look much, but soaked you through in a moment. Frank and Hoss, crouched in their trench with the rest of their platoon strung out along its length, regarded the rain with true British phlegm; not only had they grown used to it, but they were about to be rescued from it. Any minute now another group of men would come marching up to take over this particular position and they would be sent back to the rear for a rest period.

'A good 'ot barf,' Hoss said, narrowing his eyes dreamily. He hitched his puttees up and stood, head cautiously bent, looking out to the west, whence their relief would come. Frank looked up at his friend and grinned. After the war Hoss would have a permanent stoop. It came from being six foot four, which was taller than the man who had dug this trench, obviously. Hoss spent a good deal of time trying to get his height down to a decent five foot ten, with a noticeable, if understandable, lack of success.

'Tomorrow, that'll be, if we're lucky. Yes, *and* clean clothes.' Frank, crouching in the mud at the bottom of the trench patiently checking his equipment, thought of a newly ironed shirt, underpants smelling of soap and – best of all – soft, clean, sweet-smelling socks. He sighed, and picked up his war trophy. It was a German helmet of black patent leather, the brass badges missing, alas, but the spike on top still intact. An admirable trophy, and one which would be much envied by the rank and file – but what would his officers make of it? Was such looting allowed? There had been no one *in* the helmet – it had been abandoned when the Huns had left the trench — but he supposed it was still loot. He tapped the helmet, and dug Hoss in the back of the knees. 'Is it all right to take this back with us, or will some officer swipe it off me?' He grimaced at his friend. 'Think what we suffered because of it!'

Hoss grinned. It was useless to think of the real suffering which had gone into the helmet's gain — the men killed, the heavy, red-faced sergeant who had been such a brick to them lying in the mud, his face drained of colour and his right foot blown to a scarlet pulp. All he and Frank had suffered had been a nasty attack of crumbs. They had 'won' a couple of German greatcoats, thinking, in their innocence, that, propped up on a couple of rifles, the coats would make a decent tent against the weather. The greatcoats, however, had been alive with lice, known as crumbs since they looked just like fawny-white breadcrumbs, and by morning so had Frank and Hoss.

They did their best to get rid of the pests, but the older and more experienced soldiers told them it was impossible to clear them without civilised conditions, just as it was impossible to heal bleeding and blistered feet whilst out here in the soggy trenches.

'We'll be in the rear again in a day or so,' a cheerful corporal assured them. 'Then it's bathhouse drill and clean clothes. You'll not be chatty after that, or not till the next spell in the trenches, at any rate.'

'Chatty? Why not crumby?'

The corporal laughed at Frank's question.

'I'm Indian army, lad, and a chatt is 'industani for our friend the crumb. Or louse.'

Now, however, with the greatcoats hurled well clear of the trench and a bath imminent, Frank was more interested in the fate of his helmet than in his louse-bites.

'Well? Can I take my loot back?'

'Yes, if you hide it from the officers and NCOs; otherwise they'll take it off you,' Hoss advised from his own experience, for, in the backstreets of London from whence he sprang, hiding possessions from those in authority was a way of life. 'Put it in your bedroll. That'll do until we're in billets.'

Frank began to wrap the helmet with his waterproof sheet, then noticed movement at the far end of the trench.

'Hey, look there!'

Further up the trench a dixie was standing and the men were in a line by it. Steam rose and they could see hot liquid being ladled into mugs.

'Is it char? I could do with a cuppa!'

The two of them, packs on back, rifles slung, joined the queue hopefully, tin mugs in hand.

'There won't be no rum in it; we 'ad that yesterday.' Hoss held out his mug to the corporal dishing out the strong, sweet tea and grinned at him. 'Rum issue for swaddies, eh, corp? Per man, per day per haps!'

The corporal, not a man renowned for his sense of humour, grinned back. He had been a coal heaver in civilian life and was wont to compare coal heaving favourably with heaving dixies, and to accuse officers various of seeing off the rum ration rightfully belonging to other ranks. Nevertheless, this embittered man grinned at Hoss.

But the memory of yesterday's rum issue brought yesterday back too vividly into Frank's mind. It was given out before the raid. Get into a German trench, grab some equipment and a prisoner if possible; spread alarm and despondency. That was what their officer said, and Sergeant Fellowes echoed it. Frank thought that the taste of rum would always bring that moment back to life, when he and Hoss stood side by side in the rainy darkness, their faces and hands blacked out with burnt cork, the spirit coursing fierily through their veins. It was the first time he had tasted rum; having no liking for spirits but a great enthusiasm for sweets and chocolate, he and Hoss usually bartered their rum ration and their cigarettes for whatever was going in the way of sweet things.

When the rum was finished they scrambled out of the trench and crouched beside the parapet, waiting for the last man up before putting into practice all the things their sergeant had impressed upon them – spread out, crouch, move silently.

177

Even divested of their packs and the paraphernalia of the soldier on active duty, they sounded awfully loud to Frank as they clinked and clattered over the parapet and into no man's land. The mud itself was noisy, sucking at their boots, squelching whenever they moved. Darkness, of course, was a friend — but it was an enemy too, unless you kept your head, remained cool, and forced the little picture of the terrain you were crossing into your mind and kept it there. He knew that at a certain point they would probably need to crawl; the long grass would almost hide them, if it wasn't rain-flattened by now.

Hoss was close to him and the rain eased momentarily and he smelt summer on the breath of the wind and was transported for seconds back to England, a wet night in a summer lane. Then he pushed through the grass and saw Hoss rise to the crouch and suddenly this was exciting, there was a wicked thrill in it greater than climbing some-one else's flagpole in someone else's college grounds, a chamber pot clamped beneath your arm, ready to hang it insultingly above their flag.

He got his night-eyes then, and could see the treacherous terrain with the mine craters yawning at him — hungry mouths waiting to devour if you put a foot wrong. Their objective — an advance enemy trench, probably lightly held, the Staff said with the callous optimism of those who will never have to find out — was close now, on their right. They could hear soft voices, and a burst of laughter. Frank's hair prickled on his scalp and he held his rifle more firmly, his hand already fumbling for the small bomb in his pocket.

He could not have said when they were spotted, only that they were. Machine-gun fire rattled and flares suddenly illuminated the hellish night. Something went past his cheek and he flinched back before realising it was only a bird, disturbed and terrified by the sudden light and noise. He and Hoss dropped on to their bellies and suddenly the night was full of other members of the raiding party, word was passed to get back, the enemy was too strong, their wire impregnable, get *back*, damn you! Crawling now, the dark friendly, the mud an enemy, making you slip and slither. Hoss muttering, reminding Frank to keep his head down, to keep on crawling. Bullets, the wind of them over your frightened head, sweat in your eyes so that every instruction, every piece of good advice, was forgotten. Only Hoss, cool, by your side, cracking a joke of all things, about the mud. Keeping you moving, taking away the terror. Then the parapet, the slither down into the trench. Their officer, counting heads. Two dead, three wounded. Frank's thoughts taking over, full of confusion, excitement returning now that the danger was less. Could this be war? Where was the glamour, the charge, the wounded heroes, the sullen prisoners? He had imagined it all so clearly! And the other thought, which would not go away though it seemed so petty and trivial. Damn it, this is *summer,* the cricket season's in full swing, flaming June and all that. And I'm in *France,* everyone knows about France — yet it's done nothing but rain for days on end!

'Wake up, Frankie. No time for dreamin', lad! Get that char down you and I'll hump your pack on to your shoulders. We're off to the rear in ten minutes!' Hoss grinned again at the surly corporal. 'There ain't gonna be no push yet, then, or they wouldn't spare lads like us! Eh, corp?'

It took them the best part of two hours, in fact, to change places with the relieving mob and a further two hours to reach their billet. It was a good seven miles behind the lines, a farm with the men sleeping in the big barn amongst clean straw and the officers taking over the farm itself. You could still hear the shelling and see the distant smoke, but you were not woken by it. It constituted a nuisance, in fact, rather than a threat. In the trenches it was impossible to discount.

They settled in, and routine took over. Hoss's longed-for hot bath came the following day when the platoon was marched to the divisional bathhouse and thoroughly cleansed, and Frank's body knew the delights of a freshly laundered shirt and he pampered his sore and bleeding feet with whale oil and soft clean socks. The German helmet was too desirable an object to leave lying about − he hid it at the very bottom of his kit-bag. Then the kit-bag was deposited safely in a corner of the 'room' he had made for himself, walled in with straw bales.

Two days after their arrival the rain stopped. The sky was a clear, rain-washed blue and the countryside decked with its summer foliage. There was a real wood, where the trees still knew the seasons, where birds built nests in the branches and bluebells grew in shady spots. And corn-fields, green still, where larks rose straight up, singing as they headed for heaven. There was a river, with willows along its banks and a deep, quiet pool where trout lurked. Discipline was eased and the soldiers became young men again, hurling themselves into the water to bathe, eyeing the young woman who strode, sturdy and barefoot along the river path with her milking buckets on a yoke across her shoulders.

The guns still grumbled and muttered to the east but they were able to push the war out of their conscious minds, though at night the thoughts that one could rigidly control by day had it all their own way and men twitched and whimpered in sleep as they would have scorned to do when awake. June neared its end. Frank and Hoss, two tiny cogs in the great wheel of the war, waited, and knew they might die, and could not believe death could touch them.

'If this is air supremacy, let there be an end to't,' Louis misquoted, helping himself to smoked salmon. It was breakfast time in the mess and he had only been back from leave a couple of days so the smoked salmon − or what was left of it − was his contribution to civilised living. It had been a present from Ted, gloomily working for the Ministry of Defence in London and itching to be off to France, and had been much appreciated at dinner the previous night. Louis was finishing it off as a sign of ownership whilst opposite him at the table sat Nick, far more conventionally eating bacon and eggs. At Louis's words, he nodded vigorously.

'I know what you mean. We keep air supremacy, but at

180

the most horrific cost. We're losing about a hundred and fifty men a month, I believe, and the same number of aeroplanes. Seasoned men are replaced by kids, and *that* means we're hardly ever on terra firma. When this big push starts we'll all be worn out and useless.'

'That's about it.' Louis got up. 'Well, I mustn't grumble! I had my leave and spent a good deal of it in bed, one way and another. Now I've got to buckle down to knocking a few Boches out of the sky. We're on standby, you said?'

Nick nodded.

'Yes, for the next six hours. After that we can go off somewhere, if you like. We're on dawn patrol tomorrow, though, so we mustn't be late back to kip.'

'I've got a friend in the trenches, a chap I was at school with. I thought I might go and look him up later. Don't much want to go up to the line, not with so much going on, but when he goes to the rear, which ought to be around now, I'd like to see him and have a jaw.'

'I'll come with you. Better than going on the batter when we've an early start. I always feel horribly sorry for the lads in the Camel Corps, and the odd thing is, they feel horribly sorry for us! It's a good thing we don't all think alike, I suppose.'

'Yes. Ours is a solitary calling, as the poets say. I think that's what they've got against it. But those trenches!' There was a ruminative pause whilst both men thought about the trenches which they flew over so frequently and visited so seldom. 'Mind you, it was pretty grim for Cotterill yesterday and the blokes downstairs risked all sorts to get him out. We ought to nip down to the dressing station and find out how he is.'

'Christ, Louis, he couldn't have survived those burns!' Nick had a snub-nosed, cheerful face but now he looked savage. 'I hope for his sake he's gone west.'

Walking over to the squadron office, Louis reflected that Nick was right; Cotterill had been a living torch when his aeroplane had crash-landed in no man's land. In such circumstances survival would be far worse than death.

'I wonder why Cotterill didn't use his pistol,' Louis said

thoughtfully as they strolled along. 'He had one, I know.'

It was accepted amongst them that those who carried pistols did so in order that they might spare themselves the agony of death by burning. Louis, blessed with an optimistic nature, could never have carried a revolver with such intent; something would save him, something always did. But he understood that others did not have his disposition.

'I've always suspected that whatever happens, it happens too quickly for you,' Nick said. He did not carry a pistol either. 'Well, at least it's fine and dry, so we can sit on the grass.'

He drew a copy of that much coveted publication, the *Wipers Times,* out of his pocket and was soon chuckling.

Louis lay on his back on the grass and remembered his leave. It had been a wonderful ten days, mostly spent with Sarah though he had managed to arrange a brief, two-day holiday with Say and the boy. He had sent them ahead of him to a cottage on the coast and, since he had hired it for a week, had left them there too. Say was quite content in the tiny thatched house with the seashore just outside her door and a farm nearby to deliver her milk and a few groceries.

Say, sweet and fat, wanting only to make her menfolk happy, was easy company. Not so Sarah. Slim and practical in dark, well-cut skirts and jackets, she drove ambulances and practised first-aid and was proud of her achievements. She had delivered a baby all by herself, she boasted. And Louis, having just made vigorous love to her, had said that when he next came home he hoped she would be *having* a baby and not merely delivering someone else's, like a postman!

'I can't understand why you aren't pregnant already, darling,' he said rather fretfully. 'God knows, the way we spend my leaves you ought to be!'

Sarah did not care to be reproached. She allowed her voice to cool considerably.

'There's plenty of time for babies. Any woman can produce a baby. But I'm being really useful for the first time in my life, and I like it. It means a lot to me.'

'I don't like useful women,' Louis said sulkily. 'I like decorative ones.' Then, relenting, because she was so very decorative, he rolled over — they were in bed — and kissed the side of her neck, just below the ear. 'Never mind, sweetheart, you'll have a baby. I'll see to it!'

Say, on the other hand, was 'taking precautions', as she phrased it. This involved a certain loss of spontaneity whilst Say pored over the calendar, counted on her fingers, frowned and re-counted — or, almost worse, jerked away from him at the very moment when he most wanted her to lie quiet and submissive beneath him.

'Sure and I can't bear to think of it, Lou, but suppose you were killed?' she said mournfully, when he complained. 'I could support the boy, but if I had two or three more I wouldn't know which way to turn.'

Louis had to acknowledge the truth of her remark. Whilst he lived he could support her and his son, but if he were to die she would be totally alone. She would get no widow's pension because she was not married to him, his relatives would not help her because they did not know about her; her own mother, knowing nothing of her daughter's circumstances and in any event pitifully poor herself, would be unlikely to assist her.

'Very well then, Say, take your precautions. But don't, I beg of you, ever shove me back and pull away like that again at such a . . . delicate moment. Something very precious to us both might have suffered irreparable damage.'

They had laughed together, but he knew that lovemaking with Say had lost a good deal of its charm. Once fear of consequences entered a relationship, he thought selfishly, natural pleasure tended to fly out of the window.

In the mess office, the phone rang. Nick flung his paper down and got stiffly to his feet just as the door of the office burst open.

'Enemy aircraft sighted and heading this way. A number of bombers with a fighter escort. Presumably to bomb the trenches.'

Minutes later, Nick and Louis and the rest of their flight were in the air and climbing to gain height. They were over the trenches quickly, glancing below at the desolation; the trees that knew nothing of June, the craters filled with sticky mud, the thin, poisoned weeds.

Climbing still, they saw another squadron of Allied aircraft and signalled to them that enemy aircraft were approaching in force. And then, coming from the east, they saw the Huns and flew to meet them.

The action was brief but bloody. Louis was jinking, stalling, keeping his aeroplane moving briskly and, he hoped, unpredictably, firing bursts from his Lewis gun whenever an enemy appeared in his sights. He saw British aeroplanes spin out of control, spiralling down into no man's land, and a German bomber burst into flames directly beneath him. He saw the thick black smoke and pulled away from it, his heart going out to the crew of the doomed aeroplane.

Within moments, he saw Nick, gesturing, and following his friend's eyes knew that his own wing was on fire. He gauged the fire's strength and the speed at which it would travel as best he might, then turned the nose of his bus downwards. A forced landing in no man's land did not appeal, but it would be better than roasting. He began to coax his aeroplane into a long glide, taking it as slowly as he dared. The flames crept back, devouring more and more of the wing, and he knew that if he slowed too much the flames might go up the struts into the upper wing and if he went too fast he might find the flames in the cockpit with him. Why did they make the material which covered the wings so inflammable? he thought inconsequentially. Did the women who stretched the fine linen so carefully over the frame know that it burnt like a torch?

The ground, pitted and scarred, was close now, the aircraft tipping crazily. She touched down, bounced, touched down again. A crater yawned. He could not avoid it. She was travelling too fast, one wing all but consumed, the flames licking at the cockpit. He felt her tip and slide, then somersault forward. He was hurled out, felt his face smash into something yielding – and knew no more.

He awoke in bed. Hearing returned first, before he had strength enough to open his eyelids or move his lead-heavy limbs. He listened. There were voices, talking English. He felt faint amusement because he found this reassuring. Why on earth should he have expected to hear foreign words? It occurred to him next that the voices were all male. Then he heard something clicking and wanted to open his eyes, but his lids felt so heavy, like two great pillows on his cheeks. He listened for a moment longer, then drifted into sleep.

When he woke again he felt stronger. He listened for a moment, then blinked his eyes open. He was in a sort of hospital, he could tell that by the lines of iron cots and the identical regulation bed-coverings. Oddly, though, the floor was just earth, the walls greenish canvas through which he could see sunshine. He could hear gunfire too, and shellbursts. He moved his head a fraction and blinding, red-hot pain shot through it like needles being driven into his brain. It surprised an involuntary shriek from him, only the sound emerged as a moan, no more. He heard a soft voice near him and his eyes, which had clamped defensively shut as the pain struck him, opened cautiously.

A girl leaned over the bed. A fair face, red lips. He closed his eyes, then opened them again. She was still there. She had large blue eyes with thickly curling fair lashes. Her hair was almost entirely obscured by a white cap. A nurse, of course.

She spoke to him but he could not be bothered to listen, not yet, and then she stroked his cheek, her fingers cool and comforting. He wanted to laugh because she was only a child and yet she seemed to accept her role as his comforter. It was ridiculous because she was a child and he was . . . he was . . . confound it, how old *was* he?

Presently, despite himself, he slept again.

The third time he woke he did so because someone was speaking to him. He opened his eyes and there was a young man, fair-haired and freckled, with a cheerful, open countenance, grinning down at him.

'Woken up at last, eh, Louis? How're you feeling? The nurse says you're one of the lucky ones — you gave yourself a terrific bonk on the bonce and they had to shave your hair off and stitch up your scalp, but otherwise you got off practically unscathed. Some broken ribs, wasn't it? But I thought I'd pop over and cheer you up. Here, I've brought your mail and some strawberries.'

Louis smiled and murmured his thanks, taking the letters. Who was this fellow, and how had he come by his, Louis's, post? Odd, that the name Louis struck no particular bell. And who were the letters from? He recognised neither handwriting, only registering that they were quite different. One, written in black ink with flourishing capitals, looked forceful and distinctive, the other was small and sprawling, not easy to read. Women?

He turned his head cautiously to look up at his visitor. He was filled, suddenly, with panic so fearful that he could have screamed. He felt the colour drain from his face.

'What's the matter, old man?' The visitor looked concerned. 'Feeling off, are you? You've gone very white.'

'I don't know who the hell you are!' The visitor's eyes widened uneasily. 'And I don't know me! For God's sake, *who am I*?'

It did not worry the doctor nor the nursing staff that he could not remember who he was. They assured him that it often happened after a blow on the head, and when his ribs and scalp wounds had healed they discharged him and sent him back to the squadron. He knew by now that he was Louis Rose, and a good few other things about himself. He was intrigued to find that he had a wife and gazed at her photograph with lustful thoughts whizzing round in his otherwise empty head. Nick, the young man who had come hospital visiting, was his closest friend, it appeared.

'She's stunning! And you mean to tell me I've just got back from leave?' He scowled. 'I bet I had a good time with her, and I can't remember a thing! Pretty name though, Sarah Rose.'

He wrote home of course, explaining what had happened, and the family responded at once and very thoroughly. Almost too thoroughly, Louis thought, as the letters came flooding in. Sisters, brothers-in-law, nephews and nieces deluged him with photographs. His father was a grand old boy; he liked the look of him, though he was sorry that his mother had died so long ago. It would have been rather nice to get to know a mother!

The doctor said his memory would return bit by bit, and that very probably, once he got home again, everything would come flooding back. He certainly knew without any bother how to drive a car and fly his beloved aeroplane, though he could not remember one solitary detail about his crash. Friends in the squadron, who had watched, horrified, as he tipped into a mine crater, had told him all they knew, but, perhaps fortunately, the crash itself remaind a blank in his mind.

When he returned to the squadron he had been offered Blighty leave so that he could give his memory a chance, but he had refused it. The big push, the moment they had all been waiting for, was to take place in less than forty-eight hours. He wanted to be here, with his friends, guarding the trenches against German attack. It was bad enough to be down there with all the shelling going on without knowing you might be bombed as well!

In fact, he no longer worried over his memory loss. It was coming back already, as the doctor had predicted. His father's photograph could not tell him that his father walked with a stick, talked with an accent, was warm and outgoing, yet Louis knew all these things. He remembered some incidents at his own wedding, though his bride was still a mystery to him. He knew she was dark, so why did he often think of her as light-haired? She was slim, yet he remembered a delicious plumpness. It crossed his mind that he might have been a one for the girls — that would account for it. He was rather ashamed that with such a beautiful wife he still received affectionate letters from another woman, a girl called Fay, or at least that was how she signed herself. She did not seem to know he was

187

married; he ought to write and tell her, but that was not so easy. There was no address on her envelope, nor a surname. He sighed. He got tired rather easily and the doctor had warned him that straining to remember would do more harm than good. Memory would return when it wanted to and not because he tried to make it.

He read Fay's letter again, then put the whole business out of his mind. It was an odd sort of letter anyway, very domestic, talking about 'the boy' and the little, everyday things that go to make up a woman's life. It did not occur to him that it was, perhaps, a wifely letter.

'Desmond, darling!' Tina hugged her son delightedly, then stepped back, tilting her head to look up at him. 'I declare you're taller than ever, if that's possible! And you'll be home in another week or so, won't you?'

Desmond returned her hug, for they were in the seclusion of his study, and was glad that he had such a pretty little mother, one who might easily be taken for a chap's elder sister. He adored her! It made a difference, perhaps, that he was her favourite child and knew it, but he told himself he would have adored her anyway.

'Mama, what a lovely surprise! Yes, I'll be home soon, which makes it even more surprising. If I'd known you were coming over I'd have asked my study mate to buy us some cakes – he's gone into town on an exeat. But since you kept your visit a secret you'll have to ring for a taxi and take me out in style and buy *me* cakes instead.'

Tina hugged him once more, then stepped back briskly, beaming up at him.

'Des, darling, what a bounder you are! I've every intention of taking you out to tea and, what's more, out to dinner as well. I want to talk to you seriously, for once.'

Desmond, holding open the door for her, groaned.

'Not about Frank? We had that all out at half-term, surely? Daddy gave me such a dressing down, and you know I couldn't stop Frank. I gave him my word! Confound it, Mama, you wouldn't have been able to stop him, so how could I?'

'No, it isn't about Frank. We've forgiven him for running away, we write regularly, and everything's all right between us. He's young, I know, but he's a trained soldier now. I couldn't insist on the army sending him back even if I wanted to. Of course I worry terribly – and nearly losing dear old Louis made me doubly nervous – but I doubt if there's a woman in England now who isn't worried about some man over in France.'

They descended the stairs, crossed the tiled hall, and emerged into brilliant sunshine. It was the first of July, and it seemed as though summer had decided to arrive at last. Tina had ordered a cab and the driver dived out of his vehicle at the sight of them and opened the back door. Desmond ushered his mother inside, then ducked his handsome head and followed her. He shot back the partition between the passengers and the driver, then hesitated, turning to Tina.

'Where shall we go? Would you like me to take you on the river for a bit? It's a lovely day and I adore sculling a boat with a pretty woman in it. Who's to guess that you're my mama?'

She agreed enthusiastically, patting her curls. She wore a small straw hat perched on her head and a cream coloured suit with a sailor collar and dark brown piping.

'Won't it be fun? And afterwards we can have tea at that place you and Frank liked so much – the Copper Kettle, was it?'

'Yes, but I've gone off it. There's another one, awfully good, on King's Parade.' He leaned forward and addressed the driver. 'To Snidger's Yard, please.' Leaning back again, he eyed his mother quizzically. 'Now, what is it you want to talk about?'

But she would say nothing until she was comfortably ensconced in the bows of a boat and he was gently sculling upriver. Then she took her hat off, ran a hand through her black curls, and dangled the other hand in the water.

'This is blissful, Des! I wonder what Frank's doing now?' She laughed gently. 'Probably sculling up some meandering little French river, with a nice little French girl reclining

189

in the back of the boat. *Not* his mama, you dull dog!'

'Mama, he's a soldier. What on earth makes you think he might be on the river? Soldiers don't get weekends off, you know!'

'Don't they? I don't see why not. They've got to rest sometimes; they can't fight without rest, I suppose? Anyway, I've had several lovely letters from him. He's got nice billets, and a really charming friend, and it all sounds frightfully exciting.' She paused, shading her eyes with one hand to look across the glinting water. 'Oh dear, I didn't know there was a hospital near here.'

Des followed her eyes to where a blue-clad soldier strolled along the bank and nodded indifferently. He wondered why Frank was writing a lot of lies to Mama, for from the letters that he received he had gathered that life in the trenches was appalling.

'Yes, there's quite a large hospital, I believe. So you've had letters from Frank saying he's enjoying the army? I'm glad, because if he's happy who can blame me for letting him leave? But that isn't why you've come all the way over to Cambridge just for an afternoon, and right at the end of term, as well.'

'I know I shouldn't hate seeing wounded soldiers, but I do.' Tina moved carefully so that she was no longer facing the bank. 'There are such a lot in Norwich – London is worse, and I suppose they're a reproach to us civilians, living such pleasant lives really. Though of course the shortages are horrid, and then there are the raids, and conscription. Anyway, I'm *not* here just for the afternoon. Didn't you hear me say that I'd give you dinner tonight as well as tea? Your father is meeting me here tomorrow and we're having a little holiday together. He hasn't been too well, so he's got some time off from the Ministry and we thought we'd get right away from everything for a few days.'

'I see. Come on, Mama, cough it up!'

'Des, what a horrid expression!' Tina stared severely at her son, an expression of distaste crossing her face. 'All I want is your word that you won't join up. Not until you're eighteen, and then I can't stop you. Unless we've managed to get you into a reserved occupation by then, of course.'

The boat was floating gently beneath the overhanging willows which grew in the gardens of one of the colleges. Faintly, they could hear young voices in the distance, mingling with the chimes of a church clock striking the hour.

'*Stands the church clock at ten to three?*' Desmond quoted, '*And is there honey still . . .*'

'Stop it!' Tina fairly shouted the words. 'Des, don't! I don't want to think about dying!'

'Mama, Rupert Brooke wasn't writing about dying; that wasn't a war poem.' Desmond stopped rowing and leaned forward, taking his mother's small hands in his own strong clasp. 'That's a poem about Cambridge; or Grantchester, at any rate!'

'I know that, but he was killed in the war anyway, and all those lovely words . . . thoughts that no one else could have . . . he loved all this . . .' Her voice faded away. In his grasp, Desmond felt her hands trembling and knew that his mother was hiding behind a cheerful mask, the same mask she had worn when the little ones had died. She did not fool herself that Frank was safe, but she made his vulnerability easier to bear by pretending. And not only for herself; it was easier for others not to have her love and fear constantly before them. Desmond, loving her, could do only one thing.

'I won't join the army, Mama. I swear it. Not until they make me.'

It was not a great sacrifice; he had no desire to join the army, but at that moment he felt noble. He could almost feel the tension draining out of her. She leaned back, averting her face. He had never seen her cry and was glad that she was too proud to do so in front of him. And presently, when she turned to face him once more, her eyes were dry and a slight smile curved her lips. She was in command.

'Thank you, Des,' she said quietly. 'I know it's a lot to ask, but we've lost so much, your father and I.'

'It was a lovely weekend; thank you, darling!' Tina leaned across the table in the sunny window embrasure of their riverside hotel and squeezed Ted's hand. 'Do you feel better for the break?'

Ted, crunching toast and honey, smiled and nodded.

'Much better. The truth is, I get tired far too easily. And there's not a lot of time to be tired in wartime. The flat's very pleasant and I always eat well but it isn't like home.' A waitress entered the room with an armful of newspapers and he beckoned her over. '*The Times*, please, and the *Mail*, I think.'

Ted paid for the papers and Tina took the *Mail* and began to turn over the pages.

'Oh dear, Ted, doesn't life come rushing back when you see newsprint? I dread looking at the casualty lists, but I always turn to them first.' She rustled through the pages, then lowered the paper to stare incredulously at her husband over the top.

'Ted? There isn't a list in here. Is there one in your paper?' And then, as he frowned and shook his head, she added tentatively: 'Do you suppose that the war's come to an end at last?'

'I'm afraid not, love.' He put his paper down and took both her hands in his, holding her gaze with his own.

'Oh, but Ted, why should there be no lists?'

'Because there was to be a big battle at the weekend, the biggest yet. The troops have been massing along the river Somme for weeks now. I'm very much afraid that probably it's impossible to print casualty lists.'

'Impossible to . . . you mean *too many?* Oh, my God!'

The weekend crumbled to ruins as they sat there.

15

On the night following the beginning of the great push, Mark lay in a forward dressing station whilst a harassed orderly dressed a bullet wound in his stomach — the bullet had merely entered the flesh and come out again — and tried to assess the battle so far. A fiasco was the best description he could think of for his own particular part of it. Charging into smoke and a hail of bullets, he had only had time to realise that the trenches which should have been empty were not before he fell, his rifle jerked from his hand.

He must have blacked out for some moments — it could have been an hour or more — because when he came round he was amongst a sea of bodies. He had crawled, with infinite labour, back to the trench he had so lately left and when the body-snatchers came up someone had helped him on to a stretcher and seen him back to the dressing station.

'Well, lad, you've got yourself a Blighty one, by the looks!' The orderly patted Mark's neatly bandaged torso. 'Though you're a Fernleaf, aren't you? Don't suppose a Blighty one 'as much significance, eh?'

Mark sat up, gingerly, and swung his legs over the side of the makeshift bed. When he did so, the room tipped and swayed alarmingly.

'Not a lot. I've a wife and child in New Zealand, though, and they'd like to think of me in England. I've a brother in the Ministry in London, you see. I've not seen him for years.'

'Well, now's your chance, feller! Someone'll walk wiv you — if you can walk — dahn to the ambulances.'

Is this the end of my war? Mark wondered, as he limped with painful slowness further from the lines. He wondered if he would be allowed to send a field postcard to Su, then forgot everything except that he must walk forward and must not faint. And that soon, he would be able to lie down. And sleep.

Louis fell into his bed; he had never thought to fly so constantly, with so little rest, yet the days passed — they were in mid-July now — and the battle still raged. The skies were crowded with shells, screaming through the air and bursting with a sound like an express train hitting the buffers at full belt.

To be alive was a miracle. In the trenches and in no man's land the bodies piled up; a constant stream of wounded limped or were carried to the rear. Louis tried never to look down on to that carnage, but sometimes he could not help it. He flinched back, his stomach turning, when he caught a nightmare glimpse, then fired his Lewis gun into the enemy with more determination than ever. If killing Huns would bring the war to a stop, then he must kill, for what was happening on the ground was not war but slaughter.

He often thought about Frank. He knew now he had a nephew in France, and Tina had sent photographs of a fair, fresh-faced boy with an engaging grin. It seemed impossible that the lad was still alive but he could not find out. When he asked he was told that when the Staff finally decided to call off the push it might be possible to trace his nephew. But until then . . .

Once, after a particularly determined assault on a brigade which had just pulled out of the battle for a short rest, he was told by a weary, filthy, fair-haired soldier who looked no older than Frank that he knew a chap called Neyler; Nails, that was what they were calling him. He'd been wounded in the stomach right at the beginning of the push. He had no idea what had become of him.

'No, I didn't notice what he looked like,' he said wearily, rubbing his eyes with his knuckles. 'Thin and dirty, like the rest of us.'

After that, Louis saw Frank's face in his nightmares, and there was blood on the smooth, girlish skin, or wounds so terrible that they brought him out of sleep on a yell. It was not uncommon, however; few men could sleep peacefully after the first of July.

Nick of the cheerful face and freckles was dead; it ought to have been a comfort that he had taken a German fighter and a German bomber aircraft with him, but Louis only missed him. Others, too. And his memories were slow to return now, as though pleasant recollections had no place in a mind so crammed with horrors. It pleased him that he had his family more or less sorted out in his mind and he felt worried and guilty because Sarah was oddly blurred. But as soon as the heat eased off here he meant to take some leave and go back to her. Find her again. He knew he loved her, but the complexity of his feelings baffled and confused him. He would go home just as soon as he could be spared for a few days, and see her for himself. Until then he would fly, and fight, and do his damnedest to get this terrible war over with.

Frank and Hoss, alone in a crumbly, part-dug trench, lay on their backs, using their packs as pillows and their great-coats as covers. Too tired and hungry for sleep, they could scarcely even relax, for the tension which had started with the unbelievably heavy barrage on the first of July was with them still. They had not left the front lines in all that time and their weariness had reached a stage where to shut their eyes was impossible. All that mattered was resting and perhaps getting some food, the will o' the wisp of their billet seeming to have retreated past remembrance.

From the moment the bombardment had begun, Frank recalled, they had blindly obeyed orders and they had gone on doing so ever since, even when the orders seemed as if they must have been issued by madmen, or murderers, or both. They had been told, on that first morning, that there would be a tremendous artillery barrage and when it ceased they would go over the top, the officers and men equipped with wire-cutters first, and then the mass of the infantry.

They were to press forward at a run up the slope in front of their own trenches and fling themselves into the German trenches which, according to the confident predictions of their masters, would be empty, save for mangled bodies or men driven to the extremities of terror and shell-shock by the aforementioned bombardment.

It had not happened in the least like that. The effect of the barrage, which had induced a state of nervous terror in several members of their own platoon, had been minimal, for when the men scrambled over the parapets and slogged forward – Frank, a tall, strong lad, had found it as impossible as the rest to run up that hill with upwards of sixty-six pounds on his back – they were met by withering blasts of machine-gun fire which mowed down the foremost, crippling and killing, shattering the impetus which had carried them onward.

At the time, they had no idea why the wire was not cut, nor indeed that it had not been until they found themselves facing it. Beating in vain against the barbed wire, with the German gunners still very much alive, they had continued to throw themselves into the attack, wave after wave of them, until darkness had seen the pitiful remnant of that once huge army dragging itself back to its own trenches.

Men died in their thousands but still they attacked, days and nights passing like a nightmare until there was no counting them. Frank and Hoss, always together, had seen their officers and their companions killed; they had seen sick and bewildered reinforcements, green boys out from home, come up and shake and go in to attack – and be killed. Now, death-hardened before they were seventeen, they found themselves increasingly astonished as day succeeded day and they were still alive. Filthy, red-eyed, exhausted, they did as they were told without more than a grumble or two because, so far, their number had not been on any of the bullets, whizz-bangs or bombs the enemy had hurled at them, and because life, any life, was preferable to being shot. They had seen, with unbelieving horror, a young officer turn and shoot one of his own platoon who had half turned back towards the shelter of the trenches on facing the deadly hail of German bullets. On their way back, when their own officer had ordered them to retreat, they had passed the murderous officer and his victim — both dead. Such a waste, Frank had thought bitterly.

'What'll you do when the war's over, Frankie?'

Frank shifted his head on his pack and squinted across at his friend.

'Do? Dunno. Go into business with my old man, I suppose.' He sighed, rubbing his dirty face with his dirty hands. 'God, I could do with a bath!'

'An' a good scoff. Blimey, I wish me lugs'd stop ringin'! Does your guv'nor want you to work wiv 'im?'

'I don't know. But I think he takes it for granted that me and Des will work with him, one day. He's got what you might call wide interests, so it wouldn't be dull. What about you?'

'My old man thinks I'll go into the shop; there ain't no other kids, see? But I can't see me standin' behind a counter all day, slappin' jellied eels or sausage an' mash on to dinner plates. Though it's better'n this!'

His gesture included the trench, the waste of mud and cadavers that was no man's land, the enemy on the ridge above them.

'Anything's better than this. I'd rather sell jellied eels for the rest of my life than charge up that bloody slope tomorrow morning.'

Hoss grinned. Frank could see his teeth flash in the summer darkness.

'Too true, old pal. Tell you what, I'm glad I lorry-hopped into Amiens before this caper started.'

'I bet you are, you jammy blighter!'

Frank's words held no grudging note, though the two days Hoss had spent in Amiens, just before the barrage, had been the only two days they had been parted since, as raw recruits, they had stood together on the Downs, painfully learning to slope arms, to charge, to march. Hoss was more than a friend to him, dearer far than a brother, for if war did nothing else it showed people in their true light. Hoss was a tall, skinny cockney with a long face creased with laughter lines and mousy hair clipped so close to his skull that his steel helmet seemed in perpetual danger of engulfing the knobbly features beneath it. But it was not his comical face, his scarecrow figure, which made Hoss so special for Frank. It was his ability to laugh at discomfort, to joke his way through rules and regulations as prickly, and often as unnecessary, as the barbed wire which ringed the trenches, which had enabled Frank to survive the war and remain sane.

'It was jammier than you know, my son!' This, said in an effete and languid voice, was meant to amuse. What followed was not. 'It was the first time I'd ever bin off, wivout you, and I missed you suffink rotten at first, old pal. Then, later . . .'

'You were glad to be alone?' Frank stiffened like a terrier who sees a rat. 'Aye aye, here's a thing! Good little break, was it? The barrage started within thirty minutes of you getting back or I'd have asked before.'

'It was *bloody* good.'

'Enna pleace but hare's blooda good, bor!' It always amused Hoss when Frank dropped into the broad Norfolk dialect which was the *langage de guerre* of all the Neyler children. 'What did you do? Flirt with one of the nurses? Get blotto on cheap champagne?'

'Nah! Got meself . . . well, guess.'

There could be only one answer to that. For months Hoss and Frank had experienced only war and loss. They knew, none better, that a shell could come whistling out of the night sky and blow them to oblivion between one breath and the next. Tomorrow they might scramble over the parapet and die before they had even set foot in no man's land. They might make the barbed wire and be savaged by machine-gun bullets, they might actually reach the enemy trenches and be spitted on a bayonet. They might even get back safely to their own lines. But the experience which they knew, sharply, they might never taste beckoned irresistibly.

Frank dropped his voice, though they were alone.

'A woman?'

'Yeah.'

'Jee-*sus*! In Amiens? Tell!'

Slowly, choosing his words, Hoss recounted his story.

He had gone into an *estaminet* to buy a card for his mother and to have a few beers. Nothing unusual about that, save that he was alone. And then, coming out into the street again with a lacy, embroidered card in one hand, he had been accosted by a girl of no more than fifteen or sixteen. She had asked him for chocolate and, when he admitted he had none, had walked along beside him, chattering. She told him she lived on a farm just outside the town where he could buy bread and farm butter, and bacon and eggs too if he was rich enough.

Alerted at the thought of food, for he had the healthy appetite of most youngsters of his age, he had gone willingly with her to the farm whilst she continued to talk to him in a mixture of broken English and too-rapid French. She told him about her father, who had been killed in the army the previous year, and her mother, who had been killed when Amiens was bombed.

'I want to train as a nurse, one day,' she had confided. 'Or, perhaps, as a dancer.'

The farm, she explained, was merely a place where she worked in order to keep herself and her small brother, Albert.

Hoss, with money in his pocket, bought crusty bread, fresh butter, and half a dozen eggs which the farmer's wife willingly hard-boiled for him, since there was no bacon available. With this feast the two of them climbed up into a dusty, sun-speckled hay-loft where the girl and her brother slept at nights. The farm itself billeted half a dozen officers, she explained. She was very willing to accept a share of the food, and as they ate Hoss told her something about himself.

'About me dad's shop, and me mum charrin' at the big houses up west when she was a gel, and she told me about cleanin' pigsties and muckin' out the 'orses.'

'And you understood each other?' Frank said incredulously. Despite his years at boarding school his own

French was still slow and laboured.

'Well, it was a bit of a bovver,' Hoss admitted. 'We got along all right, though.'

'And then . . . ' urged Frank, longing to get to the point of the story. 'When did it happen?'

'Then. And there.'

'You were bloody lucky, Hoss. What's it like?'

'It's all right. Not like I thought, some'ow, but good. She's a nice kid, too; not like some.'

'Going to see her again?'

'I should say! But . . . Frank?'

'Mm hmm?'

'Just *see*, like. She's a good kid. If it 'appens again, good. If not, good. D'you see?'

Frank, who did not, was about to question his friend further when he heard a shell-whistle and ducked apprehensively, his head curling protectively into the shelter of his arm. There was a dull crump as the object struck the ground, but no explosion followed so he stood up and looked over the top of the trench, which was easy because it had no parapet or places to fire from but was just a digging, about five feet deep.

Bouncing leisurely downhill towards him was a smallish object, no more than a dark shape in the night. It rolled to a halt and Frank said cheerfully: 'It's a dud,' but turned and snatched up his rifle. It seemed unlikely that an offensive would start now, but you never knew.

He stood there, his senses prickling alert, for a moment. It was a warm night and faintly, on the breeze, he could smell flowers. Geraniums? It made him think nostalgically of his mother's garden. There was a bed beneath the small sitting room window which was particularly her own and he pictured her kneeling there, setting geranium cuttings in the sunshine, her hair stirred by the breeze, fingers deft and gentle on root and stem. For a moment he was off guard, relaxed; soothed out of his customary vigilance by the memories stirred by that innocent flower scent.

Then the breath caught in his throat and he coughed and with the cough shouted: 'Gas! Hoss, it's gas!'

Dropping his rifle, he dived for the bottom of the trench where his mask rested. Hoss was on his feet, peering towards the gas cylinder which Frank could hear hissing faintly now, but he too turned and with the movement came another shell-whine.

The gas, heavier than air, would roll down into the trench. Frank fumbled with the mask, knowing that he must get it on or run; there could be no safety without it in the trench. And even as he rose to his knees, all hell was let loose upon them. There was the shattering roar which presaged the shell-burst and he saw, in slow motion, the ground ascend as the shell struck and felt the precursor of the impact patter, like rain, upon his steel helmet. He had the mask to his face when something struck it from his hand and the earth rose up before him like a black curtain.

He tried to shout to Hoss to get down, but he could only wheeze as pain stabbed his lungs and throat. And then the earth descended, the weight bearing him down as he took one more desperate gulp of what should have been air but was not. He felt his face smash into the soil, felt it pressing, cold and cruel, upon every pore of him. Stifling, inexorable.

His last thought was for Hoss, who had been standing when the gas came pouring over the ground, when the shell burst.

Then, nothing.

Tina came slowly down the steps of the small hotel where she and Ted had spent the night, drawing in deep breaths of the fresh summer air. It had rained most of yesterday and most of the night as well, but half an hour earlier the sky had cleared as if by magic and the sun had come out, sparkling on a million raindrops, making the world look new-painted. And Tina, bursting with *joie de vivre*, had decided that she simply must go out and see what London looked like, after her long absence.

Her step was light, because today was a red-letter day. After all the worry of the last few weeks, Frank was to be discharged from hospital and allowed to come home to The

Pride to recover from being gassed and buried. He had been in hospital in France for weeks, but at last they were releasing him. He would come, by ambulance and hospital train, by ship and by another hospital train, as far as London, where they were to meet him with the big Daimler, the back seat covered in blankets and pillows for the journey down to Norwich.

As if that was not reason enough for rejoicing, they had heard a couple of days ago that Ted's brother Mark had made a good recovery from his wound and would be back on active service shortly. And Louis, the beloved baby brother, was being given a home posting and would be in Norwich almost as soon as they.

It was the combination of all these things that had driven her out on her solitary walk. Indeed, she could not have sat in the dining room a moment longer, sipping coffee and nibbling toast, watching the sun dazzle on the raindrops whilst Ted, reading glasses perched on his nose, worked his way through the morning papers.

Ted, best of husbands, had been quite willing to let her go off by herself. He suspected her, she was sure, of a desire to visit once again the really good dress shops in the West End, but she had no desire to shop. She wanted to walk, and think, and enjoy being in London again after so long away.

She was dressed, with wartime simplicity, in a plain, dark blue coat and skirt with a matching broad-brimmed hat trimmed with a large pink rose. Because of her small stature she had taken enthusiastically to the prevailing mode for Russian boots and today she wore elegant blue ones, with red side buttons and red heels, and she felt very fashionable and was sure that Frank would appreciate her appearance.

She tapped her way briskly along the pavements, her mind busy with her day. She longed to see Frank again, yet part of her dreaded the meeting. It was that padre, she though vindictively. He had written to her, telling her of Frank's bravery, his cheerfulness and his determination to recover completely. But he had also warned her that his experiences had changed her son; that she must do her best not to be distressed by it.

She told herself now that such experiences must change any man; surely no one who had fought in the trenches would ever be quite the same, let alone someone who had been buried and gassed and whose life, for a while, had been despaired of? Yet she was very sure that all parents did not receive letters warning that their sons had altered. Why should she, in particular, be warned? Then she shrugged the niggling little worry away. She would be seeing Frank for herself soon enough; the time to worry was then!

She came to a wide window with a display of austerity fashions and stopped, ostensibly to admire the array of gowns and hats, but really to use the glass as a mirror to check her own appearance. She saw a small, slender woman with a hat perched on a mass of glossy black hair, her skin clear as a girl's, with no hint in her figure that she had borne six children. She seldom allowed herself to think of her babies, lost to her for ever, but she thought now, examining her reflection critically, that sorrow had marked her little. Or not outwardly. To herself she hugged the scars of her loss, allowing no one to guess at the pain and guilt which had threatened to drive her out of her mind until she had come to terms with it.

She wished she had chosen something a little more dressy than her blue coat and skirt, though. It seemed severe for so joyous an occasion. And then she was visited by an inspiration. If she could buy a corsage it would make her look almost bridal. Pink rosebuds would be best, to match the rose in her hat, and it would smell sweet too.

No sooner thought than done. She was walking along a smart, tree-lined road and could see no flower-sellers, but she would probably find one easily enough if she sought in the side streets and squares. Unhesitatingly she turned a corner and hastened along a side road, for she had not the smallest fear of being lost. Like most pretty women she had implicit faith in her ability to charm any man around into assisting her. And besides, she only had to hail a cab and within minutes she could be back in the hotel with Ted, or even at the station where they were to meet Frank.

She turned another corner and, ahead of her, saw the flowers. A mass of them, spilling out from the small, rather shabby corner shop to stretch almost to the gutter, so that passers-by had to walk right round them to avoid treading on the blooms.

I'll get a rose corsage there, Tina thought.

She hurried forward, the scent of the flowers borne to her by the breeze so that her pleasurable anticipation was heightened. Lovely, lovely day, when Frank was restored to her from the jaws of death, when Louis got a home posting, and she was looking younger and prettier than any thirty-five-year-old mother had a right to look! Before her, the blooms spilled out across the flagstones, a living Raleigh's cloak of colour.

She reached the flowers and paused, arrested by their beauty and by the sheer quantity of them. Roses in full bloom, their scent heightened by the sunshine on their pink, crimson, white and yellow petals. Some were in huge bunches with ribbons of satin, gauze, velvet, others were more formally placed in bouquets. She looked further and saw lilies, white as snow with powdery gold hearts, and tall, proud gladioli, crimson, flame, tangerine. Dahlias and asters too, and all the flowers of summer, woven into hearts and crosses.

Wreaths.

Flower shops sold wreaths, of course, as well as ordinary flowers. Yet now that she thought about it, she had never seen such abundance outside a florist's, so that the flowers had invaded the pavement, the wreaths lying amongst the rest.

Her eyes went uncertainly to the legend above the shop window. 'Albert Findlay', it said in curly black letters on a white ground. And below that, 'Purveyor of Jellied Eels, Hot Pies, Sausage and Mash'.

Still she did not understand. Could it be that it was now a flower shop and the new owner had not yet painted out the previous owner's sign? She moved towards the open doorway and noticed for the first time that though the door was open the blinds were down. Through the doorway she could see small tables laid with chequered tablecloths, and a long, marble-topped counter.

There was a notice in the window, stuck to the inside of the glass. It was written in a shaky, wandering hand, the writing of someone who did not feel at ease with a pen. Peering, she read it.

> *Due to the death in France of our son, Cedric, this shop will be closed all day Thursday. We are sorry for any inconvenience to our customers.*

Tina stood there staring at the cheap, lined paper with the stiff little sentences written on it, and then she was not seeing it, nor the flowers. They had blurred together into a hot dazzle as tears formed in her eyes and spilled, burning, down her cheeks.

16

Louis was heading homewards at last. He had been in England, to be sure, for the best part of a week, but he had been busy, seeing people, taking part in discussions. And now, when he could no longer put it off, he was going home to Norwich.

The home posting, which would mean six months at least away from the Front, was by no means unwelcome, and once he had got to London and talked, with all the persuasion at his command, to the Powers that Be he had managed to arrange a secondment to the aerodrome at Great Yarmouth, where he would be principally occupied in instructing. But his actual arrival home was something to which he was not looking forward. It would be such a strange experience, to face a woman he could not recognise across the room, to take her to bed, and not to be able to recall what pleased or did not please her, yet to know she was remembering many previous nights with him.

He knew what she looked like, of course, and had managed to give the impression in his letters that his memory had returned. But when they met face to face, would she not guess?

The train was nearing Thorpe Station and Louis reached up to the rack and got down his haversack. This next bit was bound to be awkward! He had not told anyone the exact time of his arrival, but suppose someone recognised him at the station, someone he could not remember? He would just have to pretend, he supposed resignedly. He had been in London when Frank had arrived back from France and had been tempted to arrange a meeting there, because the Neylers were pretty clear in his mind now. But at the last moment he had decided it would not be fair to his wife, so had continued with his plan to arrive in Norwich un-heralded, and surprise them all.

The train slowed and he slung his haversack over one shoulder and lowered the window. The haversack was not all his luggage; there was also a canvas bag full of presents. A dusky pink muslin dress with cream lace inserts for Sarah, a big box of *marrons glacés* for Frank because he had been gassed, some pieces of embroidery for his sisters. Collars and cuffs, made of the exquisite Brussels lace and embroidered with silk so fine that the designs could have been painted on. Then there were toys for his nieces — he counted Josette as a niece — and French perfume for Tina and for his wife. And the lace stole. And the white woolly dog with the floppy red tongue. He frowned. He had bought the lace stole for . . . whom? And that toy dog must have been for someone, perhaps an employee's child. Sometimes, if he picked up the toy, a child's face seemed to blur before his eyes, becoming tantalisingly clear before it faded away. A very young child, little more than a baby, with dark hair and eyes, rosy cheeks . . . the train jerked

to a stop and Louis put a hand to his head, which was aching
abominably. Forget it, he told himself, getting down on to
the platform and lugging his belongings down too. He
glanced round, but a station was a station, it seemed. It
might have been anywhere. He handed in his pass though,
crossed the echoing hall and went out into the station
forecourt. The cabs were lined up just where he expected
them, but that might have been commonsense rather than
memory. He climbed into one, gave the cabby his direction, and settled back in his seat, half excited, half reluctant, now that the moment was so near.

The cab drew up outside an imposing house with turrets
on each corner and he got out on to the gravelled drive,
paid the fare, and then climbed the steps slowly. It was
evening, but the sky was still light. He put his finger on the
bell-push, but did not press for a second, struck suddenly
by the ghastly thought that any pretty, dark-haired woman
who answered the door would look like his wife. Nervousness had, for the first time, made him forget the photograph at which he had stared for so long.

He was sweating. He, who had been flying aircraft over
enemy territory for a longer tour of duty than most, was
afraid of a slip of a girl. It was ridiculous! He pressed the
bell, keeping his finger on it, then snatched it away as
another thought occurred to him. Suppose a maid or his
wife's sister answered the door! He was so tense he might
make an unforgivable mistake, and then . . .

The door opened. She stood there. Tall, slender, in a
clinging dark dress, her hand flying to her heart as she saw
him, the big, dark eyes widening, the soft, full lower lip
trembling.

'Louis! Oh, Lou!'

She was in his arms, slim and strong, deeply satisfying.
His body knew hers; he knew everything about her, it
seemed, as her perfume caressed his nostrils and the way she
clung brought the memories rushing back. So many things,
so many times! The touch of her mouth, the way her lips
parted for him as her body fitted neatly against him was
reminder enough of his kissing, fighting wife with her

sweetness that was spiced, always, with astringency. He groaned and buried his face in her neck, opening his mouth on her skin, tasting it and feeling her gasp and shudder as he lifted her off her feet.

He carried her across the hall and halfway up the stairs before she made him stand her down. She leaned against him then, laughing up into his face, her eyes blatantly adoring.

'Lou, you can't take me straight up to bed, no matter how much I . . . well, you've left the front door open and your luggage is still down there, and . . . well, you can't!'

'I can,' Louis said. He glanced ahead of them, to where three white painted doors were ranged round the landing. 'It's the one on the right, isn't it?'

She took his hand, stroking between his fingers in a manner which had him pulling her up the stairs two at a time. She laughed, breathlessly, but followed close.

'Louis, you haven't changed one bit. But you know I've got a companion living with me now − the house is so big, and it seemed foolish to stay here alone − and you've not met her yet.' They reached the bedroom and he closed the door and tugged her into a sitting position beside him on the bed, then began to kiss the side of her neck. 'Now just stop it. I won't be seduced before we've exchanged more than a few words. And I've some news for you.'

'Really?' He was unbuttoning the dark dress in a determined sort of way. She tried to prevent him and he captured her hands and held them out of the way whilst, one-handed, he continued to undress her. As he did so, it occurred to him that he was no stranger to the buttons and laces and hooks and eyes which fastened women's clothing. But why should he not know such things? He was a married man, after all!

'Louis, do *listen* when I'm talking! I've got some . . . oh!'

He tossed her last garment airily over his shoulder and began stripping as well. She watched, smiling. It was so typical of him and she had missed him every bit as much as he had missed him. He came over to her and took her in his arms, gentle now.

208

'Louis, I'm pregnant!'

He shouted with joy, laughing, proud as a dog with two tails, holding her away for a moment so that he could stroke the slight bulge of her stomach before he began to make love. And in the excitement and wonder of their love-making he knew complete satisfaction, a joy and fulfilment greater than any, he was sure, he had ever known before. It was a terrible thing, he thought, that such bliss could have been forgotten for so long, or that he could ever have felt confused about her. She was a marvellous woman. He would never grow tired of her, never so much as glance at another female. Marriage to such a one as Sarah was a rare privilege.

Presently, dressed again and holding hands, they went downstairs to bring his luggage into the house, to shut the front door and adjust the black-out curtains, and to make themselves a meal.

'I eat in the kitchen, as most people do,' Sarah explained. 'There's no maid, of course, but we manage very well.'

'Good, because I'm ravenous,' Louis said fervently. The kitchen door opened and he added: 'I only had a sandwich on the train . . .'

The words died on his lips. The kitchen was occupied. In a high chair by the table sat a chubby child, bibbed and busy, a spoon in one hand, a dish before him. Sitting at the table, drinking tea, was a young woman. She had very pretty golden-brown hair and blue eyes, and she was wearing a blue and white print dress with an apron over it. The dress bulged pleasingly.

'So you and Jamie have started tea, Sally! This, my dear, is my husband Louis. Lou, Sally Lewis.' Sarah seemed quite unaware of the stillness which gripped Louis in an iron hand, or of the faint colour which had surged into her companion's cheeks. 'As soon as I knew I was pregnant, I began to look in the *Eastern Evening News* to see if anyone wanted to share a house. And I found Sally's advertisement. We knew right from the start that we'd get on, didn't we, Sally? We like the same kind of things. And of course Sally can't go out to work, because of Jamie. So when my baby's born, she's going to take care of them both whilst I work. Good idea, isn't it?' She leaned over the baby. 'Jamie's got lovely dindins, hasn't he? Can Auntie Sarah have some?' Jamie chuckled and pushed the spoon inaccurately towards her mouth. 'Oh, my, what a kind boy he is!' Sarah turned back to Louis. 'Isn't he a pet? I just hope I'm lucky enough to have such a beautiful baby.'

Louis, muttering something, felt that he was caught up in a nightmare. The woman with the baby wasn't Sally Lewis, she was . . . he could *not* remember! But he knew one thing; it was the memory of this woman which had got so inextricably mixed up with his memory of Sarah that he had scarcely dared to come home. And now, to find them living under the same roof . . . he sank on to a chair and put a hand up to his head. His face felt drained of colour and he was very sure his legs would not support him any longer.

'I'm sorry, I don't feel too good.'

The women were immediately all concern. The Lewis female jumped up and made him a cup of tea, then whipped the baby out of the high chair, her face pink and flustered.

'I'll take the boy to his bath, shall I, now? Sure, and it's not easy for your husband to find a scrap of a wee boy in his kitchen when he wants nothing more than a quiet meal with his wife.' She took off the child's soiled bib and pushed it into a linen basket standing just inside the door. 'I'll say goodnight to ye both, for I'll not be down again. There's a good casserole of lamb simmering in the oven, Mrs Rose.'

'You're worn out, dearest,' Sarah said anxiously, when her companion had disappeared. 'Sit quietly there, and I'll dish up and cut some more bread.'

'I need a wash and brush up,' Louis said, suddenly seeing a way to find out a bit more. 'You dish us up a good helping of that lamb, love, whilst I tidy.'

He found his way upstairs, then followed the sounds of splashing bathwater up another flight. He hesitated outside a door, then opened it and slipped inside. It was a pleasant bedroom and Mrs Lewis was sitting on a chair with the child, towel-girt, on her lap and the enamel bath on another chair in front of her. She turned at his entry and smiled

210

without selfconsciousness. It was the smile, he saw with dismay, which one gives an old friend.

'Well, Lou? I'm sorry if you're annoyed with me, now, but I thought you were dead, see? You didn't answer my letters and I'd no rent-money, nothing. I advertised, then, and Mrs Rose offered me the job. A soldier's widow, she thought. I was desperate, Lou.'

'Well, that's all right, I suppose.' The words sounded feeble, even to himself. Deciding suddenly that truth was his only course, he added? 'Look, who *are* you?'

She still held the child and over the top of its head he saw tears fill her eyes. She said forlornly: 'I'm Sarah Sutton. I knew you'd lost your memory when I moved in, but sure I never thought you'd forget me entirely!'

She rubbed the baby dry, then began to dress him in a vest, a bodice and various other garments to which Louis could not give a name. Then she laid the child in its cot and turned once more to Louis.

'I'm sorry. D'you want me to go?'

He shook his head, frowning. He was not really listening to her.

'The baby. Is he mine?'

'That's right. James. You chose the name.'

'Does my wife *know*? Forgive me, but were you my mistress?'

She gave a watery laugh.

'Oh, Louis, what a question! I was, I suppose. You took care of me, first in a wee place in Golders Green, and then you moved us to a dear little flat right by the Coach and Horses. But when you stopped writing you stopped sending money too, and I had to do something! I thought you were dead, or never would I have come here.' She looked up at him, helplessly. 'What'll I do?'

'My wife doesn't know, then. You do realise that there can be nothing more between us? I behaved — badly — in the past, but that *is* the past. If you wish to continue to live under this roof, you must forget the boy is mine. I'll arrange that you're paid a fair sum for his upbringing, of course. My wife pays you as a companion?'

She was speechless, tears running freely down her cheeks, but she nodded, then sniffed dolorously and rubbed her eyes with her apron.

'Good. Then I hope we may be friends.'

He left the room, shutting the door firmly on her grief. I have nothing to reproach myself with, he told himself virtuously, as he seated himself opposite Sarah at the kitchen table and began to eat the casseroled lamb, for what happened between me and that girl upstairs happened to another man, in another life. He also reflected how fortunate it was that whatever had caused him to make the girl his mistress in the first place, whatever attraction she had had for him, had obviously gone. He had felt no flicker of desire for her in that bedroom upstairs, only embarrassment and a faint distaste. Eating his good meal, watching Sarah's glowing and vivacious face across the table, he was very sure that he would remain faithful to his wife.

Ten days later, Louis was sitting in the kitchen alone on the last afternoon of his leave. It was a miserable, rainy afternoon, what was more, and he felt resentful because Sarah had insisted on going out and leaving him behind.

'Darling, it's wonderful to have you home,' she assured him earnestly. 'But you're stationed so near now, you'll probably be home each weekend. And I really am needed. Trained drivers who can also do first-aid are always needed.'

'I need you as well,' Louis said fretfully. 'Tell them it's my last day and they can get someone else to drive the wretched bus.'

'No. Just amuse yourself. It's only for a couple of hours.'

She had gone, looking very pretty in her dark skirt and coat with her high boots, and Louis had mooched around the house for a bit, feeling neglected and badly-done-by. Deserted by hard-hearted Sarah and condemned to a lonely, boring afternoon at home. It was raining far too hard for visiting. Or for visitors, come to that.

He played dice for a bit, then tried to read a book, then tiptoed into the conservatory at the back where Jamie, in his perambulator, snoozed amongst the plants, with the doors wide open so that he got the air without risking a wetting. Jamie was fun to play with when he was awake but today he was most soundly asleep. He was on his side, his legs curled up, his arms clutching his faded blue wool teddy-bear, and not even when his father tentatively rocked the pram did he stir.

The thought that he was the boy's father was one which Louis did not wish to have intruding; it reminded him that, once, he had been unfaithful to Sarah. Now, having made quite sure that Jamie would not oblige him by waking up for a game, Louis decided that he might just as well pack. Then there would be less to do this evening. The other woman (he did not appreciate how apt this title was) must be upstairs in her room, either knitting for her son or for some soldier in the trenches or perhaps even resting on her bed. At any rate, she would be unlikely to appear downstairs until teatime.

Louis went to his room and got out his haversack and the canvas bag. The bag would do very nicely to hold the brand-new flying boots which Poppa had made for him; they were magnificent objects lined with thick sheepskin, and would ensure that his feet kept warm no matter how cold it might be down on the east coast.

He opened the bag and saw the lace stole and the woolly dog. Immediately, he knew they had been bought for Say and her son, though he had not known it before. Say! The very use of the pet-name brought it all back as her own stumbling words had not been able to do. The mews cottage, the sweet, plump, easy-going woman who had given him her love, her body, and a son.

How could he possibly have forgotten her? Without a second thought he took the lace stole and the woolly dog and made for her room. Up the flight of stairs and into the wide attic which had been so charmingly converted into a bed-sitting room. He did not knock – why should he do so, when this woman had been closer to him than almost anyone in the world except his wife? He knew that he must apologise to her for his former coldness, explain that

213

memory had just returned — and give her the presents he had brought so far for her.

She knew, at once. She had been lying on her bed, propped up by pillows and reading a magazine, but she threw it aside, sat up, and held out her arms.

Seconds later he was squeezing the roll of fat round her waist, teasing her, cuddling her; intending to do no more, he told himself, than to establish good relations. Unfortunately, she was only wearing a flounced white cotton petticoat — no drawers, no bodice, no corsets. And it was a double bed, with plenty of room for manoeuvre. She seemed to *expect* to be seduced, he thought plaintively, as he obliged.

When he left her they both knew that their relationship, in the fullest sense of the word, had been resumed. She was his mistress. Any feeling that it was wrong or unusual to make love to two women had completely disappeared. How could it be wrong to make three people happy instead of two? After all, he was not giving Say something which he was not also giving Sarah!

He decided to make Sarah a meal so that when she came back from driving her ambulance she would find something delicious all ready for her. It also crossed his mind that if she was not forced to cook she would have more time to give him later.

Humming to himself, he began to assemble the ingredients for a macaroni cheese, which he happened to be able to cook. As he worked his mind dwelt pleasurably on such problems as how to make sure, when he was next home on leave, that Say got her fair share of his attentions. On a weekend leave, for instance, Sarah would be very unlikely to go ambulance driving. He wondered, idly, if the attic stairs creaked; whether Sarah would notice a somewhat prolonged absence in the middle of the night. He rather thought she would; a pity. He liked the idea of stealing from the slender and energetic arms of his wife to the plump, pillow-like embrace of his mistress.

By the time Sarah arrived home, Louis was glowing with virtue and affection. Had he not used his afternoon to good effect, cooked her a delicious supper, and thought about her constantly?

When she asked, remorsefully, if he had been bored, he told her — truthfully — that he had not; packing his clothes and effects had taken longer than he anticipated, as had a little rest on the bed — he did not say whose bed — and then he had done some cooking so that they might have an undisturbed evening.

Louis, with his arms full of Sarah, was himself again.

Frank lay in the creaking wicker garden lounger with striped cushions beneath him, looking up through the branches of the cedar tree at the cloudless sky. But he was seeing the base hospital. The ward had been full of gas victims, and it reeked. He knew it and so did most of the others. The nurses were wonderful, putting up with the stench, never letting the patients see their distaste, clearing up the foul green vomit which, days later, was still being voided. But Frank had felt like a leper. He still did.

The cedar tree smelt very good; a clean, fresh smell which mingled with the scent of the crushed weed which proliferated in the grass just here. The grass was thin because of the cedar's roots and because of the carpet of needles it laid down in the autumn, yet the weed flourished; small, nameless, with a tiny white flower and little, round leaves. Frank breathed the good clean smell in, yet, stronger than the flower scent, he could smell and taste in his mouth the evil stink of the gas.

Firmly he forced his mind away from the past and into the present. To his right there were wide herbaceous borders, blurred with colour now; the scarlet of poppies, the blue of delphiniums, the vari-coloured dahlias. And behind them, like sentries sloping arms, were the cordoned apple trees. They were all eating apples — Cox's, Pearmains, James Greave — and the trees leaned decorously, linking arms, marching in splendour on either side of the long gravel path which bisected the garden, bordered with box, separating the flowers from the vegetables.

He could not, from here, see further than the apple-walk, but he knew what everything would look like. On the further side of the path there were other apple trees, mostly cookers, and beyond them the two asparagus beds. At this time of year the green fern would be fully out, the delights of the asparagus stalks themselves long over. He remembered lying in the trough between the asparagus beds once, hiding, whilst Desmond and the Sollies searched for him. The earth had been warm and crumbly beneath him, the sky brilliant above, but dimmed by the green of the fern, already turning gold in places, with the occasional hot scarlet of a bunch of berries to make the colour scheme complete. He had been the last person discovered, though who had found him, and how, had long since faded from memory.

By concentrating on the garden he hoped that it might be possible to stop seeing Hoss, outlined against the night sky, and the inside of that canvas dressing station, greenish, smelling of blood and vomit, the pain thick in the air — thicker even than the fear. He had not known, until then, that pain and fear could be seen and felt if you were weak enough — not your own pain, but the pain of others. There had been men in there much worse off than he — men with wounds so terrible that he could not now contemplate them without beginning to shake. A nurse, too, had been hit. Her face — what was left of it — would haunt him for ever, he thought.

After the dressing station came the base hospital, where they had kept telling him he would soon be going home, and then not letting him go. There had been a padre to whose hand he had clung when . . . he pushed the black thoughts back, out of his mind. No! They would give way if he thought about the garden.

Behind his closed lids the garden came to life. Wrongly. Instead of asparagus spears in the beds there were crosses — grey, crooked, mud-blackened. They moved! They limped nearer him! And there were tangles of wire around the apple trees — the trees were leafless, crucified, their branches crippled and bent.

He wrenched his lids open and sat up, sweat running down his face. Why could he not forget? Why could there be no peace for him, no clean, sane sweetness? If he relaxed his iron hold on himself the bitter memories spilled into his quiet mind, galvanising it into sick horror.

'Frank?'

The voice made him jump. He turned his head jerkily, making the wicker seat creak, and there was Mabel, standing quite close to him. She looked cool and pretty in a green and white striped cotton dress with a white straw hat on the back of her head, her hair plaited into two long tails, but the expression on her face was anxious.

'Sorry, Mabs, I didn't hear you come up. How pretty that dress is!'

'It's only school uniform.' Mabel indicated the end of the seat with a jerk of her head. 'If you were a gentleman, Frank Neyler, you'd offer me a seat. Or do you still need to lie down?'

He swung his legs round and sat, then patted the striped cushion invitingly.

'Sit down. If you can bear . . .'

She sat, then turned so that she faced him. Her eyebrows, he noticed, were beautifully shaped and now she raised them with delicate enquiry.

'Bear what? To be near you?' She giggled and took his hand in hers. 'Darling Frank!'

It was the first time he had seen her, he realised, since the Easter holidays before he had run away to join the army. Not so long really, only about five months. Yet it might have been forty years, he had changed so radically. He had left her behind. She was a carefree child still. He . . . he did not care to think what he had become.

'If you can bear the smell of gas.'

Looking into her guileless eyes, he could see no revulsion, only love and a desire to help.

'Gas? Oh, that! It's ever so faint, honestly. Is it just that?'

He loved her honesty and understood her at once. She knew it was not only the smell of the gas that haunted him. But to put into words what he felt was more than he could manage. How could one say that before, he had watched life from the point of view of an actor in the centre of the stage, but that now he watched from the back of the stalls? Once, he had been so busy *being* that questioning had never occurred to him. Now, he watched the antics that men call living and marvelled that it still seemed important to others. Even death no longer seemed so terrible; now it was merely inevitable. Did he see it simply as a sleep? He could not sleep. His eyelids would open of their own accord, forcing his starting eyes to stare into the darkness and see the past. The recent past. School might never have happened, the good times gone along with the bad. Only the war had reality.

'I can't sleep.'

He mumbled the words, incapable of explaining to this child who loved the old Frank what was happening to this new, older Frank.

'It'll come, Frank, honest. Your friend died, didn't he?'

He stared at her, surprised, for a moment, out of his indifference. How on earth had she known that? He had mentioned Hoss to no one because there was no point, now that Hoss was dead. For the first time he found himself hurting for Hoss, wanting to cry for him as he had never done before. He nodded, keeping his gaze lowered so that she would not see that his eyes were wet.

'It must be a huge thing, to see someone like Hoss die,' Mabel said.

He was surprised anew. Everyone else would say how sad, and then point out that thousands had died at the Battle of the Somme. No one else could realise that he and Hoss were almost one, that they had shared the certainty of immortality, knowing that they could not die. So Hoss's death had been a foreshadowing of his own. It had been terrible to be gassed and then buried alive, to feel the earth snapping your ribs, cracking a shin-bone, thrusting fragments of rock into soft, flinching flesh. But to lose in a blow not only one's dearest friend but one's own immortality – it was that which had finished him.

'It was a huge thing, Mabs,' he said humbly. 'I can't

explain, but . . .'

'Don't try.' Mabel was brisk now. 'Was that why you were snoozing out here — because you can't sleep at night?'

'That's right. I've never not been able to sleep before. The nights are so long, and yet I can't read or look at pictures or anything because I'm too tired. Isn't it mad, Mabs?'

He tried to grin, to make light of it, but the small face turned to his was serious.

'It's awful. Can you get out of the house without waking anyone?'

The abrupt change of subject made him smile. Good old single-minded Mabs!

'I suppose I could, if I wanted.'

'Then meet me outside your kitchen door tonight at eleven o'clock. I've got a cure for not sleeping.'

'All right then.'

He guessed that she meant to walk him around to tire him out. He had tried it himself, tried a dozen other things, but none of them had worked. Sometimes he wondered how he went on, without rest; surely, one day, he would have to sleep, like a clock that must falter as it runs down. He had nightmare-haunted naps, of course, but they left him tenser and less refreshed than ever. How long could he go on?

'Don't forget, Frank. Eleven o'clock.'

She gave his hand a last squeeze and then jumped down off the wicker chair and headed for the wood which screened her home from the big house. She was running, and her hat fell off; he could see the impatience in the way she snatched it up and let it trail and bounce behind her as she held it casually by the long, dangling ribbons. He smiled again. A nice little schoolgirl, that was his Mabel!

He was there on the dot, and so was she. It was a fine night, the warmth of the day still lingering faintly in the air. She took his hand, smiled up at him, then led him at a brisk pace across the garden and into the wood. Through the trees, never hesitating, seeing each obstacle long before he did, she led him to the tree-house. At the foot of the chestnut tree she paused, then pulled his head down to hers so that she might whisper.

'Can you climb, Frank? In the dark? It isn't too windy.'

'If you can I can, you cheeky brat! My gammy leg's quite strong now. You go first though.'

She climbed fairly slowly, and he watched and copied her holds exactly. She stopped on the second platform and to his surprise he saw that it was spread with blankets and pillows. She sat down, pulling him down beside her.

'Good thing it isn't raining, Frank! I've often slept up here. It's nice. I'm sure you'll soon drop off.'

'Literally, you mean? You're quite mad, girl, but I suppose I may as well humour you!' They both lay down and rolled themselves in the blankets. The pillows were thin but comfortable and Frank followed her lead and lay on his side. 'Of course the planks are a *little* harder than a bed, and the wind a trifle more forceful out here, but just for half an hour I'll stay up here with you.'

'Shut up and go to sleep.' She sat up on her elbow and firmly tucked in a stray end of his blanket, very much as she had tucked in her dolls when she was small. Then she leaned over and kissed him softly on his cheek. 'Goodnight, young Frank!'

'Goodnight, Mummy,' he whined in shrill mimicry of a small child. He heard her give a smothered giggle, then there was silence. She had closed her bright eyes and was obviously determined to go to sleep herself.

In his turn, Frank pushed his head into the pillow and closed his eyes. He knew it would not work, he just knew it! The wind moved the branches and there were two above him which creaked abominably. He could not possibly sleep with that noise going on, not even when Mabel moved a little closer and slipped her small hand into his. It was nice, being so close to her. He was in a room of his own at the house, because it was not fair to expect Desmond to share a room with him, what with the nightmares and the smell of gas. But this was different; he was not being selfish, because the wind would take the smell of gas right away, and he was scarcely likely to have nightmares when he knew perfectly well he wouldn't sleep. How could he, high up in the branches of the chestnut tree, for all the world like rock-a-bye baby!

Five minutes later he was snoring, his head flung back, his mouth open, little grunts competing with the creaking branches. Mabel scarcely dared to move in case she woke him. She was determined not to sleep in case he wanted her, or had a nightmare, or in case someone noticed he was missing from his bed and started a hue and cry. Of course, when morning came, she would pretend that she had fallen asleep before him and slept soundly all night; that way he would not feel guilty. And then, when the sun came up, they could both go . . . both go . . .

Two children slept on the high platform, rocked by the wind, soothed by the rustling branches of the chestnut tree. Neither dreamed.

17: 1919

Tina dipped her cloth into the bowl of warm water and applied it to the window, sponging it slowly across the four-inch strip of black paper down each side of the pane. It had been there, that black-out paper, for more than four years, and was reluctant to move; but go it must, for Ted had gone to London to fetch his sons home and they must not be welcomed by relics of the war. The years of darkness were over; light could now show around the edges of the curtains, through chinks in the shutters, could even spill out in great golden slabs through open doors! Peace might still feel new after less than five months of it, but at least one need no longer fear being seen by an enemy overhead.

Behind her, one of the twins stirred and muttered. Tina glanced round. As she had thought, the mutterer was Valentina. Nicholas slept soundly, his dark head burrowed into the pillow. It was usually thus; Valentina had been small, wizened and red-haired at birth, and was small, wizened and red-haired still and a poor thriver into the bargain. Constantly vomiting, grizzling, given to attacks of evening colic just when one thought one had a moment to relax, Valentina kept her parents busy walking her up and down, draped over one shoulder, whilst she drew up her tiny knees, screwed up her little face, and bellowed with pain.

My Armistice babies, Tina thought proudly, glancing at the two small sleepers once more before turning back to her self-imposed task. She adored them both, though giving birth to twins at the age of thirty-six had been no light matter, and presenting two sons, both in the army — for Desmond had not escaped conscription — with a tiny brother and sister had given her moments of embarrassment.

Tina caught the top of the now well-soaked strip of paper and began, with infinite care, to peel it from the pane. It came smoothly now, curling round her wrist like a cat, leaving no trace of its presence on the glass. When the window was clear she stepped down from the chair which she had used to reach the topmost pane and turned towards the children. They were peacetime babies, born on the eleventh day of the eleventh month, if not at the eleventh hour, and now that her sons were coming home peacetime could be enjoyed to the full.

The children slept and Tina turned to leave the room. She was a lucky woman. Two sons and a husband had gone to the war and two sons and a husband would return. A nagging fear that Frank had been so deeply marked by his experiences that his mind was, in a sense, injured still, she pushed to the back of her mind. Ridiculous to have such fears; Frank had gone back voluntarily after his gassing and no one had noticed anything unusual in his attitude. No official recognition of 'strangeness', at any rate. Compared with poor Cecy, she was fortunate indeed.

Cecy had lost her elder son. Brilliant, arrogant Bertie, totally unsuited to a soldier's life, had been killed just before the cease-fire. The news of their loss had reached Cecy and Abe four days after the cessation of hostilities and had been all the more stunning, harder to bear, because the rest of the world was rejoicing. Tina had had a heartbreaking glimpse of Con at that time; she had taken the girls to a bonfire which had been lit on the cattle market and had found it too rowdy for her liking, with the brewery giving away free beer and every man seeming to think it his right to kiss every woman. She had the girls clutched close and was pushing her way towards the nearest tram stop when she had seen Con. The grief on his face, the way a small circle of quiet seemed to have formed round him, was unforgettable.

There had been other deaths, scores of them, but none had touched Tina so deeply. Ted's brother Mark had been wounded twice but had gone back to his wife and daughter in New Zealand with a chestful of medals and a limp.

Tina, trotting down the front stairs, thought guiltily that other people's time always went a good deal more slowly than one's own. Mark's daughter Emily must be around two now, a little bit older than Louis's son, Simon. Yet it seemed only yesterday that Mark had written so jubilantly to announce her arrival.

Tina entered the kitchen and went straight to the oven. Since she was not sure what time Ted and the boys would be back, she had decided on a beef bourguignonne – or plain old beef in red wine, as her sons would tell her. It was looking good, she decided judiciously, and popped the casserole back into the oven, then turned to check everything else. Potatoes, peeled and in a pan of water, cabbage shredded, some dried peas soaking in a bowl.

Next she would prepare the twins' bottles and the rest of the paraphernalia which was necessary at bedtime. She had every intention of getting a nanny again just as soon as possible, and had put the word around that if Millie, her one-time nursery maid, cared to apply for the post she would be very welcome to do so. In the meantime, she managed as best she could, though Thursdays, being Ruthie's half day, were worst.

Mabel loved the twins, fortunately, and often came in to give a hand after school on a Thursday. Tina, assembling Woodward's Gripewater, vaseline for bottoms and shampoo for tops, cottonwool and bibs, tried to concentrate on her work, but it was difficult. Her mind would keep on going off at a tangent, into wild and unnecessary speculation.

One thing she kept thinking about was Ted's expanding business interests. The construction company had suffered – though he had been busy enough, in all conscience, with repairs – and the motor salerooms had closed quite soon after the start of hostilities, but Ted's cinemas, which she had gloomily thought of as a wildcat buy, were booming. People needed entertainment when things were as black as they had been for the past few years, and they had flocked to the cinemas.

She had suggested the other day that when the boys came back he could hand over some of his enterprises to them; he had grunted noncommittally but later, with seeming casualness, had said it was a good idea, particularly as he had another idea which needed working on.

Tina, with a sigh, had resigned herself to once again scarcely seeing her husband whilst he flung himself heart and soul into some new scheme. She had realised long ago that he got little pleasure out of his successes once each peak had been conquered. What he really enjoyed was the struggle to reach the summit; he was far too energetic to relax once he got there!

There was a big tray with tulips and daffodils painted on it down beside the stove. Tina fished it out and began to assemble everything necessary for the feeding, changing and putting to bed of the twins upon its multi-coloured surface. Last of all, she stood a pan of hot water, with the filled bottles in it, upon her tray. She was about to pick it up when she heard giggles and scuffling outside the door, which presently burst open so that Stella and Josette might erupt into the room.

'Hello, Mama! Have they arrived?'

Stella, very pretty in her school uniform, threw her new black felt hat on to a chair and ran a hand through her fair curls.

'Not yet. I'm going to feed the babies and put them to bed now so we can have some time to ourselves this evening. It's Ruthie's day off and she won't be back until six, and of course Mrs Walters only works until three. Would one of you . . .'

'Golly, we've got a heap of homework,' Stella said at once. 'And we've not had any tea, and . . .'

'If I helped with the twins, Mama, Stella could get tea,' Josette remarked in her clipped, precise little voice. 'You don't mind, do you, Stell?'

'Well, I'd rather . . . wait a mo., here's Mabel,' Stella said thankfully. She was turning into a lazy little madam, Tina thought, but she said nothing, only smiling with special warmth at her adopted daughter. She turned the smile hopefully on Mabel as the girl entered the kitchen. She was in her dark school coat and hat but she began to take them off at once, putting them neatly on the hooks behind the door before crossing the kitchen to Tina's side.

'Here I am, Mrs Neyler. Just in time to help to feed the lions!'

'And how glad I am to see you, my dear. As a special treat you may feed Nicky, instead of having to tease Val to drink.'

Mabel took the tray firmly from her and backed into the kitchen door as many a maid with a laden tray had done before her.

'No, don't spoil my pleasure! I'm getting quite a dab hand at persuading Val she likes her bottle, and anyway, Mum says you've advertised for a nanny. When you get one I don't suppose I'll have nearly as many chances of cuddling the twinnies.'

Tina snorted. 'I can't see one woman coping with Val, let alone Nicky as well, so I daresay you'll get plenty of opportunities to cuddle them. I've asked your mother to see if she can find Millie — do you remember Millie? She was so good with children, and I'd love to have her to take care of the twins. Nanny Sutton's with Mrs Rose now, of course, so I can't have her back.'

'No, that's true.' They mounted the stairs and turned into Ted's dressing room, where the twins slept. 'Don't they look charming when they're asleep?'

Tina's face softened as she looked down at the cots. They were her darlings, even if they were naughty sometimes!

'Yes, charming,' she agreed softly, and picked Nicholas out of his nest of blankets, then cradled him in her arm, sitting in the comfortable old nursing chair whilst Mabel handed her the bottle and made her own preparations for feeding the younger twin.

'Well, darling? What did you think?'

Sarah and Louis faced each other across the spacious living room of the house in Ipswich Road. The war had been over eight months and the house was fully lived in again, and fully staffed, so that the moss-green carpet, the delicately coloured rugs, the well-polished furniture and ornaments, had an expensively cared-for look. As did Sarah. She no longer drove ambulances or dug the garden but lived the life of a lady of leisure. She had more freedom, Louis sometimes thought, to poke her nose into the concerns of others; as she was doing now, for instance. He had gone up to The Pride to see his nephews because she had urged him to do so. Now he pulled a face, prevaricating because he did not want to have to face the truth. There was something odd about Frank.

'Think? Darling, don't insist there's something wrong with the boy because he won't pretend an interest in construction, or cars, or cinemas, when he finds them boring. Isn't it enough for Ted that Des throws himself so whole-heartedly into the family business? Look, I've told you before that shoes and boots — the whole set-up — bore me and sicken me, but you don't think I'm odd. The very *smell* of leather — ugh! But do you worry about me, say I must be ill in my mind? Of course not! I've been leading a life where

226

intense danger was part of every day, and my skills were all that saved my life. I can't expect to settle down at once, you've said it a hundred times. So why do you and Tina make such a fuss about Frank?'

'Because Frank's such a decent boy — not like Des — and he had a rotten time. Tina's blind to Des's faults, but even she's worried about Frank.'

'Why do you say Des isn't nice?' Louis said, visibly bristling. He had frequently noticed a resemblance between his own attitude to life and that of his eldest nephew. 'Just because he's attractive to women, and charming with it . . .'

'Oh, charming! That's so important, isn't it?' Sarah threw herself down in one of the deep, cream-upholstered armchairs and looked up at him ruefully. 'You think charm's important because you're so well endowed with it yourself, but you've other qualities, my dear love! And how you can deny Des's faults when already poor Ted's having to make excuses for finding him with his fingers in the till . . .'

Sarah was pregnant again and the July heat was very trying to her. He bent over her and kissed her brow, pushing the heavy hair off her face, seeing tiny seed-pearls of sweat forming on her upper lip.

'Don't talk like that, darling. Des only took a bit of money because Ted wasn't paying him enough to . . . to manage on. And you must know that he does love the business while Frank hates it so, yet Ted pays them both. I really do think he was justified in feeling a little sore with his father.'

'Oh, do you! Frank hates it, but he works hard, and Des loves it but spends an awful lot of time drinking in various bars and carrying on . . .'

Louis had been stroking his wife's shoulder but now he snatched his hand away as if she was red hot. His thick brows met in a furious scowl. He knew what was coming next: a reminder that Desmond had not just taken money, but had put a car on his father's account and expected Ted to pay all his bills, including those he ran up because of various girlfriends. If the boy has a handsome face and figure and likes women, what's wrong with showing his appreciation by taking them out? Louis thought crossly. Why did it have to be stigmatised as womanising? His own reputation in that direction had been bad once, and sometimes, when Sarah made remarks like those she realised she was about to embark on, he suspected that she knew more than she possibly could about his present peccadilloes. After all, she could not have the slightest suspicion about his continuing affair with Nanny Lewis; but there had been others. Small indiscretions, but ones he would prefer to keep to himself. There was a barmaid called Patty with a glorious fall of golden blonde hair who had been more than generous to him on several occasions. She worked in an ancient inn out at Horning and at first, he told himself defensively, it had been the hair which had attracted him, only the hair! He had longed to see her with it loose, flowing around her plump shoulders, and from there it had been a small step . . .

And then there was Rita. And Beryl. And Wilma. All employed at his father's shoe factory, all falling willing victim to his charms. In the large, quiet stockroom in the basement, between the aisles of shelving crowded with shoes and boots, he had spent many interesting and productive hours with Rita, Beryl and Wilma. Of course he had been careful to choose quiet times and had tried very hard never to enter or leave the stockroom with any of the girls, but it stood to reason that some of the bored, nasty-minded clerks must have hazarded a guess or two as to why he spent so much time checking stock. And it stood to reason that one or two of those guesses would be correct, since not only the law of averages but also his confounded reputation was against his appearing entirely innocent. He felt no guilt, of course, because nothing whatsoever would have happened if he had not been so terribly bored. He reflected now that during the four years of the war he had been faithful as faithful could be to the Sarahs. It was just that now, with no excitement or danger, and with shoes being thrust, metaphorically, down his throat all day, something had snapped. The urge to add a little danger, a little spice, to his existence had tempted him into a few acts which might, by the critical, be construed as adulterous.

' . . . with a score of unsuitable women, not even paying for his pleasure, and . . .'

'I'm going out!'

He had slammed out of the house before he reflected that her condition was probably making her critical. He was sorry then, though he felt no inclination to go back for another lecture. He had too much on his mind. Although Sarah did not know it, Say was also pregnant, as though his welcoming in of the peace had been unusually prolific. Say, of course, had been tearful and terrified at first, saying she would do away with herself or run off, sure that Sarah would guess who had fathered the child and sack her after a hair-tearing session.

'I'll have to go,' she said tearfully. 'But I'm that used to you, me darlin', and having Simon as well as Jamie to mind, that the dear knows how I'll get on without ye, and burdened by a new babe.'

It was to Louis's credit that the thought of procuring an abortion for his mistress never even crossed his mind, and when Say suggested it he was firm in his rejection of the idea. She was not to blame for getting pregnant. She must be patient for a little longer, and then he would set her up in a nice little cottage somewhere and visit her as often as he could.

'You'll have to tell folk you were widowed in the spring,' he said, after giving the matter some deliberation. 'And you'll have to change your name again and keep clear of the city for a bit. But later, when the child's a year or two old, you must bring him to visit us and pretend you've married again. See? It's quite simple, really.'

Say, poor soul, had looked doubtful, but Louis was sure it would work out. It was a nuisance that his delicious existence with two eager women would have to change, but he was sure there would be compensations.

So now he crossed over to the garage and started the car. He would go for a spin and put silly women right out of his head. He drove out into the road, hesitated, then turned down towards St Stephen's Street, heading for the Wroxham Road. He would go down to Horning and forget his troubles and Sarah's fault-finding. It was a beautiful evening and he enjoyed a drink twice as much when he could drink it sitting by the river. If it had been suggested that he was going down to Horning to see Patty he would have repudiated the suggestion righteously. He was going down to Horning right enough, and if he should happen to bump into Patty . . . but it was in the lap of the gods, after all!

Frank lay in bed staring at the ceiling and wondering why he could not pretend better. His father was being so good, dragging him around every building site, every cinema, every car showroom in the city, trying to interest him in one of them. His mother arranged for him to attend parties, brought young people to the house, made him a member of every club in sight. All he wanted – and it showed – was to be left alone.

For his thoughts, after so much anguish, were no longer a torment to him. In his own quiet way, if left alone, he simply savoured the peace. No one ordered him about, no one slung bombs at him or assailed his ears with deafening noises, no one tried to kill him. But though he preferred this life to that of wartime, he still wanted no part in it. He was perfectly content just to watch.

Others, unfortunately, thought he should participate. Mabel, for instance. She seemed to expect something from him and he was not at all sure that he wanted to give it. She snuggled up to him when they were alone, touched his hand, his cheek, yet there was no thrill of excitement, no response, in him. It was as though he had spent all his emotions in the first months of the war and now had none left to give. No enthusiasm, either, and only the mildest interest in one or two things. He was interested in the babies his mother was so proud of, for instance, but had no desire to hold them or play with them. He could not love them.

Sometimes he tried to arouse such feelings but mostly he did not bother because he was sure it was no use. Desmond and his friends who had survived the war wanted something he did not; Stella and Josette seemed almost afraid of him, giggling in corners, squeaking, enjoying a fund of private jokes. Con came closest to him, with an understanding which was strange when you considered that he had never even been in the army. But he had lost Bertie, and whatever Frank may have felt about his own brother he did understand Con's grief. However, Con was almost as detached these days as Frank was, filled with a determination to get into Cambridge University and working extremely hard, so that the two rarely met.

He worried most over Mabel, though. His feelings towards her now were so negative, yet had once been so positive. He knew he had loved Mabel and had intended to marry her one day. What was almost worse, she had known, and knew still. He could read it in her eyes, see it in the sudden way she would turn to him, feel it through her fingers when they touched him. She loved him in an uncomplicated and almost childlike way, and was waiting confidently for his feelings towards her to return to normal.

He was nineteen, yet felt ninety. No rage flowed in him, no hate. No passions, in fact. Nothing but calm acceptance of life as it was, with no desire at all to interfere. He watched Desmond's increasing greed with indifference, his frenetic affairs without even faint disgust. Sometimes he supposed, vaguely, that he too should be pursuing girls, or settling down with Mabel, but he had no desire to do any such thing. He watched.

Earlier in the evening Mabel had obviously decided to try and change things. In a few days, she explained, she would be breaking up from school for the summer holidays. She thought it might be fun to take their old bicycles and have a cycling holiday, perhaps touring down on the coast.

'Just us, Frank,' she had urged. 'I've got some money saved, and it would be so peaceful and pleasant. I know you'd like it.'

For a moment he had actually felt fear, as sharp and

acute as in the early days of the war when he had heard the approaching whistle of a shell and wondered if his number was on it. He would *not* like such a holiday, because Mabel expected something from him. A response that he did not know how to give.

Would she understand, though, that it was not a deliberate snub? He was too fond of the girl to want to hurt her, but she had to know some time. He groaned, bored by the look of the familiar ceiling, and turned on to his side. Immediately the faint, hated smell of the gas wafted up into his nostrils. He felt sick. As if any woman could want him, stinking as he did!

Presently, he slept.

'I *do* understand, Frank, honest I do.' Mabel's dark eyes were fixed earnestly on Frank's face. 'It can't be easy to fit into life at home again. I mean, there's a big gap because when you left you were a schoolboy, and now you've come back you're a man and you've been sort of catapulted into a job without any of the middle bit. Sort of.'

Frank grinned. 'You've "sort of" hit the nail on the head, young Mabs. Des had nearly a year of being in Daddy's business before he was conscripted so it hasn't been so difficult for him to pick up the reins again, but I've got no reins to pick up. All my friends were army or school and most of 'em are dead anyway. That's made things worse.'

They were sitting on the wicker garden lounger, in the shade of the cedar tree, a foot of striped cushion between them. Mabel could have closed the gap but Frank's whole attitude warned her that it would not be a wise move.

'I know. That's why I suggested you and I might go off on our own. You wouldn't have to please anyone but yourself, Frank, and it would be so restful in the evenings, just strolling by the sea or along a country lane. We needn't cycle very far or very fast. You're fit, I know, but we'd take it easy.'

'It isn't that. I feel I'm cheating you. Things have changed in a way you *don't* understand, though you come nearer to understanding than anyone else has done.' He took a deep breath and turned to face her. 'I don't think I'm ever going to marry, and once I wanted to marry you very much. *Now* do you see why I don't think we ought to go on holiday together?'

She stared, and he saw her cheeks flush beneath her summer tan. 'Do you mean . . . were you wounded *that* badly? Oh, Frank, if . . . '

He stared, then laughed aloud. 'Lord, no, I don't mean I'm incapable of . . . anything! Just that I'm not terribly interested any more. I feel so cold and detached, as if I was a different species from a different planet. How could anyone marry me when I'm the way I am?'

Mabel was nonplussed and showed it.

'What way? For goodness sake, Frank, don't you *see*? If you don't come on holiday with me I'll never understand what you're talking about! I'm not trying to tease you into marrying me or − or loving me. I just want us to have a nice holiday!'

In the end, for the sake of peace, he agreed to the cycling holiday. He knew his parents would be very relieved if he went, and he also knew that it would be pleasant to be with Mabel and away from the worried eyes of the family. In the end, he grew enthusiastic. He took over the planning and booked single rooms for them at small country pubs for the first three nights of their journey. He overhauled both their cycles, drew out his savings, accepted gracefully when his father insisted on giving him a generous sum for a holiday bonus, and at last waved a cheerful goodbye as they set off one warm, breezy morning with a drizzling rain blowing in their faces.

'We've got beds tonight at Cromer, so we shan't have to hurry.'

'Lovely. Whereabouts in Cromer?'

'The Lion. Does that suit your Majesty? And I thought we'd stop at Aylsham for some lunch, since it's about halfway. Think you can make it that far?'

Mabel beamed at him, her dark eyes sparkling. It occurred to Frank for the first time that this really was a holiday for them both, and that Mabel had never had a holiday in all the time he had known her. How selfish he had been, never considering her very real and natural wish to see a bit of the countryside and sleep under a different roof each night! For her sake, they would have a good time and enjoy themselves!

'Can I make it? I'm not soft, you know! High School girls play a vicious game of hockey, and us Walters have to walk or cycle everywhere, unlike you pampered Neylers!'

'Really? What about buses? And trams? And trains? And . . .'

She giggled and they rode on, the drizzle gradually giving way to watery sunshine which turned the wet road into a ribbon of pale, reflecting blue and the trees into faery palaces with diamond drops on every leaf. Mabel talked, sang, or was silent. Frank felt dreamy contentment steal over his senses, a feeling that soon he would know what had been wrong with him and would be able to conquer it. He would be the old Frank again, or the young Frank, rather, able to join in life wholeheartedly. For the first time, he acknowledged that it was possible to step out of his niche as audience and become an actor once more. He began, cautiously, to be happy.

'Sarah, darling, you've found a treasure in that cook. This kedgeree is first rate!' Louis beamed at his wife across the snowy surface of the dining table, then reached for the coffee pot. 'All well in the nursery?'

'As far as I know.' Sarah pushed her cup towards her husband. 'Pour me another as well, darling! I do think Mrs Bristow's a good cook, and she's longing to have a go at a dinner party, she says.'

'It would be nice to entertain again,' Louis agreed thoughtfully. 'Nothing too big, of course, because people aren't giving big parties yet, but we could invite . . .'

'All the people we owe, now we've got Mrs Bristow,' Sarah said. The servant problem at least was now fading from memory, though food was still sometimes difficult. The young Roses had a cook, a parlourmaid, a woman to do the scrubbing and a girl to help Nanny Lewis with the

234

children. 'Your sisters might like to come around and meet some young men. It's about time! Since Ray broke off her engagement I don't think she and Becky have had any fun at all.'

Louis was about to reply when the door opened and Nanny Lewis entered the room. She smiled rather apologetically at them but shut the door behind her and came across to the table.

'Good morning, ma'am, sir. Could I have a word with ye?'

It was not so long ago that they had all breakfasted together around the kitchen table. Sarah smiled and pulled out a chair, gesturing the other woman towards it.

'Of course, Sally, and sit down whilst you say it. Now then, fire ahead!'

'I'm gettin' married, ma'am.'

Louis could not prevent his involuntary start, but Sarah was looking somewhat taken aback herself and would merely have thought his surprise natural.

'Indeed? This is rather sudden! Have you known the lucky fellow for long?'

There was just sufficient censure in her tone to bring a flush to Nanny Lewis's cheeks, but she continued with her explanation though her voice wobbled a little.

'Not too long, in one way, Mrs Rose. The truth is, I'm afraid, that . . .'

'That you're pregnant? My dear girl, I've known it for several weeks! I must say I did wonder whether you were ever going to confide in me.'

It was Nanny Lewis's turn to look startled.

'You knew? Well, ma'am, I was that ashamed I should hope I couldn't say a word to ye! I'd not seen me laddo for a while, you see, so no chance of tellin' him the way I was in. Then a week ago he came back for good – he was on leave when we . . . well, anyway, he come home. And when I told him how it was he said we'd marry as soon as we could. It'll mean movin' out of the city because he wants to be near his mother, but I'm a country girl at heart. If only there's someone who can love Simon as I've loved him, ma'am!'

Louis was listening, at his ease now. This was obviously Say's way of getting out of the house without rousing his wife's suspicions, and a very clever way it was too. He hoped she had invented a good name for this mythical would-be husband, though, or they might yet be in trouble. Sarah was asking the question now – he determined to drop a cup or stage some similar diversion if Say hesitated or was at a loss.

'His name, ma'am? Well, it's Winkie Butcher. He helped out at The Pride once or twice before the war.' She turned to Louis. 'I daresay you remember him, sir? He was in business for himself, what you might call garden contracting I suppose. We've been on good terms for years, even after I met my first, but this time, when he came home on leave and found me actually in Norwich and at a loose end – well, we clicked at once, you might say.'

Louis could think of a much more basic word for it, but he was too confused to do more than grunt. Winkie Butcher? He just hoped Say was not making an almighty fool of herself, because he remembered Winkie well. A tall, well-set-up young fellow with a high colour, dark twinkling eyes, and a way with the girls. Louis knew he had survived the war and had met him in Norwich only days before, and he knew Winkie would not take kindly to Say telling people he was going to marry her. Unless . . .

But Sarah was being gracious, telling Nanny how much they would miss her, promising her a month's extra salary and some useful presents for the new baby.

'For I daresay we shall reach our time within days of each other, and last time I was given more presents than I could possibly use.'

As soon as Say had gone, Sarah began to tell Louis how hurt she had been when Nanny had not confided in her. Louis sympathised, nodded, shook his head, but underneath he was thinking furiously. Could Say have been telling the *truth*? Was she really going to marry that bombastic young Butcher? If so, he would be bitterly hurt! How could she do such a thing to him? He would have arranged something, seen her right! The more he thought about it, the more he knew he should have been consulted; he did not want Jamie brought up by some horny-handed agricultural labourer. Damn it, he would have made arrangements, given time! But he was worrying unduly; it could not be true!

It was, of course. He had believed it in his heart from the first mention of the man's name. And Say, when reproached, defended herself tearfully.

'Sure, Lou, and I know you meant well for us but you'd done nothin', and the dear knows your wife had noticed. 'Twouldn't have been long before she was puttin' two and two together and then what could we have done? And then Winkie came along with talk of gettin' a place of his own, marryin', settlin' down. So I said I'd got a bit put by. I knew Winkie liked me, you see, and I was desperate, and when he pricked up his ears and said he'd take me and the children too if I'd provide the home, it seemed just the t'ing. Oh, Lou, love, what else could I do?'

Her brogue always got thicker when she was distressed and Louis hated to see her distressed. They were in her room, not a safe place to be even though Sarah was out at a coffee morning. But he put his arm round her plump shoulders and squeezed her gently.

'All right, all right, you probably did the best thing. And fancy you having a bit of money put by! I thought you were as improvident as me!'

'Oh, I am! But you did say you'd set me and the babies up somewhere, and I thought if you'd buy a cottage as a kind of farewell present then you wouldn't need to do anything else. Well, a few shillings to buy the boy presents, perhaps, though Winkie says he'll treat him like his own. And I know he thinks the new one his, for . . .'

Louis's outraged yelp frightened him almost as much as it did Say, for in the nursery next door they could hear the two little boys murmuring as they played, and Janet, the nursery maid, would not be out of earshot. Hastily Say put a muffling hand across his lips and dropped her own voice to a whisper.

'Oh, Lou, do hush! Suppose Janet comes in?'

He tore her fingers away from his mouth but dropped his voice to a whisper nevertheless.

'His? How can it be? You're nearly five months gone! The man isn't an idiot! He couldn't . . . or are you telling me you were carrying on with him . . .' a hasty calculation ' . . . last January?'

'Sure and weren't you and the missus off to London like two lovebirds last January?' Say said sulkily. 'If it hadn't been for Winkie I'd have died with the boredom and the jealousy!' And then she, who had never reproached him, added almost sharply: 'And there was that wench in Horning, to say nothing of the girls at the factory! It's unfair of you, Lou, to be angry with me!'

'Unfair? You dare to accuse me of unfairness when it's you who're leaving me?' Louis was totally sincere in his feeling of rejection. 'Taking my child to another man — and now you tell me you were actually carrying on with Winkie back in January . . .' Another thought darkened his brow. '*Is* that child mine?' An accusatory finger pointed at Say's middle. 'Were you trying to make me responsible for another man's brat?'

Say began to cry in good earnest. She put her hands to her face but Louis pulled them down, then he tilted her chin until her tear-drowned eyes could not avoid his stern gaze.

'Well, Say? Is the child mine or his?'

'Y-yours, Lou, I th-think. B-but it's useless to say it c-couldn't be his, because it c-could!'

Louis could no longer ignore such real distress. His arms went round her and he cuddled her tightly. He kissed her brow, then her tear-wet cheeks, then her lips. Then he gently held her back from him.

'Then you want me to buy you a cottage? Well, it may take me a week or two, but I'll raise the cash somehow!'

He left her then, and went to his own room to ponder on how to get hold of some money quickly. He was fortunate in that Sarah's father paid her a handsome allowance which entirely covered the cost of running the house and paying the servants. His own salary was generous, he supposed, but somehow he had never managed to save anything. On

Monday he would have to look round the factory and see if there was any way he could raise the money. A loan from his father seemed the obvious thing, and Arthur had never been mean with his only son. It would, Louis told himself philosophically, work out in the end.

Louis leaned on the bar of the Fye Bridge Tavern and felt that the iron had really entered his soul. Despite it being a Monday he had entered the factory cheerfully enough, with a whistle, if not a song, on his lips. He had put on his best tie, a cheerful floral one, and his dark suit to please Poppa. A quiet talk with Say had informed him that what she and Winkie would most like was a small shop in the main street out at Blofield. The asking price was reasonable, the accommodation adequate. Jamie would not lack a decent garden to play in and the village school was barely five minutes' walk along the wide street, so Louis felt confident that he would be able to explain matters to Arthur's satisfaction. Sally Lewis was a faithful employee, the shop would be an investment. He would pay Poppa back in a few months and all would be well once more.

Arthur had been indulgent enough, had even praised his son's generosity in wanting to set the young woman up in business, but nevertheless he had advised his son that if he wished to purchase the place he should apply to Sarah's papa and make sure that the gift came from his wife rather than himself.

'For talk there must not be,' he pointed out jovially. 'Ah, I know you say the young couple will pay you back, my boy . . . ' for Louis had protested as much, 'but such talk we must not have, for the sake of your good little wife.' His eyes were full of affection for Louis, but there was shrewdness there, too. 'She's a good, generous girl, your Sarah. Speak to her, eh, before doing such a thing?'

Louis guessed that Poppa thought the gift of the shop was a preliminary to a relationship with Say, and was tempted to tell him the truth and get the money anyway. But there was worse to come. He had gone down to the stockroom for a legitimate purpose and was in between the shelves ticking off the required sizes of boots on an order when Wilma appeared around the corner, a gleam in her rather watery blue eyes.

'Thank God I've found you, bor! Hare's a pickle! I think I'm in the family way!'

For a moment horror froze him to the spot. It could not be true! But it was soon clear that Wilma believed it. She began to talk wildly of putting an end to it all, of how her father would kill her when he found out, of how the shame of it would probably kill her anyway.

Louis fought with and subdued an unreasonable urge to encourage her death-wish, and instead asked her what she wanted from him. It was money, of course. Money to leave the factory, to go away and have the baby somewhere where she was not known; money to set her up when she returned, having given her child for adoption.

He made enough promises to calm her, and then hurried out, not to Backs, where he would meet half the clerical staff and very probably Poppa, but to the Fye Bridge Tavern, which was a goodish walk away. There was a charming barmaid too, but for once Louis was impervious to her blue eyes and softly curling fair hair. He simply did not know which way to turn. Ghastly visions of all his chickens (so to speak) coming home to roost, of Rita, Beryl, and Patty from Horning all claiming to be in the family way, floated nightmarishly through his head. What could he do? It was going to be next to impossible to find the money for Say's shop, let alone Wilma, and to Louis's inflamed imagination the others were already lying in wait for him, ready to bombard him with paternity summonses for twins at least. What on earth was he to do?

'That'll be one and eightpence, sir, and would you kindly move away from the bar if you've finished?'

The pretty barmaid, tired of being ignored by one of her most fulsome admirers, grabbed his empty tankard and his equally empty sandwich plate and held out her hand. Louis put the money in it without one single joke, nor did he tickle her palm as he took his change.

Must be ill, thought the barmaid remorsefully as she saw

him moving – almost slinking – out of the crowded bar-room.

Later that afternoon, Louis was back in the stockroom checking off the boots once more. He was preparing a vast and extremely unexpected order for more army boots, and knew he ought to be pleased, for Poppa had been convinced that he would have the boots on his hands for the duration now that the peace had broken out. Instead, this mammoth order had been telephoned through that very morning. But he had been so sick and worried that he had not thought to tell Poppa. In fact, he might as well wait now and hand him the cheque, which would be arriving in a few days.

He blinked. Just suppose the money never appeared on Arthur's desk? It would not be in the books, of course, because he, Louis, had not thought to put the order down. He frowned. There must be some snag. It simply couldn't be that easy! Surely his father would miss the boots!

Only a little thought convinced him that this problem could easily be overcome. He would suggest to Arthur that the boots be moved into the warehousing at the back until such time as they had some use for them. In fact, there would be no need to make any such suggestion; he would get the job done now and tell Arthur that it was a *fait accompli*. And then no one would remark on the absence of army boots which Arthur had been resigned to making a loss on anyhow. The money would pay for Say's shop, perhaps even with enough left to tide Wilma over her 'trouble'.

I'll put money aside each month, as I'd planned, and pay the business back, ran Louis's thoughts. It's only borrowing, after all; if Poppa hadn't been so difficult I'd just have borrowed the money direct from him instead of having to use my wits to get hold of it.

By the time he left for home that evening, the plan had been perfected and all but concluded. The boots had been moved to the warehousing, save for those which he had sold to the army; he had even arranged for the money to be

241

paid direct to him since he was managing the sale.

Louis, without really thinking about it, had embarked on a life of crime.

18

The cycling holiday was a great success, Mabel thought as she went up to her room in the grey stone fisherman's cottage, just outside Happisburgh village, where she and Frank were staying for a few nights. Frank was laughing again, teasing her. To be sure he was not very amorous yet, but even that was improving. Better still, he was telling her more, no longer holding back his thoughts and feelings.

It was beginning to show in his face, she thought now, taking off her short, practical cycling skirt and the dark blouse which was stained with sweat and dust. He was smiling more at other people and she had heard, that very morning as they cycled through the village, two women talking.

'He's a handsome lad,' one of them had remarked. 'And she in't so dusty. Nice couple.'

Mabel was used to hearing the Neyler boys admired for their fair curls, regular features and good figures, but now for the first time she saw that Frank was really very handsome, and knew that one day other girls would envy her her tall, blond husband.

Because it was going to come out all right. The knowledge that he did love her, whatever he might say at the moment, warmed her, and she was bold enough to tell him that he must begin to battle with his self-doubt.

'It isn't just that,' he had protested. 'I'm shy, though I can't imagine why, and it's horrible to me to see Desmond acting like a randy tomcat. And then I know I smell of gas . . .'

'That smell's almost entirely your imagination,' Mabel assured him. 'I hardly notice it, truly, and if we were married and together most of the time I bet I'd *never* notice.'

He had smiled at her and it was very nearly his old smile, and then, so casually, he had put his arm around her shoulders. They were sitting on a shingle bank above the sea, which pounded the pebbles below with a surge and drag, and above them the seagulls gave their melancholy catcalls. Mabel could taste salt on her lips and, though the wind was cold, she was hot with happiness. For Frank had flung an arm round her shoulders and she could sense how near his restraint was to disappearing altogether.

'Never notice? I'll hold you to that, Mabs, one of these nights!'

'I wish you would.'

The words, almost whispered, had been going too far and too fast for Frank; she realised it as soon as they were out of her mouth. His arm had moved, absently, as though he were merely a little stiff in that position, but she felt his withdrawal keenly and would have given a good deal to have the remark unsaid. It was both fast and forward, she told herself crossly.

But it had given her a Plan, and she intended to put it into execution this very night. Frank used the smell of gas as the main reason for not making love to her; she would prove that it was no reason at all. She intended to wait until the fisherman and his wife had gone to bed in the converted shed they slept in when they had overnight guests, and then join Frank in his room. After that, she would play it by ear. If he wanted her to, she would go to bed with him. If, as was far likelier, he did not even wake, she would sleep in his room and assure him, in the morning, that the gas was nothing, a mere figment of his imagination; certainly it would not prevent a woman from sharing his bed!

She knew, of course, that it was not just the smell of gas which had made Frank so withdrawn. It was that night, the night that Hoss had died. Something had happened on that night, four years ago, which had made him believe that being close to a person would result in death. Vaguely, she believed that something had happened which had connected death and girls in Frank's mind, but what it was she had not the faintest idea. Nor did she think that it mattered. Frank was getting better so quickly that the whole worry would probably slip from his mind soon and cease plaguing them both.

Darkness was thick as she crossed her bedroom on bare feet and opened the shutters. She had donned her thin cotton nightie and now she opened the window, and then simply stared, her purpose forgotten for a moment. Her room overlooked the beach and the moon was full, painting a path across the sea, silvering the pebbles and turning the breakwaters and their long-fingered shadows into pitch. Out at sea there were lights – ships, sailing up and down the channel. And a thin cloud slipped, scarf-like, across the moon's bright disc. Beauty, and magic, were almost tangible out there.

The sleepy chirp of a bird in the lilac bush by the front gate brought her back to earth. She pushed the window wider and leaned out. She could just see the shed. The curtains were drawn, the windows tight shut. She sighed with relief and turned back into her room. Now for it! She wanted to help Frank and this was one way to do it. They had had a full and exhausting day; only excitement had kept her awake so long as this and already she could feel her eyelids drooping. Frank, she was very sure, would be fast asleep. There was no need for the fluttering in her breast nor for the sudden dampness of the palms of her hands. She rubbed them briskly against her nightgown, then opened Frank's door. It creaked. He lay facing the window, his breathing deep and even. She crossed the room and lay gingerly down on the extreme edge of his bed. There was the faintest smell of gas, but it was so faint that it could disturb no one. She made herself comfortable, and began her vigil.

*   *   *

244

It was most unfortunate that she overslept and that Mrs Mitton had walked in on them. Shaming to have her stumbled explanation of noises in the night being patently disbelieved not only by Mrs Mitton but by Frank too. He had shot up in bed, his fair curls on end, his face creased with pink lines down one side where he had slept on it, looking disproportionately astonished. Mabel had slunk from his room back into her own feeling like a Magdalen and cursing her ability to sleep through a hurricane.

Breakfast, served by a tight-lipped Mrs Mitton, was an uncomfortable meal; they agreed to move on without exchanging more than one swift, beady-eyed look. Indeed, they did not speak a word during breakfast and left almost as silently, Mabel not even wanting to thank Mrs Mitton, though she did stumble through a couple of ingratiating sentences which their hostess listened to with cynical detachment.

It had been raining, too. They rode off along the coast road towards Sea Palling. Mabel wanted to explain but she felt thoroughly misunderstood and furious with herself. Why on earth had she not told Frank what she intended to do? What did he believe, anyway? Surely not that she was trying to compromise him?

The thought made her smile and she shot a glance at Frank through her eyelashes. He was looking at her.

It was just at that moment that she noticed the rain had stopped and the sun had broken through the cloud. She raised her brows at Frank and he grinned.

'Mabs, you're a silly fool! What on earth did you do that for?'

'I wanted to prove to you that the smell of gas didn't bother me.'

'Was *that* it!' For a moment they cycled in silence. Then he spoke again, with a certain wry humour. 'Do you always sleep so soundly in a strange man's bed, then? Or were you actually overcome by the gas fumes?'

She giggled and leaned over to push his shoulder and their front wheels grazed. There was a moment of wild wobbling and then two cycles were down on the wet road and two riders, inextricably entangled, were gasping and laughing on the rain-soaked grass.

'I wasn't in your bed, Frank, I was on top of it! I don't want you to do anything you think is wrong. I just wanted you to know that if you *do* want to . . . well . . .'

Their faces were inches apart and they were laughing still, completely without guile. Frank took her shoulders in his hands and for a second they were quite still, their very breathing suspended. Then his lips grazed hers, returned with less diffidence, and then he grabbed her, holding her crushed close, the kiss burning her, devouring her so that she threw her arms round his neck and seemed to fuse against him, oblivious of the wet grass, the mud, the public highway.

He broke the kiss at last and moved back, his face reddening.

'Mabs? Oh, God, Mabs, I want . . . Mabs, could you . . . would you . . .'

A car, skidding to a halt, brought them apart and on to their feet like a pair of marionettes jerked by invisible strings. Someone jumped down and came round to the nearside of the car, leaving the engine still running.

'Whatever were you doing, sitting there on that wet grass? Honestly, Frank, if you want to ravish Mabel at least do it on dry ground!' It was Desmond, a loud chequered cap on the back of his sun-bleached hair, his shirt sleeves rolled up. He put his hands on his hips and grinned mockingly down at Mabel, dusty and dirty, vainly trying to clean the mud off her skirt. 'Hello, Mabs, old girl! Are you wounded?'

Mabel bent and retrieved her cycle with as much dignity as she could muster. She scuffed with her sandalled feet and saw that Desmond was looking at her long, bare legs. She blushed and moved round to straighten her handlebars, which were at odds with the rest of the machine.

'Shut up, Des. We had a horrible crash. What do you want?'

'Yes, and what are you doing in this neck of the woods? Not hunting for us, I hope?'

Frank sounded slightly annoyed, to Mabel's glee. So he had enjoyed the interruption as little as she!

'Of course we're hunting for you; what other reason would I have for being on the Palling Road at this unearthly hour?' Desmond sounded testy. 'I've got an old friend in the car, and she absolutely refused to come out with me unless I could find her old chum Mabs, so here we are.' He turned to the car. 'Come out, come out, you charming surprise!'

The door shot open and a vision appeared on the running board, putting back the short veil which hung over her long green eyes.

'Suzie! Oh, Suzie!'

The two girls were in each other's arms, laughing and exclaiming, neither caring that Mabel looked a regular ragamuffin and Suzie, in a green silk suit and biscuit-coloured shirtwaister, her pillbox hat trimmed with pale green ostrich feathers, looked like a model.

Presently, when their first transports were over, the girls stood back from each other, smiling.

'I've a million questions to ask you, Suzie Canning,' Mabel said severely, picking up her much-maligned cycle, which had been cast down the moment she set eyes on her friend. 'But Frank and I are having this holiday the hard way. We pedal! So why don't you meet us in Sea Palling? You'll get there a bit before us, I daresay, so you can find somewhere nice for us to have lunch. A pub, perhaps, or a small café. And you'd better think up a good excuse for not writing to me for such ages.'

The two cyclists mounted, the car shot past them, hands waved, and they were alone once more, with the road rapidly drying in the sun and Mabel thoughtful.

This had changed everything, she was very sure of that; whether it was for worse or better she could not yet say. But the ice had been broken, and Frank had kissed her. She did not think he would go back into his shell, therefore it stood to reason that though the presence of the other two might delay the cure, it would scarcely let the old illness take grip again. She had made up her mind to help Frank, and she was perfectly willing to lose her virtue to him if that would bring her old love back. No doubt Suzie and Des would spend the day with them and then go back to Norwich, which would suit Mabel very well. She and Frank had already prolonged their holiday, with everyone's approval, from one week to two, and their fortnight still had three days to run. And nights. Three days — and nights — would be time to break the spell that had so cruelly bound her love.

They made their way to Great Yarmouth in the end, having lunched at Sea Palling, and booked two double rooms at the Royal Hotel. It was all perfectly respectable, of course, for the two girls would share one room and the brothers the other. Frank did mention the smell of gas but Desmond waved this aside — with a wink and a knowing smile which puzzled Frank somewhat.

'Nonsense, old boy. The rooms are big enough, God knows, for a regiment to sleep without disturbing each other. Shall we go to the show on the pier tonight?'

But at this point Suzie looked at her friend and remarked that in no circumstances would she appear at a theatre with Mabs unless Mabs changed.

'I've brought a couple of thin dresses,' she said casually. 'You can borrow one of them, Mabs.'

And up in their room it became apparent that Suzie had planned an overnight stay, for she had a bag full of exciting things. A silk nightdress, fine as gossamer. Directoire knickers; two pairs, one in salmon-coloured silk and the other in black lace. Silk stockings. A flame-coloured voile dress with a low neckline and long, full sleeves. Another, cream-coloured, with flared sleeves and brown piping.

'Suzie, how elegant it all is,' Mabel sighed enviously. 'Your nightie's pretty enough for a ball-dress.'

She spread the garment out on the bed the better to admire. It was of palest rose, trimmed with deeper rose at the ribbon-tie waist and around the neck.

'Yes, it is pretty.' Suzie threw it a casual glance. 'It's the new Magyar style that's all the rage in town. It cost a bit, I can tell you.'

Mabel, in her darned drawers and camisole, was washing at the washstand. She rinsed the soapsuds off her face, dried it, and then turned to her own bag, pulling out a rather crumpled cotton dress.

'D'you think someone would iron this for me? We didn't mean to stay in hotels, Frank and me, and so we didn't bring anything smart.' She tossed the dress down on the bed and smiled ruefully at her friend. 'Not that I possess anything as smart as your nightdress, even!'

'No. You aren't working yet. I said I'd lend you something to wear and so I shall. The cream one is more you, I think.'

'I ought to refuse, but I'm not going to! Thanks, Suzie. I'll enjoy wearing it.' Mabel slipped the dress on over her head and surveyed herself in the mirror. For a moment she was too startled to do more than stare. Could it really be she, this elegant woman with the subtly outlined figure and the golden skin? What a lot a dress can do, she thought, honestly astounded.

'Suzie, it's so lovely it's almost wicked!'

Suzie was putting on the flame voile dress. It was too low-cut, Mabel thought, but she smiled at Suzie anyway. If her friend wanted to ask for trouble, she was quite capable of handling it. She was very glad that the cream-coloured dress was not like that, though.

'It does suit you.' Suzie patted her own slim hips, then scrutinised Mabel carefully. 'Let me do your hair, and that'll complete the transformation. I've got an ivory comb somewhere which will just make that outfit.'

Presently, looking so fine she hardly knew herself, Mabel sat down on the bed to wait whilst Suzie brushed and pinned up her own tawny locks.

'Suzie, are you still nursing? Or have you got some other job now?'

Suzie was putting lip-rouge on. She had already used some black stuff on her eyelashes, to Mabel's astonishment.

'I'm still nursing. It's a good way to meet men.' Suzie

finished outlining her mouth and stood up. 'Look, sweetie, we'll talk later, all right? Now I want my dinner!'

They had an excellent dinner and saw an amusing show on the pier, then returned to the hotel. Mabel noticed that Desmond kept sidling up to her friend but thought that Suzie was quite capable of dealing with the elder Neyler. She and Frank said goodnight, their eyes saying much more, and then they separated, the boys to go to their room, the girls to theirs.

As soon as they were in the big double bed, washed and nightgowned like two little girls again, Mabel turned to her friend, eager to talk.

'Now, Suzie, tell me everything! How did you meet up with Des, for a start, and where do you get all those wonderful clothes? You aren't married or anything, are you?'

'No. Not married or anything. Men give me clothes, or money, or even both. Dear Des said if I'd spend a few days with him he'd give me a good time and see I went back to London richer than I came down. But I'm on *holiday*, dammit! I just wanted to find you again. I daresay he's furious now, because you must have guessed he thought it would be you sharing with Frank and me with him.' She snorted. 'He doesn't know you very well, that's clear enough – or his brother. And as for me, a holiday's a holiday.'

'He doesn't know either of us at all,' Mabel admitted. 'Suzie, if you're nursing, why do you keep saying you're on holiday, as if . . .'

'As if I didn't enjoy being paid for and having presents from men? You great noodle, of course I enjoy that part. It's the going to bed part that can be boring.'

'Boring?' Mabel's voice squeaked. 'But I thought . . . you always said . . .'

Suzie laughed. It was a cynical sound. Mabel winced.

'I'm telling you now, Mabs, that if you start sleeping with someone for what you can get out of them instead of because you like them, there's no fun in it. I should know. Some of them are old, nearly all of them are married, and nine out of ten I find boring. Now you know.'

'Then why . . . ?'

'D'you want my life story? It started when I met this young officer who seemed ideal. He swore he loved me and would marry me. We slept together. Though why they call it sleeping when it's the last thing you do I can't imagine. A man thought of that one, I'll bet. Where was I?'

'You slept with the young officer.'

'That's right. And after three months or so, he told me he'd changed his mind. I was upset, but then I thought it out and it was fair enough. All I wanted from him was a nice home and plenty of money. The old how-d'you-do was fun, but it wasn't that I was marrying him for. I decided then that I'd please men for a return, not for bogus love. So I do.'

'Oh.' Mabel tried to sound sophisticated and non-chalant. 'Then you aren't really a nurse at all?'

'Bless you, I told you I was and I *am*! I meet well-to-do people when I'm nursing. And my . . . friends . . . need to be well-to-do.'

'Oh. And you said they're often married?'

'Sure. Married men need someone like me worse than single ones.'

'Oh.'

'Do stop saying "oh" like a silly goldfish,' Suzie said wrathfully. 'If you think I'm a tart why not say so?'

'You're a tart,' Mabel said promptly. They both giggled.

'Oh, Mabs, I suppose I am, but at least I'm honest. And I won't just jump into bed with Des because he wants me to. He's young and very good-looking, and I daresay he'd be good enough in bed to be a change from my present elderly admirer, but I've got a feeling about Des. I've always had it, ever since I was fourteen or so. I don't want to get involved with him. Odd, isn't it?'

'Not at all, really. Do you remember Con once, when we were kids and Des had suddenly gone berserk because he couldn't have his own way, and then he'd rushed off into the house? Frank was making excuses for him and Con suddenly looked up from whatever it was he was doing, with those bright, round eyes of his fixed on the doorway Des had just disappeared through, and he said, "Des is bad." Just like that. Everyone went quite quiet, for a moment.'

'I wasn't there,' Suzie said. 'But I know what he meant. I think Des would want his money's worth, if you understand me.'

Mabel nodded in the dark, though she had not the faintest idea of what Des's money's worth would consist.

'What about marriage, Suzie? Don't you want to get married one day?'

''Course I do. It may have escaped your notice, old Mabs, but there aren't a lot of spare men around since the war. If one wants to marry me, that's fine. Until then, I'll work hard and save up and buy pretty things.'

'I see. Look, Suzie, I don't want to seem mean, but when are you and Des going back to Norwich? Frank and I need some time on our own, and . . .'

'Mabs, you aren't sleeping with him, are you? That'd be a laugh, and me manoeuvring to keep Des from forcing you into it!'

'We aren't. Not yet. But I would, if he wanted me to. I love him.'

Mabel turned over in bed and looked into Suzie's face. She had her night-eyes now and could see quite well in the dim light. She saw the startled look on her friend's face, and then the genuine smile which followed.

'That's wonderful, Mabs! It sounds odd coming from me, I know, but why don't you marry him first? It could save a lot of heartache.'

'He hasn't asked me. Not for either, if you know what I mean. But I do think he will, if you and Des will just go!'

'That's my girl, you say it straight out! The trouble is, I think Des had planned to stay for the weekend. I can't pretend I'm keen; I want to get back to Norwich and look up some of my old friends and see how Auntie Vera's treating Gran — you know the sort of thing. How would it be if I got Des to take me home after breakfast tomorrow?'

'It would be marvellous for us, but if Des really means to

make love to you he might easily do something on the way home,' Mabel said shrewdly.

'Rape, you mean?' Suzie sniffed. 'I don't fancy that! Tell you what, Mabs, I'll steal away at dawn — very romantic — and catch the milk train up to the city. And you tell Des I've gone straight back to London, otherwise he'll probably try to catch me, and he might do it at that.'

'All right. Have you got an alarm clock or something?'

Suzie had a neat little travelling clock in her case and now she leaned out of bed and set the alarm.

'That's done. Goodnight, Mabs, and don't think you've seen the last of me, because you haven't! I'll be staying with my Auntie Vera in Bull Close Road, so you can visit me.'

''Night, Suzie. Wake me when you leave.'

When Desmond discovered Suzie's defection next morning it immediately became clear that her decision to cut and run had been the right one. He was furious and his temper grew ugly, even including Mabel in his wild threats because she had connived at her friend's escape.

'What rubbish! I didn't even wake; she left me a note pinned to the pillow,' Mabel said truthfully. She refused to hand the note over, however, since it was pinned, not only to the pillow, but to the rose-coloured nightdress.

'*When you decide to make Frank a happy man, wear this,*' the note said. '*Enjoy yourself. Love, Suzie.*'

'She's an ungrateful little trollop, that's all I can say. I paid for her meals, her hotel room, everything, and then she sneaks off without so much as a thank you . . .'

'Without paying you back in kind if not cash, you mean,' Frank said, gently mocking. 'Desmond Neyler, what would Mama think of such behaviour? And Daddy paid for the rooms and well you know it. Suzie's too nice a girl to let you have your evil way with her, so perhaps it's a good thing she's gone.'

'Well, I think she's a nasty piece of work,' Desmond said sullenly. 'Now I suppose I've got to drive home by myself tomorrow. I only meant I wanted company for the journey, you know, and perhaps a goodbye.'

'Tomorrow?' Two faces turned towards him, both fall-ing, but Desmond, not a sensitive soul, failed to notice anything unusual.

'Yes, I've got to go back tomorrow, worse luck. Oh, curse you, Mabs, if only you'd woken you could have warned me and I could have talked her round! You are too bad!'

'Don't speak to her like that.' Frank took Mabel's hand in his, caressing the inside of her wrist secretly with his forefinger until he felt her pulse speed up. Then he winked at her. 'We're going swimming, aren't we, Mabs? Coming, Des?'

Desmond had not brought a bathing dress but went and bought one whilst Frank hired a bathing hut. As a matter of fact, Mabel was extremely pleased with her bathing dress. She had outgrown her school costume so she had been forced to buy a new one before they left Norwich, and it was easily her most fashionable garment. It was navy blue with white trimming and had quite short sleeves and a daringly short skirt, a little way above the knee, though the dark blue bloomers came to just below the knee until she began to swim, when they rode up alarmingly to mid-thigh. Because it was for seaside wear, the costume had a wide sailor collar and an even wider sash tie with anchors em-broidered on it, and Mabel felt herself to be truly elegant in it, especially as she had always been a strong swimmer.

They spent most of the morning in the water, and Desmond's temper seemed to improve, though Mabel was annoyed by his persistent and oft-voiced grudge against her friend. When dinnertime came, and Desmond suggested going to a dance at one of the other hotels, she was adamant that she wanted no such thing. She was annoyed with Desmond and saw no reason why she should have to dance with him as well! Frank, she was sure, would not wish to dance. His new-found ease with her had not yet reached the heights of being in each other's arms in public.

Instead, the three of them strolled down by the harbour. There was a French ship anchored there and one of the men came over to the side and Mabel practised her French on him with some success. He blew her a kiss as she left, and both boys thought this extremely amusing, Frank teasing her with being a *femme fatale*, Desmond almost forgetting about Suzie for a moment.

Back at the hotel, Mabel pleaded tiredness and the brothers admitted that they too were tired, but would stay downstairs for one drink at the bar before seeking their beds. Mabel left them to ask at the desk that she might be woken with a cup of tea at eight o'clock next morning. As she stood there, waiting for someone to answer the bell, she noticed that Frank was standing at the bar alone. She glanced around. Desmond was making for the back of the hall, where the telephone stood. Perhaps he was going to telephone his parents, to tell them he would be back next day?

Then, in a flash, Mabel remembered that she was sleeping, tonight, in a double bed. Alone in a double bed. And Desmond had said their room was so huge that a regiment could sleep in it and not disturb each other. Or words to that effect. Which simply *must* mean that they had single beds, and were probably at opposite ends of the huge room.

To think was to act. She seized a sheet of paper and reached for the pencil which lay near at hand on the counter so that hotel guests could leave messages for the staff. She scribbled her message, folded it, wrote *Mr Frank Neyler* across it and walked a little uncertainly towards the bar. Could she go in and slip the note into Frank's hand? But there were no other women there!

'Can I help you, miss?'

A uniformed pageboy was at her elbow.

'Oh, please! Would you give this note to Mr Neyler? He's in the bar.'

'Certainly, miss.'

The boy took the note, saluted, and turned towards the bar. Mabel ran quickly up the stairs, her hands shaking a little. The die was cast! She had invited Frank to spend the night with her in Suzie's half of the bed. She opened the door, closed it behind her, then laughed at herself. She had said no such thing! All she had said was that she would miss Suzie's companionship tonight. But if he chose to construe the message as meaning the other, she would not complain!

The Magyar nightdress lay on the bed. Mabel washed, brushed out her hair and slipped the flimsy garment over her head. A quick glance in the mirror astonished her once more with her own beauty and glamour when clad in the right sort of clothes, and then she was in bed, the curtains pulled back and the window just wide enough to let in the cool sea-breeze.

She lay there, content to wait, feeling no shame, no curiosity. If she felt anything it was peaceful pleasure at the thought of a closer intimacy with Frank than she had ever known. She did not doubt that he would come, but she hoped, in her heart, that he would insist on marriage before the final intimacy. It is not that I'm a prude, she told herself firmly as she cuddled down beneath the sheets, but I do think he loves me as much as I love him, and if that's so it seems a shame to have to hide what you've done and how you feel.

She thought she was wide awake but she must have dozed a little for she came to herself when she heard the door shut gently. She glanced round and saw the light glinting on his fair hair and then he was sitting on the bed, pulling back the covers, whispering that she was beautiful, so beautiful! She lay still, her face hot as he feasted his eyes on her in the gossamer gown and then quickly, because she felt horribly shy and unsure of herself, she sat up, half turned her back on him, and pulled the Magyar gown over her head. He put his hands on her waist, then slid them round to grasp her breasts, and even as her body began to tingle into a response, everything in her died, and fear brought her heart thumping into her throat. She turned in his hold, beginning to struggle fiercely.

'Desmond! Oh, my God, I thought you were Frank! You pig! I hate you! Get out of my room or I'll scream the place down!'

He laughed beneath his breath and threw her back on the pillows, holding her still with his weight. His eyes gleamed savagely, palely burning.

'If you scream, who do you think will believe you? The pageboy gave me your note – he doesn't know one Mr Neyler from another – and it's destroyed, so no one can prove what it contained. I'll tell Frank it was an invitation and he'll believe me because he thinks he's a poor bargain. D'you want to hurt him? Because if you scream . . .'

She hesitated for long enough for his hand to gag her, then, though she squirmed and tried to bite, she could not free herself.

'You told Suzie to run away,' he said through clenched teeth. 'If you hadn't, she'd have been with me now instead of you. It's a punishment for interfering. And the more you fight the more you'll get hurt.'

She continued to fight until she could fight no more.

In the early hours of the morning, a small, battered figure left the Royal Hotel, stealing across the dark promenade, heading for the harbour. It was Mabel and she looked as if she had been fighting a heavyweight boxer all night. Her face and neck were blue with bruises, except where they were pink with abrasions. Just past the hotel she stopped to vomit, her hair hanging down unregarded, matted and lank. She knelt there for a little, and once she glanced wistfully over her shoulder, as if hoping for pursuit, but the hotel was in darkness. Frank slept, unknowing. Desmond slept too, sated.

Presently she dragged herself to her feet and moved on. She was limping and so stiff that each step felt as if it must be her last. But she must get away! It took her what felt like a lifetime to reach the harbour but she got there at last. She looked over the side, into the dark and oily water. She moved on, slowly, making for the big ship which she remembered seeing a lifetime ago. The gangplank was down. She was nearly at the foot of it when the giddy, spinning darkness which had been surging at the edges of her consciousness began to engulf her. She took two wavering steps, then knew she was beaten. She slumped across the gangplank and fainted.

19

'I don't know when a year's brought more trouble than 1919 did,' Tina remarked, from her perch on top of the stepladder in the hallway of The Pride. 'Can you take this star, Ted?'

It was Twelfth Night and they were dismantling the Christmas tree and, since Tina had no trust in servants when perched on high, she had insisted on stripping the top of the tree herself. Ted, reaching up and taking the once-a-year treasures, nodded in gloomy agreement.

'Yes, it was a bad year; let's hope 1920 turns into something really good. Though, when I think about it, I don't know that it can undo many of 1919's dirty tricks.'

'Well, Louis could come back, I suppose. And so could Mabel. And Frank could change his mind about that wretched old boatyard. And that's only the start. We could . . .'

'That really wouldn't solve many problems, darling!' Ted put a clutch of glass birds carefully into their cottonwool nest and held out his hand to his tottering wife. 'Come down now. You've got everything from the upper branches. Stella and Josette can do the rest; goodness knows they're longing to!'

'It *would* solve problems. Well, some of them,' Tina said defensively, coming cautiously down the ladder backwards, one hand holding her skirt clear of her heels. 'Oh, I know it wouldn't put back the money Louis took, or get those poor, wicked girls out of trouble, but it would be so nice for Sarah, trying to cope with the new baby and with Simon by herself.'

Ted grunted noncommittally. He was fond of his brother-in-law, and Louis's sudden flight had been as complete a surprise to him as it had been to everyone else. He thought he would never forget that dark night when the front door bell had suddenly pealed and pealed again, so that he, halfway up the stairs on his way to bed, had hurried down and fairly wrenched the door open.

Cold air had rushed into the warm hall and his breath had turned to fog, almost obscuring the figure on the doorstep. Then she had pushed blindly past him into the house and he had recognised his sister-in-law. Wild-eyed and white-faced, she had clutched his hands, her own trembling violently.

'Ted, it's Louis,' she had said. 'He isn't in London on business at all. He's on his way to Australia. He's left me!'

Even then he had been unable to stop the thought flashing through his mind: ' . . . and Sally Lewis, and Wilma, and Patty, and . . .' because it was so obvious that poor Louis had fled not so much from Sarah as from his suddenly onerous love-life. Paternity orders had been fluttering around his ears like leaves in autumn; his shocked and horrified father had thought to unveil a villain who was systematically stealing from the firm and had found the thief to be his own son. One way and another, Ted found it difficult to blame Louis, in his heart, for his abrupt departure.

But Frank's loss of Mabel had been a real tragedy, with no subsequent explanation to make it in the least amusing. She had simply gone, it seemed, disappearing into the Yarmouth night, leaving her possessions, her bicycle, and a nightgown which her mother had tearfully declared was never one of Mabel's. That mystery had not been solved, though the immediate fear – that she might be dead – had been cleared up within twenty-four hours by a letter, posted from a town further up the coast, in which Mabel declared briefly that no one was to worry and that she would be 'all right'.

After that, it just seemed that Frank had sunk back into the old apathy from which Mabel had aroused him so successfully. He was a spectator, remote from them all. Until the incident of the boatyard; and whilst Ted praised God for the chance that had flung Frank and the boatyard together, Tina, with less understanding, kept insisting that she wanted her boy home again and that he would waste his life away stuck down at Oulton Broad with never a game of bridge or a tea-dance to brighten his days.

Ted had gone to look at the boatyard partly from curiosity and partly because the man who was selling it had a Sunbeam for sale which might be just the thing to get Frank interested in driving a car. They reached the yard, and Ted was intrigued, despite himself, by the beauty of the site and by the remains of what must once have been excellent buildings.

The cottage interested him not at all, and he saw Frank poking around in it without a second thought. But his son's expression, when he began to discuss the possibility of bringing the yard back to commercial viability once more, was another thing altogether. Frank's face wore a lively, listening look.

Driving home he had ventured a question or two, and had known at once that if Frank wanted to do anything with his life it was to rescue the old yard and build beautiful boats there once more. Ted was a loving father and a man endowed with great generosity of spirit. He had wanted to invest in the yard himself, build up the business, see it prosper, but now he watched such plans whistle, unregretted, down the wind. It was far more important to him to see Frank regain his interest in life.

'Well, Frank, what do you think? A bit too much of a challenge, eh? It would take every bit of a fellow's hard work and concentration to bring that place back into shape and I've just not got that much time. I suppose someone might come in with me, but . . .'

'Could I do it, Daddy? I'd love to try, if you'd let me. I'd live down there, and I could tackle a good bit of the work. I've always loved working with wood, and if there was someone locally who could teach me . . .'

It had been as good as bought from that moment on. Of

course Ted had not bargained for a good deal of it. Frank's savings, for instance. He had put every penny into the yard and had been adamant that his father's money was only a loan, which he would pay back at the earliest opportunity. And then he had proceeded, despite Tina's tearful protests, to move into the terrible, derelict cottage. Just him and a mongrel dog he had picked up somewhere. They had been there, the two of them, for ten weeks now, and whenever Ted got the car out and drove over to Oulton Broad to visit his son he felt like an interloper. Frank had employed an old fellow who knew everything there was to know about building boats and the two of them were always busy, seldom talkative. It is hard, sometimes, to let someone else do what is best for them, Ted told himself as he pulled the ladder away from the tree and called through into the kitchen for the girls to come and finish the work. But it still has to be done.

Stella and Josette, bursting into the hall, put an end to their parents' musings upon the unsatisfactoriness of 1919.

'Here we are, girls. Mama's done the top of the tree and will leave the rest to you. And if you do a good job you may join us presently in the study and I'll give you some roasted chestnuts. I'm going to cook some for Mama and myself.'

'Oh, Daddy, what stories you tell!' Stella cried boisterously. 'You'll give us some nuts even if we make the most awful bosh of the tree and break all the decorations, so don't pretend.' She began to untangle a bell from the tree whilst Josette, dark-haired and remarkably pretty at fourteen, unwound a great mass of tinsel. 'Leave it to the experts, darlings!'

'Perfect foils for each other, those two,' Ted remarked to Tina as they settled down in front of the study fire. 'Stella's fair as a Viking maiden and Josie's got that lovely, richly brown colouring that makes her look intense and gives her skin a glow.' He cut half a dozen nuts open with his pocket-knife and spread them out on the brass shovel. 'They look very grown up this evening, for some reason.'

'I know, I noticed as well.' Tina sighed and lay back in her chair. 'They're awfully naughty — they've let their skirts down at least four inches lower than I said they might. Isn't it absurd to want to grow up so badly?'

'It's human nature, darling. My, they're going to break some . . .' He stopped, an uncomfortable pain stabbing at his own chest. How could he make such a cruel remark, when Mabel had almost broken Frank's heart?

He had liked Mabel very much and had a great respect for her father. When the letter had arrived assuring her parents of their daughter's safety, he had spoken to Frank with as much tact and consideration as he could find.

'Could it have been anything you said or did, old boy? Mabel was such a good girl. I can't imagine her leaving for no reason and frightening everyone so.'

'I think she suddenly realised she couldn't marry me, and felt ashamed to come right out with it after she'd got me round to wanting to marry her again,' Frank muttered. 'She came to my room, Daddy, and spent the night with me without my knowing until next morning. She wanted to prove that the smell of gas didn't bother her. But then, the next night, she ran away. I suppose she couldn't face telling me that she'd changed her mind. She always was a kind little creature.'

'Yes. And not stupid, either, Frank. I'm certain there was a reason for her leaving and probably it had no connection with you. We'll find out some day, I daresay, and in the meantime don't let it hurt you. I'm sure her feelings for you are the sort that will bring her back, one day.'

'I'd like to think so.'

Ted did not believe that Mabel would return. Whatever the reason for her flight it must have been serious. He could not imagine what had happened, he just knew that something had. And in the meantime, there was the boatyard. If Frank could make a go of it he might come back to them again. Ted prayed nightly that the miracle would happen.

Louis stood at the ship's rail as she steamed into Sydney Harbour. The water winked in the sunlight and the city on the shore looked wonderfully inviting, the very place to start a new life.

It was hot, though it was early January. Louis thought wonderingly of the land he had left, of the people muffled in coats and scarves and boots. Yet here there were bathers in the surf and even at this distance he could see the light cotton clothing of people walking along the front.

Looking back, he could only wonder what miracle had made him suddenly cut and run. He knew, really, that it had been misery and desperation as his troubles increased, backed by the boredom, the soul-destroying hours spent in the factory, with its smell of hides and leather, of feet and sweaty humanity. He had left for all the wrong reasons and had found much more than he deserved even before he put a foot on shore. Peace of mind and clarity of self-vision had come to him; he had seen himself, idle, pleasure-loving, lazy, and had not liked what he saw. Of course he had loved Sarah, she was beautiful, witty, and an ideal wife and mother. His children were grand kids. But he had been content to let Poppa pay him a wage for being bored. He had not worked for his money! Here, in this new country, there would be no one willing to pay him for doing nothing, no one to wait on him hand and foot, pay his bills, see to the preparation of his favourite meals.

Oddly enough, too, stories of Poppa's came back to him. Stories of the American west, the great stretches of prairie, the mountains, the sense of being part of the country. Before, he had not really understood the wistful note in Arthur's voice as he told of these things, but now he thought he did. To go out into the burning blue distances of Australia and to survive by his own wits and muscle; that really would be something!

He wanted to work manually, to make roads or dig for coal or round up cattle. He knew now that he had been playing at life, playing at being a man even, and that even the war years had been cushioned for him. Out here, for the first time, he would be given the opportunity to come to grips with reality. He must seize it with both hands or regret for ever.

He leaned on the rail, symbolically gripping it hard. The challenge would be accepted! He would not regret!

I am a deserted wife, Sarah said to herself as she held Cara
to her breast and watched her suckle. I am a deserted wife,
she told her reflection as she applied skinfood to her face
before going to bed. I am a deserted wife, she reminded
herself as she got behind the wheel of her car. But she did
not really believe it. Louis had been away so much during
their marriage that she never quite got over the feeling that
one morning she would turn over in bed and he would be
there, that look of loving affection dawning on his face and
his mouth quivering into a teasing smile at her surprise.

She missed him horribly, but she was an independent
young woman with a good deal of courage and was determined not to show anyone how she felt. Her father, equally
determined that she should divorce Louis, could not persuade her to make any move yet.

'I'll make arrangements when I'm ready and not before,'
she told him coolly. 'I'm not unhappy, living alone with the
children − I'm too busy to be unhappy.'

It was not quite true, of course. She would have had to be
a good deal harder than she was to have taken his defection
as anything but a near-mortal blow. At first, it had seemed
that her world had come to an end; her cosy coffee mornings, her bridge parties, her good works, all needed a
husband somewhere in the background, though she had
never realised it. And then there was the letter. Louis had
left her a letter, and if confession was indeed good for the
soul then Louis's soul, she thought, must be in mint condition! The letter had Told All: the story of his long affair
with the other Sarah, including the admission that he,
Louis, had fathered both the nanny's children; the beget-
ting of children on two females at his father's factory and a
barmaid out at Horning; the seduction of a landgirl, a
chorus girl at a London theatre, another factory worker.
And his embezzlement. The deceit and the lies necessary to
get the extra money for his women. All written down in his
six-page letter, almost proudly.

At first she had reacted as any woman would. The letter
had been like a knife in her side; the pain had felt physically

real so that for days she walked carefully, moved slowly, as if a sudden jerk or an incautious step might open the wound and bring the blood pouring out.

She had been saved from despair by something which still caused her family a good deal of distress. She had seen an advertisement in the *Eastern Evening News* for a lady to help in a small coffee shop, 'hours by arrangement'. She had applied, agreed that she would work three mornings a week, and got the job. What was more, she loved the work. Her three mornings might be a source of embarrassment to her relatives, a time when they felt they could not go into Dorothy's for fear of being served by Sarah in a frilly apron, but to her they were escape from household routine and a feeling that she could, if she wished, be completely independent of everyone.

At first, she had tried to blame Louis's weakness on the war, but she was far too honest a person to lie to herself and she soon saw that it *was* a lie; the war had scarcely affected her husband. The war had hurt Frank terribly, but he was neither dishonest nor immoral. In fact, of all her relatives-in-law, Frank was the one with whom she was most in sympathy. She knew how Mabel's sudden disappearance had shattered him; even Desmond had been affected. He had got his car out on the fateful morning and had searched the countryside for hours, not even pausing for food. Of course, it had only been a temporary worry with Desmond; he had forgotten the girl in a couple of days. But Frank, she knew, would not forget. He had moved into a derelict cottage in the middle of the derelict boatyard and was said, by his fond father at any rate, to be working miracles there.

I do the same, in my small way, when I'm serving coffee and cakes at Dorothy's, Sarah told herself. Frank builds boats to forget and I serve impatient ladies with delicious food. And both of us, whether we know it or not, are building up a life for ourselves which the deserter knows nothing about, and that is good for our self-respect. Across the gap in their ages and the miles that separated them, she mentally saluted Frank. His was much the harder lot. She only hoped he would reap a rich reward of forgetfulness.

Frank was in the boathouse, waxing the first craft to go out of the Neyler yard. She was a little beauty, commissioned by a man called Claud Grundy so that he could teach his son to sail, and everyone who saw her was impressed.

'We won't hurry over her, Mr Frank,' Benjamin Coates said when Frank first read him the customer's requirements. 'He in't going to want to sail her in mid-winter, so we've plenty time. When we're established, then we'll ha' to work fast, but now it'll pay us to be leisurely.'

So they had taken great care and worked with pride, and the result pleased them both. Gleaming with careful polishing, every plank − for she was clinker built − smooth as satin, with the name *Dancing Lady* picked out on her bows in gold and black, she was a first-rate advertisement for the yard.

Frank hunkered back on his heels and glanced around him. The waxing was finished and it must be nearly time to repair to the cottage for a cup of tea and a chat over the next day's work, but since there was no sign of Benjamin yet he could afford to stay where he was and dream a little. Staring out of the boatshed door he saw the sight he loved most − the Broad, steel-grey and calm as evening galloped over the flat country, the sky as pale as the water, birdsong lulled, only the occasional *plop* as a fish rose disturbing the silence.

To this place he had come last year, and in the time he and Benjamin had worked on it improvements had been made almost daily. Their first task had been to make the big boatshed, the one he was in now, watertight and fit to work in. They had done so, and it was now a good deal more weatherproof than his cottage. But he spent hours working in the boatshed, and he only slept in the cottage and spent the long, dark evenings there. Then he built up a roaring fire, lit the lamp, and read or figured or just stared, dreaming, into the flames. Rain came through the tiles and drove in at the gaps beside the windows but it bothered him not at all. He slept downstairs, so what did a bit of rain upstairs matter? And after living in the trenches the cottage was luxurious in the extreme. He had a roof over his head, a fire, and a couch to sleep on. And, best of all, he was happy.

For he had never expected to be happy again, after Mabel's defection. He had moved here to get away from the family, puzzling over his inability to enjoy the same things as his brother, his quietness, his lack of friends. And he had found happiness. And Patch. Patch was a skinny mongrel with guilty eyes and the air of abject apology common to most dogs who have been unwanted and unfed since puppyhood. He was a sly, furtive little animal but he adored Frank and Frank adored him. He slept on the foot of the couch at night and could be found with his nose an inch from Frank's heels during the day. Despite the fact that he was now well fed he stole whenever the opportunity presented itself and slunk away from raised voices as if perpetually conscious of wrong-doing. He remained aggravatingly skeletal too, apparently quite capable of wolfing down two enormous meals a day and never gaining an ounce. But he was all the company Frank wanted.

Apart from the invaluable Benjamin, of course. Benjamin had worked for one of the big boatyards, a foreman, invaluable to the firm. But they had not wanted Donnie. Frank, desperate for someone who really knew about the business, would have taken on a dozen Donnies provided that Benjamin came with them, and anyway Donnie was a hard worker. It was just that he had to be carefully watched and carefully instructed. His father knew that Donnie was simple so he was prepared to take the trouble, and Frank was prepared to follow suit not only because he was genuinely fond of Benjamin but because he liked Donnie, and saw no reason for making the lad's life difficult by giving him orders which he could not carry out.

Without saying much, Benjamin watched Frank with Donnie, and then threw himself, heart and soul, into the new yard. It would succeed because Benjamin wanted it to, and with this in mind he taught Frank everything he knew, everything he would have taught Donnie if his son had been normal.

''Tweren't the bosses,' Benjamin explained to Frank once, when Frank had shown curiosity over the other yard's rejection of Donnie. ''Twas th'other men. They couldn't leave orf teasin' the lad. When he done something wrong everyone lost time horsing around with him, and they teased him into doin' wrong.'

It was not difficult, as Frank well knew, to fluster Donnie into doing peculiar things. Once, his father, visiting the yard on a muddy, rainy day, had asked Donnie casually to 'pass a cloth over my windscreen, lad, to clear off the mud splashes'. Two hours later, when Frank accompanied Ted out to the car, Donnie was still there, standing drenched in the downpour, the cloth going automatically over and over the shining clean windscreen. One had to be a lot more definite than Ted had been when giving Donnie orders!

There had been other occasions. Asking Donnie to chop some logs and finding him patiently trying to cut them up with a kitchen knife because he did not know where the axe was kept, finding the lad weeping dolorously because a frog had glanced at his sandwiches and he thought they were now unfit for eating – these were samples of Donnie's behaviour when rattled.

But they had no trouble with Donnie if they phrased their commands with care and kept an eye on him. Indeed, some of the finest polishing on the *Dancing Lady* had been done by Donnie, because he was endlessly patient, never fretting to get on with the next job, always content with what he was actually doing.

'Mr Frank? The boy Donnie and me, we're finished. See you tomorrow, shall us?'

'What about our cuppa?' Frank, guiltily aware that he had quite forgotten to put the kettle on – or to light the fire for that matter – scrambled to his feet and clicked his fingers – needlessly – at Patch. 'I'll go and light up and put the kettle on.'

'Not tonight, Mr Frank. You've a visitor,' Benjamin said gruffly. 'She've been here a moment or two, I reckon. We're orf.'

Recognising a note of finality in the other man's voice,

Frank knew better than to press the invitation. 'See you in the morning, then. Goodnight!'

He hurried across to the cottage as soon as the Coates had gone, conscious of faint curiosity mixed with annoyance at an unsolicited visit. He much preferred being alone, but no doubt it was his mother, or one of his aunts. He knew it would never be the only woman he would have welcomed.

He stepped into the kitchen and blinked. The lamp was lit, the fire roared up, lighting the whitewashed walls and the low ceiling criss-crossed with blackened beams. Good old Benjamin. He must have done the necessary before leaving.

'Hello, Frank!'

A slim, smart young woman sat on the easy chair by the fire, with a slice of bread impaled on a fork held out to the flames. She was smiling at him though her eyes were watering and her cheeks flushed from the heat.

'Suzie! What on earth . . .?'

'I've come to see you. Mabel asked me to.'

'Why?' The smile left Frank's mouth and he felt his heart begin to bump unevenly in his chest. 'Why couldn't she have come herself?'

'I'll tell you in a moment, if you'll just fetch me some butter for this toast. I suppose you *do* have butter? And a knife would be useful, too.'

Frank went into the walk-in pantry and picked up the butter. It was a big pantry because the family who had lived here last had half a dozen children, or so he had been told. For himself, it was useful because he could buy in large stocks of food and this made trips to town rare events. With the butter in one hand he went over to the dresser and got down two plates with pink roses all over them − his mother's gift − and then fished a couple of knives out of the drawer in the table.

'Here you are.' Frank put the butter down and held out his hand for the first round of toast. 'You can eat it, since you suffered for it, and I'll make the next bit.'

Suzie smiled but shook her head. 'No fear. This bit got

scorched. You can have it. Besides, I'm getting used to being part toasted myself. Just sit down and eat the meal I've cooked for you and don't be ungrateful, and if you'll pass us another slice of bread I'll have the next one.'

Without another word Frank picked up the loaf which Suzie must have brought with her and cut a thick wedge. He handed it to her, watched her impale it on the fork, and then began to butter his own slice.

Presently, the task done, he sat down in the easy chair opposite hers and began to eat, staring at her as he did so. She was thinner than she had been in the summer, and he sensed a brittleness about her which he had never noticed before. As though she was made of fine glass and might easily be broken. Her glorious hair was not bobbed, he was relieved to see, but left unfashionably loose and just tied back with a piece of narrow velvet ribbon. She had always been very pretty but now she was something more. Her intelligence was showing, Frank thought confusedly, and smiled at the thought. Absurd! But she was lovely to look at. He could sit here and enjoy watching her as he enjoyed watching the Broad when sunshine and wind bedevilled the water into a multiplicity of dancing, sparkling ripples.

'Well? Aren't you going to ask me why I'm here?'

He shook his head, and smiled when she pouted.

'Oh, Frank, where's your curiosity? You're unnatural!'

'I'm not.' He took an enormous bite of his scorched toast and tasted the salty butter and the charred bread with a gourmet's pleasure. 'This is delicious, Suzie! I don't ask because I already know what you've come to tell me. Mabel's alive and well and isn't coming back.'

She stared, delicate tawny eyebrows climbing.

'How did you know? *Did* she write to you, after all? At The Pride, I mean? She wouldn't know this address. Do you know where she is? If so, why . . .'

'She hasn't written, not as far as I know. She writes to you, then?'

He could not prevent the hurt from sounding in his voice and Suzie spoke quickly, eager to soothe.

'No! She's only written once and that's why I'm here. She

said to tell you there was a good reason for leaving and a better one for not coming back. She said she's sorry.'

He continued to munch. Silence drew out until the kettle, on Suzie's side of the fire, began to sing and spit droplets of water out on to the fiery logs. As Suzie reached to take it off the flames he seemed to recover from his abstraction.

'Sorry? What for? She's done nothing to me. It's her parents she should apologise to, going off like that. I believe her mother nearly went insane with worry. It was unforgivable.'

'She's been in touch with them now, and they've forgiven her.' Suzie turned away from him, looking into the heart of the fire, her green eyes reflecting the gold as it danced so that they seemed to have a life of their own. 'She's married, Frank.'

The silence stretched out. Frank just sat. Suzie waited a moment and then panic filled her. His eyes looked so empty! She jumped to her feet, dropping her toast and the toasting fork in her haste, and came to stand close to Frank, her hands on his shoulders.

'Frank? Are you all right? Did you . . .'

'I heard.' He sounded composed, a little amused, even. 'It came as a bit of a shock, that's all.' He pushed her gently away, then gestured to the floor. 'You've dropped your toast. Don't waste good food.' He waited until she had picked up the toast and was pouring the tea, then added: 'Bit quick, wasn't it?'

Reassured by his calmness, Suzie nodded and passed him a cup of tea.

'Yes, it was. He's a Frenchman, apparently. I expect she'll come home one day, but not yet. Not so soon. He's a bit older than her, I gather, and . . . well, that's why she said to tell you she was sorry. Because of getting married on the quiet, I suppose.'

'Very understandable. Did she give you an address to write to? Because if so, do write and tell her I'm not furious, or anything like that. But I would like to know . . .'

271

'No. No address.' She sipped at her tea, then glanced at her watch and jumped. 'Gracious, look at the time! I've a car picking me up here in five minutes. I must drink up and go.'

'You've got to leave now? That was a very short visit!'

'That's your fault, old Frank, for living in such an inconvenient neck of the woods! But I'll come and see you next time I'm home. If you want me to, of course.'

'I'd like to see you, but warn me next time. If I'd known you were here I'd have come in sooner, for a start.' He put his empty cup down. 'Are you still nursing, Suzie?'

'Yes. I don't know whether I'll go on doing it for very much longer, though. I get terribly tired.' She grinned at him, a naughty grin. 'I lead a very full social life, you see, and nursing is becoming little more than a time-consuming and exhausting hobby.'

'I can imagine.' He spoke drily. 'You're terribly thin, girl, but I suppose it's fashionable.'

'It is. But actually I'm not being fashionable, it's the result of burning the candle at both ends; one tends to lose weight. It suits me, however, so I don't repine.' She pulled a face. 'Better than being fat!'

The car, tooting outside, brought her to her feet. She was wearing a brown wool dress with a belt of plaited gold silk, and now she flung her coat across her shoulders and picked up her hat and gloves. The coat was a pale, rich fur. It looked very expensive and Frank said as much as he helped her into it.

'Yes, it's mink. And before you ask me what I did for it, I'll tell you. I was very kind indeed to a very boring old man – the husband of one of my patients. There, now you know that I'm a scarlet woman!'

He could not tell from her tone whether she was serious or not but he bent and kissed her cheek, then pushed her out through the door, back into the cold and the winter dark.

'Yes, you always were ever so wicked. Goodbye, Suzie, and thank you very much for making the effort to come and see me. Don't forget to come next time you're in Norfolk!'

He stood and waved until the cab had disappeared down the long drive and then turned back into the kitchen. It was not until the sound of the engine had faded into silence that he began to cry.

20: 1924

The twins were in the sandpit, which was tucked out of sight between the vegetable garden and the wood which hid the Walters' cottage. It was a delectable spot, made especially for them by their father and William Walters, and whenever the weather permitted Nicky and Val could be found there, digging, lugging slopping buckets to and from the standpipe, building towering edifices, or just sitting and dreaming.

Today was hot, so they were clad in bathers, and June, so they were eating cherries. The cherry tree overhung the sandpit and dropped an abundance of fruit on the white Yarmouth sand, and though this brought the hazard of flies and wasps the twins were quite ready to put up with the trifling inconvenience for the sake of unlimited cherries.

Their nanny, who had not thought much of the sandpit at first, now frequently blessed it. To be sure, it meant sand in everything, but the sand was clean and regularly changed and it kept the twins happy and relatively mischief-free for hours on end. As witness today; a bright and beautiful Sunday when the rest of the family were attending a cocktail party at Frank's yard, to launch his latest boat. Val had bargained briskly for today.

Their mother had been dressing for dinner when they had tackled her about it. Sitting on the little round stool in front of her dressing-table in a slim-fitting black georgette dress with fringes that swished gently when she moved, she was fastening around her neck a beautiful string of topaz stones, yellow as cat's eyes. She raised her eyebrows when they appeared round the door and smiled at them.

'Hello, bandits. Has someone broken it to you that we're not taking you to Frank's party tomorrow after all? You'll be much happier at home with Nanny, though. A quiet lunch, nothing which will give you tummy upsets, and then a walk to the park perhaps. Far better for you than a grown-up party.'

'We want to come with you!' Val's voice was calculatingly close to a wail. 'We don' wanna be left on a Sunday! Nanny won't let us do *anything* except the park and picture books!'

'Oh, but you'd hate it at Frank's party, pets,' Tina replied, her eyes widening with horror at the thought of being saddled with two five-year-olds. 'You'd be so bored!'

'We want to come!' Nicky said in a high whine.

Val was opening her mouth for a fresh onslaught when their father, coming through from his dressing room, called their bluff.

'Nonsense! You'd hate it. What do you really want?'

Nicholas glanced at Val. She always knew what they wanted. That was the advantage of being a twin!

'We want to play in the sandpit all day in our old things. We want strawbs for tea, please, and late bed, because the rest's at Frank's party, having fun.'

'It's a deal.' Their father was already dressed for his dinner party, in white tie and tails, but he bent down and shook hands on the bargain in the approved manner. 'I'll see to the details. All you have to do is be good.'

And now, the day having been won, so to speak, they were enjoying the fruits, both of their endeavour and of the cherry tree. Their mother disapproved of greed and would have forbidden cherries had she thought of them, but the twins, bitterly used to seeing delicious, indigestible food being borne into the dining room and steamed fish and macaroni pudding making its way nurserywards, believed

274

in striking whilst the iron was hot. Last year Val, stricken by sickness after an excess of cherries, had thoughtfully rushed out and vomited behind the coach-house sooner than draw adult attention to the whereabouts of the cherry tree. This year she was too sensible to over-eat. Besides, it was a leaner year for stoned fruit.

Everything had gone well, with cold chicken at luncheon followed − treat of treats − by icecream and by Stella, returning early from the party, with a present for them from Frank. A beautiful little sailboat, carved and rigged just like his own boat, *Sayonara*.

Since the stream was forbidden territory to them, their mother showing signs of going into strong hysterics if they mentioned playing there, they had a galvanised bath full of water in the sandpit. On this hot afternoon, having first buried the bath up to its rim in sand, they filled it to overflowing with buckets of water, threw in some shells to add verisimilitude, and floated their new acquisition on its gleaming surface. One at each side of the bath they crouched, each with a hand in the water gently stirring to keep the model boat on the move.

They were sitting thus, dreamily playing, when the boy found them.

He was a very little boy, with bleached fair hair and tanned skin. He must have been about three, Val thought. He came through the trees and there was something in the way he looked over his shoulder which led them to suspect that he had escaped from a parent or a nanny who would presently hotly pursue him.

Val's maternal instincts were not pronounced, but he was a charming little boy. She lifted him over the stout little brick wall and sat him down on the soft sand.

'Hello! What's your name? I'm Val and that's Nicky.'

The boy stared thoughtfully from one to another but vouchsafed no answer.

'He's too little to talk,' Nicholas said condescendingly. 'Much too little, aren't you, old chap?'

'No he isn't. Babies know their own names ever so young. Come on, tell Val your name.' The little boy's mouth curved and a small, plump hand shot out and tugged at her limp red hair.

'*Tu es fillette,*' the small boy said solemnly.

'What?'

'*Je m'appèle André,*' the little boy said in a squeak. 'Ooh!'

The last exclamation was caused by a slim young woman in one of the very short skirts which caused their father to roll his eyes and their mother to purse her lips. She came quickly out of the trees and addressed the erring André in a torrent of quick and angry-sounding French. Then she turned to the twins and spoke to them in perfect English.

'Hello! I thought at first that you must be Mrs Neyler's twins, but I believe I'm wrong because you aren't a bit alike.'

'We're the twins.' Nicholas spoke rather gruffly. He and Val were very different because of Val's flaming red hair and his own light brown thatch, but it always annoyed him when someone showed obvious scepticism over their relationship. Twins did not have to be identical, after all!

'I'm sorry.' The lady sank on to the sand as though she were well used to sitting on the floor and pulled the little boy on to her lap. She was very thin, Val saw, and her eyes were huge, black and sparkling with long straight lashes. 'I ought to know better than to make remarks like that, because people annoy me by saying that André and I don't look like mother and son.'

'He is your little boy, then! But he's French!'

The lady had a small velvet purse dangling from her wrist. Now she rummaged in it and brought out a packet of cigarettes and a gold lighter. She turned courteously to the twins. 'Yes, he's French. Do you mind if I smoke?'

'Please do,' Val stammered. She was intrigued by this lovely lady who actually asked children if she might smoke in their sandpit! 'How can he be French if you aren't? You aren't, are you?'

'No, only by marriage. My husband's French, you see, so I'm called Madame de Recourte.'

She put the cigarette between her lips and snapped the

lighter. The cigarette was pale blue and the paper between her lips was gold. A faint flame appeared, then she inhaled and the tip of the cigarette glowed red. She sighed luxuriously and blew a thin stream of smoke towards the upper boughs of the cherry tree. Val had already noticed that the lady's fingers were tense, gripping the lighter, and now she took in the rest of her appearance. The sleek, black hair was short and held close to her head by a band of amber-coloured velvet which matched the long beads round her neck. Her dress was a fine black voile, sleeveless, tubular, ending just above her knees as she sat. Her shoes were very elegant, with high heels. They were made of shiny leather and had huge velvet bows on the toes. She wore a tiny gold wristwatch on one wrist and on the other three or four thin gold bangles. Around one ankle was a fine gold chain with a heart hanging from it. Her stockings were the sheerest silk that Val had ever seen.

'Well, will you know me again?'

The lady's voice was teasing, but Val knew herself understood; her staring was a compliment and had been taken as such.

'You're very pretty, and you have lovely clothes. But I don't know you, and you don't know me. Do you?'

'I did tell you my name was Madame de Recourte.'

'Oh, yes, and I told you we were the Neyler twins. But I don't know who Madame de Recourte *is*!'

The lady laughed and let the little boy down on to the ground, where he sat down with a thump and proceeded to scoop sand into a pile with great energy.

'Nor you do! Well, would it help if I said I was . . .'

'Children, Nanny says tea's ready. She doesn't want to wait too long, because . . .'

Tall and slender, as blonde as Madame de Recourte was dark, Stella stood there, one hand fluttering towards her mouth. She stammered something more about the tea, then, with her eyes fixed on the twins' new friend, added: 'Is it . . . can it be you, after all this time?'

Madame de Recourte got to her feet and held out one hand, dropping the cigarette on to the path and letting it smoulder there unregarded. She was smiling, but Val could tell that the easy air which she had begun to wear had gone, and she was, for some reason, on her guard. Against Stella?

'Yes, the prodigal daughter's returned for a few days. I wondered whether you'd recognise me, Stella. Four years produce many changes. I didn't intend to visit but my son ran away and when I followed him I came across the twins and we got talking. I'd better be getting back, or Mother will worry.'

'Oh, Mabs, hang on for a minute! It's so good to see you. You look terribly chic and elegant. We were all awfully worried when you went away, and curious too, I suppose. Is the little boy really yours? He's — he's very nice.'

The Fench lady bent down and picked André up, ignoring his shout of annoyance and his pleas to be let alone. She held him close to her chest, almost defensively, and continued to speak to Stella over the top of the lint-white curls.

'Yes, he's mine. My husband, Matthieu, wanted André to meet his grandparents and he was coming to England on business so he brought us. I truly didn't mean to come near The Pride. I knew we could stay quite safely in the cottage. Your parents have always respected our privacy, and I should have let Mum run after this chap . . . .' She squeezed her son, kissing his neck and making him squeal and giggle. 'Please forget you've seen me, Stell.'

'Mabs, I can't! Please come up to the house! Not today, because everyone's away at a party, but tomorrow. Mama would be terribly hurt if she knew you were here and had gone without seeing her, to say nothing of Daddy and the boys. Desmond's married now, you know, but Frank . . .'

'No!' The word was said so sharply that it sounded like an expletive. 'I'm leaving almost at once and I know better than to open old wounds. It's only by chance you've seen me, so please don't tell your parents or brothers that I've been home. If you *knew*, Stell, you'd understand! Please?'

There was a noticeable pause before Stella said sulkily: 'All right, if you feel so strongly. Though how you intend to keep the twins quiet I can't imagine!'

Madame de Recourte turned to the twins, sitting in the

sand and staring from her face to their sister's. She smiled at them and dimples peeped for a moment.

'It's rather important, Val and Nicky, that no one knows I've been here. You won't tell?'

Nicholas glanced at his sister, waiting for her lead, and Val shook her head decisively. She had taken a liking to this French lady, whose profile reminded her of an Indian maiden in the nursery picture at home.

'We won't tell.'

'Thank you.' She bowed her head at them, then turned back to Stella. 'One day, Stell, when the wound's not so raw, I'll come home properly and we'll meet and talk about old times. But it's too soon. I couldn't face the explanations and exclamations. Try to understand, there's a darling!'

'I can't,' Stella wailed irritably. 'When you ran away I was only a kid and the hushed voices defeated me. Frank went round like a ghost and Des was too bright and cheerful, and we were told not to mention your name. It never occurred to me that there might be a rather . . .' She hesitated, glancing uneasily at her small brother and sister. 'Well, more in your sudden flight than met the eye. Oh, well.'

'Don't jump to conclusions, Stell, and don't worry. I really am very happy. *André, chéri, dis adieu.*'

Then she was gone, the child in her arms chattering away in French nineteen to the dozen as he was borne off. Stella stood for a moment, gazing after them, then rounded on the twins.

'Gracious, you two always seem to be in a mess! Nanny wants you for your tea and what she'll say when she sees your faces I don't know. Where did you get jam from out here?'

'It's not jam, it's cherries,' Nicky corrected placidly. 'We'll wash in this water if you'll go and tell Nanny we won't be long.'

As soon as Stella, grumbling, had disappeared behind the apple trees, he and Val leapt from the sandpit and grabbed the still smouldering cigarette.

'Turn and turn about,' Val said crisply, sucking frantically at the gold-coloured filter. 'Ugh, it's strong. Worse than those leaves you and Simon smoked.' She removed the cigarette from her mouth and regarded it thoughtfully. 'Lots of the papery stuff's got left on my lips,' she concluded balefully.

'You can have it *all*,' Nicky said. 'You've chewed it! You aren't supposed to chew it. I heard Uncle Frank showing Stella how to smoke a cigarette and he kept saying "Don't chew it, girl!" which is how I know it's wrong. Go on, hurry up and finish it and then we can have some tea. It'll be strawbs, because Daddy promised.'

Ten minutes later, tottering back to the house, Val remarked that she really was not hungry and thought she would miss out on tea; twenty minutes later Nanny, holding Val's head over a basin in the nursery bathroom, remarked sourly that sooner or later young ladies who made pigs of themselves with cherries would get their come-uppance.

And Val, sheet-white and still pathetically heaving, could only snivel and curse the demon tobacco whilst endeavouring to assure a frankly unbelieving Nanny that it was nothing to do with cherries!

'I shouldn't have come back.' Mabel faced Suzie across a small table in the window of the Corner House. 'It was just that you said you'd be in the city this week and Matthieu really did think we should have "*des petites vacances*" with my parents. It seemed meant. If only I'd sent Mother chasing after André into the Neylers' den! All I can think of is that Stella will blab and great unhappiness will result. She wasn't very reliable as a child. And at the back of it all, I suppose I hoped that if I came home a miracle would happen and everything would come right again.'

'Mabel, that's for babies, dreams like that. How can it "all come right", as you put it, when you're married to Matthieu and happy too? For all I know, Frank may be pursuing some girl, and no one can just roll back the years like a cheap carpet that's worn badly! Beds have to be lain on, dear.'

'I didn't mean anything like that,' Mabel said, colouring.

'I'm not that stupid! No, I meant that Frank and I might meet and be friends again and understand each other without having to mention Des. But as you say, it was just dreams.'

Suzie nodded rather abstractedly. She was examining the large plate of cream cakes on the table between them and now her hand hovered, unwilling to select too quickly.

'Cream cakes are my biggest failing! I love those éclairs but they're gone in no time, and the cream puffs with coffee icing don't last much longer. Cream horns, on the other hand, are quite substantial *and* they have jam at the bottom.' She took a cream horn and bit into it, continuing with a full mouth, 'I've never really understood why you left! Oh, I know about Des, but you couldn't have known you were pregnant then! I really thought Frank was nerving himself to pop the question, you know, and it was plain as the nose on your face that you loved him. So why, Mabs? Why let Des spoil it all? And then why on earth did you slam the door on Frank by marrying Matthieu? It really mystifies me.'

'I ran away because I didn't want to hurt Frank by admitting what Des had done; at least, that's what I told myself. But I think it was instinctive, really – you're badly hurt, so you crawl away and hide. And having left, I didn't know how to go back without entering into explanations which would probably be disbelieved and would certainly bring great distress. Then there was Matthieu. He really is the kindest man, Suzie, and he really did love me. And I him, though in a different way from the way I loved Frank. When I told him I was pregnant he was so good, so generous! It made no difference that the boy wasn't his. He insisted that we marry and he's treated me so well. He adores André; nothing is too good for his son. Well, one day you must come and visit us and you'll see for yourself how lucky I am!'

'Mm hmm. How did you meet this paragon, anyway?'

'I worked for him.' Mabel smiled. 'The classic case, my dear! He has an import-export business and a flat in Paris and a beautiful country home, rather like a farm. I worked at his Paris office for a few weeks, translating English into French and French into English; languages were always my strong point. Then I found I was pregnant and Matthieu came in to pick up a batch of translating and found me weeping over the sheets. He was wonderful. It was Friday evening and I expected him to give me a week's notice – I hadn't even started the translations, you see – but he told me the work was rather important so I must go back to my room, pack a bag, and he would take me down to his country house where we could work on the translations together.

'Once there, I saw that I'd have to explain, so I did, and he asked me if I'd be prepared to stay at the château, do some translating for him there at weekends, and keep the place nice during the week. He said it would be less arduous than the job in Paris, and that I could have my baby quietly, with the village doctor and midwife in attendance, and then put the child out for adoption, or at least write to my parents after the event. But no more than three weekends later he proposed. And I accepted. And we've lived happily ever after, I might add!'

'A château's a castle, isn't it?' Suzie said, seizing on the most important detail. 'Is he immensely rich, your Matthieu?'

'Yes. But that isn't why I'm happy with him!'

'I'm sure it isn't. But doesn't it coat the pill?' Suzie murmured mischievously. 'I'd bet a considerable sum of money on the fact that he's older than you.'

'He's forty-four, actually, though he doesn't look it. If you're imagining a bloated sugar-daddy, forget it.' She opened her purse and produced a small photograph. 'See?'

Suzie took the photograph and pursed her lips in a soundless whistle of admiration.

'Cripes and blimey! All that and money too. *Now* I know why you don't dream of Frank any more!'

'I do.' Mabel snatched the photograph back, her cheeks flaming. 'Oh, God, I dream of him! Just to see him in the distance, in a crowd, anything . . . that's why I came home!'

'You want to have your cake and eat it, my girl,' Suzie said severely. She shook the coffee pot and then beckoned to the waitress. 'Could we have more coffee, please?' And then, her attention reverting to her friend once more, 'Frank's doing his best to forget you, my dear, and the kindest thing you can do is to forget him as well. I don't think Frank could share friendship with you, not when he'd hoped to become your lover. Perhaps in a few years' time, when he's married himself, it might be different.'

'Marry? Frank? He wouldn't!'

'I think he will. You wouldn't want to deny him the happiness you've found, would you, Mabs?'

'Oh, no, but now that I'm married I shouldn't think it would even cross his mind.' She put her hands to her hot cheeks, aware of Suzie's censorious look. 'Look, I had to marry for André's sake, otherwise I should probably have bided my time and then come back to Frank. But I couldn't, not with his brother's child, and with Desmond stamped all over his face, poor little devil. So you see, it was different for me.'

'It always is. You leave Frank alone, Mabs. Now let's change the subject. I've got a brand new flat in London in a brand new block; why don't you bring Matthieu to visit me there? When my man-friend's not around, if you prefer.'

Mabel glanced pointedly at her friend's outfit. The honey-coloured fur cape, the pale gold voile blouse, the dark brown accordian pleated skirt, exactly matching the high-heeled leather shoes with their big brass buckles.

'Your man-friend's obviously not short of a copper or two, dear! What do you use your salary as a nurse for? To buy nail lacquer?'

'Miaow!' Suzie grinned appreciatively at her friend. 'I never thought you'd turn out so elegant though, love – you've got chic since we last met. I won't ask where you got your suit, or that divine little hat, because they shriek Paris, but I *have* to suggest that Matthieu and my friend Ronald must have one thing in common!'

'If you mean they both spend their money on bad women, I suppose I can scarcely deny it, now,' Mabel said quietly. 'You've always been proud of being a naughty girl, but I've been brought up to see what I did as . . . oh, Suzie, as ever such a sin! And it was all pain and humiliation, every moment!'

'I didn't mean that! Honestly, Mabs, how you take one up! I meant they both enjoyed spending money on pretty women!' Suzie cried, leaning across the table and catching Mabel's hands in hers. 'I just wish Ronald would decide he wanted to marry me and then I could be comfortable, instead of having to be careful never to offend him! It must be lovely to be cherished by a man whether he's rich or poor.' She glanced at Mabel through her long, tawny eye-lashes. 'I'm going down to Oulton in a day or so, to see Frank.'

'Oh, are you?' Mabel stared at her friend, her eyes hardening. 'If you're thinking of trying to wheedle Frank to cherish you, you'd better stick to your sugar-daddy, because you'll just be wasting effort on Frank!'

'You really think Frank's yours, don't you,' Suzie said slowly. 'And it was true, once. But you've forfeited any rights, Mabs; you forfeited them the day you agreed to marry Matthieu. However, if you'll go down to Oulton and live with Frank as his mistress I certainly shan't go and visit him. That's fairly said, isn't it?'

Mabel caught the waitress's eye and asked for the bill, then turned back to Suzie.

'Frank deserves better than you can offer. Why should he take such *very* shop-soiled goods when he could have the best? I wouldn't go to him because of one man, so why should you go to him after a dozen? You leave him alone, Suzie Canning!'

Both girls were on their feet now, hissing at each other across the remains of their morning coffee.

'Shop-soiled goods? What did Matthieu get, then? It's marriage that's in question, remember. And at least I'm not trying to palm another man's child off on Frank.'

'You, have a child? When you've been sleeping with men since you were thirteen without producing one? I very much doubt if you're capable of giving birth!' Mabel's face,

284

which had been pink with temper, suddenly drained of colour and she caught at Suzie's arm as the other turned to leave. 'Suzie, I'm sorry, that was a wicked thing to say! I didn't mean a word of it, I swear I didn't. It's just that I can't bear the thought of anyone else having Frank.'

'I know.' Suzie linked arms with Mabel and the two of them walked over to the cash-desk together. 'You might be right at that, and I'll forgive you anyway, because of the compliment you just paid me.'

'Compliment?' Mabel pushed the money across the desk and raised her brows at her friend. 'What was that?'

'You said if you wouldn't go to him after one man, why should I do so after a dozen? My dear Mabs, it must be nearer fifty!' She laughed as Mabel protested, but continued seriously: 'I know what you mean; Frank's an extremely eligible bachelor and could have his pick of bright young things – bright young virgins, if we're being honest. But he *likes* me, Mabs. I've been going over to the yard about once a month for ages now and I'm breaking down the barriers and giving him back his self-confidence and I do think that one day he may want to marry me. I'd hate to think that you grudged him a normal life.'

'I'm being a bitch in the manger, you mean,' Mabel said ruefully as, arm in arm, they turned right along Gentleman's Walk. 'I wish you good luck, Suzie, and happiness too. If those things go with Frank, then I still mean them. There, wasn't that big of me? Now I'd like to pop down to Garlands for some voile to make my mother a rather special dressy sort of blouse, and to Fullers for one of those oozy, gooey fudge cakes. Are you coming in that direction?'

'Yes, I'm coming; at least I'm not going anywhere else,' Suzie said. 'Can I tell Frank I've seen you and that you're happy? Or is that asking too much?'

'Tell him,' Mabel said, and, arms linked, they set off towards Garlands. They were a striking sight. Desmond, strolling along with his hat tilted jauntily on his blond locks and a rose in the buttonhole of his pale grey suit, stared and halted, one hand at his tie, the other held out, his most ingratiating smile directed at Suzie.

'My dear Miss Canning, it's been years! You must introduce me to your friend . . .'

His voice died away as Mabel, her cheeks flaming, brushed past him and hailed a taxi-cab. She was in it and being whisked off down the road before he had collected himself. Desmond blinked and rubbed his nose ruefully.

'What've I said to offend the little lady? I only meant to have a few words with such a pretty couple!'

'I daresay she's got a thing against being accosted in the street by an Englishman,' Suzie said consolingly. 'Madame de Recourte − that's her name − has been pretty strictly brought up, by all accounts.'

'Oh, French, was she? Well, she looked topping. Those very dark, silky sort of suits can only be worn by the French. I know you girls don't like to show your figures any more, you all want to look like sixteen-year-old youths, but the way that silk clung . . .' He whistled expressively. 'Oh well, there's no accounting for tastes, I suppose. But I'd like to meet her properly − be introduced, and all that.'

'Well, perhaps you'll meet her one day, though I believe she's going back to France tomorrow. And I'd better go too. I've got some shopping to do; some voile and a cake. So if you'll excuse me, Desmond . . .'

'Oh, Suzie, don't rush off!' Desmond's smile was engaging but the look in his eyes was predatory; Suzie remembered what Mabel had told her and shivered, despite the warmth of the sun. 'Let me buy you luncheon, for old time's sake. It's years since we met and we've not had a chance to talk yet, and . . .'

'And you're a married man with two children,' Suzie said briskly. 'Goodbye, Desmond. Give my regards to your family.'

The smile had left Desmond's face and there was a sharp glint in his eyes which Suzie recognised. She continued to stare unflinchingly up at him, however, reminding herself that he could scarcely do anything, not out here on the Walk with people everywhere!

'You've a sharp, nasty tongue, Suzie. I remember how

you let me down all those years ago, and I've not forgiven that yet. Now there's another set-down to add to the score I'm reckoning up against you. It'll be paid off though, one day.'

She turned away, unable to hide the distaste she felt, and hurried towards Garlands. Behind her, she heard him strike his cane viciously against something, probably the nearest lamp-post, but she did not turn her head. Was Desmond really dangerous, or just a foolish, greedy young man? Not so young, either; he must be twenty-three or four. He had slipped up in his amorous dealings about three years ago, Frank had told her, and got a girl of good family pregnant. Forced to marry her, he seemed to be acting in the belief that a pregnant woman was a happy woman – or at any rate, a quiet woman, for his wife had had three babies in three years, and was expecting a fourth, though Suzie knew that she had miscarried of her second child.

And Beryl was not his only responsibility. He had a mistress, a sharp-faced, avaricious, henna-headed woman called Zelda who owned a gown shop on Davy Place and lived in a small flat above it. Desmond had bought her the shop and set her up in business but she was shrewd and hard-headed and had soon gained her financial independence, though even Frank had no idea whether she was still in his brother's debt or had paid him back.

'I don't say anything to Des,' Frank had told her when they discussed the uneasy alliance between Desmond and Beryl and the torrid affair between Desmond and Zelda, 'because in a way it's to Beryl's advantage that he keeps the other one. You see, he's so busy with the pair of them and all the kids that he doesn't get up to other mischief.'

'Like what?' They were at the Swan, in Horning, eating strawberries and cream by the river and watching the passing boats – a busman's holiday, Suzie had teased him.

'Like cheating Daddy,' Frank said ruefully. 'He used to enjoy the devious methods he employed, I'm certain of it. Now he doesn't have time – he just demands.'

'And gets?'

'Usually.' Frank sighed and pointed to a passing yacht.

'That's one of ours. Beautiful, isn't she? The third . . . or was it the fourth? . . . that we built. Where was I?'

'That Des gets what he wants.'

'Oh, yes. Well, the only time I *did* say something to him about Beryl and Zelda he said it didn't matter, because neither minded about the other and, in fact, each was happier to receive only half his attentions.'

Despite herself, Suzie giggled. 'Your brother is an unmitigated cad, and terribly conceited; but he's probably got a point!'

And now, entering Garlands and realising that she could scarcely buy voile for Mabel's mother when she had not the slightest idea of the quantity or the colour required, she also realised that it might not merely be Desmond's amorous attentions which were best divided between his wife and his mistress. It was quite possible that Desmond was a bully.

On this disagreeable thought she turned out of the shop again, and headed for Fullers.

21

Louis sat on the third park bench in the gardens nearest the medical school, reading a letter. Balanced on the bench beside him were three more, as yet unopened. It was a hot day and sweat kept running down his forehead and into his eyes, making them sting. From his chin the drops descended on to the letter, making the ink run as though someone had wept over it. And, thought Louis, that might yet happen.

For the letter was from Sarah, and it asked for a divorce. She had waited for five years and still he said not a word about returning. For the first couple of years she had understood; he was working on a sheep station, living in a bunkhouse, messing with men like himself; there could be no place for her or the children there. But then he had written that he was moving to Sydney.

'You never really said why,' the letter said a trifle plaintively. 'Only something about a little boy called Sam falling into a turnip chopper. And still no word that you would either come home or send for us. Finally, Lou, dear though you will always be to me, good sense has prevailed. Simon is terrible naughty. He needs a father's firmness, and Cara needs a father's love. To save more time and heartache, would you please provide me with evidence? It need not even be real – just you and Another, booking into a hotel as Mr and Mrs Rose.'

Sitting on the bench in the shade of the acacia trees, Louis remembered his life on the sheep station, so abruptly shattered by Sam's accident. He had been the only man on the homestead that afternoon and he had driven the station wagon, with Sam's body tightly clasped in one arm, all the way to the nearest village where he might find a doctor.

The doctor had been there – drunk. So drunk that he had sat in a chair, boozed and bleary, and told Louis, step by step, what to do for Sam and how to do it. And at the end of what had been both the worst and the best three hours of his life, Luis had known one thing. He wanted to be a doctor. He had gone with Sam into Sydney when the boy was well enough to be moved, and had entered his name at the medical school there. Doubts had been expressed at his ability to do the course at his age, until they had examined Sam. Then he had been allowed to enroll, and since then he had never looked back with any sort of regret to what his life might have been.

Until this moment? But could he even say that? He knew now the deep satisfaction of somebody making something of his life, for he was well on the way to becoming a doctor, and a good one. His social life was almost nil, for in every free moment he worked to keep himself, to buy books, and instruments, and respectable, though not smart, clothing.

For a moment he thought about home, and his family. There was pleasure and pain in such recollections, yet both were faint, faded by time and by a life so much more interesting and important than the life he had left. He still knew that Sarah was a beautiful woman and that his children would be handsome and intelligent. But bringing them out here would never work – Sarah was used to a different sort of life altogether and would not appreciate having to live in cramped lodgings and work for her living when she could be at home in the Ipswich Road house, a gracious, relaxed hostess, a fond though never over-anxious mother, a generous and loving wife. Here, she would have to be breadwinner for herself and the children because he could not support them all and continue with his degree and nothing, not the love of his wife, not the cries of his children, would deflect him from his course now.

He looked at the letter again, half believing that he had misread it, but he had not. She wanted a divorce, and he knew she was entitled to ask for one. He grinned ruefully as he thought how far from easy he would find it to provide her with the 'evidence' she spoke of – she would not believe it, but he scarcely knew any women save for a few fellow-students. And the money to buy a 'companion' for a night would have to be earned.

But he would do it. It would cut the last link with England, and he suspected that it would hurt badly, but for Sarah's sake he would do it. He had never faced his own complete determination until this moment, but now, confronting it, he knew that his work had been made easier by the fact that, subconsciously, he had felt he could always drop his life here and return to Norwich; take up again his job in the factory, slip into the once-familiar role of Sarah's lover, the children's father.

He put Sarah's letter down on the park bench and picked up the next one; Tina. He would know that neat, decisive handwriting anywhere. She would know about the request for a divorce since she and Sarah had always been close. He opened the letter, half hoping that Tina would refer to the divorce, half hoping she would ignore it. He skimmed across the first page; his younger sister Rachel had married a middle-aged widower called Adolphus Siegal and much to everyone's surprise, since 'middle-aged' was a euphemism for a man in his late fifties, she had recently produced a son named Caspar. Tina enthused over the baby, over the motherly way his own daughter Cara behaved with the tiny cousin. She told of a party at Cecy's house, The Towers, on Unthank Road and for a moment Louis was back in the garden on a summer's day long ago, when, as quite a young child, he had hidden himself in a patch of pampas grass during a game of hide and seek. He had been unharmed but one of the little girls, searching for him when he had giggled, had cut herself quite severely on the razor-sharp pampas blades.

The house had not been Cecy's then, nor the garden; it had belonged to the Solstein parents. But they had moved out several years ago and the 'young people', as Abe and Cecy had been called by them, had moved in. Louis, dreaming, saw again the broad, daisy-speckled lawn drowsing in the sun, the wide herbaceous borders with their clumps of blue cultivated thistles and the huge Himalayan poppies, the air soft with the scent of flowers, sleepy with bee-hum. He blinked and shook himself back to awareness of the gardens where he was sitting, the acacia and eucalyptus trees, the parched grass, the brassy heat of the midday sun. Different — but every bit as beloved, he realised with surprise. Oh, England called him, of course she did! But so did Australia. England had been his dearly beloved home, but now so was Australia. And he knew which country would win, because Australia had won already. He might go back for holidays but he would never live in England again. In his heart, he did not even want to, save as a sentimental journey to a time when he was younger, seeing things with the clear, uncomplicated vision of a child. Here, life was harsher perhaps, but it was more real, more earnest. A quicker pace, a fiercer struggle for richer rewards.

He laid Tina's letter down and picked up the pad of paper and the pencil. He wrote firmly, not really thinking of anything but the need to get the deed done.

> *Dear Sarah, thanks for your letter. I'll do as you want, of course, and as soon as I can arrange it. Kiss the children for me.*

He hesitated over the signature; he always signed himself 'Your loving husband, Lou' when he wrote to Sarah, but would it be appropriate in view of the impending change in their relationship? He thought about it, then shrugged and signed off as usual. He folded the letter, put it into his pocket and then picked up the last envelope. Without opening it, he knew it was from Say. He could see her penning it so clearly, sitting behind the post office counter in the village shop he had only ever visited once, but which was still engraved on his memory. The post office was just a bit of the counter, of course, but Say had a tall wooden stool and a pink blotter, and it was there that she sat and wrote her long, rambling, surprisingly shrewd letters to him. He loved receiving them. Say never asked for anything, not for vows of love, not for interest in her brood, not even for replies to her letters. She wrote because she wanted to, and it showed. Bits of village gossip, a fragment of talk she had heard which might interest him, the marks Jamie had got in his latest arithmetic test, all jostled with the weather, the state of her garden, the hen who laid astray, the flimsiness of the new sugar bags and how was a body to sell sugar when it come out at the seams of the bag the way it did?

He could see her so clearly, a little plumper, probably, with her pretty hair carefully tied back yet always coming loose, a curl bobbing against her broad, calm brow. She would be writing with one arm curled protectively round the letter, so that no one else could read it, and the tip of her tongue just peeping out from between her white teeth. Behind her, the sacks of flour and sugar, the tub of margarine with its scoop, and on the shelf, the big jars of boiled

292

sweets, the colours inviting even in the gloom. Slightly to one side, there was a door, propped half open. Behind it was the wide, low-ceilinged kitchen where Say cooked their meals, did their washing, coped with her brood. She had a girl to help her now, Maureen Jarvis, and across the kitchen was the back door, also quite often open, affording Say a glimpse of her garden.

'Country children don't want nor need much garden,' she had written proudly once, 'because they've all the meadows and woods to play in. But we've got a sandpit and a swing and one day Winkie's going to build a slide.'

He settled down, after a quick glance at his watch to make sure that he still had plenty of time before his next lecture, for an enjoyable read, and as he read his contentment grew. For Sarah might cut him off, slam the door, take another man to her bed and her heart, but Say never would. She would always be there, cushiony, welcoming, his friend if he needed one, his lover if he wanted one. She was Winkie's wife, and a good wife too, he had no doubt of that, as he was sure that she was an excellent mother. But she could not give Winkie her love, because that had been handed to Louis, lock, stock and barrel, a dozen years ago.

Is it possible that I've ceased to love Sarah yet still love Say? Louis wondered, as he stood up at last and folded the letter back into its envelope, to be enjoyed over and over in the days to come. Surely that was not possible! No, the truth was that he loved both women in different ways, and probably would until the day he died. And he did not believe that Sarah no longer loved him; she wanted her freedom, but that was because she could scarcely do as Say had done, and marry again, without first obtaining a divorce.

Sarah's the same, really, he comforted himself as he entered the cool hall of the medical school. She loves me as much as ever, but she needs a father for the children, just as Say did.

The thought comforted his vanity, if not his intellect.

Suzie closed the door of Mr Abbott's room behind her and

then looked around the hall. Gleaming tiles, cream-washed walls, the hospital smell she had known for so long all about her, even here; antiseptic, carbolic, illness. She gave a little sigh and made for the front door. The last time! For Mr Abbott had told her, pretty bluntly, that if she wanted to get rid of the cough that had haunted her for the last six months, and put on some weight again, she must give up nursing for a reasonable length of time, if not for ever.

'Take a job in the country, if you can't take a long holiday,' he had advised. 'And don't do anything more than you have to; you've been burning the candle at both ends for far too long, nurse. How old are you?'

'I'm twenty-two, sir.'

'Hmm. D'you want to be twenty-five? Hey?'

'I do indeed, sir. But not for three years or so!'

She had smiled perkily but he did not smile back, frowning down at his blotter as though he had not heard her reply. His heavy, pink and white face looked solemn in a way she had seldom seen it and suddenly she was afraid. Was she really ill?

'That's right, keep cheerful, but I'm serious, y'know. If you don't give yourself a chance you won't see twenty-five. Nor twenty-four, either.' He had thick, bushy eyebrows and he glared at her through them in a manner she had often found comic when she was being lectured by him on some small point of hospital procedure. Now it was not funny. 'Take a year off from nursing, perhaps two. If you could get a job in the country, where the air's clean and the pace of life is slower, it would give your lungs a chance. Nurses are practical people, in my experience; daresay you could make a go of light housekeeping, eh? Giving orders, that sort of thing?' He leaned forward across his desk and smiled, the ends of his waxed moustache tilting upwards. 'What d'you think, eh?'

'Are my lungs diseased, sir?'

She got the words out through a horrid thickening in her throat, a fluttering of panic in her breast. Her palms were pressed to the side of her uniform skirt and she could feel them moist and hot, as she could feel the now familiar tightness beginning in her chest.

'Diseased?' He shot her another glance. 'We've all got Londoners' lungs; yours aren't any worse than mine, I daresay. But you're a nurse; you should've guessed that all the wheezing meant things aren't right.' He got to his feet and moved around the desk, putting a huge, well-manicured hand on her shoulder in a fatherly fashion. 'Hey now, missie, don't look so frightened! I'm not condemning you to anything but a change of scene for a while, and then you'll probably be fit as a fiddle again. Fit as a fiddle.' He paused, as though searching for the right words. 'If the cough doesn't clear up after you've been in the country for a few months you'd best come back, have a few tests done. All right?'

'Yes, sir. If you think that's all I need. Country air and rest.'

'Nothing better for the lungs than clean air and plenty of rest.' He cleared his throat. 'You're a pretty girl; got a beau? Any chance he'd marry you, hey?'

'I've got a – a friend, but he's an elderly . . .'

He interrupted her, his face reddening. 'I don't want to know any details, nurse! Does he have a place in the country? Any chance of you staying down there?'

Suzie laughed and shot the doctor a mischievous look. 'I wouldn't get much rest, sir! But I come from a country city, if there is such a thing – Norwich, down in Norfolk. I've a friend there who might need a housekeeper.' Her eyes dreamed. 'It's a lovely spot, quite near the coast, and the air couldn't be purer. I think I'll be able to go there.'

'Good, excellent, couldn't be better. I've a great fondness for Norfolk. Punting on the Broad, bagging a couple of wild duck – ah, yes, that's for me when I retire.' His relief showed in the way he pumped her hand and called his good wishes after her as she left his room, and Suzie wondered how far the doctor's kindness would have carried him had she not made it clear she knew a refuge. His gruff manner hid the most generous heart – indeed, it had been at his suggestion that she had consulted him over the wretched, niggling cough, the weight loss and the attacks of lethargy which no one else seemed to have noticed.

And now, she reflected, walking along the pavement in the general direction of the tube station, she had been condemned to idleness. Not that she would be idle, she would rather anything than that! She qualified this fool-hardy thought by dodging across the pavement and touching wood on the façade of a small grocery shop. An elderly woman, booted and fur-coated, came out of the shop with a frown which melted into a smile as Suzie beamed at her; it was a cold winter's day but Suzie's stunned initial reaction to the doctor's advice was rapidly dissipating in delight and anticipation. She was going home! After all the years she was going home to Norfolk, and, what was more, she was going to stay there.

With Frank. Strangely enough, she had no doubts or fears about her destination. She would go back to the flat now and tell Ronald that she was leaving him – and London – for medical reasons. He was fanatical about his health and the slightest hint that she was ill would be enough to persuade him that she must, indeed, go away. Then she would go down to the station and get herself a single ticket to Norwich Thorpe. She would stay with her aunt for one night and then the next day she would go down to Oulton Broad and tell Frank he needed a housekeeper.

At the entrance to the tube station she bought a large bunch of freesias for an exorbitant price from the flower-seller sitting nearby, then dived down the steps. The freesias smelled of spring and despite her precarious position – no job, very soon no lover, no home – her heart was light. She had loved Frank quietly for so long, and now, at long last, she was going to be near him so that he, too, might fall in love with her!

The boatyard had turned into a roaring success; one had only to glance around it to see that. All the sheds were either repaired or rebuilt and there was a double garage housing a large truck and a shiny new Hudson-Essex, whose gleaming black bonnet paid a silent tribute to the hours the boy Donnie had spent waxing it.

Frank walked across the immaculate yard in the increasing dusk of the rainy afternoon, and pushed open the door of the cottage. It had changed very little in the past five years, though the roof no longer leaked and the window frames had been renewed and reglazed. But a glance round it would show that it was a bachelor abode, for it completely lacked the woman's touch despite all Tina's motherly efforts to see that her son lived in some style. Frank merely suffered the turkey rugs, the satin sofa, the modern pictures, until Tina had gone home and then sent them back to Norwich on the next conveyance city-bound. Once this had been a brewer's dray and Tina had suffered the shock of having the vehicle arrive outside The Pride, complete with the beautiful modern gold and white divan bed she had sent her son, just as six members of the Bridge Club arrived for dinner. It had been her last gift. Now, when she came to visit Frank, she might glance at his shabby rugs and worn sofa and cast her eyes towards the ceiling whilst tutting her disapproval, but further than that she did not go.

He stood on the doorstep, just inside the shelter of the small porch roof which he and Benjamin had added, removing his rubber boots and thinking rather mundanely about his supper. It would have been nice to settle down in front of the fire with a hot cup of tea, knowing that a meal would presently be brought in, but he would have to either stir himself into action with a frying pan or go into the village and order dinner at the Wherry. He took off his waterproof and hung it on a nail just inside the door, then turned for his last look at the Broad. He did this every night, and the sight never failed to soothe him and to give him a deep sense of satisfaction. Tonight was no exception. There was something fascinating in the sight of the Broad under rain, that mirror-smooth surface dimpled and pitted so that it resembled frosted glass, making the steel-dark sky above it seem lighter in contrast. And tonight, despite the lateness of the hour, there was a boat making its way across. Like a waterboatman, one of those Christ-like insects that skim the surface of the Broad, their bodies the boat, their elongated legs the oars, it came nearer and nearer to his mooring, partly obscured by the grey mist of the rain falling straight and mild into the water.

Frank paused. It could not be coming to the yard, not at this hour! He went through in his mind the number of people who might come to him across the water, rather than down the lane, but they were few and none of them would have ventured out in such a downpour without a good reason. He was on the telephone – it was essential in a business such as his – and even the most casual caller usually rang him since he was so often out, or too busy to attend to unexpected visitors.

Then a hand was raised in greeting. So he had best abandon thoughts of settling down for the evening just yet!

Only an idiot would have gone out again, into that relentless wet, yet Frank felt vaguely guilty, standing in the shelter of the porch, watching his visitor get rather clumsily out of the boat, shake masses of water off a huge, ankle-length water-proof cape and hand it to the boatman. No money changed hands and Frank guessed that only a substantial advance payment had lured old Pat Paterson out on such a night.

The boatman turned his craft and began to row out into the Broad once more, and the visitor turned and crossed the yard with quick steps.

'Hello, Frank. Can I come in?'

'Suzie! Come in, girl, you'll catch your death!'

He pulled her into the kitchen, closed the door, then surveyed her. Her dark tweed coat was soaked across the shoulders and hem despite the cape and her hair clung to her head, beads of moisture pendant on each lock, but she smiled up at him gallantly, though she was shivering and her lips showed blue beneath their paint.

'I've c-come to visit you, and you're s-so difficult to reach unless one has a car, which I've not! May I go to the fire for a minute?'

Her fingers were at the buttons of her coat and, seeing that her efforts to remove it were making no headway because her hands were numb with cold, Frank unbuttoned her like a child, threw the coat carelessly on the floor, and snatched the roller towel down from behind the door. He rubbed her hands until the fingertips began to glow pink, then turned his attention to the soaked gold of her hair, wielding the towel to such good effect that presently her hair, short as a boy's, stood up, soft and fluffy, like chick's down.

'There! Better? Now you can sit down!'

She sat down, smiling up at him. She was wearing a lemon jumper suit with a green chiffon scarf in the low V neck, caught in at the waist with a green and gold leather belt. The skirt was straight and very short and her legs were clad in such fine silk stockings that for one horrified moment Frank thought they were bare.

'For a moment I thought you'd come out bare-legged, in this weather,' he remarked, sitting down opposite her in the sagging but comfortable chintz-covered armchair. 'Anyone who's mad enough to cross the Broad in this sort of rain is mad enough for anything.'

'Bare legs are unfashionable, and you couldn't accuse me of *that*,' she protested. She held out her hands to the fire and Frank could not help noticing that her fingers were so thin he could almost see the flames through them. 'I didn't mean to come over until tomorrow, but then I decided the sooner the better. I would have hired a car, but someone was ahead of me. It would have meant waiting for ages, and then I remembered Pat.' She cocked a bright eye at him. 'Why? Aren't you pleased to see me?'

'Of course I am. But did you arrange for the car to pick you up later?' Belatedly remembering his manners, he added: 'I could run you to the station in the Essex, of course.'

'Never mind later!' She sounded impatient. 'Is there anything to eat in this place or have I got to face that rain again? Because I'm starving, I warn you!'

'There's some cold chicken, I think,' Frank said, guiltily remembering the inroads he had made on the bird during his lunch-break. 'Probably some potatoes – cold boiled ones, I mean – and half – nearly half – a marmalade pudding. And I've tinned stuff, of course.'

Suzie pulled a face. 'Marmalade pudding? But even in your beloved Essex, I'd have to get out and stumble into the Wherry. No, don't try to persuade me to let you buy me an expensive dinner; I'm too tired. A little cold chicken and some boiled potatoes will have to suffice for tonight.'

'There's no need for that; we'll go to the Wherry,' Frank said, grinning at her. 'And then I'll take you to the station and you can sit in the car until the train arrives; how does that suit you? We can talk over dinner.'

'No. I'm determined not to go out again tonight,' Suzie said firmly. 'I'll fry the potatoes and do the chicken in a sauce. I'll even heat up the marmalade pudding, if that'll please you.'

'It sounds delicious,' Frank said slowly. 'But Suzie, you said you didn't want to go out again tonight!' A tide of colour engulfed his face and he stared at her. 'Good God, you can't very well stay *here*!'

'Why not? I call it very inhospitable of you, Frank, not to insist that I stay. I even brought a nightie, to keep me snug.' She reached for her dull green leather handbag and produced from its depths a wisp of what looked, to Frank, like cobweb. 'See! Wasn't I sensible?'

'Is that a nightgown? My dear girl, you might as well be . . .' He thought better of it and cleared his throat. 'Look, of course you can stay! But I've no spare bed and I can't offer you mine because I don't know where the clean sheets are! Mrs Coates changes it for me, and takes most of the heavy washing home with her. But you're very welcome to the couch and a pile of blankets.'

She smiled and nodded. She looked very pretty now, flushed from the fire, and as he smiled back at her he noticed that her makeup had all been rubbed away when he vigorously towelled her dry and was touched that she had made no effort to re-apply powder and lipstick, as most girls would have done. She trusted him, even without the defence of her paint. It did not occur to Frank that girls were generally thought more attractive with makeup than without; he knew that, for his own part, Suzie was far more

300

appealing with her skin clear and clean, her tawny lashes untouched by mascara, the line of her lips her own pale, soft pink.

'Then I'll go and check our supplies.' Frank got up and went over to the pantry. Suddenly he felt like a kid, flushed with the excitement of this new venture. It would be fun to have a visitor, fun to know that Suzie was going to share his breakfast next morning. 'I say, how about making a chicken curry? There's a jar of curry paste!'

'Yes, I think I could manage that, if you've got some vegetables.' Suzie got up and came across to the pantry. 'And you've got cheese, so I'll have cheese and biscuits whilst you guzzle marmalade pudding.'

'Except that I don't think I've got any biscuits. And what have you got against marmalade pudding, anyway? I think it's delicious; Mrs Coates nearly always makes me one when she comes in.'

'Well, I could learn to tolerate it, I suppose.' Suzie began to collect ingredients for a curry, ignoring Frank's startled glance. 'Here, you go and peel some onions. We'll talk over our meal.'

But once at the table with their soup in front of them, Suzie seemed to have lost her tongue. She began to speak, took a spoonful of soup, blushed, and then turned accusingly on Frank.

'Now that it's come to the point I'm nervous as a kitten! And why I can't imagine, considering some of the things I've said and done in my time!'

'Then nervousness becomes you, because you look very pretty, stuttering and stammering there,' Frank said. 'Go on, girl, cough it up!'

'I've given up nursing.'

'Really? Now that does surprise me. I thought you'd only give up nursing for marriage, and if you'd got married you'd have blurted that out first, not last.'

'No, I'm not married. And I've left the chap I was living with. I don't want to go back to him.'

'Why should you? Nurses are always wanted; get a job nursing in Norwich, then we could meet more often.'

Suzie sighed and put down her soup spoon.

'Frank, are you deliberately being dense? I don't *want* another job in nursing. I want to be a — a housekeeper for a change.'

'Lord, I didn't know you were so domesticated,' Frank said mildly. 'Have you any particular part of the country in mind for this new venture? Or any would-be employer, for that matter? Do you want me to speak to someone? Is that why you've come visiting in such foul weather?'

Suzie tried another tack. 'It's got to be fairly light work, that's the trouble. To tell the truth I didn't so much leave nursing as get told I must leave.'

'Sacked, you mean? Why, for God's sake?'

The long green eyes met his. Their sparkle was a little too bright.

'A doctor at the hospital said I must have rest and country air. Otherwise, I might . . . might . . .'

'Suzie! Are you ill, love?'

'Only a little ill. But I don't want it to get worse, which is why I'm here.' Suzie took a deep breath and squared her shoulders. 'Frank, wouldn't you like a housekeeper? A living-in housekeeper who just wants board and lodging? I'll sleep on the couch until I can get into Lowestoft to buy a bed, and I wouldn't be any trouble, honestly.'

'You're ill! Why didn't you tell me straight away? What did the doctor say? What is it? If you need treatment I'll pay for you to go into a nursing home, I'll do something!'

'I'm not terribly ill. It's just that I've been overdoing it, what with heavy nursing and — and everything. If you'd let me come here and take it easy for a few months, then maybe I could go back to nursing after all. The doctor seemed to think . . .'

Frank got up and lifted her carefully to her feet, then pulled her round to face him. He shook her gently and, when she tried to speak, put a finger across her lips.

'Shut up and listen for once, you bossy young ex-nurse! You'll come here as my guest and I'll see you get rest and fresh air and everything else the doctor says you need. What do you think Mabs would say if I let you get ill?'

Suzie flinched, then laughed, though tears stood in her eyes. 'What do you think she'd say if she knew I was living in the cottage with you?'

'Yes, that's true. And my mother! It'll be best if I pay you a fair wage and let you prepare the odd meal now and again. We'll go into Lowestoft and buy a bed tomorrow – there's a second bedroom, though it's full of lumber at the moment. I'll have Donnie clear it out. We'll be very snug, I'll be bound.'

He was grinning, his cheeks flushed, his eyes blazing with excitement at the plan. He had not known he was lonely until Suzie had made her proposal, but now he acknowledged that he would enjoy her company, that it would enrich his life. Patch, who had been snoozing in front of the fire, was woken by the excitement in his master's voice and gave a blurred half-yelp-half-yawn, and then, when they laughed, got staggeringly to his feet, tail wagging, and butted Frank with his head. What goes on? his eyes said.

'I'm going to live here with you and your old man, Patch,' Suzie said, kneeling down to pet the dog. He suffered it gracefully but his eyes never left Frank. 'How will you like not being the only pebble on the beach, old lad?'

'Two people to beg from, two people to take him walks – he'll be in clover,' Frank said at once. But it was a mistake. At the sound of the word 'walk' Patch rushed to the door and fixed the handle with a beseeching gaze. 'Hey, don't take me so literally, Patch. We're in the middle of a meal. Later!'

But Suzie walked to the door and opened it. Outside, the rain had stopped and a frosty moon rode high over the Broad.

'To hell with later, Frank. Nothing's going to spoil and the soup's gone cold already. Let's celebrate in all that wonderful romantic moonlight!'

'Well, just down to the staithe and back,' Frank conceded. He took her arm as they walked and was a little shocked by its fragility. In the darkness she clung close and her happiness was so strong that even the dog was affected by it, capering ahead, diving into clumps of bush, rousing the sleepers therein to a sleepy chirp.

'We'll buy that bed tomorrow.' Frank was planning busily as they returned to the lamplit kitchen. 'And a piece of carpet, some curtains — all the things you'll need.'

'Do you have a double bed, Frank?'

He had been eating curry in between sentences but when she spoke she saw him stop for a moment, perfectly still. Then he glanced up at her. There was a warning in his glance that she did not fully understand.

'Yes, I do. Why?'

The warning had been too open to ignore; she said feebly: 'Then may I have one too? In case of — of one of your sisters or — someone wanting to stay?'

'Certainly. And now you've got to try my marmalade pudding. I think you'll find it's quite delicious. You've been put off by the thought rather than the taste.'

As she ate the pudding and commented favourably, Suzie told herself not to be so brassy and brash. Frank was only human. It would not be long before he was as eager to share her bed as she was to share his. It was just that he was a decent, law-abiding man with a sense of responsibility and with a deep respect for the right way of doing things. He had seen what happened to promiscuous men — his Uncle Louis, far away in Australia, and his brother, with a whining and discontented wife and a demanding mistress. Frank would think very carefully before taking a step as profound as sleeping with her — but that he would do so in the end was a certainty.

So Suzie ate her marmalade pudding and then helped Frank to make up the couch in front of the fire, and when he had left her, she snuggled down quite contentedly on its narrow cushions. It would all turn out the way she wanted it to, now that she had been accepted as a member of the small household.

22

Frank telephoned Con's chambers in Cathedral Street from the alcove on Guildhall Hill, just beside the Public Benefit Tailor's shop. As luck would have it, however, Con's secretary informed Frank crisply that her employer was at the Guildhall today, prosecuting in a motoring offence.

'I'm not far from the Guildhall,' Frank told her, squinting sideways to where the façade of that building could be seen. 'Do they break for luncheon, or do they carry on, munching sandwiches or something when no one's looking?'

'If the case seems likely to be a long one, they usually adjourn at about one o'clock, Mr Frank. But if the magistrates see that the case may be brought to a speedy conclusion then they may well continue on past that hour. In my judgement, the court will probably adjourn at one o'clock today, since it is a somewhat complicated case. But I could be wrong, of course.'

'I see.' Frank consulted his wristwatch and saw that it wanted but ten minutes to one o'clock. 'I suppose I can pop in, can I, and take a look to see how things are proceeding? I very much want to speak to Mr Solstein.'

'I'm sure that would be acceptable, Mr Frank; it's not as if it were a matrimonial or were being heard in camera. Goodbye, sir.'

Frank replaced his receiver and emerged from his alcove, wondering how Miss Barker spoke when she was not being the perfect young solicitor's secretary. Probably very much as she had just spoken to him, for she was a middle-aged spinster who adored Con and seemed to live for her work.

He glanced up towards the Guildhall just as Con, beautiful in a dark suit and a dazzlingly white shirt, came round the corner of the building. He headed for the line of cabs opposite the market but heard Frank's shrill whistle and grinned, crossing the road to greet his cousin.

'What's all this? You up on the spree, old boy? I thought you'd have been ankle deep in sawdust at this hour, or munching your way through one of Suzie's ploughman's lunches!' He shot a penetrating look at Frank and his manner changed. 'What's up?'

'If you've got a moment, I thought we could lunch together and have a talk. I rang your chambers and Miss Barker told me where you were. Look, Backs is pretty close. We could have a beer and some sandwiches. Or if you want a proper luncheon there's White's.'

Con took his cousin's arm. 'Backs and sandwiches will suit me fine; I've got to be back here in an hour. Unless it's something very confidential, in which case you may find Backs full of friends.'

'I'll chance it,' Frank said briefly. 'And I don't have any friends who'd come up and interfere between us – they'd get pretty short shrift if they tried!'

They reached the Haymarket and turned into the Elizabethan room, with its panelled walls and ceiling, all dark and smelling of food and beer, crowded with men perched on every available surface, munching and drinking.

'There's my partner – he's just finishing. We'll grab that corner table,' Con muttered, steering Frank through the crowd. 'Hello, Symons, Felton; may we bag your places?'

Mr Symons was whitehaired and wore *pince-nez*, and Andy Felton, an extremely able barrister, was a tanned young man whose favourite recreation was sailing; and though so different the two of them were close friends. They greeted the cousins, then slid out of their settle behind the small round table.

'You're more than welcome, Solstein; I recommend the beef and pickle sandwiches,' Mr Symons said primly.

'Good day to you both.'

Behind his senior's back, Andy winked, then they were lost in the crowd.

'Nice chaps,' Frank ventured as he and Con squeezed on to the high backed settle and gestured to the waitress. 'I wouldn't change the boatyard for anything, but sometimes — just sometimes — I feel I need someone to talk to, and Ben isn't much of a one for conversation, though his grunts sometimes speak volumes.'

Con's eyebrows climbed. 'I thought you had someone? If I lived with Suzie I'm sure I shouldn't complain that I'd no one to talk to — does she ever stop for breath?'

'I can't talk to her about this.' The waitress came up and took their order, then left them again. 'I need to be told what to do!'

'I see; I hope you aren't after free professional advice, because if so you'd best not tell Symons, nor Felton neither; they'd both of them charge the Archangel Gabriel if he asked the way to heaven — and they don't belong to the Chosen People, either, so they've no excuse.' Con grinned his crooked, monkey grin. 'Now I wouldn't charge you — or not above a tenner, at any rate!'

The waitress, obviously harassed, dumped two foaming pints of beer and a plate of chunky sandwiches in front of them. Frank fished out the money and tossed it on to her tray and she gave him a distracted smile before disappearing into the crowd once more.

'It's about Suzie. You know she came to housekeep for me because they wouldn't let her go on nursing? Said she wasn't fit enough?'

'I know that was the story. True, was it? Your sister assured me that Suzie had been after you for years, and that it was just an excuse to get into your house. Well?'

'She's ill; in fact quite a lot worse than she knows. I took her up to London a couple of weeks ago,' to see that doctor chap she's got such faith in — Mr Abbott. He did a lot of tests, told her to rest and get plenty of fresh air and good food, and told me to take her home. But when he rang through on Monday he got put on to me, out in the shed, and it was a different story. He told me she's going down-hill, and of course he recommended me to see that she took his advice. But he said there were traces of blood in the sputum samples. The summer's a bad time for consumption, it seems, but he said if she made it through to the autumn she might regain a measure of health during the winter months.'

There was a short, shocked silence. Then Con spoke, his voice hushed.

'Consumption! And Suzie, of all people! Frank, I'm sorrier than I can say, but surely he doesn't mean she's going to *die*? Not if she takes care, heeds his advice? Damn it, she's only our age!'

'Have you seen her lately, Con? I swear I'd not noticed how thin she's got, how slowly she moves, until he pointed it out. And then I knew that the improvement she talks about is just an illusion.'

'Yes, but . . . did he hold out no hope? What about a sanatorium? I've heard there are places in Switzerland which do miracles. We'd all help with the cost, you know that.'

Frank shook his head. 'Mr Abbott seems to know and he says it's a disease that moves either slowly or very fast, and she's deteriorating fast. He doesn't think she'll last much longer than next spring.'

'Does she know?'

'She knows she isn't a lot better, but she definitely doesn't know she's worse. I think it's because nursing was such a strain that she finds the quieter pace of life easier and thinks she's getting stronger. But I'm afraid she'll notice, unless I can do something to take her mind right off it.'

Con took a huge bite out of a sandwich. 'Such as? You could send her to Switzerland under some pretext.'

'It wouldn't work. I've already suggested it and she just laughed at me. I thought . . . marriage.'

'Marriage?' Con's eyebrows shot up almost into his hair. 'But she's living with you — isn't that enough?'

Frank's voice sank to a mumble. 'I'm not sleeping with her, Con. I've never even tried to make love to her. I've found a thousand excuses for myself but the truth is I didn't believe I could make love to anyone. Ever since the war I've kept clear of women because I've thought that the gassing and the other business had combined to make me impotent − or different, at least. The way I see it now is that if I married her, showed her she was the one person I really cared about, then she wouldn't mind so much − that I've never seduced her, I mean.'

'I'm sorry as hell about Suzie, Frank, you know that.' Con regarded his cousin with open curiosity. 'But are you trying to tell me that you've never done it? Not even once, when you were sixteen or so?'

'That's right.'

'And you think that marrying Suzie will convince her she's the one you love? If so, she's remarkably obtuse. I've known for ever how you felt about Mabs, even when we were kids.'

'Yes. But Mabs is married. Gone. It's taken me a while to come to terms with it, but I think I've done it. She isn't going to come walking across my yard one day, like in a romantic novel, to tell me she can't live without me. She's happily married to her Frenchman and probably never spares me a thought.'

'Then Desmond's oft-voiced suspicions that you'd had a crack at Mabs in Yarmouth and it was that which made her bolt were false?'

'False as hell. If Des and Suzie hadn't turned up I don't say things would have continued so − so platonic, but as it was I didn't have a chance to blot my copybook. I meant to marry her; you know that.'

For a moment the two young men sat in silence, contemplating what might have been. Then Con sighed and spoke.

'Right, Franko, then I take it you want advice of a purely emotional nature. You want to know if it's right to marry a woman just because she's dying.' He paused, but Frank said nothing so he continued. 'Morally or ethically it might be wrong, I don't know, but in your shoes I'd marry her.'

'You would? I'm glad, Con, because I'm going to. Will you stand by me, old fellow? We'll have a quiet wedding, but I'd like you to be there.'

'Wild horses wouldn't keep me away.' Con took the last sandwich, then wagged a finger at Frank. 'One thing, though; have you thought that she might not . . . oh, hang it, that she might . . .'

'Might not die? I'd give my right hand to have her live, but if there was no danger to her life I wouldn't have considered marrying her. I'm selfish, I suppose. But having considered it, it's what I want. I'm fonder of Suzie than anyone bar Mabel. And I told myself last night when I was lying in bed and wishing I could sleep that Mabs is probably completely different now. Fat, with a family of spoilt little French kids and down-at-heel shoes. I might not even recognise her, let alone want her. No, I'm not afraid of regretting the marriage, even if it lasts a normal lifespan. I — I dread losing Suzie. It's going to be hard anyway, but I've a shrewd feeling it will be harder after we're married.'

'That's something you'll find the strength to face when it happens,' Con said sombrely. He pushed the table back and stood up. 'Walk back to the Guildhall with me? On second thoughts, I've got another thirty minutes before I'm in court again, so I'll walk back to the Essex with you — where did you park her?'

The two cousins walked companionably back along the Haymarket to where Frank had left his car.

Suzie crossed the yard, nodding to the men at work in the big boatshed, and dived into the woods which surrounded the yard. She had a special place down by the water which even Frank did not know about, where she went sometimes to be alone.

She reached the glade and settled herself comfortably on the fallen tree-trunk with the clear view across the water, deserted in the October sunshine, reached into her pocket for a packet of cigarettes and drew one out, then hesitated.

Frank hated her smoking and she had all but given it up, to please him. Only when she was very unhappy had she come here to smoke and weep, and now she was happier than she had ever been. She put the cigarette back, then knelt down and scraped at the soft, peaty earth until she had a fairly deep hole. She put the packet of cigarettes into the grave, laid her lighter on top, then snatched the lighter back before burying the packet and patting the topsoil into firmness once more. No point in destroying a perfectly good lighter along with the demon tobacco!

The gesture having been made, she leaned back on her tree stump and let her thoughts wander. Marriage! She had dreamed of so many things; of the moment when Frank would realise that he wanted her, would steal across the landing into her room, slip into her bed, make love to her! Or sometimes she would imagine herself at a party, the belle of the ball, with men vying for her attention and Frank at last realising what he was missing, so that he came to her, cast himself at her feet . . . yet strangely enough, marriage itself had never entered into her imaginings because it had seemed too unlikely!

For a long time, she had been unable to believe that he could resist her. She had worn her most provocative dresses, had planned 'accidental' meetings on the landing when she was in her négligé. She had tried dressing up and not dressing at all. And whatever she did he behaved with perfect friendliness and courtesy. She could not even reproach him for his apparent indifference to her, because he had made it crystal clear that she might live in his house as a guest or a housekeeper, but never as his mistress.

And now she knew that he was not indifferent! He had taken her to London to see Mr Abbott and insisted that they book into an hotel for a couple of nights so that they could take in a show. To be sure, they had had single rooms, but he had been sweet, putting his arm round her in the theatre, taking her to tiny, candlelit restaurants and buying the most exotic food on the menu, going with her to the smart clothes shops and splashing out his money on an absurd but gorgeous Chinese garment with a high collar and long, full sleeves, vividly embroidered, the soft silk of the skirt whispering right down to the floor so that when winter came she could be warm in the draughty cottage.

He was different himself, more relaxed, with a softening

of his attitude towards her. It was because she was better, of course. Mr Abbott was determined to get her right so had insisted on another year's rest, but he knew she was better too. In a year, she thought hopefully, when Mr Abbott told them, Frank will be used to me around his house and won't want me to leave. In the meantime, she would be very careful. Her cough had improved a little and she scarcely ever got breathless now, or wheezed when she hurried. Smiling to herself, she thought that she hurried so little — and would hurry less, for yesterday, when Frank had returned from a business trip to Norwich, he had stopped off in the village on his way home.

'There's a girl, Madge, coming in for a few hours each day in future to do the rough work. And I've brought you something pretty.'

'A girl to help with the rough work — goodness, Frank, I do little enough now; just a bit of cooking and cleaning!'

'You'll do less, then, because I want you fit again. Aren't you going to ask to see what I've bought you?'

She nodded, and he drew a small box out of his pocket.

'Close your eyes then, and hold out your hand.'

She obeyed, holding out her left hand palm uppermost. She felt it gently turned over, and then a ring was slipped on to the third finger. She opened her eyes and saw that it was a cluster of emeralds on a narrow gold band, and that his fingers still held her own.

'Oh, Frank, it's beautiful!'

She was still admiring it when she suddenly saw that it was on her engagement finger. She looked up at him, not daring to ask the question which hovered on her lips. Was it an accident, or . . . ?

'Darling Suzie, will you marry me?'

With true feminine logic she had promptly burst into tears and it was during his efforts to stem the flood that Frank had kissed her for the very first time. And then his arms were round her, he was cradling her against his chest, telling her that he had been *afraid* to ask her to marry him!

'Because of the gassing I've never been with a woman, my darling, and you've never pretended to be an innocent.

312

I'd begun to doubt whether I could be anyone's lover, and you – you were so beautiful, self-confident, that you frightened me!'

She remembered the evening with dazed pleasure. He was going to marry her. They would continue to live in the cottage unless there was a good reason for moving out – his face looked so shy and proud when he said that – but he would have the whole place redecorated and refurnished, and she should choose how it was to be done.

'I like the cottage the way it is,' she had insisted stoutly, and was rewarded by his relieved grin.

'So do I, but it isn't very smart or modern, I know. We'll do the bedroom up, though, with some pale sort of carpet and matching curtains, like my mother's room at home. And I'll buy a new bed, one of those divan things Mother wanted me to have. You deserve the best!'

'I've got the best, or will have once the knot's tied.' She reached up and kissed his chin. 'When can we get married? You said a quiet ceremony, just for family; but I don't have any family now except my aunt!'

'Share mine; goodness knows there are enough of them! Stella's got the most frightful bounder in tow now, Paul something or other, and then there's Josette – you always liked her, and she'll leave her social work in London for our wedding, I'm sure. Des and Beryl can't very well be left out, nor their batch of runny-nosed kids, and there's Auntie Sarah and Simon and Cara. What about your friends? Wouldn't you like to invite some of 'em from London? We'll have a cosy supper party at the Wherry after the ceremony, and we'll hire every available bedroom for the night so that no one has to drive home. How about it?'

'Not the London crowd, but a few schoolfriends.' She hesitated, glancing up at him, her eyes exactly matching the emeralds on her finger as he had known they would. 'You know Mabs was almost my only friend at one time, certainly my dearest friend; but she won't be able to come, so might I ask her parents?'

'You don't think she'd leave France just for a wedding? Probably you're right. As for the Walters, you don't imagine any Neyler could get married and not ask them, do you? I don't want any hurt feelings either, so Ruthie and Edie must come, and Alice – she's part of the family – and then there's Nanny Sutton, only she's Mrs Butcher now, and the Sollies, and Auntie Becky, and the Siegals . . . did I say a quiet wedding?'

And now, sitting on her tree-trunk with the cigarettes symbolically buried beneath her feet and a new life opening up before her, Suzie vowed that she would make Frank forget Mabel. She had seen the way his fingers had clenched when she had mentioned her friend, how the air had seemed, for an instant, to be charged with an emotion she did not understand. Love of a sort for Mabel still lingered, but she would dispel it! She would show him that real love was a two-way emotion with physical as well as mental harmony essential to its blossoming, and it was real love that they would share!

Through the belt of trees which hid her from the yard she heard a dog yap once, sharply, and knew that Patch had spotted Frank. She got to her feet. In a couple of weeks they would be man and wife and there was a lot to plan still, including the honeymoon. Frank was insistent that they honeymooned in style and had offered her the choice between a cruise, a month in France or a month in Switzerland. At the mention of a honeymoon she had cried again. She wanted so much to be a virgin for him, nervous of the thought of being alone with her lover in some strange hotel room. He knew the reason for her tears without being told and had hugged her and laughed at her, telling her that the Suzie he wanted to marry was the same Suzie who had delighted him with her naughtiness when they were children, and that her many love affairs were only the result of her sweetness and generosity.

She emerged from the shelter of the trees and saw Frank carrying a tin of paint from the boat which he had just rowed across the Broad to the shed. He called out: 'Hello, gorgeous; miss me?' and her heart thumped so hard that it made her cough, for he had said it in front of the men working in the shed, had proclaimed his partiality aloud for

314

all to hear.

When he had delivered the paint they went indoors and Suzie made scones and then they sat down by the fire and discussed honeymoons, bedroom wallpaper, and where they should hold the reception. And Suzie tried to forget the niggling fact that never, for all his own sweetness and generosity, had he said he loved her.

'Didn't Suzie look charming? I'm sure she was delighted to have a proper wedding, even though Frank kept insisting they wanted to be married quietly. All that white satin, and the veil so fine it seemed to float after her down the aisle. Didn't Stella and Josette make charming bridesmaids, too, one so fair and the other so dark! Ted? Are you listening?'

Tina was sitting in front of her dressing-table, brushing her hair. The room had just been redecorated in pale green with a mossy carpet and curtains and bedding the colour of young beech leaves. Tina, her glossy black locks outlined against the reflection of an alcove of soft, dull sage colour, looked at Ted in the glass and frowned. Despite Frank's early objections it had been a very big wedding indeed, with a marquee on the lawn and two hundred guests thronging the garden and reception rooms of The Pride. It had been a great deal of work, Tina reflected now, quite a society wedding, but she was not one bit repentant, for naturally Frank and Suzie had preferred it, in the end, to a dull family affair.

Ted put his hands on her shoulders and grinned at her reflection. He touched her hair with his chin, thinking that it was still dark and thick, though there might be a white hair here and there if one looked closely. He never looked closely. He did not need to; he knew her as he knew himself and he knew, too, that her remark had been caused by guilt, that she had spoken because she wanted his reassurance that they had done the right thing by giving their son a big wedding.

'Yes, Suzie looked charming, and what's more she'll remember her lovely wedding all her life, and that's the object of the exercise, isn't it? But that dreadful Cunningham youth was drunk as a newt, and it grieves me to see Stella ignoring decent young men and taking up with bounders.' He smoothed down his hair with one hand and sighed. 'She'll marry in haste and repent in leisure!'

'Marry in haste? At twenty-two?' protested Tina. 'It's high time she was married. I just wish she'd never met young Cunningham. But I don't want to think about them. I want to think about Frank and Suzie. They're spending tonight in London, aren't they, and catching the boat-train to France first thing in the morning?'

'That's right. Remember our honeymoon? And that awful journey up to Inverness, and you falling asleep with all your clothes on and waking up in a bate because you'd had no grub? And blaming me for everything?'

'I remember.' Tina turned and rubbed her head against his striped pyjama jacket. 'I was so nervous, you know. That was why I smacked you, and shouted. They're much more sophisticated these days, though. I expect Suzie's quite experienced already. But I daresay Frank doesn't mind.'

'I daresay you're right. Come to bed, darling. We can lie in tomorrow, and let someone else bring us breakfast for once.'

They climbed into bed and presently Tina heard a small snore, then a deeper one. Sighing, she drove an elbow briskly into Ted's well-covered ribs and then, when he merely grunted, heaved him from his back on to his side. The snoring stopped. So much for romance, Tina thought ruefully, and curled round her husband, snug against him. How long ago was it? Getting on for thirty years ago he wouldn't have gone to sleep so promptly! She thought of Frank, in bed with Suzie in some large, impersonal London hotel. She hoped they would be as happy as she and Ted, but secretly she thought that theirs was a state of bliss which could only be achieved in rare cases. A housekeeper, however much Frank might pretend that she was a fully trained nurse, was still a housekeeper. Any girl who managed to woo Frank into matrimony had Tina's approval, but she was still a very ordinary girl. Unlikely to be one of those rare women who achieve complete matrimonial bliss.

Content with her lot, Tina joined Ted in slumber.

'Well, Suzie, home in three more days. Enjoyed it? What do you think of the sunny south?'

Frank and Suzie were strolling along the harbour at La Coquel, a tiny but increasingly popular fishing port on the Côte d'Azur whose shingle and sand beaches and tiny cafés had conquered the young Neylers' hearts. It was a day of peaceful, golden sunlight, the blue sky flecked with white overhead, the breeze no more than a whisper. Suzie smiled up at her husband and squeezed his hand.

'It's wonderful, and the holiday's been wonderful, and *you're* wonderful! But home's pretty good too, so I shan't be unhappy to leave. And to tell you the truth, I keep wondering how Patch is getting on and whether he's eating properly. Suppose he's a skeleton when we get back? Would you ever forgive me?'

He put his arm round her waist and hugged her to him. 'Naturally I'd blame you for insisting on a French honeymoon! Fool! Now look, are you sure you don't want to come with me to see this fellow? It's mean to transact business on our honeymoon, but this Bernard's got a new way of putting his cruisers together which interests me, and he's perfectly willing for me to glance at his plans and talk things over. It might mean business for the yard too, because there are one or two things we do which he's intrigued about. You know you can come if you like, but I don't want to bore you with technical discussions.'

'I shan't be bored because I'm not coming to the offices with you. See that café? The one with the green and white striped awning and the orange trees in tubs? I'm going to sit down at one of those little tables, order coffee and cognac and be peaceful. I'll write some letters and when you come out we can stay there and have a spot of luncheon. Does that sound nice?'

'Lovely, if you're sure.' He walked her to the café, then pointed to the other side of the harbour. 'See that tall building with the blue door? If you want me, just go through it into the reception place and ask for Monsieur Bernard. I shan't be long, if you're sure you don't mind?'

She laughed and that made him laugh too, then he raised a hand and set off along the cobbled quay and she watched him disappear behind the blue door where, if she was any judge, he and Monsieur Bernard would be engaged in dull discussions for a good deal longer than the hour or so he had promised. However, it did not worry her, for first she would drink the lovely dark coffee and follow it up with a tiny glass of sparkling cognac, and then she would nibble some of those delicious little biscuits, salty on the outside, sweetish on the inside. Then she would write some letters, whilst the pigeons who lived in the old warehouse buildings opposite came down and squabbled with the gulls for any scraps she might throw them, and finally she would walk further along the quay, to where the taciturn, bearded, bereted French artist usually sat, and buy a picture of the harbour to hang in Frank's office when they got home.

Her morning planned, she sat back in the surprisingly comfortable wicker chair in the dreamy sunshine and contemplated the harbour. Because of the increasing popularity of the place there were several yachts moored incongruously amongst the fishing boats bobbing on the dirty harbour water. One of them had only lately docked, she realised — a sleek navy blue and white hull, the sails already folded, and aboard the bustle which obviously preceded a party coming to land. She could see a man, a boy, some sort of golden retriever which barked once and was sharply reprimanded in French. Idly, she watched as the man and the boy crossed the deck and came ashore. They were strolling towards her now, the man tall and distinguished-looking, with dark hair winged with silver, deeply tanned skin and dark eyes which regarded the little boy affectionately as the child hurried beside him, chattering in shrill accents. Something about the man caught her attention. He was extraordinarily handsome and his clothes were good — a dark blue silk shirt and a pair of cream slacks. Of whom did he remind her?

She gave up the puzzle and looked instead at his companion, a little boy as blond as the man was dark. Blue-eyed, too, unless she was much mistaken, and with a look of . . . she nearly gasped with shock. Frank! How odd to see a little boy who could have been Frank's double at the same age in France, of all places! She was just thinking how funny it would be if the boy were a by-blow of Frank's, how she would tease him, when without any conscious effort she knew who they both were. A glimpse of a photograph years ago, a fragment of talk, and she knew without a shadow of doubt that this was Mabel's husband and her son by Desmond Neyler.

Suzie jumped to her feet. She must stop them, speak to them! If Mabel was here too, now was the time to lay the ghost, for surely Frank would accept her loss if he saw her with her handsome husband and beautiful little son? But in jumping to her feet she overturned her cognac, which splashed all across the peach-coloured linen of her skirt, and then the glass rolled off the table and shattered on the paving. Two waiters appeared, one with a cloth to sponge madame's skirt, the other with a brush and pan to clear up the glass. It only took a moment or so, but that was enough. When she looked up again, the couple had disappeared.

Slowly sitting down again, Suzie realised that she was bathed in perspiration and that her heart was beating uncomfortably fast. She felt as if a band enclosed her chest, squeezing her ribs, constricting her heart, and she could feel heat flooding her cheeks. She sat very still for ten minutes, feeling her heartbeats gradually slow to normal, the perspiration cool on her skin. Consciously she forced herself to relax, not to think, and only when the tension had ebbed completely did she allow herself to consider the situation.

What on earth would she have said, for a start, had she reached Monsieur de Recourte? It was a blessing that she had spilled the cognac. But the Recourtes had come off that yacht; she glanced towards it. If they had done so there was a good chance that Mabel was still aboard. She considered the question of what to do calmly. The town was a small one, and the yacht would probably remain moored in the harbour for the rest of the day at least. Should she suggest to Mabel that they behave in a sensible, civilised way and meet for luncheon, all five of them? Or should she cut her losses and try to persuade Frank to leave?

She turned to glance at the yacht and went cold, then hot. Standing on the deck, leaning on the rail, was a slender figure in a navy blue and white suit. She was staring across at the building into which Frank had disappeared not twenty minutes earlier as if she could sense that somewhere inside it was the man she had once loved. Or loved still? Suzie could not say, but neither could she sit here and wait for Frank to emerge and see Mabel.

She got up and went into the café, paying the waiter who was leaning against the bar and having a quick swig from a bottle of red wine. Then she sallied forth into the sunshine, heading with determination towards the yacht. When she neared it, she moved across so that she could see Mabel's face. It was calm enough, but her gaze never moved from the blue door, and the look in her eyes made Suzie ache for her. But she could not allow Frank to see that expression!

'Hello, Mabs. I thought it was you! I spotted you from the café over there, where I've been drinking cognac. Would you care to join me?'

Mabel started violently and one hand flew to her throat. Suzie's eyes flickered over her friend's glossy hair, the deep golden tan of her skin, the slim fingers loaded with rings, the nails, polished ovals of perfection. She looked very beautiful, and not old enough to be that little boy's mother.

'I'm sorry if I surprised you, Mabs, but I was sure you'd seen Frank, and would guess I was somewhere in La Coquel.'

Mabel shook her head, then came over to the gangway, gesturing to Suzie to join her.

'No. That is, I thought I saw Frank, but I often think I see . . . people. It didn't occur to me that it really was him, nor that you'd be with him. But just in case, I stayed aboard when Matthieu and André went ashore. I wouldn't want to bump into him accidentally, not with André in tow. Look, come aboard and have coffee with me. We can't stand out here all morning.'

She ushered Suzie on board and down into a large, airy

320

cabin where the remains of a continental breakfast still littered the table. A manservant was clearing away at lightning speed but in response to a volley of French from Mabel he picked up his tray and vanished in the direction of the galley.

'He'll bring us fresh coffee presently, and croissants. Do sit down and tell me why you and Frank — I take it you're with Frank? — are in France?'

Suzie lay back in her chair and looked coolly across at Mabel.

'Certainly. We're on our honeymoon. Didn't you know?'

'I believe my mother did write something about a wedding, but it seemed such ages ago, and I thought . . . well, let me wish you both happiness.' Mabel's smile was brief and barely changed the look of stunned disbelief on her face. She turned towards the door. '*François, le café vite, s'il vous plaît.*'

'Thank you. We are happy. Look, Mabs, I thought it might be better if we all met for luncheon, André as well, of course. But . . . I wonder now if it would be wise? It would be difficult for me to persuade Frank to leave here, but perhaps you might tell Matthieu that you'd prefer somewhere brighter, with more nightlife? I find I'm — I'm afraid.'

The manservant brought a tray with a silver coffee pot, a tall silver jug of hot water and another of milk which he placed before Mabel, then returned with another tray laden with a variety of bread and cakes. Mabel thanked him dismissively and when he had gone turned to Suzie once more.

'I don't want to meet. It seems incredible that you've forgotten who fathered André, but I'm trusting that you've never told Frank?' And then, as Suzie dumbly shook her head: 'Well, you goose, what do you think Frank would feel? To know, for certain, that I'd run away because his hateful brother had raped me? And even if you can bear to contemplate that, just think about Matthieu for a moment. He's never met Des, so he'll naturally assume that Frank is

321

the man who treated me so badly, because André's very like both boys. As for leaving, Matthieu's come all this way to see a man who builds yachts and cruisers and I can't think of a single convincing reason for just abandoning the place without seeing Monsieur Bernard.'

'Oh, God!' Suzie felt the band begin to tighten round her chest. 'Monsieur Bernard is Frank's contact too. He's there now, in his offices.'

'No!' Mabel abandoned her pretence of calm and began to wring her hands. 'Suzie, what are we to do? I dare not let Matthieu see Frank. He might kill him! I beg you to go!'

Suzie put a shaking hand to her head. Her skin felt cold and clammy. She reached for the coffee which Mabel had just poured and raised the cup to her lips. The china chattered against her teeth for moments before she could summon the strength to sip it, but it helped. After half the cup had been laboriously drunk, she felt the band begin to loosen its grip.

'I c-could pretend to be ill. If I did, and said I wanted to go home now instead of in three days, I think Frank would take me.' She shot a look at Mabel, half defiant, half pleading. 'He's very fond of me – loves me – and he wouldn't make me stay here against my will.'

Mabel was staring at her friend. A shade of anxiety crossed her face, then she leaned over and put a hand on Suzie's forehead.

'You don't have to pretend; you *are* ill! Suzie, what's the matter?'

'Oh, I'm all right now, but I've had food poisoning. I adore lobster, but I do believe it was that.' She watched the concern leave Mabel's face. 'Very well, I'll persuade Frank to leave.'

She got up, and had to cling to the table for a moment before turning towards the door which led on to the deck.

'Suzie. I wish you didn't have to rush off, but I do understand.' Mabel had risen too and now she crossed the room and touched the other's arm. 'I know it's silly, but I would love to see Frank, just for a minute, close. To see how he's changed, and so on. Could you bring him past the

yacht? I promise I won't come on deck or let him see me,
I'd just like to see him again.'

'I can't tell which way he'll go when we leave Monsieur
Bernard's office,' Suzie said guardedly. 'But I'll do my
best.'

She left the yatch with a brief wave to Mabel, then made
her way over to the blue door. As luck would have it, Frank
had finished his business and greeted her warmly.

'Darling, how kind of you to come and meet me! Monsieur Bernard has recommended an excellent place for
lunch, right round by the mole. We can stroll along the
harbour and look at the boats and then try the seafood at
Pierre's.'

Suzie's heart skipped a beat. 'Oh, not that harbour
again! Why can't we strike into the centre of the town and
then drop down that road with the vines growing on the hill
and reach the mole from there? A change of scene.'

He agreed without demur and she led him away, past the
artist, who scowled at them because they walked across his
little length of cobbles, away from the yacht and Mabel.
She thought of Mabel, pressed close to the cabin window,
hungry for just a glimpse of Frank, and knew a pang of pity,
but her steps did not even falter. Frank was hers now, and
she dared not risk him so close to Mabel. Suppose he
sensed her presence, as she had thought at first that Mabel
had sensed his? Resolutely, she walked on.

23: 1926

Suzie had a bed downstairs in the main living room of the
cottage, and Frank had a lean-to kitchen and a downstairs
lavatory built on so that she should not have to climb the

stairs. Today she was sitting up, writing a letter, with the pale spring sunshine flooding in through the small windows which looked out on to the yard. When it was really warm, Frank usually propped the door open so that he could keep an eye on her, call across, but it had been chilly when he left so the door had remained closed.

When the door opened, she put down her letter and at once smiled joyously, for she thought that Frank must have returned earlier than expected from Lowestoft, but instead Con came into the room.

'Good morning, my love! Frank rang yesterday and said he'd be in Lowestoft this morning so I thought I'd steal a march on him and come and visit you.' He crossed the room, put his hands on her shoulders, and surveyed her solemnly. 'You make an incredibly pretty invalid!'

'Oh, Con, not an invalid! Frank says that quite soon . . .' Her voice faltered, then picked up strength again. 'Quite soon I'll be up and about again, now that spring's come. However, I'm beautifully spoiled at the moment, what with Frank fussing, and Mrs Fennell coming in to cook when Madge is off for a few hours, and visitors bringing me pretty things.'

Con laughed and took off his coat, then produced from his pocket a small, square box with a cellophane lid. Inside it, a miniature rose tree with perfect tiny roses, each one no bigger than a fingernail, grew in a tiny pot.

'Oh, Con!' She took the rose from him, devouring it with her eyes. 'Isn't it perfect? Put it near me, so I can enjoy it. June roses in April! I told you people spoiled me!'

'Next time, it'll be a bird in a gilded cage,' Con said teasingly. 'You may be tied to your bed, but the cage gets prettier each time I visit you.' He sat down on the chair by the bed and examined her. Her hands were transparently thin, her face was shadowed by the illness, but indomitable courage shone from her green eyes and her smile showed only her genuine pleasure in his company.

'I'm not caged, not when kind gentlemen leave the door ajar!' She shook her head as he went to move. 'No, I was teasing. I want to know all the gossip, and you can't talk freely with half the yard listening! Go on, amuse me!'

'Why else have I come over? But what about your letter? If you've nearly finished it shall I leave you and go and make a cup of coffee whilst you sign off? Then I could post it for you on my way home.'

'My letter?' Suzie's voice was vague. 'Oh, it's nearly finished, but it's not urgent. I'll finish it tomorrow. To tell you the truth, Con, I find writing terribly tiring. I read a lot though, especially now that I've stopped trying to knit or crochet.' She picked up her letter and leaned across to put it on her bedside table and caught her breath on a cough. As Con watched, she froze into a dreadful stillness, deathly afraid to move, even to breathe, until she had mastered the urge to cough, when she sagged against the pillows, then pulled out a large handkerchief and pressed it against her mouth. Speaking through it, she announced cheerfully: 'Mustn't cough! Now, Con, tell!'

Con became aware that he was tensed on the edge of his chair and leaned back too, pretending to consider. 'What should I tell you this time, I wonder? You know that Sarah's changed her mind about the divorce? Women are fickle in some ways and towers of strength in others. I admire Sarah immensely, and when you think what she's put up with . . .'

He continued in this vein for a while, then switched to an account of Stella's wedding to Paul Cunningham, which had been held two weeks previously despite great uneasiness in the family. He described Grandpa's new lady friend, for Arthur was turning out to be a regular lady-killer in his old age and favoured spats, violet hair oil and gold-topped canes, accompanied by flappers who hung on his every word and voiced the opinion that he was a 'darling old gentleman'. There was nothing even faintly unpleasant in all this elderly gallantry, but it caused his grandsons a good deal of amusement.

He told her about Ted's latest brilliant idea, which had been to stage a mannequin parade at the car saleroom and to serve champagne and pâté de fois gras to his customers. One of the mannequins, perched on the bonnet of a brand-new 11.9 Bean (ridiculous name for a car, Suzie remarked), had got oil on a gown valued at over a hundred guineas, and Ted had calmly taken it from her and lent her a pair of mechanic's overalls in its stead, gone down to the kitchen, and scrubbed it clean with a mixture of petrol and carbolic soap.

'It worked, too, which was what infuriated the designer,' Con told her. 'Whilst she was raving about the fine fabric and the delicate material and the cost of every stitch, Ted was treating it like a bit of old sacking and getting away with it!'

Suzie gave her tiny, breathless chuckle and Con remembered with a pang her old, carefree laugh and knew that he would never hear it again, for Suzie dared not laugh too freely. Or move too suddenly. Or cough.

'Hasn't your hair grown?' he said idly, in a pause. It was shoulder length, as thick and glossy as ever, waving luxuriantly across the pale skin of her shoulders, for her nightgown was sleeveless and low-cut.

'Yes, hasn't it? They say hair goes on growing . . .' She paused. 'Well, it goes on growing whatever your health is like,' she concluded breathlessly. 'Tell me more, Con!'

Con began to rattle on inanely, about his mother's spring cleaning, about Grandpa's Alice, who had turned the house upside down to find her birth certificate because she could not remember whether she was fifty now or next birthday, and, when she did find it, insisted on giving a party because she was only forty-nine. And all the time he was speaking his heart was aching for Suzie, because he knew all too well what she had been going to say. Hair goes on growing even after you're dead, that was what she had choked back. Yet she did not know on how slender a thread her life hung, Frank had assured him of that.

Presently, he saw she was almost sleeping. There was a lovely smile on her face, but her eyes were closed and presently the smile faded and she turned her head into the pillow. He leaned over to pull the covers up across her bare shoulder, and sent her letter fluttering on to the floor. He tucked the blankets round her, then picked up the sheet of paper. She must tire easily, he thought, for there were only a few short sentences, written in Suzie's round, childlike handwriting. He read them at a glance, without any intention of prying on her.

For a long moment afterwards he just sat, the page in his hand. So simple the words, and so practical.

> *Dear Mabel, Frank married me*
> *because I was dying. It will be*
> *soon. Could we meet before I go?*

Presently, his composure regained, he put the letter softly down on the bedside table and leaned back in the chair. Of course she knew. She had been a nurse, she was a sensible girl still. And how much harder it must be to pretend ignorance, to join joyfully in the game of 'getting well' which Frank played so determinedly! After about ten minutes she stirred and gasped and he heard the wheeze and gurgle of her chest as she struggled against a cough. It was unbearably painful to sit there helpless whilst she fought her lonely, hopeless fight and Con's courage suddenly drained away. He got up and stole over to the door. His hand was actually on the doorhandle when she spoke.

'Con? Have you got to go now?'

He turned back. The game needed two people, and it must be played to the finish.

'No, I'm not leaving, I was just slipping out for a word with the men whilst you slept. I'm not used to people dropping off in the middle of my best stories, I might tell you! I hear noises from the kitchen, so I'll ask Mrs Thing to make us some tea, and then I'll tell you about Val's unanimous letter . . .'

Mabel came. She received the letter and read it, then cried all over Matthieu, who patted her and petted her and insisted that she should go back to England to see her friend for the last time. It was painful, perhaps, but it was his wife's duty and he knew she would not shrink from it.

Nor did she. Ten days after Suzie had despatched the letter Mabel walked into the living room.

'Suzie? Oh, my dear!'

The two girls embraced and Mabel felt the skeletal thinness of the body inside the frilled pink nightgown and tried to hide the shock that Suzie's appearance had given her. That lovely hair had been cropped short again and was dull and lifeless, the once-glowing skin pale and waxy, and her eyes and teeth seemed far too large for her small face, fined down to bone by the disease.

'It was good of you — to come so far, Mabs. It's taken some — arranging!'

Suzie's voice was a thread, but the mischief was there, the life-force. It seemed impossible that she could be dying, yet Mabel had been aware of the nearness of death as soon as she touched her friend.

'Yes, I'm sure it did. I do hope, darling Suzie, that you managed to send him off with Con for the day? Con said it was all arranged when he spoke to me on the phone.'

Suzie winked conspiratorially. Death parodying life. Mabel clutched her handbag tightly and tried to listen and not to think.

'Yes. We had to think of — something really good. I pretended I wanted — one of the new mattresses.' She paused. It was clear that she could not talk for long without rest. 'He won't be back till late.'

'I see. Is there anyone else in the house?'

'Yes. I'm never — left. Madge is in the kitchen. She'll bring in — the trolley — presently.'

'That's fine, then.' Mabel was wearing a suit in what was described as crushed strawberry wild silk, and a dull pink cloche hat. She saw Suzie's eyes taking in every detail of her appearance and was glad she had not worn dark clothes. Taking off the hat she shook her hair free and then shed the suit jacket, for it was a warm day. The blouse beneath was a paler shade of pink and admirably tailored. She caught Suzie's eye and grinned.

'Paris, and fiendishly expensive! But Matthieu takes a pride in my appearance.'

Suzie touched her frilly nightgown.

'London. Frank likes me to look — nice, too.'

328

Mabel sat down on the edge of the bed and took her friend's hand. It lay in her own warm palm like a little claw, so cold and dry it felt.

'Darling Suzie, I know you asked me to come here so that we could talk about more important matters than Paris suits and London nighties! Is there anything I can do to help you, make things easier? I'll do anything within my power, or within Matthieu's.'

The head on the pillow nodded.

'Yes. I want to know — about your — marriage.'

'Very well.' It was more or less as she had expected, though she had not realised that Suzie would come straight out with the question. But time was short and they both knew it. 'Matthieu wanted a wife and, even more, a child. He's a fine person, Suzie, but he doesn't make love to women. Not to any woman. He *isn't* a sissy, really, but ours has always been a — a marriage of convenience, and the agreement is that he'll treat André as his own son and me as his wife in every sense but one, if I'm faithful to him and treat him as I would a more — more ordinary husband.'

'I see. I'm not terribly — surprised. Men that — handsome usually — marry young.'

'I suppose so. Matthieu hurts me sometimes by his jealousy and suspicion, though it's obvious why he's jealous and suspicious, even though I've not given him the slightest cause. He knows I once had intercourse with a man and gave birth to a son. He's afraid that one day I'll want what I'm obviously missing.' She sighed. 'He can't believe that my one and only experience of sex was horrible and frightening beyond belief. So he's safe, my poor Matthieu. I've got no desire to let anyone . . . well, anyway, that's our secret. You won't tell.'

'I won't. But you're still — in love with — Frank.'

It was a statement, but Mabel nodded.

'I suppose so. When we met last autumn I envied you so much! I feel terribly guilty now, but then all I could see was a normal marriage to a loving husband, the very things I had once wanted and needed, and which fate has denied me. I saw you touch, kiss, walk away with your arms round each other, and I knew you were in love. Then, for a moment, I wanted it *all* – the pain, the closeness, everything I can't have.'

Suzie's eyes closed. 'And me. And me.'

'I know, love. I know. But at least you've *experienced* these things, even though you've got to lose them! Frank loves you wholly, not . . .'

'No.' It was just a faint, husky whisper. 'It's the same – with us. All goodness, kindness, but no – physical marriage.' A tear slid down the pale cheek and one frail finger wiped it away. 'Dear Christ, Mabs, do love him! For me.'

'I do.' Mabel could not see Suzie's face through the shimmer of tears in her eyes. 'You know I do. I always have, and I can't change now.'

'Yes. But love's no – good from five – hundred – miles away.'

There was a clatter, then the kitchen door opened and Madge wheeled the tea trolley into the room, beaming at them both.

'In't that nice to have a friend come calling all the way from France? Afternoon, ma'am, I've made a foo of my own scones, what no one else don't know the recipe for, and thass as nice a cuppa tea in the pot as ever I made.' She swung the trolley dexterously around the rug and brought it alongside Mabel. 'Shall I pour, ma'am, or will you do th'honours?'

'I'll pour, Madge. Thanks very much. Everything looks delicious.'

Mabel poured tea into delicate china cups, arranged a slice of thin bread and butter, a dab of jam and a scone on a plate for her friend, and all the while she knew that Suzie would be fair; she would not make any deathbed wish to demand that she, Mabel, should desert her husband and come rushing back to look after Frank when she died. But she had left her friend in no doubt whatsoever that that was what she wanted. One day. When the time was ripe, she hoped and expected that Mabel would return to Frank, and she wanted Mabel to know that it was not only all right with

330

her, it was her dearest wish.

'Here's your tea, love. You know I'll do my best. Is there anything else?'

Suzie sipped her tea. Her eyes had a dreamy, contented look, as if now the plea had been made she could stop worrying and rest. At her friend's question, she shook her head.

'No. There's only one other thing, and — Frank will see to — that.'

There must have been two hundred people at the funeral. All the Neylers were there, of course, and the Roses, the children subdued and miserable with black bands round their arms, for children had loved Suzie and she them. All the villagers came, showing their sympathy in the only way they knew, by wearing their best and subduing their voices; for East Anglians don't wear their hearts on their sleeves. And then there were friends. From London, from Norwich, from hospitals all over the country they came. And schoolfriends. Men, women and children who had loved Suzie in their different ways came to pay their last respects.

Con, standing at the graveside as the body was committed to the earth, thought bitterly that it should have been raining, then chided himself. A pale blue sky, new leaves clustering on the trees which surrounded the country churchyard, clouds scudding overhead gilded by the May sunshine and driven by the sort of breeze every yachtsman loves, that was the sort of day Suzie would have chosen to say goodbye on. She had been so full of life and laughter that it was fitting her last party should take place on a beautiful day.

The funeral tea was to be held, not at the cottage, but at the largest house in the village. The Matthews family had been good friends to Frank and Suzie, and when they offered the use of their house Frank was glad to accept, knowing he could not have faced making the necessary arrangements himself.

Supporting his mother who had wept steadily throughout the very moving service, Con caught Frank's eye and they both grinned, the same thought occurring to each – how Suzie would have giggled to see Cecy, who had never approved of her, behaving like a human sprinkler!

Once they were all at the house protocol took over. Frank moved about being a good host, Con settled his mother in a chair between Auntie Tina and Auntie Rachel, and went off to fetch them some of the excellent buffet set out in the dining room. People were losing their diffidence now, and were beginning to talk, even to smile, and once again Con thought that this party was the poorer for Suzie's absence and blinked at his apparent inability to accept the fact of her death. Even in the churchyard, when Frank had stepped forward with a handful of the peaty black soil and dropped it on the coffin, he had been unable to convince himself that it was really Suzie down there, cold and silent in the dark.

A group of villagers were talking to Arthur and his Uncle Ted and he went towards them. Grandpa looked patriarchal and splendid in an old-fashioned black suit with his spade-shaped beard white as driven snow. He greeted Con cheerfully enough, but there was sadness and bewilderment in his eyes.

'A child so young, and the boy so new married,' he muttered to Con. 'A sad and terrible thing. Will you with your cousin stay, tonight? Eh? Would you do that for the old man? Alone he should not be, not tonight.'

'If he'll let me, Grandpa.' Con squeezed the old man's hand. 'I don't want to sound trite, but Suzie wouldn't want any weeping at the bar, you know. She'd have told you to have a drink and enjoy her last party.'

Ted, standing back, nodded and moved to stand between them. 'She was a good girl, and a gay one. It seems wrong that . . .'

'That the old man, who more than his share has seen, should drink at her funeral,' Arthur said. 'I would have gone to let the lass stay. Unfair, that I should live to see this day.'

'I know.' Con patted Arthur's arm. 'But consumption isn't fair; it doesn't attack only the elderly. Let me get you

332

both a drink.'

After a couple of hours the rooms were thinning of people. Mrs Matthews pressed Frank to stay the night, but he refused, saying he had work to do and would be the better for doing it. By the time he and Con left, however, it was dark, and he was obviously glad of his cousin's company.

'You can keep mum or you can talk, old chap,' Con told him as he slid into the passenger seat of the Essex. 'But you've been on your best behaviour for hours; it'll do you good to relax and talk. I know more about the business than most, which might make it easier.'

Frank nodded and started the engine. 'Thanks, Con.'

They drove to the yard in silence, but as they walked into the cottage Frank spoke in a startled tone.

'There, Madge came back and I told her not to! I told her I'd probably get you to stay and that we . . .' His voice choked up and he stopped in the doorway for a moment. The kitchen door was ajar and through it they could hear Madge moving about and humming beneath her breath. A good smell of cooking reached them. The cottage did not have electricity but there were oil lamps which the girl had kindled and the fire crackled merrily in the grate.

'Madge? That you? I've brought my cousin home and the smell of cooking's very welcoming, but you shouldn't have come back. You've worked like a beaver for weeks and more than deserve your evenings free.'

The singing stopped and Madge put her flushed face round the door. 'You din't think I'd leave you hare alone tonight, without so much as a hot cuppa tea?' she said indignantly. 'Nor no fire nor lights? Fine thing that'd be!'

'We ate quite a lot at the Matthews',' Con began, but Madge brushed this aside.

'I saw what you ate, a foo sandwiches! Thass no food for a working man! I done you a casserole of beef with dumplings, plenty for both. And the fire's lit and Benjamin and Donnie and me set to and – and cleared the place.'

For the first time Con realised that the bed which had dominated the living room for so long had gone. He saw

333

Frank's glance go round the room and for a second his cousin's eyes closed as though he could not bear to contemplate the change. Madge saw too, but she spoke with determined briskness.

'That don't do to hang on to memories, even when they're happy, so we cleared through. Just you sit down to your teas, now.'

They ate, then helped Madge to wash up despite her insistence that she could manage alone, and just as they finished a knock on the door revealed Madge's 'steady feller', come to walk her home.

When she had gone, with promises to arrive in good time next morning to get them 'a bit of breakfast', the men sat down, one on either side of the fire, and leaned back in their chairs. Patch, close against Frank's leg, whined and pushed his nose into his master's hand. Frank's fingers began the automatic caress that Patch loved – fingers along the jawline, up round the ear, across the dome of his head, round the other ear, down the jawline again. Patch sagged, eyes half-closed, an expression of sloppy bliss on his furry face.

'Frank, do you want to talk about it?' Con said presently, when he had got his pipe going.

'Frank nodded. 'It's odd, but I do. Right at – at the end there was something so strange that I'd like to tell you. Couldn't tell anyone else, of course.'

'Fire ahead then.'

Frank sighed and nodded at Patch, comatose against his knee. 'He missed her fussing, that last week. She'd put her hand over the edge of the bed, and he'd push his head under it, but she didn't have the strength left for pulling his ears and tickling him. Poor chap, poor old Patch.'

Silence stretched. Con, looking at Frank, saw that his cousin was remembering, had forgotten his presence, the new emptiness of the room. His lips wore a half smile, his lids drooped, his hand caressed Patch automatically. But presently he sighed and came back to the present.

'Last Saturday, that was when I think she began to know. You remember, she decided she wanted a special sort of

334

mattress and despatched us to Norwich to order one. When I got home she was quiet and peaceful, but next day I took one look at her and knew she'd never lie on the new mattress. Dear God, she went downhill fast once she loosed her hold.'

'Loosed her hold? That's a weird way of putting it!'

'Is it? It's what she did, you know. As if she'd hung on and told herself she'd make it if she kept up her spirits. And then, that day we were in the city, it seemed as if the strain of holding on was too great, and she'd decided — well, to let go. She wasn't miserable or depressed or anything like that. It was as though she'd stopped fighting and was saying, "I've done my best but now I'm tired; let me sleep."'

His voice broke on the last three words, but Con said nothing. He sensed that Frank would tell what had to be told in his own way and his own time.

'She slept a lot on Sunday,' Frank went on. 'But on Monday she woke up really early. It was one of those rare, absolutely still mornings, when a mist hovers above the Broad and sounds travel like billyo. I could hear the Franklyn boys squabbling over a bicycle pump as clear as if they were in our yard instead of right across in the village.

'She looked up at me when I took her a cup of hot milk — there was blood on her chin, Con, and on her pillow, and you know how fastidious she was — and she said, "Frank? Will you do something for me?"'

There was a painful silence. Con knew that Frank wanted to tell his story unemotionally and kept his eyes on the flames of the fire. Let the words come, he prayed silently. Let him find the words. To tell can often ease the pain.

'Of course I said I'd do anything,' Frank continued. 'And then she asked me to pick her up, wrap her in a blanket, and take her outside. Said there was a place down by the Broad where she'd been very happy, happier than she deserved, and she wanted to die there. I can tell you, it came as one hell of a shock, because I didn't know she . . . damn it, she'd let me believe she was as ignorant as — as I wanted her to be. Of course I thought how frail she was, and how chilly it can be before the sun comes up, and I kept telling her it wasn't wise, but she just fixed those great, tired eyes on mine, and when I'd finished waffling she said, "Please, Frank." '

This time the silence stretched on too long. Con spoke gently.

'Did you do as she asked?'

'Of course. I wrapped her in a blanket and carried her out. Hardly daring to put one foot in front of the other, she felt so light and brittle. She loved the air on her face, and when she felt the breeze she gave a tiny smile, just a tiny one. Then she pointed to the trees and whispered – she was past talking by then – where I was to go. Said you could see the whole Broad from there and that it looked so – so heavenly when the sun rose.

'I had an awful job to get through the undergrowth. It had grown a good deal thicker because no one went there once Suzie was bedridden, but I got through at last. It – it was a good place, Con, as good as she'd said. The sun came up red as blood, and the mist stirred and began to lift, and then she . . . she . . .'

Con spoke quickly, seeing Frank's haunted eyes, the way his hands shook.

'You did right, old chap, don't let it get you down! She died as and where she wanted to die, and that's a lot more important than being comfortable or getting another hour of life!'

'Yes, I suppose . . .' Frank stopped and shook his head violently. 'No! You see, I took too long, I was doubled up over her, shoving my way through blasted willow saplings and undergrowth, and just as I reached her clearing I looked down into her face. She'd closed her eyes and her face had sort of smoothed out. She looked young and blank and . . . and terrible. Oh, God, Con, she never saw that sunrise! She died before . . . before . . .'

And he was crying, painful, tearing sobs, whilst Con hugged his shoulders and knew himself powerless to comfort him.

24: 1927

Louis woke early, with a pleasurable sense of anticipation bringing his eyes open even before he had remembered what morning this was, in what way it was special to him. He rolled over in the big divan bed, and viewed his bedroom, newly decorated, with complacency. Pale wallpaper scattered with blue morning glory blossoms, a carpet whose colour had been described in the shop as 'midnight velvet', curtains of dark cobalt with silver embroidery, with a matching counterpane for the bed which reposed, at the moment, on the floor, the night having been a warm one.

Until ten days ago, it had been the bachelor apartment of any fairly successful man living along the North Shore. But then the telegram had arrived and, in a blaze of excitement, he had examined his bedroom. Fawn walls, brownish carpeting, mud-coloured drapes. He had acted at once, getting in touch with the most expensive interior decorator in the whole of Sydney and putting himself unreservedly in the fellow's hands. The result had been a bedroom of undoubted blueness, the bill a nine days' wonder at the hospital where he worked.

Fortunately, the other rooms had not been nearly so bad. There was a wide-windowed living room overlooking the harbour, and because he entertained there and, presumably, the man who owned the flat before him had done the same it was pleasantly decorated in creamy gold colours, with the carpet a square of brilliant orange and the curtains some sort of bronze silky stuff.

A white tiled bathroom and a yellow tiled kitchen completed the apartment and now Louis jumped out of bed and

337

went through to run himself a bath. Naked, he admired his physique in the mirror, then began to wash. Humming, he soaped his thick, curly black hair, then rinsed it clean with handfuls of water. No doubt about it, he was a pretty good bargain for a man in his mid-thirties. When Sarah had written to him telling him that she had changed her mind about the divorce he had been rather pleased, expectant almost, but then the telegram had arrived and he had decided that he would not lose her twice! For she was coming to visit him in Sydney, and he knew that this was his opportunity. If he could not make her fall in love with him all over again – and with his new city – he would be extremely surprised!

Moving out of the bathroom and back to his bedroom, he picked up the telegram and studied it, though he knew it by heart. *Arriving Thursday 10th Tasmanian Queen stop Book hotel three week stop Sarah.*

He smiled scornfully at the very idea of booking a hotel room for Sarah whilst he had his apartment and his double bed! It would be absurd, for she was no longer suing for a divorce and she was still his wife! Oh, he had little doubt that she would try to get him to return to Norwich with her, but when she saw his work, his life, when she understood that there could be no question of his leaving his career and his home, he was sure he could persuade her to stay with him, send for their children.

He dressed quickly in white trousers and a white shirt, with a silk handkerchief knotted in the neck, for the day would be a scorcher or he was no judge, and then made his way into the kitchen. He poured himself orange juice, adding ice and a sprig of mint, then cut a thick slice off the loaf and put it under the toaster. When it was light brown, he added butter and a generous spoonful of honey and carried his meal through into the living room, sitting down in a comfortable chair in front of the sweep of the view.

My last breakfast alone, he was thinking sentimentally, when his cleaner, Klara, rattled on the door and then came through it, puffing, to announce that it was a good drag up the stairs.

338

'Too true,' Louis agreed. 'Morning, Klara! When I've done here you can tidy up my brekker things and then do the bedroom and bathroom. I'll be off presently to meet Mrs Rose.'

'Ain't that great, Mr Rose? She'll love dis apartment, she'd be a foolish voman else!'

He smiled at the Germanic turn of her words and got up to take his dirty plate and glass back into the kitchen. Klara was no younger an Australian than himself, but they shared both a tremendous love for their new country and an inability to lose their accents. Louis still spoke English as if he had never moved out of Great Britain in his life.

'You're right, Klara, so get it nice for her. Here . . .' He fished in his pocket and drew out a handful of coins. 'Before you leave, would you go down to that place on the corner where the flower-sellers sit and get me some roses? Red ones. Put half in the green glass vase in the living room and the rest in the blue and white china bowl in the bedroom. All right?'

'I'll do that, Mr Rose. There ain't none of your younk people coming, then?'

He shook his head, remembering that Poppa, too, said 'younk' like that, as did several members of the Jewish Congregation. He had scarcely thought about religion over here, though he did attend Shul if he had the time and felt in the mood. A man without a woman, he reminded himself now, could not afford the luxury of kosher eating, let alone slavish regard for the sabbath, not when he was a working surgeon at the biggest and best hospital in Sydney, at any rate!

'Not yet, but I'm hoping to persuade her to send for them. Don't forget the roses!'

He left the flat and ran down the two flights of stairs to street level, then regretted his haste as sweat broke out on his skin. It would never do to arrive at the quay sweaty and over-eager. He wanted Sarah to be impressed by the new Louis, the one who held lives in his hands and was trusted and respected in the community; he wanted nothing to remind her of that impetuous, idle young man she had married. Or nothing but his lovemaking, he amended. He was very sure that his performance in bed had been near-perfect when he left England, and it had probably improved as much as his general character had in his new country!

On the way to the hospital he popped into a florist and bought a bunch of white lilies with powdery gold hearts. The girl behind the counter smiled at him and added a pink satin bow *gratis,* and Louis pinched her cheek. Nice girl, nice flowers, nice morning.

He met a ward orderly just outside Casualty, a chap called Fred Biggins. Louis thought Fred a scrounger and a lazy blighter but this morning everyone shared a halo. He greeted him cheerfully, and was rewarded by his immediate response:

'Mornin', boss! Today's the day, then?'

Going through reception Mr Cargill came out of matron's office with a pile of papers and also stopped in his tracks.

'Morning, Rose. It's little woman day, I see!'

Louis flourished the lilies and admitted that Mr Cargill had guessed it, then went on his way to his secretary's office. Miss Shelley Porter sat at her desk, typing with incredible speed, working her way through the letters and reports which he had dictated to her yesterday. She looked up at his entrance and smiled beatifically.

'Today's the day, then?'

'That's right. Some flowers for you, my lovely!'

He had meant the flowers for Sarah, but he could soon buy some more, and it brought Shelley out of her seat, skipping round the desk to take the flowers, squeaking and burying her nose in their scented petals, then bending down to select a vase from the multitude tucked away in the bottom cupboard. She liked flowers. And she liked Mr Rose. Louis, who had not, if the truth be known, lived the life of a celibate since qualifying, admired her bottom as she bent down to get the vase. It was a charming bottom, satisfyingly plump, and he knew from experience that it would be encased in french knickers made of softest silk. It was a good bottom to stroke, to pinch. Miss Porter was a bright young thing and thought it a great feather in her cap to be having an affair with the best looking surgeon in the hospital. But now, of course, he would be a model husband. He knew he could be such a thing — indeed, it would be difficult to fall from grace once Sarah was installed because there was no opportunity for dalliance in the busy wards and he would be too tired after work to satisfy any woman other than his wife.

Shelley chose her vase and came out backwards. Louis put his hands behind his back, out of harm's way. He watched as she straightened and began to put the lilies lovingly into the container.

'Everything all right, Miss Porter?'

Shelley replied that everything was fine, thank you, sir, then glanced out of the window and towards the door. Having taken these elementary precautions she promptly threw herself into his arms. She was a satisfying armful too, for a man who had once spent five years without a woman. Louis tried to forget how successfully he had made up for those five years since! She had firm, high breasts which she could not subdue as fashion demanded, and lovely legs with well muscled thighs and calves. As he held her now, he thought irrelevantly that it was nice that she had decent calves. I could never make love to a woman with skinny calves, he told himself piously, nor with those awful bulging ones like Sister Watson's!

'Louis? Do you think you should, darling?'

His hands, quite without conscious thought, had moved round and were pushing themselves past the barrier of her waistband to grasp the tempting, melonlike curves of her bottom. He pulled himself together and stepped away from her. Today of all days!

'Sorry, sorry, I don't know what came over me. Because this is goodbye to all that, my dear. You do know that?'

'If you say so, Louis.' She smiled up at him, the tip of her tongue just peeping between her small teeth. He swallowed, and she moved closer again. 'Shall I get the photo of your wife out of your desk and put it on top? Or aren't you going to bring her back here?'

She was so close that he automatically put out his hand and patted her bottom. Oh. Hell. Think of *Sarah*, damn it!

'You're a thoughtful girl, my dear. Yes, put it on my desk. In fact, you can be the ideal secretary and nip into town for me and buy some roses to put near the photograph. Red ones. All right?'

'Will do, Mr Rose.' She took the money he offered her and went round to sit behind her desk once more, every inch the efficient secretary in her white blouse and dark skirt. 'Good luck with your meeting, sir, and give my regards to your wife.'

'Thanks.' He nodded to her and let himself out into the corridor again. It might be as well to agree to matron's suggestion, now that Sarah would soon be here. Matron, a lady with a weight problem and a rather fine moustache, disapproved of Mr Rose and said – loudly – that Mr Rose's secretary ought to work in the typing pool, with the other medical secretaries. Yes, he rather thought he would agree to the change; there was nothing like removing temptation – far more efficient than merely promising oneself to fight it.

As he walked through the streets towards the docks he found himself trying to conjure up a picture of Sarah's bottom, and was a little shocked, then comforted himself with the thought that it was probably a sign that he was settling down at last. At least if he took to staring at feminine bottoms the owners would almost certainly be unconscious of his admiration – he remembered a teenage obsession with breasts which had proved almost equally embarrassing to himself and to the owners of the breasts!

He lingered once he got near the docks, having a cup of coffee and a wedge of heavy fruit cake at a scruffy little corner shop, then set out, having first purchased a large bunch of red roses. It would please her to find her way strewn with red roses – they *were* the flower of love, and two hearts beating as one, and so on, weren't they? Then he saw the ship and his doubts and fears vanished, to be replaced by almost unbearable excitement. She was coming, the *Tasmanian Queen*, bearing down upon her mooring, heading for the shore! It did not matter that she was old and salt-stained, with rust showing around her Plimsoll line and barnacles encrusting her plates, she was carrying Sarah! Thoughts, lascivious and loving together, filled his mind. Sarah on their honeymoon night, pure and pale, first frightened, then generous. Fighting, kissing Sarah. With their first child in her arms. Walking across the bathroom naked turning to laugh at him. Weeping when he left her. Sarah. Sarah.

The ship docked, passengers thronged the rail. He stared until his eyes ached, but could not pick her out from the crowds. It occurred to him that she might have aged in six years, her hair might be grey, her figure fuller, less lissom. He grew anxious that she might find the heat too much, and pushed forward to the foot of the gangplank. Fat or thin, dark or grey, she was his own darling Sarah, and he would welcome and protect her as such!

'Louis? Lou, my darling! Over here!'

He looked. She had come down the gangway and was hurrying towards him, her hair coming down from its bun, her face shiny with perspiration and love. Plump, pretty, carelessly dressed in blue gingham which was stretched over her wonderful, expansive bosom, her hands held out to him, a tender smile curving her generous mouth.

Louis's heart faltered. Shock stopped his forward progress, mouth at half-cock, the roses tumbling from his nerveless arms to lie on the paving. Then she was close and he was grinning, grabbing her warmly to his chest, kissing luxuriously, then hungrily, the soft, eagerly parting lips she offered so ingenuously.

'Say! My darling girl, to come all this way alone! Say, you're more beautiful than ever and I adore you!'

They walked away towards the city, Say hanging on to his arm, chattering, looking up into his face as he, indulgently smiling, looked down into hers.

The wrong woman.

Or the right one?

The whole family were gathered in the Green Room at The

Pride, with most of their friends and all the Congregation. Ted, looking fondly round him, wondered why it was always The Pride. It was his father-in-law's seventy-fifth birthday, and 'Where else should we hold the party?' Tina had demanded. 'I'm the eldest child, darling, and this is the family home when it comes to a real get-together. We couldn't expect Cecy to help, with her tiny garden and cramped reception rooms. I know Rachel's home is quite spacious, but it's so tidy and dull, and besides, Adolphus is an elderly man, the planning and excitement wouldn't be good for him. And Bishopsgate wouldn't be fair because all the planning would fall on Poppa himself, and there isn't room in the drive for more than three cars, they would have to be left out on the road, and . . .'

The arguments were needless, of course. Ted liked to entertain and would have been hurt had the party venue been moved to anyone else's home. He just liked to ask, that was all! He got a considerable thrill, if the truth were known, out of looking round the motley crowd of Jews and Gentiles, family and business associates, knowing that each one of them saw him as one of themselves. They never thought of him as that young man from the Colonies who had done well for himself, he was just Ted Neyler, one of the best.

Ruthie had outdone herself with the cake. It was gigantic, and on the topmost tier seventy-five blue candles would presently blaze. Arthur was getting emotional of course, trumpeting down his nose, making extravagant promises of how he would mark his three-quarter-century by blowing out every single candle at the first attempt − if his grandchildren and great-grandchildren would help him!

'Simon mine, you're the eldest so you bring the little ones to the old man.' He beamed round at the assembly. 'Come on, don't be shy! Beryl, bring the cottontops over here. Come along, I shan't eat 'em!' Desmond's tired-looking wife pushed her three eldest children towards their great-grandfather but clutched the two youngest to her, as if to blow out a candle might cause them to disappear as well.

'Here we are − I'll hold baby Cas, eh, Rachel?' The

344

two-year-old Caspar had a strong-featured face and a tetchy expression, but he clutched Grandpa's beard and grinned to himself, a dark imp. Arthur counted heads. 'Simon, Cara, Val and Nicky, and little Dessy, little Art, Maudie.' Seeing the children clustered around him suddenly reminded him of that other party when other children had come running to blow out his birthday candles. David, Henny, and Kitty, who would come running no more. He felt tears come to his eyes, but smiled through them at his beloved family. 'Ach, how I wish my dear Deb could have lived to see this day!'

The Rabbi was a new one, a small, square man with glasses, a salt and pepper beard and a great sense of fun. He put one hand on Arthur's shoulder and indicated the children and their parents with a jerk of the head. 'What a family, Arthur! What a grend femily you got!'

Arthur, blowing his nose vigorously, agreed, but there was a shade of enthusiasm missing, for Louis was not here. The others were lovely boys, but Louis was his only son and he missed him sorely, thinking wistfully of him every day, writing to him, talking about him. However, it would not do to think about Louis or he might make a fool of himself. He turned Caspar so that the imp faced the candles which Ted was lighting even now.

'A grand family; you're right, Rabbi. And now, children, you've got to give an old man a hand with all these candles!' They were ablaze now, and someone had drawn the curtains so that the only light came from the cake and its brilliant burden. He drew the children close.

'Now then, some strategy we must have! Our attack we must plan, eh?'

The young heads drew close to the venerable one and Frank, watching indulgently, remembered himself, fifteen years before. How Grandpa had planned the great blast of breath which would send each group of candle flames into oblivion, how even he and Des, though telling themselves they were too old for such nonsense, had nonetheless done their part with gusto.

'Now, *bubelehs!* At the count of three! One . . . two

. . . wait for it, Simon . . . and *three!*'

The candles went out to a man and the singing started, the whole assembly starting with 'Happy Birthday', and then, to wild applause, breaking into 'We all wish you *mazel tov*' whilst the children capered and clapped and the adults reached for their glasses, so that they could toast Arthur when there was a pause in the singing.

Frank noticed that the servants had joined them and were standing, singing and clapping, but obviously waiting for the moment when they could get at the cake. He moved towards them, meaning to congratulate Ruthie on her magnificent catering, when he heard, faintly, the chimes of the front door bell.

No one else heard, and after only a moment's hesitation, Frank slipped from the room, closed the door softly behind him, and went across to the front door. He opened it, and a tall man stood there, with a small woman holding his arm. Both were smiling, albeit somewhat nervously.

'Hello, Desmond! I've seen photographs of you, but I don't suppose you can guess who I am?'

The twang was somehow familiar, yet Frank knew he had never seen the man in his life before. He frowned, then laughed, standing aside and gesturing the couple into the hall.

'I'm sorry, but I'm not Desmond, I'm his brother, Frank. Do you want to see Des, or is it my father? You see, there's a family party going on, and . . .' At that point, it came to him. 'Good God, I thought your voice sounded familiar! It's Uncle Mark, isn't it? And you must be my Auntie Su!'

'Too right, and I suppose Ted's miles away, and we'll miss each other, like we did in America,' the man said ruefully. 'We're here for a bit this time, mind, so we could always come back . . .'

'No, no, he's right here, behind that door!' Frank was almost gabbling with excitement. 'You don't know how marvellous this will be for Daddy, Uncle Mark, because he's never had any family of his own at one of these great unwieldy gatherings, and . . . oh, he'll be so excited! Do you mind if I take you in right now and introduce you?'

Su, clinging to Mark's arm, spoke for the first time. 'Yes, but it's a family party, and we aren't family, not strictly speaking.' She cocked her head as a mass rendering of 'Seventy-five today', more generally sung as 'Twenty-one today', assailed their ears. 'It sounds like a birthday party.'

'Yes, it's my grandfather's seventh-fifth birthday,' Frank said. He had just realised that his Auntie Su was Chinese and was still trying to assimilate this extraordinary fact and to wonder why his father had never mentioned it. 'Look, they've quieted down now, so I suppose they're cutting the cake. Come on!'

He crossed the hall without more ado and flung the Green Room door open wide. The Green Room was separated from the conservatory by wide glass doors but this afternoon these were open to give the guests more space. As Frank entered, Ted was just about to propose the toast. He turned to gaze enquiringly at his son.

'Yes, Frank?'

'Two visitors to see you, Daddy,' Frank announced. 'They've come one hell of a way to be at this party – half a world away. Can you guess?'

For a moment they faced each other, the two brothers who had not met for nearly thirty years. Greying red hair, a thin, intelligent face, quiet grey eyes faced greying blond hair, a broad, jovial face, bright understanding blue eyes. Then the two men moved as one and were in each other's arms, thumping each other's backs, talking both at once, whilst tears streamed down Ted's face and Mark kept gulping.

'I never thought . . . it was mad to come all this way . . .'

'Mark! Nothing matters but that you're here!' Over his shoulder Ted roared: 'Edie! Get the bed aired and made ready in the yellow room – we've two guests who'll stay for ever!'

For the first time it occurred to Frank that his father was growing old, hair thinning, waistline thickening. He was barely twelve months older than Mark, but it could have been twelve years. Then Ted turned and beamed at him, and no critical thought could survive against the depth of affection he always stirred in his second son.

'Well, Frankie? What do you think of that? After all these years!'

'I think that you and Uncle Mark, and probably Mama and Auntie Su as well, ought to take your cake and your champagne and sit quietly in the study for a bit and catch up on things.' They went eagerly, the two women eyeing one another with open interest. They were really rather alike, Frank thought, two small, slender ladies with night-black hair and backs like ramrods. Su was a good deal younger than Uncle Mark, obviously, and a good deal younger than Tina, but his mother had kept her youthful figure and much of her youthful exuberance as well.

When they had bustled from the room, Frank turned to Desmond. Des was leaning back in a chair, gazing cynically at the now closed door. He had not, Frank realised, uttered one word of greeting to his uncle and aunt.

'Well, Des, what do you make of that? After all those years!'

Des pulled a face. 'Oh, they're after something, you may be sure of that. It's a long way to come to scrounge, but I daresay they know him too well back home. And Daddy'll shell out, that's for sure.'

Frank gave him a look of complete disgust and walked out of the room. It was so typical of Des, who always had his hand in someone else's pocket, to assume that everyone else was the same. Frank had only seen Mark for a few moments but he felt he knew him already. A strong, independent man, who would ask for help from nobody but would be quick to offer it.

He found himself outside the study door and hesitated, then made up his mind. He tapped and walked in. The men were standing by the window, deep in conversation, the women were sitting by the fireplace, equally engrossed.

'Thought I'd just tell you I'm off home now,' he said cheerfully. 'I've got some work I'd like to finish before the light goes. But I'll be round here first thing, to get to know

348

my newly acquired relations!'

'Must you go?' Ted knew that Frank had intended to stay for the family dinner party, but he also understood his son. 'Well then, drive carefully. Come to luncheon tomorrow!'

'I will.' He turned and was immediately aware that they were engrossed once more before he had closed the front door behind him. It was right and proper that it should be so. As he gunned the car down the drive he found that he was thinking about Mabel. He had not thought of her properly since Suzie's death. She must miss family parties, too. He had looked for her at the funeral, half ashamed of looking yet unable to stop himself hoping that she would come. She and Suzie had been such close friends, after all. She had not come, though one of the most beautiful wreaths bore her name. And since then he had stopped thinking of her, had concentrated on his work, on a newer, faster boat that he was designing, and on living alone in moderate comfort.

He drove along the summer lanes and into the yard, parking the Essex in the end shed which served him as a garage. He went into the house and realised that there was no food in for an evening meal since Madge had assumed he would be dining at The Pride. Never mind, he could make do with cold stuff; or he could always nip across to the Wherry and get himself something hot.

He made himself a cup of tea and took it outside. The yard was quiet although the Broad itself was not — holidaymakers, yachtsmen and little boys in scruffy skiffs plied their way across its glinting surface beneath the hot sun. He felt content, sitting still for once, whilst a bee buzzed drowsily and gathered honey from the climbing rose near his head and the tea in his cup cooled. Patch pushed a cold nose into his hand, then sighed deeply and curled up at his master's feet. Frank slept.

When he woke, evening had come and the weather had changed. It was cold, and above his head dark clouds gathered ominously. He took his chair indoors and lit the fire, for the cottage could be chilly in the evenings even in the height of summer so the sticks and coal were always

349

ready in the grate. Outside, it began, quite gently, to rain. Frank went into the pantry and began to assemble the makings of supper, for he would not bother to go across to the Wherry on such a chilly night. There was half a ham, some cold potatoes, a jar of home-made chutney and a wedge of marmalade pudding. He piled everything on to a big dish, stood it in the middle of the table, then went over to the window. The rain was really coming down now, fairly bombarding the water, turning the surface of the Broad to frosted glass. It was rather nice when it rained as if the heavens had opened, and one was snug indoors, with a fire burning, and food ready to eat.

And then he saw the boat. Who on earth would be coming here on such a night? It could scarcely be family or friends, for most of them would believe him to be still at The Pride, enjoying Grandpa's seventy-fifth birthday dinner. It could be Con — Con did not like him to be alone on family occasions — but why should Con come across the water, in Pat Paterson's row-boat, with Pat straining at the oars?

The boat had swung towards his landing stage now; there could be no doubt that he was about to receive a visitor. Someone small, swathed in oilskins, sat in the stern of the boat. Frank's heart began to beat a steady tattoo against his ribs. There had been another occasion once when a boat had come across the water in appalling weather, bringing someone very special to him. He had thought, then . . .

He walked out, straight into the storm, with the thunder rumbling overhead now and, far distant, lightning stabbing at the unseen hills. He was soaked to the skin in seconds but he walked steadily on as the boat drew in to the landing stage and someone clambered out, shed the borrowed oilskins and turned, a little uncertainly, towards him.

Frank quickened his pace. He grinned foolishly, even though she could not possibly see his expression through the driving rain. And in his heart, the sun came out.